THE CARNELIAN LEGACY

CHERYL KOEVOET

WestBow
PRESS
A DIVISION OF THOMAS NELSON

WestBow Press books may be ordered through booksellers or by contacting:

WestBow Press
A Division of Thomas Nelson
1663 Liberty Drive
Bloomington, IN 47403
www.westbowpress.com
1-(866) 928-1240

ISBN: 978-1-4497-8089-0 (sc)
ISBN: 978-1-4497-8090-6 (hc)
ISBN: 978-1-4497-8088-3 (e)

Library of Congress Control Number: 2012924219

Printed in the United States of America

WestBow Press rev. date: 03/19/2013

THE
CARNELIAN
LEGACY

In loving memory of my father,
Frank Hettick Jr., who always taught me
that one person can make a difference.
And for my mother, Shirley,
who continues to demonstrate daily
what it means to love unconditionally.

Your beginnings will seem humble,
so prosperous will your future be.
—Job 8:7 *(New International Version)*

CHAPTER 1

JACKSONVILLE

It was the last place in the world she wanted to be.

Marisa MacCallum wiped away the tears that blurred her vision and stared at the mahogany casket. Maybe he was waiting for them at home. Maybe tomorrow she would wake up to find it had all been a dream. But it wasn't a dream.

It was a horrible nightmare.

Already a week had passed, and still she couldn't believe he was gone. Her dad's bright blue eyes and infectious grin were still fresh in her mind. Sure, the doctors had been surprised by how fast the cancer had spread, but they couldn't have predicted he wouldn't last another six weeks. His death had taken everyone by surprise and she secretly wondered if he'd just given up in the end.

Somehow, someway, Marisa had to move on. The tall, slender high school graduate had been accepted to the pre-med program at UC Irvine the year before, but when her father's cancer had appeared, her dreams of becoming a doctor shattered in an instant. She made countless trips to the hospital and tried to keep their home functioning as normally as possible. She'd been so busy managing their household that senior year at South Medford High now seemed like just a blip on the radar.

And she had no clue where her life was headed.

As the bagpiper's final stanza of "Amazing Grace" melted away into peaceful silence, she dotted her cheeks with a crumpled tissue. It had been

1

his favorite hymn. She leaned back to check on her brother Mark. But his puffy eyes and quivering lip made her feel even worse. Still, no one was going to see her cry.

She heard Uncle Al sniffling next to her. It couldn't be easy losing a twin, she thought. Now that her dad was gone, she and her brother Mark were the only family the forty-eight-year-old real estate agent still had left. She took her uncle's hand in hers and gave it a loving squeeze.

Alistair MacCallum glanced down at his niece. She was so much like the sister-in-law he'd lost years ago in a car accident. Before his brother Alan had discovered he had cancer, she'd been a beautiful, bouncy teenager with freckles, long chestnut hair, and hazel eyes that sparkled whenever she dropped the punch line of her latest joke. But almost overnight, Marisa had been thrown into the adult world of hospice care, cooking, cleaning, changing light bulbs and balancing checkbooks. The twinkle had all but disappeared from her eyes and instead they reflected a wisdom that stretched far beyond her years.

Alistair had grown accustomed to losing loved ones in his life, but saying goodbye to his only brother at this stage in his life was unbearable. He had always been highly protective of his brother's kids, but now that both parents were gone, Alistair was determined to be there for them. He wanted to make sure they still reached for every opportunity that life had to offer them.

"Amen," said Pastor Holman.

Marisa buttoned her dark wool coat and hurried down the hill toward the parking lot, anxious to avoid her father's co-workers. Although the staff of Rogue Valley Realty meant well, she just couldn't stand to hear over and over again what a terrific guy her dad had been.

For the past decade or so, the real estate duo of Alan and Alistair MacCallum had helped several families purchase homes in their sleepy southern Oregon town of Jacksonville. Most of the people in the area even knew the brothers by name. Both of them, but especially Alan MacCallum, were known around town as honest men of integrity and all-around nice guys.

But no amount of kind words could ever bring her father back. And since her dad wasn't here anymore, Marisa just wanted to get out of the creepy cemetery and never come back.

"Risa! Wait up!" It was Danielle. She had been Marisa's best friend since third grade. The short brunette with a pixie haircut panted, tried to catch her breath as she studied Marisa's face with concern.

"Are you leaving already?" Danielle asked.

"Yeah, sorry—I didn't know that you'd come."

"I got here late. You okay?"

Marisa shook her head. "I gotta get outta here. Call you later?"

"Sure. And again, I'm really sorry about your dad."

"Thanks."

Marisa hugged her briefly and hurried off toward the parking lot. She slid into the passenger's side of her uncle's Land Rover and quickly shut the door. She sunk down in the seat as she scanned the crowds for her uncle and Mark. They must have stopped to talk.

She groaned. They were chatting with Mrs. Finchley. The way that woman liked to talk, they could be there for a while. Marisa wanted to go home. But it wasn't really home anymore.

Not without Dad.

Minutes later, her uncle and brother finally managed to slip away. Not a word was said as the trio drove down to their historic brick home on the north side of town. The autumn foliage that colored the hills reminded Marisa of her rapidly-approaching eighteenth birthday, but a big celebration was the last thing on her mind.

Uncle Al covered the distance in less than ten minutes and parked the car in the street in front of their house. Mark said nothing as he stepped out onto the curb and loosened his tie. At sixteen, he was already an inch taller than his sister and people who didn't know better were starting to think he was older.

"I'll go make us some lunch," said Uncle Al.

Just as he was unlocking the front door, Marisa spotted her father's weather-beaten rocking chair on the porch. She bolted up the stairs toward her room and collapsed onto the window seat, burying her face in her arms. A moment later, there was a soft knock at the door.

"Aren't you gonna eat?" her uncle asked, peeking in.

She wiped her eyes. "I'm not hungry."

"Risa, you haven't been eating much lately and I'm startin' to worry."

"I'm okay, Uncle Al," she said, grabbing her jeans.

"Just come and sit with us then."

"I'm going for a ride. I'll grab something when I get back."

"Honey, I don't think you should be alone so soon after"—he didn't want to say it—"everything."

"I'm fine. I just need some space."

"Well, if you're sure..." he trailed off. He studied her for a moment. "I'll make some sandwiches and pasta salad and stick them in the fridge for later."

"Thanks."

He stopped. "Oh, and Marisa?"

"Yeah?"

"I hope you're not planning to ride up into those woods above Gold Hill. You know your dad didn't want either of you two up there by yourself."

"She's always going up there to ride," Mark said, barging in.

"Not *always*," she said. She glared at her brother. "C'mon, Uncle Al, everyone knows it's just a bunch of superstitious nonsense."

"It's not nonsense. And don't think for one minute I'm gonna let you do all the things your dad didn't let you do," he said, wagging a finger at her. "You two may think that you're adults, but you're still underage and still under my protection."

"You don't have to worry—I'm not seven anymore," Marisa said. "Besides, I've got my phone with me." She gathered her long, wavy hair into a ponytail and grabbed her riding boots.

"I know you're not," Uncle Al replied quietly. "In fact, you remind me more and more of your mother every day."

And every bit just as stubborn, he thought.

"Why don't you two go eat your lunch?" Marisa suggested.

Mark shrugged and headed down the stairs.

Uncle Al hesitated as he studied her reflection in the mirror. Maybe she was right. Maybe all she needed was a little bit of space. He shook his head and closed the door behind him, still muttering to himself.

She grabbed her One Direction concert tee out of the laundry basket and slipped it over her head. She pulled on her track sweatshirt and skinny jeans and rummaged in the closet for her riding cape. It had belonged to her mother years ago, and she always wore it whenever she went out on Siena. Danielle thought the cape was frumpy, but Marisa didn't care. It was warm and comfortable. She threw it around her shoulders and grabbed the leather satchel she'd bought for ten bucks at a flea market in Portland.

"Ugh," she groaned. The battery was drained on her iPhone. She dug her solar charger out from under some papers on her desk and slipped it in its vinyl case.

She turned to leave but stopped when she spotted the purple book that shared shelf space with her track ribbons and equestrian trophies. Her father had given it to her the same day he had been diagnosed with stage four prostate cancer, but she'd carelessly tossed it aside. It had meant something special to him, so the least she could do was read it.

Marisa grabbed the book, dusted it off, and shoved it into her satchel as her feet flew down the creaky old stairs. "I'll be back in time for dinner," she called to her uncle. She snatched her riding gloves lying neatly on the coat rack.

"Be careful!"

"I always am."

She jogged down to the beat-up Mustang her father had bought over in Coos Bay the year before, hoping they could fix it up. But with all the doctors' visits and chemotherapy eating up every spare moment, there just never seemed to be enough time. She loved that beat-up ride and never wanted to get rid of it.

She turned the key in the ignition. The low rumble of the Mustang broke the silence of their sleepy neighborhood as it crawled up toward the north side of town. The air smelled crisp and fresh. It was still a bit misty from the rain showers that had saturated the asphalt the night before.

With one hand on the steering wheel, Marisa watched as the sunlight reflected off her diamond ring in the form of tiny rainbows flicking and bouncing across the dashboard with every turn in the road. The ring had been her mother's. Her father had given it to Marisa the same day he'd given her the book.

Marisa wore the ring on her right hand to prevent the town gossips from starting some wild rumor that the MacCallum girl had gotten engaged. Her father had always joked that whenever a person on the north side of town sneezed, the south side already knew about it before someone even had the chance to say "God bless you."

As she cruised north up the old highway through the beautiful Rogue Valley, she glanced in the rearview mirror and noticed a silver car in the distance. She'd seen the same expensive-looking car around town a lot lately, but she didn't recognize the driver. They lived in a tourist town that was constantly under invasion by rich Californians and it was probably just some hotshot photographer up shooting nature pictures for a few weeks.

When the Myrtle Ranch Stables homemade sign came into view, she slowed down and turned off the highway onto the familiar gravel road. Hers was the only car in the lot as she hopped out and hurried up the dirt path. She slid the stable door open and a smile spread across her face when she saw the chestnut-colored mare in her stall.

"Did you miss me, girl?"

Siena snorted, blinking softly. Marisa quickly saddled up and headed out on the trail. After she had reached the edge of the meadow, she concentrated on the steep path that wound and twisted its way several hundred feet up the mountain. Soon they reached the top and the terrain started to level out. She admired the incredible view out over the valley and took a couple of deep breaths.

The familiar smell of fresh cedar comforted Marisa after the emotionally draining morning, and for the first time in weeks, she finally felt at ease. Siena trotted at a comfortable gait as pine, cedar, and sequoia branches blotted out the last rays of summer sunshine. A chilly breeze blew down from the mountains and stirred the dead leaves on the path.

She closed her eyes and exhaled deeply, forcing the suppressed emotions from the past several weeks to rise to the surface. Now that it was too late to start at UC Irvine, she'd have to wait until the spring semester. But first, she'd have to save enough money by then. She'd start looking for a job on Monday. It was going to be an uphill climb since the pickings were slim and lots of people were already out of work.

From out of nowhere, memories of her sixteenth birthday two years earlier came flooding back. She remembered it like yesterday when her father blindfolded her and lead her down to the stables. He'd chosen the horse because of its reddish-brown hair that matched Marisa's exactly.

She wiped her eyes with the sleeve of her jacket and wondered if the pain would ever stop. Uncle Al had said that grief couldn't be turned off and on like a faucet but that people should just allow their tears to flow whenever they came. Marisa never liked to express her emotions in front of others, but now that she was alone, she could have her long overdue meltdown in private.

As Siena trudged deeper into the forest, Marisa pulled out a tissue and blew her nose. She thought about her uncle's warnings. Every kid in the valley knew the stories about the forest the Latgawa tribe had referred to as the Forbidden Ground. It had been nicknamed that because horses and other animals often refused to enter the woods.

Ever since the mining town had been established back in the late 1880s, the folks of Gold Hill had been baffled by a series of unexplained phenomena and some even went so far as to call the woods cursed. Every now and again when a person went missing, the townsfolk whispered that they'd been taken by the woods. Amazed that people could be so easily misled by superstitious folklore, Marisa didn't buy any of it.

She searched for a fallen log or rock where she could sit and read underneath the trees and suddenly remembered the perfect spot. A few weeks before, Marisa had noticed a new picnic table that the National Park Service had just installed. It must be somewhere just up ahead—

Flash!

Siena reared up suddenly as a blinding flash of lightning struck the forest less than fifty yards away.

Marisa braced herself for the clap of thunder but it never came.

She opened her eyes and scanned the trees but saw nothing. Her gaze swept to the rear.

No movement.

She sat still and listened. An eerie quiet settled over the woods, and it occurred to her that not a single bird was chirping or whistling. Leaves clinging to the branches rustled in the breeze. The leather squeaked slightly as she shifted her weight in the saddle.

She froze. She wasn't alone.

"Hello?"

Silence.

Clenching the reins tightly in her fist, she sniffed the air. The acrid smell of static electricity penetrated her nostrils and her heartbeat quickened. She could feel Siena trembling underneath her. She dug her heels into her belly, but the animal began to edge backwards.

A twig snapped somewhere in the bushes.

"Is somebody there?"

No answer.

Her mind raced. The nearest house was still a few miles away. She could outrun almost anyone on horseback, as long as they didn't have a gun.

She spotted the picnic table a few feet ahead of her and dug in her heels. Siena just bucked and turned in circles.

Flash!

A blue-white starburst struck the ground once again, but it was much closer this time—only ten feet away. Siena whinnied and reared up on her hind legs. Marisa lunged for the pommel to keep from falling off.

She stroked the horse's mane as her eyes darted around the forest. A wisp of gray smoke rose from the path where the bolt had burnt a strange, circular pattern into the ground and shrubs.

Knowing that her only chance was to make a run for Sam's Valley just a few miles east, she tugged furiously at the reins and dug her heels into the horse's belly but the poor animal wouldn't move.

All of a sudden, a bone-jarring shockwave rattled through the forest and she glanced over her shoulder.

Something *big* was coming her way.

Without warning, a bolt of blue energy struck the trail right behind them. The forest canopy lit up like a thousand flash bulbs as a rush of wind swirled around them with a deafening roar. The ground shook like an earthquake as she yanked on the reins to steady her horse.

Leaves, branches, and pinecones pelted them as dead limbs broke off and flew through the air. Siena bucked and jumped in a total state of panic.

She struggled to cling to the horse and remain in the saddle. She ducked and shielded her head with her free arm, terrified of being hit by flying debris. She felt her body being sucked up into the air and she grasped the pommel as tightly as she could.

Bracing her feet inside the stirrups, she fought against the force of the wind. But after a minute or two, she knew it was no use. Her grip weakened until at last she could hold on no more, and her fingers slipped, finally releasing the pommel.

As Marisa screamed, the sound of her voice mingled with the horse's terrified whinnies. Her cape whipped across her face and blinded her as she was sucked up and separated from Siena.

With no sense of up or down, she spiraled helplessly in circles through the air as the wind roared in her ear. Her arms groped for anything to grab onto. Unable to see the individual trees but just a spinning mass of blurry green, she was overcome by dizziness.

I'm going to die.

She felt a sharp blow to her temple and landed with a hard thud just before she drifted off into a dark, dreamless sleep.

CHAPTER 2

CARNELIA

MARISA'S HEAD THROBBED WITH pain as she slowly opened her eyes. Two young men were crouched down on either side of her, discussing something in a language she didn't recognize. A dark-haired man was supporting her head with his arm when suddenly his eyes locked on hers.

"*Marken mat rede fynchel sit?*" he asked her softly.

Stunned by his perfectly chiseled features, Marisa couldn't help but stare. He had a strong square jaw that was covered with a couple days' worth of dark stubble and his skin was lightly bronzed. The color of his hair was so dark it was almost black, and his eyes were framed by thick eyebrows. His face was marred only by a half-inch scar along his cheekbone.

She sat up quickly but became dizzy and sank back down again. Her temple felt wet and sticky. She touched her glove to her forehead and was horrified to discover that the wetness was blood. The dark-haired man released her gently and strode over to his licorice-colored horse. He removed a piece of cloth from his saddle bag and returned. He pressed it firmly against the wound.

Not to be outdone, the red-haired young man jumped up to retrieve a flask from his horse's saddle. He offered it to her and stroked his beard thoughtfully.

"*Hesen myrd akin limh?*" the redhead asked.

It dawned on Marisa that they were probably tourists in town for the Ashland Shakespearean festival. Gold Hill was pretty far from the festival, though, and she wondered what were they doing so far up the mountain.

"Are you lost?" she asked finally.

The men exchanged bewildered glances, and the redhead turned the question back to her with an amused smile.

"Are *you* lost, milady?"

"No, I'm not lost," Marisa said, relieved that he could speak English. "Who are you?"

"We mean you no harm, milady. We are on a journey."

She looked around. "Where is Siena?"

The redhead looked puzzled. "Siena? Hmm, I don't know of any village around here called Siena. Is that where you are going?"

"Siena is my horse!"

"Ah, of course! Darian found your horse down the road and brought her back here. We had quite a time calming her down. She's over there, just beyond those trees." He pointed off into the woods.

"Who's Darian?"

"Oh, do forgive me. We've not yet introduced ourselves. My name is Lord Arrigo Macario, but my friends call me Arrie." He bowed low and swept his hand in a fluid gesture. "The tall man with the suspicious eyes is His Excellency Darian Fiore."

The dark-haired young man nodded slightly but didn't lower his eyes. He kept them fixed squarely on Marisa.

"And might we know your name, milady?"

She cocked her head. Lord? Milady? This guy seemed to be taking the Shakespearean act a bit far. "My name is Marisa."

"*Din rew fynchel sit Mar-isa*," said Arrie, translating.

Darian nodded again but remained silent. His eyes narrowed suspiciously at her as he examined her from head to toe, soaking in every detail.

"So, what's a young lady such as yourself doing out in these woods alone?" Arrie asked.

"I'm just out riding Siena like I do every day."

Arrie jumped up. "If you would excuse me—we are actually in a terrible hurry. I was just about to replenish our water supply when we stumbled across you. I shall return in a moment."

Marisa said nothing, but just nodded. She watched in amusement as he took off through the trees. The tourists that flocked to Ashland for the festival tended to go overboard with their costumes and funny accents, but these two seemed to have the Shakespearean act down to a science.

She propped herself up against the base of a nearby tree and lifted her gaze. The dark stranger was still watching her like a hawk.

Roughly twenty-three years old, Darian was unusually tall and broad. He was dressed in a strange but elegant uniform with a metal breastplate and dark cloak. He wore knee-high boots and carried a large sword at his side.

Is this guy for real?

"Do you speak English?" she asked nervously.

Silence.

He crossed his arms and watched her in curious silence. His eyes guarded her tightly, as if he were spring-loaded and ready to jump at the first sign she tried to run away. There was no hint of a smile on his stony expression.

Marisa glanced off into the trees where Arrie had disappeared. At least he had acted civil toward her. She scanned the forest around her and quickly weighed her options. Her shoulders sank as she realized there was nothing she could use as a weapon. Darian, on the other hand, carried a gigantic sword, and he didn't appear as if he would hesitate in using it.

She wondered if she should try to run for it but quickly decided against it. She was no match for either of those men. Even if she did manage to get away, she wouldn't get far.

What did they want with her? Would they try to rob her? Arrie had said that they weren't going to hurt her. Neither of the two young men seemed to be the criminal type, but one could never tell. She didn't have her wallet or anything else of value on her.

Except her mother's ring.

Marisa's heart sank. Her father had warned her not to let anything happen to the ring, but she'd been dumb enough to wear it out riding. She glanced down at her hand. Her gloves were still on. At least for now the ring was safe.

Arrie hurried towards her and snatched her satchel off the ground. He tossed it into her lap. "Come, we need to move quickly. The *rijgen* are known to hunt in these forests."

"Who are you guys? Are you from Europe?"

"No, milady."

"Well, obviously you're here for the Shakespeare festival."

"We need to see to that wound on your head," Arrie said, helping her to her feet. "It appears you have bumped it pretty hard."

She brushed the dirt off her jeans. "I'm okay. I just need to call my uncle."

"Might I please inquire as to where you are from?" he asked.

She fiddled with her phone. "Uh, yeah—I'm from Jacksonville, about eighteen miles south of here. Hey, do either of you guys have a cell phone? I need to call my uncle, but my battery is dead."

Arrie smiled. "I thought as much." He grabbed the reins of his dapple gray horse. "Come, let's move quickly out of these woods, and once we reach the village, we'll talk."

She shoved her phone in the satchel. "Wait, you didn't answer my question. Who are you guys?"

"There's no time to explain. Come with us now if you want to leave these woods alive."

"Leave the woods *alive?*"

Darian was scanning the trees as Arrie glanced around nervously. "It's highly likely they've already detected our presence here. Are you able to ride?"

"I'm okay. Just point me in the direction of my horse."

"Be quiet until we are out of the forest," he whispered.

"Why are we whispering?"

"Shhh!"

Arrie led Siena over to Marisa and handed her the reins. As she mounted her horse, he grabbed his leather pouch from a nearby rock and quickly climbed up into the saddle. He motioned to her to be silent and all three started down the mountain toward Gold Hill.

They had only been riding for a few minutes when the weight of Darian's stare started to bug Marisa. She spun around to give him an earful, but the moment their eyes met, she remembered Arrie's instructions for her to be quiet. She had no idea why he was acting so strangely toward her, but maybe he was one of those Europeans who despised Americans.

Marisa shielded her eyes from the sun. It had already sunken low on the horizon, so she must have lain unconscious on the path for a few hours. As the horses clipped along at a brisk pace, she studied the trees carefully. Suddenly a sinking feeling spread from the pit of her stomach.

Something didn't *feel* right.

Although she knew those woods like the back of her hand, she just couldn't seem to figure out where they were. Perhaps Siena had wandered further up the mountain than she'd thought. But she remembered seeing the new picnic table right before she blacked out.

Marisa knew exactly where they *should* be.

Once they reached the end of the forest, she followed Arrie through a clearing and squinted when she saw a small town a few miles away. Had they come out on the other side of the mountain? It looked as if it might be Sam's Valley, but she couldn't be sure.

The two men seemed to relax a bit. Darian took the lead as they rode down the steep mountain trail single file. When they reached a grassy meadow at its base, Arrie passed her and maneuvered his horse next to Darian's. Marisa heard them quietly discussing something, and quickly brought Siena to a halt.

"Okay, you guys, I need some answers here."

The two men exchanged silent glances but they didn't stop.

"You'll have your answers soon," Arrie said. He eyed her with a torn expression, but he kept moving.

She took a deep breath and closed her eyes, recalling the sequence of events from the time she'd woken up. "We should have reached Gold Hill by now," she said.

"Milady, it's not safe out here after dark. We need to get to the village quickly," said Arrie.

"What village? Where the heck are we?"

"We're near Andresis. Please hurry!"

"Um, okay, Andresis. Never heard of it."

She whipped out her iPhone to track her position. Darn! She'd forgotten the batteries were dead. It was too dark to use her solar charger.

Marisa felt the two men's eyes on her. They had stopped in the middle of the road and Darian was glaring at her impatiently.

"Okay, you win," she said finally. "But at least tell me who you are. My uncle would kill me if he knew I was going off with two strange men."

"As I said before, I am Arrie Macario, and this is Ambassador Darian Fiore. We are on a diplomatic mission to Abbadon and must reach Andresis by nightfall. So you can either accompany us to safety or remain here and take your chances."

"Are you two for real?"

Arrie shifted uncomfortably. "Marisa, I know this will be difficult for you to accept, but there is no easy way to say it. You are no longer on Earth, but on Carnelia. I shall explain everything to you shortly, but we really must get inside." The men moved on with a sense of urgency.

She hurried to catch up. "Wait—where is Carnelia?"

"No time to explain now, just hurry."

The sun slid behind the mountains just as they reached the entrance of the village.

Marisa's jaw dropped.

The village of Andresis was surrounded by a wooden structure fifteen feet high. The gate was guarded by gigantic men dressed in black armor with long spears and shields. The man who Marisa guessed must be the captain of the guard motioned for them to dismount, but when he noticed the crest on Darian's breastplate, he bowed and quickly waved them through.

Although the village might have been plucked out of some scene from The Late Middle Ages, something about it appeared almost futuristic to Marisa. The suits of armor worn by the men weren't like the crude tin cans and cumbersome chain mail displayed in heritage museums and old British mansions. Rather, they were elegant, unrestrictive, and tailored to fit each owner. Each man carried some sort of weapon, whether it was a sword, dagger, or bow. The women were clothed in understated yet elegant dresses with hems that lightly brushed the ground and flattered the female form.

Marisa followed closely behind Darian and Arrie and tried not to gawk. As the townsfolk nodded and bowed to them as they passed, she noticed them staring at her casual attire. It was then that she realized none of the women were wearing pants. The whole scene made her feel like she'd stumbled onto some elaborate movie set in Hollywood.

The quaint, black-bricked houses and shops had green, glazed roofs and appeared old yet cozy. A shepherd guided a herd of livestock down the main road, but she couldn't determine what sort of animal they were. They appeared to be some sort of goat/deer hybrid, and she watched in amazement as the black-horned beasts meandered past them.

Marisa closed her eyes and paused for a moment, forcing herself to consider the possibilities. It could be some sort of weird, vivid dream. It felt too real to be a dream, though. Perhaps she had somehow ingested poisonous mushrooms in the woods and it was all just a hallucination. But she was too aware of her surroundings. She felt too alert to be hallucinating. And she would have remembered eating mushrooms.

Am I dead?

Darian stopped in front of a building with a curved metal lantern above the door and a weathered wooden sign with strange writing on it. She dismounted and tied Siena's reins around a pole as Darian opened the door and motioned for her to enter.

Inside the dimly lit reception hall, glass bottles of every shape, size, and color filled the shelves lining the walls. A small fire glowed in the fireplace and the air smelled of smoked hickory and old wine. Several male travelers rested in sturdy wooden furniture with their drinks and pipes—all of them staring at Marisa's strange attire.

They hadn't been inside for more than a minute when an old woman wearing a long skirt, dark apron, and white cap approached them. Darian bowed politely and gestured toward Marisa as he handed the woman two copper coins.

17

She grabbed two spiral-shaped keys from a row of hooks behind the counter and handed them to Darian before disappearing into the back. A moment later, she returned and handed Marisa a neat stack of clothes.

"Thank you—"

"*Aur smyden,*" Arrie interrupted, bowing deeply.

The old woman eyed Marisa with a startled expression as each grungy traveler in the darkened room watched the scene with interest. The old woman waved them off and returned to her post behind the desk.

"Perhaps it would be wise to let me speak on your behalf from now on," Arrie whispered. He motioned toward the back. "Are you thirsty? Let's have something to drink and discuss this calmly, shall we?"

"Yeah, okay, sure. A drink. Why not?"

Darian led them into a large room beyond the lobby with wooden tables and chairs and an ancient-looking bar.

Noticing they were the only ones in the room, Marisa quickly turned to Arrie. "Okay, maybe you can explain now what the heck in going on. I thought you said back there that I was no longer on Earth. You're kidding, right?"

"No, I'm afraid not. You are in Carnelia," Arrie said.

"Right. Where exactly is that again?"

He smiled. "You speak English, so obviously you are from Earth, which lies in a different dimension from ours. Judging from your accent, I'd wager that you're from somewhere along the West Coast of the United States, perhaps Canada."

Her eyes narrowed at his. "If I really am in some other world, how is it that you know about Earth and can speak English?"

"You are, in fact, still on the same planet and physical space but in another dimension. Obviously, you've traveled through a vortex."

"*What!* Are you sayin' that I've traveled back in *time?*"

"Shhh! Please keep your voice down. We don't wish to draw any unwanted attention," Arrie whispered.

"Oh, right, right, I forgot," she said.

18

"No. Time travel is something entirely different. You are one of the few people to have traveled through a vortex from one dimension to another..."

Arrie broke off as a woman brought three tankards of a strange drink, plunked them down on the table, and hurried off. Darian quietly took a sip.

"What is it?" she asked, pointing to her mug.

"It's ale. Go ahead and try it."

"No thanks." She pushed it away. "What's a vortex?"

"Let's see, how do I explain this?" Arrie tapped his finger on the table. "Did you see three separate flashes of lightning? But without the thunder?"

"Yeah?"

He nodded. "Most definitely a vortex. You can imagine it as an invisible tube or funnel, shaped like a tornado, but you can't see it until just before it's about to open. Animals won't go near them. They sense them better than we humans do."

"And that's why Siena freaked out?"

"Indeed," he said, taking another sip.

"So that's how I got here? Through a vortex?"

"That is correct."

"Can you hold on for a sec?"

"Certainly."

Marisa pushed herself away from the table, stumbled outside, and quickly glanced around the bustling main street. With no idea where she was going, she headed down a narrow alley. She spotted an octagonal-shaped rain barrel against the wall and hurried over. She inhaled a deep breath and dunked her head under.

She gasped from the shock of the icy water and collapsed on the ground. A few bewildered passers-by stopped to stare. Coughing, sputtering, and finally convinced she wasn't dreaming, she ran a hand through her wet hair and glanced around.

"Where am I?" she shouted.

19

"Marisa, what are you doing back here?" Arrie said, hurrying over. He removed his tunic and threw it around her shoulders.

"I—I..." she began, her teeth chattered.

"Are you trying to make yourself sick? Come back inside." He guided her shuddering frame back up the alley toward the main road.

She ran her hand along the rough-hewn stones in the wall. As she felt their roughness, she forced herself to accept the truth of her new reality.

"Arrie, am I dead?"

He shook his head and smiled. "You've had quite a shock, milady. It would be best if you rested for a while."

They stepped back into the dimly lit reception area. The lounging travelers stared at them as they clutched their tankards, frozen in the same positions as when she'd left.

Darian pointed silently toward the stairs. She followed him up a narrow staircase and to the end of a dark corridor where he stopped to unlock a door.

The guest chamber was small but quaint. A single, octagonal window overlooked the busy main road. Darian opened it and fresh air drifted into the room along with the sounds of people, horses, and wagons. Marisa peered out across the valley up to the mountains from where they'd come, still trying to figure out where she was.

Arrie coaxed her into the chair as he leaned over to examine her temple.

"It's just a small gash which should heal fairly quickly. Nothing to worry about," he said with a smile. "Will you be all right here by yourself?"

"I guess so," she managed.

He patted her hand. "Stay here and rest for a while. We'll be back to fetch you for supper a little later. The proprietor was kind enough to find some clean clothes for you. Rest well, milady."

Arrie followed Darian out into the hall and shut her door.

Marisa studied the strange, dark green walls of her room. Where was this Carnelia, anyway? She stared at the pile of clothes on the bed. What had she gotten into this time? What would her uncle think when she didn't return after her ride?

Her head was pounding, and the blood pulsed through her neck. She closed her eyes, forcing herself to calm down. Then she remembered the bottle of aspirin in her satchel and removed a little white pill. She found a crude water pump in the bathroom and pumped it up and down, collecting just enough water to wash it down.

As she glanced up into the mirror, Marisa was startled by her pale, grimy reflection. There was a streak of dried blood on the side of her face, and her hair was disheveled.

She grabbed a small linen towel and moistened it to scrub the blood and dirt off. A tear ran down her cheek and then another. Unable to stop the flow, she threw the towel in the sink and collapsed onto the bed. Was it really only just this morning that they had buried her father?

She sobbed into her pillow and a wave of exhaustion consumed her. Her body, mind, and spirit had all been stretched past their breaking point.

CHAPTER 3

ANDRESIS

MARISA AWOKE TO THE sounds of soft flute music drifting up from below. The fact that she was no longer in Oregon came flooding back like a tsunami. She stood to look out the window.

The soft glow of street lanterns pierced the darkness. The street was still busy below, but all the shops had been closed. She peered up into the hills where they'd emerged from the forest and wondered what Mark and Uncle Al were doing. They were probably worried sick about her by now.

Marisa shut the window and spotted the pile of clothes still folded neatly at the foot of the bed. The two men would be returning for her soon and she needed to get dressed. She slipped into the corset-like underwear and pulled on the long-sleeved shirt. It felt odd until she realized it was on backwards. The dress was a scintillating shade of deep ocean blue, with a rich, royal feel to it, like thick velvet. When she tightened it around her waist by pulling on the drawstrings, she noticed how it flattered her figure.

A loud knock at the door startled her. It was Arrie.

"How are you feeling, milady?"

"Honestly? I feel as if I've just been hit by a Mack truck."

"Trust me, that's a perfectly normal reaction," he chuckled.

She followed him down the stairs and through several other rooms before they entered a noisy, crowded dining hall.

The beamed ceiling was nearly fifty feet high. Gigantic wrought-iron chandeliers hung down and emitted a warm glow. A large stone fireplace created a welcoming, cozy atmosphere in spite of the enormous size of the room.

Marisa gasped when she spotted several trophy heads of a hideous, apelike wolf hanging along the walls. Each of the heads varied in size, but they all had the same sharp teeth and menacing yellow eyes. She hoped never to see one alive.

Arrie motioned toward a table in the far corner of the room where Darian chatted with a pretty young woman. The woman set a jug down on the table and when he said something to her, she smiled shyly at him.

As Arrie and Marisa sat, the woman quickly curtseyed and left to attend another table. Darian poured the ale into three large mugs and handed both of them one before raising his own.

"*Ap eirie*," Darian said.

"*Ap eirie*," Arrie said. "It means 'here's to fulfilling your destiny.'"

"Cheers."

Marisa was finally able to get a closer look at the handsome young ambassador as he sat across the table from her. At least six feet six, he had to have been one of the tallest men she had ever seen. She quietly admired the way his armored uniform emphasized his athletic physique.

He grasped the tankard with a strong hand and raised it to his lips. His square features were softened by the candlelight, but his countenance remained suspicious of her. His eyes intrigued her as they shifted nervously between staring into his cup, roaming around the room, and gazing directly at her.

"You seem to be in shock, milady. Are you well?" Arrie asked.

Marisa blushed. "No—I'm not. In fact, I think I may be going crazy," she said. "How can I still be on the same planet but in a different dimension?"

Arrie took his napkin, folded it, and wrapped it around his tankard to demonstrate. "Think of it as many layers of cloth compressed tightly around a planet. The fabric is made up of hundreds of threads running parallel and perpendicular to each other. Each strand is distinct and separate from the others, yet they are all weaved together.

"If you were able to look down closely on those threads, you'd see that they lightly touch each other in certain places. Where they meet, they are compressed—overlapping slightly and essentially occupying the same space. Are you still with me?"

"Barely."

"The thread or strand you are living on is one dimension, and we are on another. The vortex is the physical location in space and time where both worlds meet and overlap. You slipped through that vortex from your world into ours."

"So according to your explanation, it's possible for two different worlds to coexist in the same space at the same time?"

Arrie's face brightened. "Not just two worlds—but *many*. You can't see the other dimensions even though they're right here, converging through the same space we're occupying."

She digested that for a moment. "So right now, there are people in other dimensions all around us?"

"Probably. We are oblivious to them, and they to us, and yet, they exist. Some call them parallel universes, but they aren't skewed tangents of our own universe. In other words, there aren't multiple versions of Marisa or Arrie running around out there as scientists in your world like to claim..." Arrie broke off as the woman returned with plates of steaming food.

Marisa was starving. She grabbed her fork and started to dig in but stopped when she noticed the others weren't eating yet.

"We always give thanks to Garon before a meal," Arrie said.

"Who's Garon?"

"He is the author of the universe and of all things."

She said nothing but set her fork down, bowed her head, and closed her eyes.

Darian began to pray, and although she couldn't understand what he was saying, the sound of his voice was captivating. Commanding and deep, it matched his face perfectly. She listened as he spoke their strange language, noticing how well it flowed, without any harsh or guttural sounds.

When he finished, she opened her eyes. "So basically I came through some black hole?"

Arrie swallowed a mouthful. "No. You wouldn't have survived a black hole. Those will rip you apart right down to the subatomic level."

"Oh."

"The vortex of which I speak is really more of a wormhole—except you didn't go forward or backward in time, you simply passed from one dimension to another."

She shook her head. "This is—nuts!"

"I understand your skepticism, milady, but I'm afraid it's true. What most people fail to recognize is that they are constantly overlooking other dimensions all the time and don't even realize it."

She stopped. "What do you mean?"

His eyes narrowed. "Have you ever felt like you were being watched? Even though you knew you were alone?"

Marisa shuddered. "Yeah."

"You just *sense* it. You know something is there even though you cannot see it, but you just *feel* a presence. Some people swear they've seen a ghost. Others call it paranormal activity or having a sixth sense. But in reality, these people have actually just caught a glimpse of someone or something in another dimension."

"That's just creepy."

"Indeed. Most people choose not to believe in spiritual anomalies beyond their comprehension. It scares them to open themselves up to the possibility, so they simply deny their existence."

"So a vortex is the only way between worlds?"

Arrie nodded. "As far as we know. Of course, we cannot predict exactly when and where a vortex will open—we only know certain areas have a higher rate of occurrence than others. Still, the chances of being in the right place at the right time to be drawn into a vortex are extremely small."

Her eyes widened. "Do you mean to tell me I'm *stuck* here?"

"Perhaps not," he offered. "Some have traveled there and back again."

"Okay—but Arrie, there's something that just doesn't add up. How can a guy living in a world without cars, computers, or any kind of technology explain the theory of the vortex?"

"But it isn't just a theory, it's a scientific fact..." he trailed off.

She cornered him with her eyes. "You didn't answer my question."

Arrie shrugged. "The truth is, I traveled through a vortex into your world purely by accident. I lived there for a few years and attended a university where I studied quantum mechanics. Then, most unexpectedly, I was drawn back to Carnelia through another vortex."

"Wow. And that's why you can speak English so well—because you've been to my world?"

Arrie nodded sadly.

Darian eyed her suspiciously as he whispered something to Arrie. He hadn't said much all afternoon, but she noticed that he couldn't seem to take his eyes off her.

"Did anyone accompany you through the forest?" Arrie asked.

"No, I went riding alone."

"Alone? What were you doing in those woods unescorted?"

"I'm almost eighteen. I can take care of myself." She raised her tankard and took a sip.

Arrie shifted uncomfortably. "Indeed, milady. I meant no disrespect." He quickly changed the subject. "That is quite a remarkable ring you're wearing. In Carnelia, a ring such as yours symbolizes ownership. Does it hold particular significance for you?"

"Yeah, it was a gift," said Marisa. Her eyes moistened.

"A gift from whom?"

"From a man I love very much."

"Ah, I see." Arrie and Darian exchanged glances.

Marisa gazed down at the magnificent ring made of rose gold. In its center, an exquisite teardrop-shaped diamond sparkled in the candlelight. Curled around the stone on both sides of the band were flowers containing three small diamonds nestled within.

"So, you say you'd just come from earth when we discovered you?" Arrie asked.

"Yeah—I think so. I mean, I may have been knocked out for a while before you found me."

"Did you happen to see us before you fell off your horse?"

"No." His question irked her. "And I didn't *fall* off my horse. Something sucked me up into the air. I must've hit my head because it knocked me out. Next thing I know, I'm waking up to find the two of you above me. Why are you asking me that anyway?"

Arrie looked sheepish. "Our friend over here wants to make sure you're not a spy."

"A *spy*? He thinks I'm a spy?" She turned angrily to Darian. "Look, dude, I'm really sorry you're stuck with me, but I'm not a spy!"

Darian glared at her for a moment and slammed his tankard down hard on the table. People stopped to look as he stood abruptly and headed for the door. He shoved a few coins in the proprietor's hand and stormed outside.

Marisa's jaw dropped. "What *is* that guy's problem? I'm starting to think you should have just left me back in that forest. It's pretty obvious I'm puttin' you two out."

Arrie sighed. "There are some things you should know about Darian, and if I were you, I would not be so hard on him. He's been through some very trying times, and there are undoubtedly many more ahead."

"Well that may true," she said, drumming her fingers on the table, "but it doesn't give him license to act like a jerk."

"Do not take it personally. That man has a tremendous burden to bear for this country, and he is only trying to discern his friends from his enemies."

"He seems pretty young for an ambassador," she said. "Maybe he can't handle the pressure."

Arrie downed his ale and looked at her. "Marisa, we will do everything we can to help you return to this Jackson's Ville; however, we have a job to do and must be able to see it through."

She smiled at his mispronunciation. "What job?"

"A very important job. And I am here to protect him."

She was intrigued. "Protect him?"

"Yes, you see, Darian comes from a very influential family—the most powerful house in our country, as a matter of fact. He is of noble blood, with rank and a title, and must demonstrate absolute discretion with those whom he chooses to associate."

She held up a hand. "Listen, Arrie—I don't expect Darian to *associate* himself with me, but really, some common courtesy would be nice."

"But if you would just—

"And I don't appreciate the rude way he stares at me like I'm some kind of freak. I thought ambassadors were supposed to be, uh, you know—diplomatic!"

He shook his head. "It's not like that. Darian's duty is to protect our lands from those who are trying to tear it all apart. He has some very dangerous enemies, and there are even some in his own family who are trying to destroy him."

"So what does all that got to do with me?"

"I'm only trying to show you things from his perspective. I happen to believe that you are just an innocent bystander in this scenario, but Darian, well—he can be slightly paranoid. He tends to err on the side of caution."

"*Slightly* paranoid?"

"Milady, you must understand that he has every right to be suspicious of you."

"Why? What do you mean?"

"Well, after all, it was a remarkable coincidence that we just stumbled upon you as we did up in those woods. It would be just like his opponent to send a beautiful woman to spy on him."

Realizing that she may have been too quick to judge him, her shoulders sagged. Her father had always warned her about pre-judging people before she knew their background and circumstances.

"Marisa, I must caution you that this mission is vital to the survival of our society. At the very least, Darian must assume you're a shrewd spy for the enemy disguised as a damsel in distress. At best, you're an unnecessary distraction he cannot afford to have at this point."

Arrie leaned back as a young man removed their plates.

"Okay, I get it," she said. "I need to give the guy a break. But he can't honestly think I'm a spy. Isn't it pretty obvious that I'm not from around here?"

He shrugged. "He's just being cautious. Darian is an extremely complicated man. And to those who do not know him well, he can appear distrustful and cold. He's a lot like his father was."

His father.

"Arrie, I really appreciate that you're explaining all this to me, but—" she choked up, unable to get the words out. "You should know that my father just died, and we only buried him this morning."

"Oh, no," he groaned.

"I was already having the worst week of my life before I wound up here. I just want to wake up from this surreal nightmare."

She buried her face in her hands and wept softly.

"Oh, Marisa, I'm so sorry about your father. Believe me—I know what you're feeling. I lost mine when I was ten years old."

"I just don't understand why this is happening."

Arrie handed her a napkin. "Come, it's time that you got some sleep. You've had a rather long day and week from the sound of things. But first, let's go find Darian and make amends."

He offered her his arm, and they left the people, music, and dancing behind and stepped out into the chilly night air. She blew her nose with the napkin. She didn't feel like talking to the unfriendly young man.

She followed Arrie down the main road, and when her eyes had adjusted to the darkness, she spotted a tall figure standing on a bridge a few hundred feet away. It was Darian leaning over the railing, staring down into the water in quiet contemplation.

Arrie stopped her. "Let me go talk with him first. You wait here and come down in a few minutes."

Marisa said nothing but just nodded and watched as Arrie hurried down to Darian. She gazed up into the heavens, stunned to see millions of stars. The sky was pitch black. Somehow the skies seemed so much darker than on Earth.

She waited impatiently as the men discussed something for several minutes. Each of the men took turns glancing up at her. Darian's arms were crossed in defiance as he shook his head at Arrie.

At last Arrie motioned to her, and she walked to the bridge.

"Mar-eesa, I am sor-ry," Darian began, emphasizing her name.

"*What!* You can speak English?" she exclaimed. "You made me think you couldn't understand anything I was saying!"

"I must first make sure you are not a spy," he said, his rich accent enveloping each syllable. "And it has been a lit-tle while since I spoke English."

"Darian, please, I'm not a spy, okay? I can barely manage my own life right now."

"I am very sorry about your father," he offered. "Please ac-cept my, ah—condolences."

"Thank you," she said, loving the way he pronounced her name. "Listen, I don't know yet what is going on, but I'm just a high school grad with an uncomplicated life. Or at least that's what I used to think." She smiled shyly at him. "You probably have no idea what I'm talking about, do you?"

"I think I do," Darian said, revealing a stunning grin.

Arrie stepped in. "Pardon my intrusion, but Your Excellency, the hour is getting late, and we need to get some rest. Tomorrow we have a long journey ahead of us," he said.

Darian hesitated but finally nodded. The three exhausted travelers returned to the inn and trudged up the stairs.

As they reached the door of Marisa's room, Darian stepped up to unlock it for her. She stood close enough to feel his warmth and noticed that he was a full head taller than she was. He opened her fingers and gently placed a small key in the palm of her hand. She looked up into his face and his eyes locked on hers. In only a fraction of an instant, she saw an intense sadness buried somewhere in their depths.

"Good night," he said softly.

She paused before entering the room. She quickly turned to say goodnight, but they were already down the hall, quietly discussing something in their own language. She closed the door and slipped out of her dress and into her T-shirt before climbing into bed.

As she laid waiting for sleep to fall, Marisa's thoughts drifted back to Darian. He was unquestionably the most attractive man she'd ever seen. Truth be told, there weren't very many fabulous-looking guys in the small town of Jacksonville. But even if there were, none could match his striking appeal.

Beyond his good looks, he had an air of quiet sophistication about him. It was almost as if he had already seen and done far more than most people in their entire lifetime. She listened to the music still playing below in the tavern and was haunted by the image of his piercing eyes. Their color reminded her of the seaweed she and her dad used to find washed up along the beach.

Marisa drifted off to sleep and dreamed she was galloping on Siena through the forest. As she tried to dodge the lightning bolts striking all around, she kept hearing her father's booming voice call out to her from somewhere deep among the trees.

CHAPTER 4
ARRIE

MARISA STARED AT DARIAN in defiance. She wasn't about to get left behind. There was no way he could force her to stay in that godforsaken town all by herself.

"I'm coming with you, and that's final," she said, untying Siena's reins.

"This isn't a good idea," Darian said angrily. "It's much too dangerous and you'll only slow us down."

Her hazel eyes flashed at him. "What am I supposed to do around here in the meantime?"

"You'll only end up complicating everything!"

"But I don't know anyone around here. Who's gonna understand my gibberish in this town?"

"She's right, Darian. We can't leave her here," Arrie said as he mounted his horse. "I don't think we have a choice."

Darian scowled at him and unsheathed his sword. He pretended to examine the blade before finally shoving it back into its scabbard. He shook his head in frustration and climbed up onto his horse, seizing the reins a bit rougher than necessary.

"Well then, we'd best be on our way," he replied coolly.

Marisa followed the two young men out of the village. She was at a complete loss to understand why Darian wanted nothing to do with her. He clearly saw her as a threat to their mission, but she couldn't figure out why he seemed so intimidated by her.

After leaving the edge of the village, they traveled through hilly country for more than an hour. Marisa was amazed by the breathtaking landscape as she listened to the sounds of birds chirping and whistling high in the trees. She strained to listen to their beautiful songs, but Arrie kept chattering away, pointing out the various plants and trees and famous battles that had been fought in the area.

After a while, her mind began to wander. She wondered what the two young men were trying to accomplish on their diplomatic mission but decided to ask Arrie about it later. The main thing occupying her thoughts, however, was how she was going to return home. She remembered Arrie's explanation of the vortex and decided she needed to know more.

"So, Arrie, just how many different worlds do you think exist out there?" she asked.

He looked at her with surprise. "Well, there could be an infinite number of worlds in coexistence. Scientists in your world theorize there are probably a total of eleven different dimensions according to their string theory."

"Eleven? How did they arrive at that number?"

He shrugged. "It's a complicated concept, but it's just a theory. We're only certain of four distinct realms in the multiverse of which we have firsthand accounts. Your world Earth is one dimension, then there is Carnelia, of course, and there are still two others. There is also a fifth dimension called Syion, but it's more of a spiritual realm—forbidden for humans."

"A spiritual realm?"

"Yes, but we know very little about it. No one alive has ever been there and returned."

"Well, then how do you know it even exists?"

"Oh it exists. But one may only enter in spirit once the body has died."

"You mean like heaven?"

He nodded. "Heaven, yes, that's right."

"So once a person dies, they go to this Syion?"

"Only those who believe in Garon may enter," Darian interjected. "Those who do not believe may not enter."

"What do you mean? They believe that he exists?"

Arrie shook his head. "No, it's much more than that. Believing in Garon is not just believing he's out there somewhere. One must sincerely seek to know *who* he is. If you know him and follow his ways, you cannot help but love him and be thankful. That is what it means to believe."

She didn't know how to answer that. Although her parents had been pretty religious and had taken her to church almost every Sunday, Marisa wasn't sure what she believed anymore. She wasn't convinced that there was a God out there who even cared about her.

They had been traveling for a couple of hours when Marisa started to feel drowsy. She watched Arrie as he stroked his horse's mane.

"Both of you have really beautiful horses—especially Darian's. What's his name?" she asked.

"Obsidian," Darian answered.

Marisa stared at him for a moment, waiting for him to say something else. When he didn't, she shrugged and turned to Arrie.

"And what do you call your horse?"

"Horse," Arrie said with a smirk.

"Seriously? You don't have a name for him?"

Arrie shook his head.

"Well, that's just wrong. I'm gonna give him one." She gazed at the dapple-gray horse. "Spot? Stormy?" She snapped her fingers. "Wait—I got it! Why don't you call him Concrete?"

"Concrete? But isn't that—"

"Yeah! And it's perfect," she said, laughing. "He's the same color as our driveway."

"Well then, Concrete it is!"

After they traveled for another hour, they stopped to rest in a beautiful wooded area. Marisa spotted an old tree stump and climbed down to stretch her muscles that were already becoming stiff.

She untied her satchel from the saddle and headed toward a large grove of trees. Arrie dismounted and led the horses down through the forest to a small stream to drink. Darian strolled over to where she was sitting and leaned against a tree.

"So tell me about your family, Mar-eesa."

"There's not much to tell. I had an awesome father and we were real close. He helped me through some pretty tough times."

"How did he die?"

"Cancer," Marisa said. She noticed his puzzled expression. "He got sick last year, and it worsened to the point where his doctors couldn't do anything anymore."

"I am very sorry for your loss," he said.

"Thanks. The last two months have been the worst of my life."

"I cannot tell you that the pain lessens any because it doesn't. But after a while, it no longer consumes your every thought."

"Yeah, that's what I've heard."

"Do you have any siblings?" he asked.

"I've got a younger brother, Mark. He's sixteen. I also have an uncle who's like a second father to me. He is my father's twin. Everybody always says they look exactly alike, but I can—could always tell the difference."

"What about your mother?"

"I can barely remember her. She died when I was six."

"Such a shame," he said, shaking his head. "That is much too young to lose a mother. How did she die?"

"Car crash." Marisa looked at him. "Do you even know what a car is?" Darian shook his head.

"I didn't think so. Anyhow, my father broke the news to us one night. After that, he never wanted to talk about it. I think it was too painful for him."

"I am very sorry."

"I was so young when she died. Mark was only in kindergarten." She closed her eyes as she tried to remember her mother's face. "Our mother was such a kind person, but she was always very sad. I've never been able to understand how a person could be so sad."

"Sadness comes in all shapes and forms to all people. It is how a person chooses to deal with it that matters," he said, leaning his head against the tree. "Did your father ever tell you what the reason was for your mother's sadness?"

"Nope. He never wanted to talk about her death. He used to tell me a neat story about how they first met, but not much else."

"It must have been very difficult for him."

"Yeah. It was."

He gazed down at her hand. "I must say, that is a most extraordinary ring. Is your husband back on Earth?"

She looked at him, puzzled. "My husband?"

Darian nodded and pointed to the ring.

"But I'm not married," she said in a puzzled voice.

As Marisa looked down at her mother's ring and a realization suddenly came over her, she looked up at him and smiled.

"When I told Arrie that I'd received it 'from a man I dearly loved,' the man I was referring to was my father, Alan MacCallum. I'm not even engaged," she joked.

He grinned slowly. "Ah, I see."

"It was my mother's."

Arrie hurried over. "Come on, you two. We need to leave now if we want to make it through the Mychen Forest before dark."

Darian nodded.

They quickly mounted their horses and continued down the road. The beautiful landscape began to change from gently rolling hills into much steeper mountains and rocky cliffs. Marisa noticed there weren't many trees but mostly just shrubs and bushes. The majestic scenery reminded her of a coffee table book they had at home on Scotland.

The vistas were breathtaking, and once she was finally able to charge up with her solar charger, she snapped a few photos on her iPhone. She even managed to sneak a few candid shots of Darian and Arrie.

"Okay, now it's my turn to ask the questions," she said, slipping the phone back in her satchel.

Arrie grinned. "What would you like to know? I must warn you, though—I have no secrets that are worth hiding."

"You said you lived on Earth. How did you get there?"

"Well, a few years ago I happened to be visiting Terracina, the country where my father was born. I made my way up into the hills to take in the magnificent view from Pescara Hill. All of a sudden, there were flashes of light all around me and I got sucked into a vortex, same as you. I landed down by the river in a small village called Resteigne, near the Ardennes Mountains in Belgium."

"You probably had no idea what was going on," she said with a chuckle.

"What an understatement! I thought I'd died," he said. "But after the initial shock wore off, I did everything imaginable to fit into my new surroundings. I learned three different languages: French, Flemish, and English. I attended the École Polytechnique just outside of Paris and met a remarkable woman on the Avenue des Champs-Élysées. Her name was Astrid."

"You've been on the Champs-Élysées?"

Arrie nodded.

"Incredible!"

His eyes grew distant. "Astrid and I were to be married in a little less than a month when I was unexpectedly transported back to Carnelia."

"*Married?*"

"Married."

"Gosh, Arrie, I'm so sorry. Talk about lousy timing."

"Indeed, I must admit I was quite heartbroken."

"Okay, I know this is probably a stupid question, but you said that the chances of a person being drawn into a vortex are fairly small. Just how did you manage to get sucked in twice?"

"That is one of life's riddles that I may never know the answer to. By now I know what to expect, but back then, I'd only heard about vortices in stories and legends. When I was in your world, I studied quantum physics at the university hoping to gain a better understanding of them."

"Why have I never heard of a vortex before?" Marisa asked.

"That is because the powers that be do not want you to know."

"You're not saying it's a conspiracy, are you?"

He chuckled. "No, I'm not suggesting that. Your world has bigger problems to worry about. All joking aside, some people believe that there is an unseen force out there, controlling the gateways, opening and closing them at will. So you see, Marisa, I must have traveled to your world and back again for a reason."

"Can a vortex be predicted?"

"Can you predict the path of a tornado?"

"No."

"Well, neither can you predict a vortex. They don't usually open up in the same place twice. Of course, all the information we've managed to gather is based solely on firsthand accounts. I'm afraid it isn't very scientific."

"So there are others who have traveled between worlds?"

Arrie nodded. "We've actually made discoveries of new technologies by traveling to some of these other worlds. When we return to our home in Crocetta, we'll take you to visit Celino. He's a sorcerer from Earth and may be able to help you."

She brightened. "You mean there's someone else from Earth who can help me get back to Jacksonville?"

"Perhaps."

"But then, why haven't you tried to go back to Earth?"

He didn't answer.

"This fiancée of yours—Astrid, does she even know what happened to you?"

"I never told her about Carnelia, only that I came from another country," he said. "I'd already mastered French when I met her, so I don't think she suspected anything."

She pressed him. "And...?"

"That's all there is to tell. I still love her, but I've since come to realize that we are just not meant to be together."

"But you went through a vortex twice, so maybe it could happen a third time, right?"

He smiled sadly. "That's not likely to happen." His face clouded over as he reached down for his flask and took a sip of water.

"I'm sorry, Arrie. I don't know what to say."

"The worst part is that Astrid has no idea what has become of me. After I disappeared, she must have concluded that I had no desire to marry her. There is, in fact, nothing I would rather do more."

Although he avoided her gaze, Marisa could still see the moisture in his eyes as he fought to keep his composure.

"Time to stop for a rest," Darian said.

Arrie climbed off Concrete, quickly tied him off, and hurried off into the trees, still visibly shaken.

Marisa watched him disappear. "Is he going to be okay?"

"He'll be fine," Darian answered softly.

CHAPTER 5

DARIAN

MARISA RUBBED HER BEHIND, exhausted from being on Siena so long. She was accustomed to riding her almost every day but never for this long. Her thighs ached and so did the bruised hip she'd fallen on the day before. The wound on her temple was beginning to heal, but her head still ached. She followed Darian to a large tree and sat down at its base.

"How far is it to wherever we're going?" she asked.

"At least another full day's journey." Darian pointed to the snow-capped mountains some thirty miles away. "You see those high mountains in the distance?"

"You mean those jagged peaks?"

"Yes. Abbadon is located inside that mountain range. We must find a place to camp tonight because there aren't any more villages between here and the castle."

She stared at him in horror. "We're camping out?"

"Of course."

Marisa had loved sleeping in their family's camper at the coast. There was something so cozy about roasting s'mores around a driftwood campfire on the beach. But somehow camping in Carnelia didn't seem quite so carefree and she was pretty sure it didn't involve a Winnebago.

"We must be cautious, though, and ensure that we aren't too"—he searched for the right word—"vulnerable."

Marisa didn't like the sound of that. She didn't know how to shoot a gun and had no weapon to defend herself. Something told her that these two young men could hold their own, but the idea of camping outdoors with hidden dangers lurking behind every tree was a bit unnerving.

She quickly changed the subject. "So what exactly is your connection to Arrie? He seems like a nice guy, but he's had quite a bit of drama, hasn't he?"

"Indeed," Darian replied. "He's been in my service for as long as I can remember. Actually, we're distant cousins by marriage. Our whole family was extremely sad when he disappeared to your world. We thought we'd never see him again."

"It sounds like he didn't really want to come back here."

"He was quite happy with Astrid."

"Does anyone else know about his trip to Earth?"

He shook his head. "Only a few family members know. He rarely ever talks about it, even with me. I think it's still too painful for him."

"So why did he tell me? I'm almost a complete stranger."

"I don't know." Darian lowered himself down next to her and leaned against the tree. "Perhaps since you've traveled through the vortex to another world you can understand how he feels. Maybe he thinks he can trust you."

"What about you? Can you trust me?"

He avoided her eyes. "There are still many questions that need answers. No doubt Arrie has told you about me, and why I may seem a little, uh"—he tapped his head in search for the right word—"paranoid?"

She smiled. "Yeah, I think he may have mentioned it."

"I am a little bit, ah, how do you call it in your language? Ah yes—perfectionist. I just cannot afford to trust people I don't know."

"But why?"

He twirled a twig between his fingers. "Many people only get close to me because of what I can do for them. They are insincere and only using me to get what they want. For all I know, you could be one of them."

"Me?"

"Certainly. You could be one of Savino's spies, hired to keep an eye on me."

"Who's Savino?"

He sighed. "Someone who desperately wants to see me fail."

"Okay, so you're a control freak. I know lots of those. I have to admit that sometimes I'm a bit of a control freak."

"Control freak?"

Marisa gave him a sidelong glance. With his stunning looks, wealth, and power, he was probably used to getting whatever he wanted. Goodness knows this young ambassador had probably never been in short supply of female admirers.

"We all have our faults you know, Darian. But you can't hide behind your own prejudices as an excuse not to trust people. In my world, people are presumed innocent until proven guilty. Maybe you should just learn to trust a little more."

He shook his head adamantly. "My situation is different."

"It can't be *that* different. So okay—let's say you inherit some castle and a hefty chunk of land. You do all your duties, you fulfill all your obligations, and in the meantime, you learn how to lighten up and live a little bit. Once you've done all that and everybody's happy, you can call your own shots, right?"

"Unfortunately, no—I cannot."

"Well then, can't you just—"

"Milady, believe me, I want to trust you, but things just aren't that simple. You have no idea who you're talking to!"

Darian stood up and stalked off into the woods. She watched him disappear before she finally jumped up and hurried after him.

"In the end, it doesn't matter if you trust me or not," she said. "But I will tell you this—you need to learn to trust people a bit more, or you're never gonna be happy. My father always said that if you never take the risk, you'll never take the triumph."

He spun around and stabbed angrily at her with his finger. "You don't understand anything about my life or the people who are trying to control it! If you knew the truth, you'd know why I must be suspicious of every single person I meet."

He turned on his heel and marched away.

"No, I don't understand! Why don't you explain it to me?" she yelled, trying to catch up. "Learn to trust someone besides yourself for a change!"

"Trust someone? Hah!" He stomped through the woods, ducking to miss the low branches as he shook his head and muttered to himself. She hurried to keep up with his long strides.

Suddenly Darian stopped, sucked in a deep breath, and wheeled around to face her. "Do you truly want to know just how tightly I am bound? Then I shall tell you. I'm not even allowed to choose the woman I am going to marry!"

"Why not?"

"I had a, ah—did have, an arranged marriage."

"What do you mean *had*? Did she break it off?" She snorted. "Now there's a shocker for ya!"

"No," he shook his head sadly, "she died."

Marisa froze.

"Oh, Darian! I'm so sorry," she said, touching his arm. "Really, I'm so sorry for joking about that just now. I had no idea it was something awful like that."

"Don't trouble yourself. It happened a long time ago," he said, dismissing it with a wave. He resumed his brisk pace through the woods as if he was trying to put some distance between himself and his painful memories.

"But who was she?" she pressed, wishing he would slow down.

He stopped in his tracks and slowly turned toward her.

"Her name was Princess Maraya Fiore. She was the daughter of Queen Elyse Fiore and King Macario. We were betrothed by our parents and would have ruled together after she ascended the throne."

"You were engaged to a *princess*?" Marisa gawked.

He nodded sadly.

"Wow, that's so—tragic. How did she die?"

"Her ship hit a terrible storm in the Sea of Pyrgos, and it sank. There wasn't a single survivor. Her mother, father, brothers—all lost. Several members of the royal family went down with the *Carnelian* as well, including Arrie's father."

"That must have been awful!"

"After we received the news that the ship never made it to Terracina and pieces of the wreckage had been recovered, our family was devastated. That one event pushed our country into a state of turmoil that has plagued it ever since."

"So what happens now? Can't you just marry someone else?"

Darian shrugged, plucking a leaf. "It's not that simple. According to Carnelian law, I must marry a Fiore princess in order to ascend the throne. But there are no suitable matches. It would be impossible for me to choose my own bride unless the law is changed."

"Is there anyone who can change it?"

"The man who is currently the power behind the throne is determined to steal the crown. He would never change the law so that I could marry whomever I want and ascend the throne." He rubbed the stubble on his chin.

Marisa shook her head. "I still can't get over the part about the arranged marriage. I could never marry some guy my parents had picked out for me."

"Why not?"

She looked at him, astonished. "I don't know—what if he was the ugliest guy on the planet? How can you just marry someone you don't even know?"

"You might be surprised. Most arranged marriages work out better than when the couple is allowed to choose for themselves. Family members are extremely practical when it comes to selecting mates for their children."

She shook her head. "Nope, sorry. I could never marry some guy I didn't know. Don't people here ever marry for love?"

"Some are fortunate enough." He shrugged. "My options as far as a spouse go have always been extremely limited, however. You might say it comes with the job. Perhaps it's my destiny never to marry."

"So what happens if you just decide to marry a common girl?"

"That is quite out of the question," he said, quickly dismissing the idea. "If I do not ascend the throne, then Savino will. If he were to succeed, it would mean utter disaster for our people. I must do everything in my power to stop him from taking the crown."

"You would sacrifice your own happiness just to keep this guy off the throne?"

Darian's eyes locked on hers. "I have been raised to put duty first. It is who I am. In the end, the privileges of being a member of the royal family always balance out with responsibilities."

She did a double take. "Wait—what? You're a member of the royal family?"

"Of course, my duties take top priority, and I am determined to succeed, which is precisely why we are on this diplomatic mission. Once we have been to Abbadon, I am confident things will work out."

"I hope they do."

He shifted uncomfortably. "We should be getting back now so we can move out."

As they walked back up the hill toward the horses, Marisa thought about his comment of being a member of the royal family. It certainly would explain his arrogant attitude toward her.

When they reached the grove of trees, Arrie was patiently waiting on top of his horse for them to return. Darian mounted his horse and looked thoughtfully at her before his face reverted back to its stony expression.

She replayed their conversation in her head. Something about him intrigued her, and her strong fascination with the young ambassador surprised even her. Although she had only known him for a day or two, she had already seen a lifetime's worth of sadness in those eyes.

All the boys she knew back home in Jacksonville were just that—boys. But this young man just a few years older than she seemed to already carry the weight of the world on his shoulders.

The company of five large warriors crouched behind the jagged rocks several hundred feet above the valley floor. Two of them carried longbows and quivers full of arrows while the other three harbored shields and long swords. Each man was poised to attack the second their leader gave the command.

The copper-haired leader motioned silently to his men with a closed fist, warning them to remain alert. Hidden from view, the warriors watched as the two men and one woman on horseback made their way along the road toward the Mychen Forest.

One of the younger archers quietly drew his bow and aimed it at the tall, dark man in the lead. From his perched position up on the rocks, the soldier could easily take the man down with just one shot. When the copper-haired warrior saw where he was aiming, he slammed his bow to the ground in anger. He grabbed the arrow and snapped in two, quietly but firmly rebuking the young man.

The band of warriors watched as the three travelers stopped just short of the edge of the forest. They waited in silence for their commander's hand signal which came a moment later. They quickly retreated down the far side of the hill just as fast as they could run.

The order to attack had been given.

CHAPTER 6

MONSTERS

DARIAN TUGGED GENTLY ON the reins, bringing his horse to a stop at the edge of the forest. Without a word, he sniffed the air and watched for any movement among the trees but saw nothing. He maneuvered his horse around to address Marisa in a voice only slightly louder than a whisper.

"Marisa, for your own protection, please listen carefully to what I am about to tell you. We will proceed in single file with me in the lead, then you, with Arrie bringing up the rear. You must remain in a defensive position with your horse between mine and Arrie's.

"Do not speak. You must not make a sound of any kind, but continue as quickly and as quietly through the forest as possible."

He paused for a moment and scanned the clearing for any sign of movement. When he saw none, he turned back to her.

"If we are fortunate enough not to encounter the rijgen, it should take us about twenty minutes to reach the safety of the clearing on the other side. If we are attacked, run your horse as fast as you can until you are clear of the woods. Whatever you do, do not stop, and do not try to hide in the forest." He removed a small dagger from his saddlebag and handed it to her. "Please take this and pray that you will not need it."

Marisa glanced down at the weapon encased in a black leather pouch. She removed it carefully from its sheath. There was an intricate coat of arms engraved in the upper part of the blade.

She looked at Arrie. He was stroking his mustache anxiously but still tried to reassure her with a smile.

"Darian, isn't there any other way without going through the forest?" she asked. "I mean, if it's so dangerous, shouldn't we just try to go around?"

"Unfortunately, this is the quickest way through. There is one other way, but it's up and over a treacherous pass with its own set of dangers. We just don't have the time."

"But is it worth the—"

"We must cross this forest if we are to reach Abbadon by tomorrow," Darian said impatiently. "Stay close and you'll be fine."

He drew his sword from its sheath, bowed his head in a short prayer, and moved forward with determination. He turned, motioning the others to follow.

They entered the forest, and the trio of horses settled into a steady trot. Marisa scanned the forest but only saw tall trees and dense brush consisting of unusually large ferns. The vibrant green moss covered the trees and fallen logs like a thick carpet. She would have marveled at the beauty of the woods had it not been so unnerving.

The deeper they went, the darker the woods became. Marisa felt a chill as the temperature suddenly dropped several degrees. She wrapped her cape tightly around her body and listened to the horses' hooves hitting the muddy road with a clippity-clop sound. They were making too much noise.

A bird cawed somewhere in the trees, startling them.

She turned to glance at Arrie. He was sweeping the forest with his eyes, back and forth, up and down between the trees. He stopped his scan just long enough to give her a small smile and put his forefinger to his lips, motioning for her not to make a sound.

A familiar fear gripped her. They weren't alone.

She couldn't see Darian's expression, but in the defensive way he held his sword, he seemed prepared to slice through anything that made a move toward them. His tall frame and broad shoulders were tense as he leaned forward on Obsidian.

Darian's head jerked to the left and then he spun around. He gestured to Marisa and Arrie to increase their speed, and the horses' accelerated into a bold canter. As their hooves pounded the ground, Marisa winced. Her eyes scanned the brush for anything unusual. At first she didn't see anything, but then she happened to be looking in just the right place.

Something was disturbing the ferns.

Off to her right a few hundred yards, a dark shadow darted through the forest, moving parallel to them. Her eyes tried to follow it, but it quickly disappeared.

Darian motioned to go even faster. Obsidian broke into a full gallop with Marisa and Arrie following close behind. The horses thundered down the road at a furious pace to escape their predator.

In the corner of her left eye, Marisa saw something accelerating between the trees. The ferns bent and swayed in its wake. Was it the same thing she'd seen before, or was this a different one?

Her heart was pumping as she struggled to cushion her body from Siena's muscles exploding underneath. She clutched the reins tight and arched her back as the adrenaline coursed through her veins.

So this is how it feels to be hunted.

She spun around to check on Arrie. A wave of terror gripped her as she spotted the frightening monster chasing them. It was a hideous, three-way cross between a wolf, a bear and an ape. The giant mass of dark fur bared its long fangs as its beady, yellow eyes darted around in search of the easiest prey.

Marisa opened her mouth to scream, but no sound would come.

Seeing the look of shock on her face, Arrie followed her gaze and glanced behind him. When he turned around again, his face was as white as a sheet. The beast snarled, lunging at Arrie with his razor-sharp claws and only narrowly missing him.

From out of nowhere, a second animal raced toward them and tried to slice Arrie's head with its claws. Arrie ducked just in time and shouted something to Darian who spun around without breaking his lightning-fast pace. He saw the two creatures racing behind the horses as their vice-like jaws took turns snapping at Arrie's head. Arrie unsheathed his half-sized sword and swiped at them as they growled and hissed at their prey.

Completely numb with fright, Marisa shut her eyes and ducked her head flat against Siena. From somewhere out of the depths of her memory, the image of her mother praying with her as a little girl flashed through her mind. She hadn't prayed in years and wasn't sure if Garon even existed. But she felt utterly helpless and it was the only thing she could do.

Dear Garon, if you are out there, please save us. Please help us make it out of here alive and away from these horrible beasts. Please... help us...

She lifted her head and spotted a sliver of light up ahead in the distance. Galvanized with fresh hope, her heart immediately sank when she turned to see four creatures chasing them. When she saw another two running parallel on either side, she knew their chances of being able to outrun the racing monsters were slim. The terrified look on Arrie's face only confirmed her fears.

Rising up in his saddle, Darian lifted his saber high, preparing to attack. A creature lunged at Obsidian's legs, but it howled and fell away after Darian sliced off its arm. Marisa forced herself to look away as the bile rose in her throat.

When she looked back again, another creature was rearing up on two hind legs to run just like a human.

This is my worst nightmare, but I'm actually wide awake!

At least nine feet tall, the beast turned its ugly head toward her and snarled. It was agile and fast, and the monster's sharp claws looked as if they could sever a man's arm as cleanly as a knife through butter. Its hellish, yellow eyes glowed in the darkness of the forest as they locked on hers. The creature raised its snout as if it were smelling something.

It *smelled* her fear.

Her shaking fingers curled around the handle of the dagger. She slowly unsheathed it, praying all the while she wouldn't be forced to use it. She glanced down at the blade and prayed silently once again.

Without warning, the beast pounced through the air and flew directly toward them. Marisa's scream penetrated the forest just as something whizzed past her ear. She felt a rush of cold air. The animal's body slammed against a tree and fell onto the road, dead.

Stunned, she looked around, puzzled as to what killed it just as it was about to attack her. But with all the other monsters still on their heels, she didn't have time to stop and think about it.

Ahead of her, Darian stabbed repeatedly at the creature running next to him, but each time he missed. With one final grunt, he sliced through its midsection with a broad, sweeping motion, and the beast shrieked in pain.

Now there were only two beasts still chasing them. Arrie had managed to stave off the remaining two behind them using only his small sword. As the horses thundered closer to the edge of the forest, the slit of light became bigger and brighter.

Suddenly a man screamed in pain.

Marisa whipped around just in time to see Arrie tumbling off his horse. She watched in horror as he fell to the ground and rolled a few times before finally coming to a stop in the middle of the road.

She shouted to Darian and pointed behind her toward Arrie. He was lying in the mud on his stomach, crumpled up and not moving. Darian shouted for her to get to safety as he pointed toward the clearing. In a flash, he wheeled Obsidian around and thundered away toward Arrie.

Siena bolted on with tremendous speed toward the gap in the trees now less than fifty feet ahead. She glanced back and saw Darian stabbing at the two beasts as they circled around Arrie and hoped they would make it out alive.

Just before Siena reached the clearing, a creature leapt out onto the road right in front of her, poised for attack. She shrunk back in fear, knowing it had her right where it wanted her.

Game. Over.

Shhhhwwwooooooop! An arrow pierced the creature's chest right below the heart. Marisa yanked Siena's reins hard to the right to sweep around the animal as it writhed on the path. Her eyes darted around the forest, searching for the arrow's origin, but she didn't see anyone.

Once Siena broke through the opening and had reached a safe distance from the forest, Marisa steered her toward a grassy meadow where she dismounted and fell to the ground. She gasped, fighting to catch her breath and struggling to focus on her next move.

She glanced around the sunny, peaceful meadow as worry began to consume her. She thought about Darian and Arrie still back in the forest. Should she go back and try to help them? No, Darian had told her to get to the clearing and wait for them there. But what if they'd both been killed by those horrible creatures? She didn't even want to think of that possibility. If both of them were dead, then she soon would be too.

Without warning, a man's scream erupted from somewhere in the forest. Recognizing Darian's voice, tears formed in Marisa's eyes.

Think—think!

She had no clue of where they were headed. The sun was already beginning to set, and Darian had said there weren't any more villages until they reached Abbadon. Although Marisa had aced the mandatory outdoor survival class way back in sixth grade, she doubted she could survive even one night alone. She was on her own.

With nothing to do but wait, she wiped her tears and tried to collect her thoughts. She rolled over on her back into the soft grass that had been warmed by the sun. With her arm resting across her eyes, she didn't see the giant warrior glaring down at her.

He didn't look happy to see her.

Darian had no time to stop and check if Arrie was still alive. Lunging with his sword, he stabbed at the creature hovering over Arrie while the other monster attacked him from behind. Fighting one of these creatures was already a challenge, but defeating two of them was nearly impossible. He screamed loudly at the beast attacking him, which seemed to confuse the creature temporarily. But then the monster realized it was just a bluff and resumed his attacked, swiping at Darian with his massive claws.

Just as Darian felt his strength beginning to wane, his blade finally found its mark. He stabbed the growling creature in the heart, and it fell away dead. But it was too late. Before he could strike at the other beast, it was already lunging for him.

Shhhhwwwooooooop!

An arrow split the air and struck the creature's back. The hairy monster yowled in pain and fell sideways, badly wounded but still alive. It gnarled and snorted, swiping at Darian and only narrowly missing his left leg. But before Darian could kill it, another arrow split through the forest. This time it struck the creature under the rib cage, and it stopped moving.

He sprinted back to where Arrie lay still on the ground. His arm had been wounded and he was unconscious, but Darian sighed with relief when he discovered his friend was still alive.

He scooped up the red-headed young man, draped him over his saddle, and grabbed the reins of both horses as his eyes scanned the forest. They had to get out of there before more beasts could arrive.

Startled to see the towering warrior glaring down at her, Marisa felt her waist for the dagger, but it wasn't there. She spotted it on the ground just a few feet away and quickly scampered over the grass toward it, but it was already too late.

The soldier seized her arm and twisted it behind her back. Then he grabbed the other one and bound them both together with a piece of rope. Lifting her up as easily as if she were a rag doll, the warrior held her at eye level. As he sneered cruelly at her discomfort, she noticed that he had one gold tooth in front.

She had heard fairy tales about giants, but she'd never seen anything like him. Although she was nearly six feet tall, she only reached the height of his belt.

"*Lawraken er rynchen omon id defin?*" the giant bellowed.

Terrified, Marisa shook her head. He was too powerful to fight, and she didn't have the strength or will at that point to resist. The man dropped her down to the ground and let out a low whistle. Three more warriors emerged from various hiding places at the edges of the forest and approached them.

Each of them was incredibly muscular and just as big as the gold-toothed warrior. They were outfitted in sleek bronze breastplates, sturdy boots, and bronze helmets. Three of them had bows strapped across their backs, and the gold-toothed warrior carried a sword and a large shield.

As the warrior eyed her suspiciously, she decided her only chance of staying alive was to keep her mouth shut. She listened quietly as the men discussed something among themselves in their own language.

A man's voice shouted from the edge of the forest. She saw Darian and a fifth warrior emerging from the clearing. Relieved to see that he was unharmed, her heart sank as soon as she saw Arrie slung unconscious over his horse. After all the tragedy that he had already endured, she prayed that he wouldn't be doomed to die a terrible death too.

When Darian saw that Marisa's hands were tied behind her back in submission, he became enraged. He shouted at the lead warrior as he pointed angrily at Marisa. Reluctantly, Gold Tooth untied the rope and released her. Darian hurried over to Marisa, his face a mixed expression of anger and concern. Without a word, he gently but firmly steered her toward a large grove of trees.

Only when he was certain that they were out of earshot of the others did he speak to her. "Are you all right, Marisa? You are not hurt?"

"I'm okay. Just a bit shook up, I guess. Is Arrie going to be okay? What were those nasty things in the forest? And *who* are those very big men?"

"There's no time to explain. You must just trust me—"

"Trust you? Wow. Didn't you just lecture me on all the reasons why I can't be trusted? And now I'm just expected to trust you, no questions asked?"

He said nothing but just stared at her, frustrated.

"I'm sorry, Darian. I should be thanking you for saving my life. Forget I even said it."

"No, no—you're absolutely right. I suppose I deserved that," he said, looking a bit sheepish. "First of all, you can rest easy as Arrie will recover. He has sustained a minor flesh wound, but it isn't life-threatening. Those 'very big men,' as you call them, are warrior guards sent from Abbadon."

"Warrior guards?"

"Yes. They had specific orders from Savino to escort us safely through the woods, but the company arrived too late. The older warrior with the copper-colored hair is Talvan. I've known him all my life and he can be trusted, but the other men are loyal only to Savino."

"I've never seen anyone so big in my entire life."

She shook her head and wondered how much more of this craziness she could take. Her life back in Jacksonville seemed pretty darn tame compared to all this.

"Marisa, please, this is extremely important. Did you say anything to the warriors?"

"No. I didn't even get the chance. They—"

"Good! From now on until we arrive back at Crocetta, you must not utter a single word in the presence of others."

"What! Why?" She stared at him in disbelief.

"Savino must not know that you are from Earth. If anyone in Abbadon discovers the truth, it will get back to him and that would be bad."

"Well, how the heck are you gonna explain me, then?"

"We shall say that you are a mute. You can hear, but you cannot speak. Do we have an accord?"

"Arghh! This is crazy," she groaned, covering her face with her hands. "I don't understand anything that has happened since yesterday."

Darian looked at her patiently, still waiting for an answer.

"Okay, I promise—mum's the word. I am only going along with all this hoping that it will turn out to be some elaborate dream."

"Good, thank you."

"But can I still talk to you and Arrie?"

"Yes, but we must be extremely cautious. You may only speak when we're confident no one else can hear." He noticed her gloomy face. "It will only be for a couple of days. You'll be able to speak freely once we've left Abbadon."

"Yeah, whatever," Marisa mumbled. She turned to go.

"Wait a minute," he said, stopping her. "I have something for you." He fumbled around inside his uniform before finally producing an oval-shaped, transparent device no larger than an almond.

With his thumbnail, he pressed a green button several times and gave it to her. "Here—put this in your ear."

"What is this thing? It looks like a tiny hearing aid."

"It's a language translator. It will allow you to hear every conversation in English."

"Really? Wow—that's pretty cool!" She pushed her hair behind her ear and carefully inserted the device.

"If you put it in your right ear, you'll hear a simultaneous translation of whatever you're listening to. You'll still hear the foreign language in your left ear, but you must learn to block it out."

"Won't that drive me crazy? Like watching TV and listening to the radio at the same time?"

"After a while, you will become accustomed to it. Just concentrate on what is being said in your right ear. If you cover it with some hair like this, no one should be able to detect it. All right, let's try it out."

As Darian spoke to her in Crocine, Marisa could hear a man's voice translating the words into English.

"Ha—it actually works!" She was amazed by the tiny piece of modern technology. "Where in the world did you get such a thing?"

He smiled mischievously at her. "Actually, the correct question to ask is 'in *which* world did you get such a thing?' Do you remember Arrie saying there are four known worlds that can be entered through a vortex?"

"Yeah?"

"Well, this little instrument found its way into our world from one of the other three dimensions. It is extremely valuable, so whatever you do, please don't lose it. Now, come—we need to return to the others."

She gave him the thumbs-up that she could understand what he was saying, but remained silent as she followed Darian across the meadow to where the warriors waited.

Although she hadn't seen much yet of this strange new world, one thing was for certain—life in Carnelia certainly wasn't dull.

CHAPTER 7

TRUCE

"NOT TO WORRY, SHE'S all right now," Darian said loudly as they crossed the meadow. "Talvan, find a spot to set up camp." The copper-haired man gave him a quick nod and hurried off.

Marisa spotted Arrie lying on the ground several feet away and saw he was still unconscious. She desperately wanted assurances he was going to be okay, but she didn't dare ask about it in front of all the other men. Keeping her mouth shut was clearly not going to easy.

The tawny commander returned within a couple of minutes and ordered his men to set up camp on a flat, grassy terrace not far from where they stood. It was a strategic location that would allow them to observe anything or anyone approaching the camp, and there was a river where they could get fresh water just a few hundred feet below.

Marisa led Siena down the hill to a bucket of drinking water and removed her satchel. Exhausted and emotionally spent from their terrifying afternoon, she sat down on the grassy, sloping hillside and breathed deeply, glad for a few minutes alone. She watched the men up at the campsite as they hurried about, completing their preparations to settle in for the night.

With a minimum amount of effort, two men cleared the area and pitched the tents. Another warrior got a fire going within just a few minutes and began to make some stew. The gold-toothed warrior stood guard high on the hill above them, but there was no sign of the lead commander or Darian.

The temperature dropped as the sun slid down over the horizon. Marisa shivered and pulled her cape tightly around her. A wave of relief washed over her as she realized armed guards would be watching over them during the night.

She lay back in the grass and watched as the clouds slowly changed from their orange, pink and purple hues the further the sun disappeared. The view was spectacular, and she tried to remember the last time she'd actually taken the time to watch a sunset. It had been a long time ago—too long, in fact.

It was just starting to get dark when she spotted Arrie reclining against a dead tree stump closer to camp. Relieved to see that he had regained consciousness, Marisa stood up and led Siena back up the hill to the others. She plunked down next to Arrie and stared bleary-eyed into the smoky fire. As it crackled and hissed, she listened to the comforting roar of water rushing somewhere below them.

"You look as if you've had a rough day, milady," Arrie said, smiling weakly.

Completely forgetting Darian's instructions, Marisa opened her mouth to speak but quickly closed it again as soon as she remembered. Noticing Arrie's puzzled expression, she giggled softly. She tucked her hair behind her ear, tilted her head toward him and pointed to the small device before subtly raising her finger to her lips.

Arrie nodded and smiled in understanding. Together they sat in silence and watched as the soldiers organized the camp according to their standard military procedures.

When Darian and Talvan finally returned, the warriors gathered to sit around the fire as one of the men passed around plates heaped with food. Marisa avoided the gold-toothed warrior by sitting as far away from him as possible. She tried to eat in a ladylike manner but her hunger made it difficult not to gulp the food. She practiced using the translator by listening to the men's discussions.

Darian remained silent for most of the evening and she pretended not to notice his stare. The orange glow of the flames danced in his eyes as he studied her from across the fire. The rest of the men lounged around the fire pit, slurping their ale and belching loudly. A couple of them had already drunk too much and their conversation was slowly sinking into the gutter. Talvan offered her a mug of ale, but she promptly refused.

Disgusted by the three men slowly sinking into a deep state of intoxication, she decided that it was time for her to go get some sleep. Marisa stood up and dusted herself off. Darian quickly downed the last of his ale, scooped up the lantern and sidestepped the lounging warriors to approach her.

"Milady, allow me to escort you down to the river."

The men stopped their drinking and stared at her. Marisa hesitated, but she took Darian's hand and they walked down the hill away from camp. She didn't know if her heart was beating faster because of their brisk walk or if it was because he was holding her hand.

Unable to see where she was going, Marisa stumbled over a rock in the darkness and almost fell, but Darian quickly caught her. She stole a glance at his handsome profile in the low light of the lantern as he guided her down a steep, narrow path. The roar of the water continued to grow louder until they finally stopped several feet away from the river's edge.

She gazed up into the night sky, amazed to see millions of stars. They seemed to twinkle in 3-D like tiny shards of glass, dotting the heavens all the way across to the horizon. It comforted her to see the same familiar moon nearly two-thirds full. She glanced over at Darian and noticed that he was quietly studying her in the moonlight.

"Do you think we might be able to call a truce?" he asked.

"I didn't realize we were at war."

"Not really war, but I still haven't made up my mind if you're a spy or not."

"I'm not a spy, Darian," she said softly.

"You probably feel like Alice in Wonderland by now."

Marisa's jaw dropped. "How do you know that story? And how is it that you can speak English so well? Or have you been to Earth too?"

"No, I have not been so fortunate as to have visited your world. I learned to speak English and a few other languages from Celino, the man of whom Arrie spoke yesterday."

"But why would you even bother learning to speak English?"

"To the privy members of the noble class of Carnelia, Earth is known for its, uh, its—what's the word again? Soph—sophisticated cultures. My mother felt that learning English would enrich my education, so she hired Celino as my tutor. He encouraged me to read all sorts of English books and literature."

"Sophisticated cultures?" Marisa raised an eyebrow.

"Do you not come from a sophisticated society?"

"Me?" She snorted. "Definitely not. I'm from a small hick town in Oregon that most people have never even heard of."

"Have you mastered a trade, or are you a gentleman's daughter?"

"If you're asking me whether I have a job or if I'm rich enough not to need one, the answer is neither. I just graduated from South Medford High last June and had hoped to get out and see the world. I just had no idea it would be a different world altogether."

Darian smiled.

"In fact, I was all lined up to start med school this semester, but then life sort of got in the way."

"Med school?"

"Medical school. I want to become a family practitioner—uh, doctor."

"Ah, a doctor. That's quite impressive," he said, giving her a sidelong glance. "Do you think you are well-suited for that kind of work?"

"What do you mean? Because I'm a woman?" she asked archly.

"No, no—I didn't mean it that way." He chuckled. "It's just that I have fought in many battles and have seen terrible things I never wish to see again. You would see horrible things all the time if you became a doctor."

"Yeah, the blood and gore doesn't bother me so much. Before my dad got sick, I had considered joining Doctors Without Borders. You know, travel around and see the world? Help third-world countries. That sorta stuff."

"Have you traveled much?"

"Not really. I've been to California and Washington and skiing up at Whistler, Canada a few times, but I've never been further east than that. My dad took us to Hawaii one year and he was planning on taking us to Scotland for Christmas. But now that'll never happen."

Darian led her downstream and motioned for her to sit next to him on a large rock. He picked up a few small stones and threw them into the water one at a time, watching each one as it splashed.

Marisa huddled to keep warm under her cape and avoided his eyes. She was starting to fall for him but knew that wasn't a good thing. He was completely out of her league. There was something so irresistible about him that made her wonder how many hearts the handsome young ambassador had already broken during his short life.

"I brought you down here so that I could explain some things to you before we reach the castle tomorrow," Darian said, interrupting her thoughts. "We must conduct our duties as soon as possible and then get out quickly again. I don't plan on staying for more than a couple days."

When she realized that he'd brought her down to the river to discuss business, Marisa felt embarrassed and was relieved that he couldn't see her flushed face in the darkness.

"The man we are visiting is called Viscount Savino da Rocha. As I told you earlier, he is the real power behind the throne, and he also happens to be my cousin. However, he is not the *rightful* heir to the throne."

"He's your cousin?"

"*Distant* cousin," he corrected. "Savino's father, Count Gregario da Rocha is currently the king, but not our legitimate monarch. Gregario was supposed to assume the throne only temporarily until the rightful successor could be crowned, but he actually has no desire to renounce the throne."

"And now you're having trouble getting rid of him?"

He nodded. "When Gregario's illness worsened a few months ago, his son Savino stepped up to serve until his father passes. However, we are certain that Savino has no intention of yielding the throne once his father is dead."

"Can he do that?"

"Politically speaking, it would be extremely difficult. Theoretically speaking, it would be nearly impossible. But that won't stop him. Savino has hired some shrewd advocates who are investigating the issue of succession as we speak. Gregario does not belong to the Fiore bloodline and was never the true and rightful heir."

"Then I don't understand Savino and the Fiore connection."

"After Queen Elyse perished in the shipwreck, her younger sister, Sophie, became queen. Sophie was Gregario's wife and Savino's mother. When Sophie passed away unexpectedly five years ago, her husband Gregario assumed the throne."

"Then why *shouldn't* Savino inherit the throne?" she asked.

"Because he does not carry the Fiore surname. Savino is a da Rocha, receiving his name from his father."

Marisa stared at him blankly, struggling to connect the dots.

"Let me explain it another way. Since the time of our common ancestor, King Petrus Fiore, the Fiore dynasty has ruled over all the lands of Crocetta and Abbadon right up until Queen Elyse. Had the royal family not perished in the shipwreck, according to the laws of succession, Maraya Fiore would have inherited the throne. I would have married her, and so—I would have now been on the throne."

Slowly his words registered and Marisa giggled as she imagined telling her best friend Daniela the entire story.

"What are you laughing at?"

"Oh, nothing," she answered, shaking her head. "It's just that my friends back home would never believe me in a million years if I told them about all of this."

"Come, we should be going back now. We have a full day ahead of us, and we need to be well-rested." He led her slowly back up the hill toward the camp but just before they reached it, he stopped her.

"Marisa, I know how difficult it is to lose a father. If you ever need someone to talk—"

"Thanks, but really—I'm okay."

Darian nodded and spun around to go back. As Marisa watched his tall silhouette quickly climb the hill toward his tent, she felt bad for cutting him off. He was only trying to help and she should be kissing his feet for saving her life more than once.

Knowing that she wouldn't be able to speak once they reached the campsite, she hurried after him and slipped her arm around his neck.

"Darian, thanks for saving my life today," she said softly. "I would have been dead now if it weren't for you."

Marisa stepped back, but Darian grabbed her arm and pulled her toward him. "You are most welcome, milady," he whispered in her ear. The hairs on Marisa's neck stood on end as he kissed her softly on the cheek.

As Darian and Marisa approached the campsite, the men eyed them with interest. They hadn't moved an inch since they'd left and Arrie was nowhere to be seen. Marisa guessed that he had probably already gone to bed.

"Here is your tent, Lady Marisa," Darian said with a bow. "Sleep well, and we shall see you in the morning." His face was solemn as he lifted her hand to kiss it, but his eyes twinkled. He winked at her, and she smiled in amusement.

Marisa entered her tent and sighed. She had probably been too bold in her manner of thanking him, but because she had felt so attracted to him, she simply couldn't help it. She lay on her mat waiting for sleep to come and chided herself. How could she allow herself to fall for a guy when she knew that it could never go anywhere?

Even if Darian had been attracted to her, he could never let it show. It was nothing personal. It's just that his fate had been sealed long before he'd even met her.

CHAPTER 8

ABBADON

MARISA AWOKE THE NEXT morning to the clatter of pots and pans. She stuck her head out of the tent and squinted in the brightness of the morning sun. The warriors had already taken down all the other tents and stored them on their saddles.

Ducking back into her tent, she groaned. Her muscles were sore from the strenuous run the day before, and sleeping on the cold, hard mat hadn't helped, either. Although she hated the idea, she knew she had to get up and get ready to go.

She rubbed the sleep from her eyes and spotted the leather satchel in the corner of the tent. She took out her father's book and ran her hand across the soft texture of the purple fabric.

Opening it gently, she leafed through the pages. The book's writing contained fluid, controlled strokes, except for the final page where the script was cramped and labored as it angled down off the paper. She flipped between the first and last pages and noticed a striking difference in writing styles.

Her knowledge of Scottish Gaelic was far too limited to be of any help in deciphering the book, but she was determined to have it translated once she returned to Earth. If she ever returned, that is.

"Good morning, sleepyhead!"

Marisa jumped as Arrie stuck his head inside the tent. Remembering not to say anything out loud, she just smiled and waved to return his greeting, and he quickly excused himself again to make sure all his gear was properly stored on his horse.

Darian's head popped in. "Milady, we are preparing to leave now. You'd best be getting ready to go."

She set the book down on the mat, stood up, and walked down the hill to the bucket of fresh water to splash some on her face.

Darian glanced around and noticed that Marisa's was the only tent still standing. He entered it and bent down to roll up her bedding but hesitated when he spotted the book lying on the mat. He touched the velvety softness of its cover and rubbed the black stubble on his chin in quiet thought.

Finally, he opened it and quickly skimmed through the pages but stopped when he noticed a strange drawing. While he was studying it, a thin slip of paper fell out of the book. He bent down to pick it up and unfolded it just Marisa entered the tent.

"Hey, what are you doing with that?" she asked.

"Milady, I apologize. I was just rolling up your mat when I found this beautiful book." Flustered, he quickly folded the paper, slipped it between the pages, and handed the book to her.

"Thanks," she whispered, slipping it back in the satchel.

"Did you write it?" he asked curiously.

"No."

Darian said nothing but hastily rolled up her mat and left the tent. She watched as he hurried down to the grove of trees where Talvan was barking orders and couldn't help but admire the way his muscular body filled his uniform.

She saw him pointing to her as he discussed something with one of the warriors and her heart stopped. As the soldier walked up to where Marisa stood and began to take her tent down, she sheepishly stepped aside.

A few minutes later, Darian announced that they would be leaving immediately. The small company of seven men and one woman mounted their horses and began the last leg of their journey toward Abbadon.

With no desire to be a part of the warriors' lewd conversations laced with male humor and raucous laughter, Marisa stayed on the outermost edges of the formation and focused on the beauty of the magnificent nature surrounding them. She stared up into the sky and noticed that the heavens were such a brilliant color of blue with only a few puffs of clouds here and there. The leaves were turning into their fall colors just as they had back in Oregon and as far as she could tell, Carnelia's seasons were the same as on Earth.

Her focus on the breathtaking scenery slowly drifted as thoughts of the handsome young ambassador invaded her mind. The fact that she could not stop thinking about him bothered her. Since Darian rode behind her on the opposite side, she was grateful not to have his handsome form as a constant distraction within her range of vision.

As Marisa turned to peek at Darian, she was once again met by his unsmiling, stony expression. She looked away. Why did he act so pleasant to her one minute, only to flip over to extreme coldness the next?

She remembered Arrie's comment about how complicated Darian was. Obviously, there was much more to this young man than meets the eye. No matter how attractive he was, though, she just could not fall for him. Her heart had been shattered once before, and she didn't care to relive that again anytime soon.

Just one week before graduation and on the night of their senior prom, Marisa had been humiliated in front of the entire school when Troy Matthews had taken off with her good friend Michaela Adams. Looking back now, it had been nothing more than a brief obsession, but at the time, it had seemed like the end of her world.

But with Darian, things were different. He wasn't some hick-town quarterback with a pickup truck and his daddy's credit card. Darian was already a key player in the power and politics of the country and he was more than capable of doing serious damage to a girl's heart.

She shifted her attention back to their surroundings. For the next few hours, the group climbed higher toward the snow-capped peaks. They crossed alpine meadows where flowers in every color of the rainbow dotted the pastures like colorful mosaics. Later, they passed through narrow valleys where emerald hills climbed steeply at sixty-degree angles.

As the men's chatter eventually fell silent, Marisa closed her eyes and listened to the horses' hooves meeting the road. Birds squawked high in the air, and for a few minutes, none from the party disturbed the majestic stillness.

No car horns, no sirens. No jet planes overhead, no throngs of people yammering into their cell phones or shouting to hail a cab. The breathtaking beauty engulfed and soothed her, and for a little while at least, her soul felt at peace.

As the party descended over the rocky terrain, Marisa leaned out around the soldier to check on Arrie. Although his face was pale from exhaustion and he winced each time the horse stepped into a rut, he seemed to be recovering. One of the warriors had bound his wound to help prevent it from becoming infected.

Satisfied that he was okay, her thoughts turned to Mark and Uncle Al. They must have gotten really worried when she never came home the night before. Members of the Jacksonville police, neighbors, and other friends in their tight-knit community had probably been up all night combing the area for her. Her uncle had probably figured out early on where she'd gone. If she ever made it back home, she could expect a serious grounding. She didn't care, as long as it meant getting back home safe and sound again.

Her eyes moistened as she thought of all the people worrying about her. The burden of what her friends and family must be feeling made her cry. As the tears began to overflow and run down her cheeks, the bottled-up emotions from previous days erupted to the surface. For the first time in her life, she couldn't go to her father to make it all better. She leaned her head against Siena's and cried.

Talvan spotted her slumped over her horse and removed his helmet. When he saw Marisa sobbing, he quickly spun around and motioned to Darian.

"Time to stop for a break," Talvan shouted. The men saw Marisa's head buried in Siena's mane and exchanged knowing glances.

Darian turned to the youngest warrior. "Take the horses down to let them drink."

"Yes, sire."

All of the men except Arrie and Talvan left with their horses to go down to the river.

"Why don't you two rest by the river for a few minutes as well?" Darian suggested.

Talvan and Arrie both said nothing but just nodded and hurried off.

Marisa wiped her eyes and climbed down but clung to her horse. She pressed her cheek against Siena's as her weeping turned into sobbing.

All of a sudden, strong arms enveloped her and Marisa turned her tearstained face toward Darian's. As he gazed down at her, she thought he was going to kiss her but he pulled her tightly into his chest instead. He stroked her hair softly as she mourned the father she'd never see again.

"Marisa, I'm truly sorry. The worst kind of pain the world has to offer can be found in losing a loved one."

As her cheek pressed firmly against him, she could hear his heart beating, solid and strong. Slowly, she opened her eyes and saw that they were all alone.

"Sit here while I fetch you a drink of water," he said.

Once he was out of sight, she wiped her tears on her sleeve and groaned, knowing that she must look awful.

From out of nowhere, a distant memory flashed through her mind. Marisa was only seven when she was out walking in the woods with her father after the death of her mother. He had explained to Marisa that there was no such thing as coincidence and that everyone's fate was ruled by their destiny. Wondering how her coming to Carnelia figured into her fate, destiny, or whatever one wanted to call it, Marisa was starting to doubt that she had any sort of control over anything at all.

Darian hurried back with a cup of water and handed it to her. The men were starting to return and he commanded Arrie to take Siena down to the river. As they waited for him to return, the gold-toothed warrior smiled smugly at her.

"Like I was saying before, women should stay in the kitchen where they belong—not on a man's journey!" He snickered as the other warriors roared in laughter.

"Deimos!" Talvan shouted, "That's enough!"

Marisa covered her face with her hands. Something inside of her snapped and she decided it was time for her to stop relying on others. From that moment on, she would be on her own.

Silently telling herself to toughen up, she climbed back into the saddle. As the party continued along the mountain road, Marisa fought the urge to look back at Darian. Starting today, she would only look forward and not back, both literally and figuratively.

Hours later, a weariness caused by a lack of sleep began to weigh Marisa down. She started to nod off, but as soon as one of the men whistled, she sat up quickly. They were just rounding the final turn in the mountain as Talvan gestured toward the imposing fortress at Abbadon.

Perched high on a rocky cliff like a crouching cougar surveying its domain, the ominous, gray castle did not appear either welcoming or friendly. A small city cowered against the fortress on all sides, and the entire region seemed enshrouded in a cloud of darkness.

Darian ordered two warriors ahead to inform the castle of the approaching delegation and to request that preparations be made for one extra female guest.

When Marisa saw the castle looming in the distance, the surreal nature of the situation smacked her head on. The fantastical notion of being escorted by an ambassador and giant warriors up a mountain ridge toward a medieval castle was simply impossible in her mind. Although she knew by now that she wasn't dreaming, she still fought the logic in her even being there.

The company reached the town at the foot of the castle and weaved its way through the narrow streets as people stopped to bow and curtsey. Darian smiled politely and waved, even stopping to shake a few hands.

They made their way up the hill and approached the main gate of the castle. An old woman stepped forward and offered Marisa an apple. Smiling gratefully, she took it from her. But before she could take a bite, Deimos ripped it from her hand and hurtled it through the air. The piece of fruit bounced off a rooftop, rolled down into the gutter, and disappeared.

"Stupid, foolish girl! It might be poisoned," Deimos snapped.

Marisa glared at him, angry and confused. She didn't think the woman was trying to poison her, but she wasn't in a position to protest. The old woman cowered back in fear from the angry soldier.

The screeching noise of metal scraping metal caught everyone's attention as the iron gate of the castle slowly raised in front of them. As the horses moved under the stone archway, Marisa looked up and saw the giant spikes of the portcullis. The small company entered the cobblestone courtyard where two rows of warriors stood to receive them.

Once everyone was inside, the gate was lowered and Marisa glanced back just in time to watch it clang shut. She couldn't shake the feeling that they'd just been locked inside a prison.

Darian dismounted and strode over to assist Marisa. She ignored him and climbed down by herself as he stared in bewilderment, stunned by her obvious snub.

Sensing the awkward moment, Arrie bowed and ushered Darian to the inner courtyard, where their host waited to greet them. Marisa trailed a few steps behind and tapped on her earpiece, not wanting to miss a single word.

"Ah, Your Excellency, you have arrived at last," said a rich, baritone voice. "Was your journey long and tedious?"

Curious to see the man addressing them, Marisa leaned around Darian's full frame. Her eyes widened and her jaw dropped.

CHAPTER 9

SAVINO

A STRIKING YOUNG MAN with pale blond hair, fair skin, and electric blue eyes stood to welcome them. Dressed in an elegant suit of charcoal armor, the master of Abbadon Castle stood almost as tall as Darian. Displaying an air of superiority and confidence, the man wore a devilish grin that made her wonder what nasty thoughts he was thinking. After he had gazed briefly at Darian and Arrie, his eyes settled on Marisa and he strolled over to meet her.

"But pray, who is this most gorgeous creature you have brought with you? Is this the celebrated beauty, the Princess Adalina?"

"No, Your Grace," Darian said. "Allow me to introduce to you the Lady Marisa. She is a distant cousin of Lord Arrigo from Terracina."

Marisa and Arrie exchanged bewildered glances. Aware of her dirty clothes, grimy shoes, and tear-stained face, Marisa stepped forward and curtseyed awkwardly.

"Milady has joined us on our journey and will be accompanying us to Crocetta at the conclusion of our stay in Abbadon," Darian added matter-of-factly.

The blond man kissed her hand. "So, did you enjoy your journey here, Lady Marisa?"

Marisa quickly looked at Darian, flustered. Without missing a beat, he stepped up to answer his cousin. "Your Grace, unfortunately, Lady Marisa is a mute. She cannot speak, but she can hear and understand you perfectly."

77

"A mute? What a perfect tragedy! A beautiful woman such as this with no voice to speak or sing?" A mischievous grin spread across his face. "Still, I'm sure there must be some rather compelling benefits to having a woman who cannot speak." He turned to his aides, laughing at his own joke, and several other men joined in.

Marisa muttered something under her breath.

Savino bowed deeply. "Milady, I am the Viscount Savino da Rocha. You are most welcome in my castle. I am certain you must be tired and in desperate need of freshening up."

He motioned to a group of women.

"Helinda will show you to your chambers where you can bathe and change into something more"—he appraised her filthy dress with obvious disgust—"appropriate."

Marisa smiled nervously as three ladies dressed in beautiful gowns led her away to a large doorway on the other side of the courtyard. She was a little nervous about the whole mute act and hoped that she wouldn't blow it for Darian by accidentally opening her mouth.

The women entered a dim, windowless corridor where a few flame torches provided the only source of light. The air was cold and damp and Marisa shivered as a chilly draft blew past them.

Helinda motioned to her to ascend a circular stairway and Marisa noticed that each of the stone steps had been worn down in the middle from centuries of use.

Halfway up to the second level, she saw a slit in the stone cornice of the wall. She moved up close and peered through the narrow gap. Feeling a rush of cold air, she gasped as she saw a beautiful waterfall a mile away that cascaded several hundred feet down into a rocky cove.

Realizing that the others were waiting for her, she turned to climb the second flight of stairs. They reached a massive oaken door that looked as if it had been there for centuries, and Helinda removed a large key from her pocket to open it.

When she entered the chamber, her eyes were drawn up to the magnificent vaulted ceiling and opulent chandelier hanging from its center.

As big as the entire first floor of her house back in Jacksonville, the room's walls were a mixture of black rock and polished grey stone. Several stained-glass windows added color to the room, and a large stone fireplace provided enough warmth for the entire suite.

Dominating the room was a king-size canopy bed covered with an array of satin and velvet pillows in all shapes and sizes. There was a dressing table, night stand, and separate full dressing room, including a full-length mirror. Beyond the dressing room, two women poured hot water into a bathtub.

Helinda started a fire in the fireplace by striking two stones together and after a few minutes, the area became cozy as soothing warmth spread throughout the spacious chamber.

Marisa was admiring the exquisite tapestry hanging above the bed when she realized that Helinda was speaking to her. She turned her head toward her and listened.

"...all your clothes were lost on the journey. This cabinet contains clothing for your personal use during your stay," Helinda said, riffling through the dresses.

"Some of them are likely to be your size, but you'll have to see what fits. The viscount is holding a ball in honor of Prince Darian tomorrow night, so I would suggest that you start searching for a dress appropriate for the occasion."

Prince Darian!

Did she seriously just say he was a prince? Marisa gasped as those two little words registered in her brain. Up until then, he had only been referred to as Ambassador Fiore. He had mentioned that he was a member of the royal family and was required to marry a princess, but he'd never said anything about being a prince in his own right.

She let out a deep sigh. No wonder he looked down on her. Not only was she falling for a guy she could never be with, but he happened to be a prince too.

"Supper will be in the dining hall in one hour, and you mustn't be late," Helinda shouted on her way out the door. "His Grace does not appreciate tardiness."

79

Marisa shut the door and let out a deep sigh, glad to finally be alone. She sank down onto the bed and admired the elegant furnishings. The expensive-looking fabrics and priceless objects of decor made Marisa wonder what it would be like to live in Carnelia as a member of the noble class.

She spotted a beautiful evening gown hanging on the wall and studied it, trying to determine to which clothing era the styles belonged. She finally decided that the evolution of clothing had taken a different path than on Earth. She liked Carnelian clothing because it made her feel better about herself. Her posture had even seemed to improve just in the few days since she'd arrived.

As Marisa perused the dresses in the cabinet, she began to feel incredibly insignificant. She'd been raised in an average, middle-class family and didn't know anything about royalty, diplomats, or even the way rich people lived. Everything and everyone she'd encountered in this world seemed so far out of her solar system.

Darian is a prince?

She stared in the mirror and shook her head angrily. Darian had lied to her about his position. Why was he trying to hide from her the fact that he was a prince?

She removed her clothes and settled into the bathtub. She missed her uncle and brother and longed to return to Jacksonville. At a time when she was badly in need of her father's advice, it was him that she missed the most of all.

Arrie had said that there was a man who might be able to help her return to Earth, but the doubt had already started overshadow hope in her mind. The possibility that she might never go back began to sink in. She stepped out to dry off and slipped into an understated but beautiful brown dress.

As she brushed her long chestnut hair, she gazed out the windows overlooking the mountains and watched the sun dip down behind the horizon. Peering below, Marisa could see the village they'd come through on their way up to the castle.

She noticed the street lanterns flickering in the darkness below and pondered the slower pace of life without TVs, movie theatres, video games, and freeways. She spotted a family out walking after supper and imagined how different life must be not to have all the modern technical distractions eating up one's time.

A loud knock startled her. She opened the door to find Arrie smiling and offering her his arm.

"Good evening, milady. I've come to collect my *cousin* for dinner," he said with a wink and a smile.

Marisa giggled and curtseyed mockingly. "Thank you, kind sir, but I'm afraid I'm not up for a fancy dinner this evening. Do you think our host would mind terribly if I respectfully declined his request?"

Arrie chuckled. "In the manner you bowled Savino over this afternoon, I'd wager he'll be quite disappointed if you don't show," he said dryly. "However, I will tell him that milady is too exhausted after our journey, and he shall not be able to argue with that now, shall he?"

"Thanks, Arrie. I'm goin' to bed early tonight and try to get some decent sleep for a change."

"Cousin, I think that is a splendid idea. I'll ask the cook to send something up for you in a little while."

"Good thinking. I'd appreciate that."

Arrie nodded and disappeared down the corridor. She shut the door and smiled to herself. He seemed to possess the knack for being able to put a smile on her face no matter what.

She stepped out of the dress and stiff undergarments, pulled a thin, linen nightdress out of the top drawer, and slipped it over her head. As she passed by a full-length mirror, she gasped and then giggled when she saw that the nightgown didn't leave much to the imagination.

Grabbing her satchel, she rummaged around in it and took out her father's book. She tossed a couple of logs on the fire, propped up the pillows, and climbed into bed. The mattress felt soft but firm as she snuggled under the comforter.

She leafed through the pages and studied the Gaelic script. It was obviously someone's diary, but whose? Could it be her father's? She doubted it. Her father had always written in boxy, squarish script, but this was more curved and flowing. Each entry began with what seemed to be a date followed by several paragraphs. There were small drawings, diagrams, and even a couple of small flowers pressed between the pages.

Halfway through the book, she found a piece of linen paper that she had missed before. She carefully unfolded it and saw that it was some sort of letter with writing so faded it was almost impossible to read.

Then she noticed a piece of stationery stuck between the pages near the back. She unfolded it and gasped when she recognized her father's handwriting.

August 12

Dearest Marisa,

Doctor Martin got the results of the MRI back this morning, and he told me that the cancer has spread again. I know now that I don't have much time left. I'm making the most out of every day I have, but it hurts me more than you'll ever know that I won't be around to watch you grow up, get married, and have children of your own. I hope that you will come to realize someday just how much you are loved.

You are such a treasure and a joy to me, serving as a constant reminder all these years of my love for your mother. She was a remarkable woman, and now I see so many of her incredible traits shining forth in you.

It's so hard to sum up all the wisdom of my whole life into one tiny bit of advice to pass on to you, but if I had to, it would be this: you will be confronted with numerous choices in your life, but always strive for what is good and right and never settle for less than that which is worthy and worthwhile.

I am giving you this book and your mother's ring. These treasures are the last remnants of the beautiful life we shared long ago. Please take good care of them and never forget that it is by choice that the ordinary person decides to live a life that is extraordinary. I love you so much, my dearest lassie. Happy eighteenth birthday!

Love, Dad

Marisa stared into the fire as the tears spilled from her eyes. She wiped them with the sleeve of her nightgown and placed the book on her nightstand. She shut the drapes but stopped abruptly as she peered through the window. There was a group of men strolling across the main courtyard below and she saw that it was Arrie, Darian, Savino, and one other man she didn't recognize. Hopefully they had been successful in conducting the business they had come for, and she knew she'd made the right decision not to join them for dinner.

All of a sudden, Darian glanced up at her window and she quickly hid behind the drapes. Marisa didn't want to reinforce his suspicions that she was spying on him. She peeked out again a moment later, but the men were already gone.

Knowing that the next day would be another busy one, she shut the drapes and sighed. On her way back to bed, she blew out the candles as her thoughts turned to their adventures in the woods when the horrible beasts were chasing them. She'd never been so scared in her entire life, but Darian had displayed remarkable courage in killing the monsters that had attacked Arrie. As her heart began to burn once more for him, she tried to force him from her mind.

Mesmerized by the fire, her eyelids drooped as the remaining flames died down into nothing but glowing embers. Just as she was drifting off to sleep, she was startled by a solid knock at the door.

She groaned and rolled out of bed in search of a robe. When she couldn't find one, she tiptoed across the cold stone floor and remembered Arrie's promise to have the cook send up some food.

She opened the door and was surprised to find Darian standing in the doorway, holding a tray of food in his arms. Cleanly shaven and wearing a different uniform, he seemed distracted when he saw her in the sheer nightgown.

"Good evening, milady. May I come in?"

"Uh, yeah—sure. Come on in." She crossed her arms nervously and her face flushed with embarrassment.

"Arrie said you weren't feeling well. We thought some food might make you feel better." He set down the tray and removed the cloth.

"Thank you, Your Royal Highness."

Busted. "You're welcome," he said sheepishly.

"That was, um—very thoughtful."

Awkward silence.

"Yeah, okay—so why *didn't* you tell me you're a prince?"

Darian checked the hallway to make sure no one was listening and quickly shut the door. He leaned against it and sighed.

"It was a minor detail that wasn't important at the time."

"Not important?" Marisa shot back. "I'd say a detail like that is pretty darned major!"

"Would it have made any difference when you were nearly killed by the rijgen?"

"That is not the point! You lied to me and made me believe that you were just an ambassador. I had to find out from the maid that actually you're a prince!"

"I did nothing of the sort. For all intents and purposes, while we are on this journey, I am His Excellency Ambassador Darian Fiore. That is my official capacity until we reach Crocetta!"

More awkward silence.

He lowered his voice. "Would you have treated me differently had you known that I was a prince?"

"Of course I would have!"

"Then perhaps you will understand why I did not tell you."

She turned her back and walked to the windows.

"Marisa, it was not my intention to mislead you in any way—"

"But?"

"But it has just been my experience that fancy titles such as mine build up walls that can hinder most inconveniently."

"Believe me, I'd rather have a wall to climb over than be lied to any day," she said angrily. Darian looked as if he'd just been slapped.

He cleared his throat. "The Viscount Savino da Rocha kindly requests that you join him tomorrow morning for breakfast and after that a day filled with hunting and sports."

"I would be honored to join him, Your Highness."

"Then I bid you a pleasant night's sleep, milady." He bowed hastily and hurried down the corridor.

As his brisk footsteps grew fainter, Marisa slammed the door in frustration. She hadn't meant to be so hard on him, but he seemed to bring out the worst in her. She was falling for him but didn't know how to stop it from happening. He wasn't the type of guy that a girl could be just friends with. Darian Fiore was the sort of man that most women would have trouble remembering to breathe whenever he was around.

As she climbed back into bed, it occurred to her that Darian was like a bar of chocolate she knew she shouldn't have. And the only way for her to avoid giving in to temptation was to keep the chocolate as far away as possible.

CHAPTER 10

CONFESSIONS

THE NEXT MORNING, MARISA awoke from a well-rested sleep just as Helinda was making a fire in her fireplace. The middle-aged, heavy-set woman seemed cheery as she chatted, but Marisa couldn't understand a word of what she was saying. She grabbed the earpiece off the nightstand and shoved it in her ear.

"...really would be quite something, don't you agree?"

Marisa just nodded and smiled sweetly. The woman quickly disappeared, leaving her alone to dress. Obviously the hunting and sports activities would be taking place outdoors, so she needed to bundle up unless she wanted to freeze.

As she scoured the closet for something warm, Marisa finally grabbed a chocolate brown dress and slipped on a camel riding coat with fur edging and a matching hat. She didn't know how to braid her hair into an elaborate hairstyle like the other women in the castle, so she just twisted it into one long braid down her back.

Marisa was starving. After her quarrel with Darian the night before, she'd been too upset to eat anything from the tray. As she headed down the steps toward the dining room, the heavenly scent of fresh-baked bread and cooked eggs wafted up the stairwell.

As she entered the dining salon, Marisa saw that everyone had already been seated and was eating. Savino noticed her immediately and quickly rose from the table.

"Ah, how marvelous it is to see your pretty face again this morning! Are you feeling better after a full night's sleep?"

Marisa just smiled and nodded. He pushed her chair in for her, and signaled the server to bring her a plate filled with bread, cheese, and eggs.

As soon as the food had been set down in front of her, Savino returned to his seat at the head of the table with Darian on his right. To Savino's left and on Marisa's right, the same middle-aged man she saw in the courtyard the night before was quietly sipping his tea. Arrie sat at the opposite end from Savino, enjoying the hearty breakfast.

Directly across from Marisa and sitting next to Darian was the most beautiful young woman she had ever seen. Dressed in a pale-blue beaded dress that matched the color of her eyes, the woman had long, golden hair swept up onto her head with soft wisps that hung loose.

Her crystal earrings sparkled in the morning sun, and her refined, dimpled smile bore a strong resemblance to their host's. Appearing to be about twenty years old, the blonde beauty had that stuffy, unmistakable air of aristocracy about her.

Savino rose from his chair. "Ladies and gentlemen, may I present to you the Lady Marisa, cousin of Lord Arrigo of Terracina and our special guest this week." Everyone nodded and smiled politely at Marisa.

"Lady Marisa, I would like you to meet Lord Gaspar, my chief advisor." The man sitting to her right bowed his head slightly and pursed his lips in what she guessed was meant to be a polite smile.

"And the young woman seated next to Prince Darian is my lovely twin sister, the Lady Matilda da Rocha." The blonde woman bowed her head and smiled sweetly.

As Marisa admired her impeccable beauty, she wondered where this delicate young creature figured into the complex scheme of intrigue.

"Matilda arrived home late last night from a trip to visit family in Vermanlys," Savino explained. "Unfortunately, she was not present in time to greet you upon your arrival yesterday afternoon, but she shall join our party during the rest of your stay here in Abbadon."

Marisa took a bite of bread and casually glanced over at Darian as he whispered something to Matilda. The young woman smiled back at him and nodded in agreement as if they had just shared some private joke.

As she watched the two of them side by side, Marisa decided that they made a lovely couple and wondered why Darian hadn't mentioned her earlier. He had said there weren't any suitable Fiore princesses to marry, but since Matilda was Gregario's daughter, Marisa wondered why he couldn't marry her and ascend the throne.

"This morning I have a wonderful shooting party planned for us all," Savino announced. "Once everyone has had the opportunity to change into appropriate clothing, we shall set out together."

Shooting party? Marisa remembered the monstrous beasts that chased them through the forest and shuddered. She grabbed Arrie's hand under the table and gently gave it a squeeze.

When he looked at her and saw the silent protestation in her eyes, Arrie's lips curled in amusement. Without missing a beat, he turned to their host.

"Your Grace, since the Lady Marisa does not consider herself accomplished enough in the sport to take part in the hunt, would it be all right with our host if I stayed behind at the castle to assist her in practicing her skills?"

Savino frowned. "Well, yes—yes of course. Whatever you wish," he answered, dismissing them with a wave of his hand. "The rest of us shall set out in half an hour and return before lunch. You may both join us later when we shall all walk up to the falls together."

She mouthed a silent thank you to Arrie as everyone rose from the table and disappeared to different rooms around the castle. He pulled out her chair and escorted her down the two flights of stone steps into a cool, dark chamber.

Marisa stared in amazement at the enormous size of the armory where equipment and all kinds of strange weapons hung on the walls. Picking up a straw target and two longbows, Arrie pointed toward a quiver containing several long arrows in the far corner.

"Marisa, would you please take those arrows for me?"

"You mean you're really gonna teach me how to do this?"

He chuckled. "But of course! The next time we encounter the rijgen, I fully expect you to be the one to defend us! Now, out you go."

He led her out through the main courtyard toward a smaller courtyard on the west side where he set up the target. He glanced up at the cloudy skies above.

"It's going to rain," he said.

Sure enough, just as he was helping her aim the arrow at the target, light drops of rain began to fall. They ran for cover under a nearby stone archway as it began to come down harder and faster.

"I'm sorry for dragging you away from the hunting party, Arrie, but I just feel so out of place. I didn't feel like tagging along as a dumb mute with people ten times more important than me." Marisa watched the dark gray storm clouds race across the skies as she huddled under the archway. "I just can't pretend to be someone I'm not."

"Nonsense. I should be thanking you for pulling me away from that dreadful outing. I'm always playing fifth wheel, and I don't enjoy trudging through the mud in the cold, damp woods in search of the most pathetic creature to shoot at."

She smiled weakly as she watched the rain spatter across the stones in the courtyard. Somewhere up in the mountains a bolt of lightning struck, and the thunder crashed a few seconds later. The pouring rain was quickly drenching everything in sight as they hunkered down under the archway.

Arrie gazed at her thoughtfully. "Marisa, I do understand what you're feeling, and I am sorry. I know what it's like to try to fit in where you don't belong, but you must believe me, it does get easier. You shall find your place here and get on with your life."

"But I have no idea *what* I'm supposed to do. I had plans, but when my dad got sick—well, everything just got shoved onto the back burner. But now, all I've ever known and loved is gone!"

"Look at this as being the start of a new life. True, it is a very different world, but you can make it here just as well as where you came from. Perhaps even better."

She stared out at the misty mountains.

"Marisa, look at me."

Slowly she turned.

"Nothing happens without a reason. Some way or another, a solution will present itself. Maybe it won't be the same one you would have chosen and it might not happen in your timing, but it will come."

"How can you be so sure?"

"I know it sounds daunting, but you are a very capable young woman," he said, touching her nose gently. "You just need to build up some confidence and stop worrying so much. Years from now you shall look back on this time and state with confidence that everything worked out for the best."

"Now you sound like my dad. How did you get to be so smart?"

"Ah, it comes from experience," he said with a wry smile. A clap of thunder broke somewhere in the skies overhead.

"Can you honestly sit there and tell me that your separation from Astrid was for the best?" she asked.

"I have to believe it is. I gave Astrid up in my mind because I had no choice, but my heart still hopes. Perhaps I'm just a fool, but I'm a firm believer in finding love the second time around."

"You will, Arrie," she said softly. "I know you will."

Marisa studied the tiny streams of water running through the grooves in the cobblestones. All of a sudden, she felt the need to confide in him.

"Arrie, I'm afraid."

He stared at her in mock amazement. "You? The woman who charged her horse full speed through a pack of bloodthirsty rijgen? Whatever could *you* possibly be afraid of?"

"Now that you mention it, I've been meaning to ask you about those awful monsters. Are they in every forest here or just certain areas?"

"No and yes. The best way I can explain the rijgen to you is that they are kind of a three-way cross between a bear, wolf, and ape, but several times more ferocious than any. They seldom attack humans on their own but usually move together as a pack. They remain in certain forested areas and are never spotted outside the cover of the forest."

"Hmm, strange we don't have them on Earth."

"Who says you don't?"

She stopped. "What do you mean?"

"Surely as a native of the Pacific Northwest you've heard of the *Sasquatch?*"

She raised an eyebrow. "You mean Bigfoot?"

"That's the one. Same thing."

Marisa looked at him, skeptical.

"Oh yes, it's true. Not only do people travel through vortices, but animals and inanimate objects can also get caught. Your horse Siena came through with you, correct?"

She nodded slowly.

"Well, although the rijgen are indigenous to Carnelia, down through the centuries, some have gotten trapped and transported through a vortex into your world. The Native Americans have insisted on their existence for years now, but there are just too many skeptics out there ready to quash the truth."

"But that's just an urban legend. Somebody declared years ago that Bigfoot was nothing but a colossal hoax."

"Well, I can assure you, milady, that was no hoax that nearly ripped my arm off," he said, rubbing his shoulder.

"Nevertheless, they're out there in your world too, wandering through the forests, along with many other strange animals people from your world like to believe are myths."

"Unbelievable," she muttered.

"Now stop avoiding the issue. You were just about to tell me what frightens you."

She looked at him sheepishly. "I—I'm afraid of falling in love with the wrong person."

He crossed his arms and smiled. "And would this *wrong person* happen to be a certain tall, dark-haired gentleman saddled down with ruling a country?"

"Yep, that's the one."

"Ah, yes. That is a difficult question, isn't it? I'm afraid I don't have a quick and easy solution for you. Why is it that we always seem to want the things we cannot possibly have?"

"I've never met anyone like him, Arrie. He's the kind of guy I could seriously fall for—so hard that I don't think I would ever recover."

"Impossible love. I can tell you a thing or two about that."

The rain still hadn't let up, and more water rushed down the gutters, overflowing and spilling over the sides. The hem of her skirt was already soaked.

"Arrie, why didn't Darian mention Lady Matilda to me before? He told me that there weren't any Fiore women he could marry to ascend the throne. Is that true, or was he just saying that?"

"I do not think it likely that he has deceived you, Marisa. However, if Darian had wanted to marry Lady Matilda, there would be nothing to stop him. Unless perhaps, if Savino were to chain his poor sister to the wall. But even then, Darian would find a way. He always does, you know."

"Ughhh," Marisa groaned, smacking her forehead. "So not only do I have to endure being around a guy I like but can never be with—I have to watch him while he courts little Miss Perfect. This is like senior year all over again. The only thing missing is the prom where I get dumped."

"Now, Marisa, do cheer up. There are, after all, many other fish in the sea. Or so I've been told. You know that the Viscount da Roca admired you from the moment you arrived at the castle. He was attracted to your charm and beauty alone. That must offer you at least some assurance that you are quite capable of securing another man's love?"

"I guess so," she said, shrugging. "What do I know about love anyway? I've never even had a boyfriend for more than a couple of months. The guys I know back home aren't worth the time or trouble."

"Give yourself a little bit of credit, my dear. You are still very young. Sometime and somewhere, you shall meet the right person. He is out there, of that I am certain."

"Believe me—I'm in no hurry to rush into a relationship," she said quickly. "But what's a girl to do with a guy like Darian? I can't get him off my mind. You can't turn feelings like that off and on like a faucet, you know."

"Indeed, this is true. I will grant you that Darian Fiore is quite a remarkable specimen to be had. But you must simply find other distractions to get him off your mind."

Arrie nudged her softly. "I assume that you're aware of the formal ball this evening where plenty of eligible young noblemen shall be in attendance?"

"I don't think that I can look at another guy as long as he's standing right there. Everyone pales in comparison."

"If I'm right, and I know I am, you'll knock them all over in that pretty frock of yours. There will be plenty of dukes, lords, and barons to choose from, and by the end of the night, you'll be chasing them all off with a sword. Perhaps you might even dance with your future spouse tonight, hmm?"

"Dance!" Marisa exclaimed. She jumped to her feet. "Oh, Arrie, the ball is this evening, and I don't even know how to dance! I was team captain of our dance squad back home, but that was totally different. Do you think you can you teach me?"

He offered her a hand. "Come—let's get out of this rain. It doesn't appear as if it's going to stop anytime soon." Grabbing the archery equipment, they hurried back into the castle out of the rain.

Arrie put his finger to his lips, and she nodded as they passed a man polishing a statue in the hall. As they entered a large salon, he spotted a servant arranging some flowers on the table.

"Would you please be so kind as to leave us?" Arrie asked.

The maiden smiled shyly before closing the door. He led her to the dance floor and took Marisa's hand, placing it on his forearm.

"Now we don't have any music, so we'll have to do without. It's actually quite simple. First, I bow to you and you curtsey." He bowed formally to her with his heels touching as Marisa curtseyed gracefully.

"Fine, that's fine. Now, placing your left hand on my arm, you give me your hand, stepping one step backward with your right foot and I move forward with my left foot. One, two, three, four — good!

"Now, I turn you sideways with one hand, like this, and you move forward with your left foot, and I go back with my right foot. Perfect! Now raise your hand above your head and hold it against mine and we circle around. Well done—you do catch on easily!"

"Well, this is nothing like our halftime dances back home, but I think I've got the hang of it," she said, giggling. Though Marisa was secretly hoping she wouldn't have to dance at all, she knew that she probably couldn't avoid it.

Arrie practiced with her for a full hour, and when she had all the steps down for three different dances, he suggested they both return to their rooms until the hunting party returned for lunch.

Marisa quickly grabbed his sleeve. "Arrie, please don't say anything to Darian. I don't want to complicate things between us. I know that he could never settle for someone like me. Will you please promise me?"

"Marisa, if you really do care, you should be honest with him. He deserves no less, even if his hands are tied as far as his own future is concerned."

She stared at him, pleading with her eyes.

"All right, I promise," he answered finally. "I won't say anything, but you should still tell him how you feel."

"No way!" she said, shaking her head. Arrie just shrugged as he left the salon and hurried down the corridor.

Marisa glanced both ways down the hall and tried to remember how to get back to her room. She walked down to her right, but when she wound up in an unfamiliar, darkened corridor, she was confused. She continued around the corner but, after realizing that it didn't lead to the main hall, she double-backed around again and smacked right into Darian.

"Oh—" she exclaimed, her heart racing.

"My apologies, milady. I returned from the hunt early since the rain wouldn't let up and there wasn't much game to shoot at." He smiled sheepishly at her as a maid approached them.

Darian quickly slipped her arm under his. "Allow me to escort you back to your room, Lady Marisa. You've just enough time to change before lunch."

She smiled politely and nodded for the sake of the maid. He led her down the main hall and up the two flights of steps to the guest quarters. When they reached the door of her room, he opened it slightly but blocked her from entering.

"Will you be coming to dinner tonight?" he asked softly.

She nodded slowly, keeping her gaze lowered to the floor. He was hard to resist, but she didn't want to encourage him in any way. One look into those dazzling eyes of his and she just might cave.

A smile played on his lips. "You are planning to attend the ball in my honor tonight, are you not?"

She hesitated slightly but nodded once again.

"Wonderful!" He grinned at her. "Then I shall see you at lunch, milady." He stepped aside to allow her to enter, but not before he took her hand and kissed it.

Darian turned to leave and she watched his dark cloak billowing out behind him as he strode down the hall.

Superman, she thought. *I've actually discovered Superman.*

Her heart beat quickened as she closed the door and collapsed against it. Was it only flirting, or was he really interested in her?

She shook her head. Who was she kidding? An attractive, incredible man like that would never be interested in a plain Lois Lane like her. Superman didn't exist. He was just a fictitious character in one of her brother's graphic novels.

He wasn't real.

The luncheon plates were heaped high with fruits and vegetables, salads with breads and meat and cheeses. Each guest had a shining bronze goblet filled with wine.

Marisa tried to concentrate on the two animated discussions taking place around the table, but finally gave up when she realized both of them were about the morning's shooting party. She shifted her focus to the interaction between Darian and Lady Matilda. He refilled her water glass twice, and when she whispered something to him, he chuckled.

A sickening feeling squirmed in the pit of Marisa's stomach, and she felt like a complete idiot. She lived in a world where couples chose each other based on mutual attraction, not like Carnelia where matches were predetermined based on rank, pedigree, and duty.

"Will you join us on our walk up to the falls, milady?" Savino asked, interrupting her thoughts. Startled, Marisa turned to him and nodded.

"And may I have the pleasure of escorting you there?"

She smiled shyly and nodded.

Savino pulled out the chair for her. "We shall meet in the courtyard in a quarter of an hour."

The young viscount beamed at Marisa as he kissed her hand.

Fifteen minutes later, Marisa descended the stone steps to find Darian, Lady Matilda, Savino, Gaspar, and Arrie all assembled in the courtyard. Fortunately, the blue sky had reappeared after the morning thundershowers had moved on.

Marisa's heart fluttered when she saw Darian's striking figure leaning against the wall as he chatted with Arrie about something. Out of his usual armored uniform, he was dressed in tall riding boots, dark gray trousers, a fitted tunic, and a black cloak.

Matilda was beautiful in a dark green ensemble with fur edging, and somehow Marisa knew that there was just no competing with the vogue style of Lady da Rocha.

Savino had exchanged his dark, armored suit for the more suave, sophisticated look of a fitted blue tunic and cloak. Clearly, he was the sort of man who always dressed impeccably no matter what the occasion.

"Milady, shall we go?" he asked with a pleasant smile.

She nodded.

Savino took her hand and guided her down a back stairwell. They passed through an iron gate where they entered the forest directly behind the castle.

Trailing a few steps behind the host and his partner for the afternoon, Darian, Matilda, Arrie and Gaspar kept in tight formation as they chatted about trivial subjects.

The mid-afternoon walk through the alpine woods was a refreshing change from the decidedly somber mood of the castle. The familiar smell of fresh pine permeated Marisa's soul and lifted her spirits. But as the party meandered up the path through the misty forest, the scenery reminded her of Oregon and she began to feel homesick once again.

Savino held Marisa's hand as she climbed over fallen logs and helped her cross a small stream. Chattering enough for the two of them, he described his life of privilege in nauseating detail.

As he droned on about the responsibilities of ruling a country, she just nodded politely in even intervals before finally tuning him out altogether.

For the next hour, they continued to climb the steep mountain slope as the roar of the waterfall became louder. When they finally reached the base pool of the falls, Savino had to shout to be heard above the roar.

"Milady, might I have the honor of escorting you to the bridge to take in the magnificent view?" He offered her his arm and Marisa smiled in acknowledgement.

Complaining that the spray from the falls would soak her clothes and cause her to catch a chill, Matilda kept a considerable distance from the pool. Always the perfect gentleman, Darian remained at her side but eyed Savino carefully as he guided Marisa up the hill.

It was a steep, brisk hike up to the falls, and by the time they made it to the top, she was panting as she tried to catch her breath. They approached a wooden bridge that straddled the gorge where the upper runoff from the waterfall passed underneath.

"Close your eyes, milady, and allow me to lead you."

Savino took her hand in his as he put the other on her waist and guided her toward the middle of the bridge. The moss-covered planks were slippery from the mist, and she shivered as the waterfall roared loudly behind them.

"Well, milady, you should feel very flattered," he shouted. "It's not very often that I bring a woman up here."

Marisa just nodded, her eyes still shut.

"So, tell me—what do you think of the view?"

She opened her eyes and gasped at the spectacular vista from their high vantage point. The mountains were covered in a sea of evergreens that stretched as far as the eye could see. The setting sun cast a rainbow between the clouds that had dumped so much rain on them earlier. As she spotted Savino's castle about a mile away, the view reminded her of the time she had gone hiking with her father and brother at Multnomah Falls.

If only Dad was here to see this now, she thought.

She closed her eyes and listened to the roar of the falls behind her as the delicious scent of wet pine filled her nostrils. When she opened them again, Savino was standing very close.

Marisa gazed into his electric blue eyes in search of any understanding but sighed when she realized he couldn't begin to comprehend what was going on inside her. He had no idea that she'd just lost her father and that this breathtaking landscape reminded her so much of the beautiful world she'd left behind.

Without warning, he slipped his arms around her and pulled her close to kiss her long and full on the lips. She tried to relax as he kissed her, but by the time Savino released her, Marisa was struggling for air.

"I apologize, milady, but I just could not help myself. You are so beautiful standing there, and your spontaneous tears warmed my heart." He pulled her close again and kissed her for what seemed like a long time. His hand gently stroked her hair, and as they parted, he caressed her cheek.

Something in the corner of her eye caught her attention and she turned to see Darian's stunned expression. From where he stood watching them on the path just a few feet away, he appeared to be frozen in shock.

With the deafening roar of the waterfall behind them, neither Savino nor Marisa had heard him approach, and she wondered how long he'd been standing there.

"Your Grace, I apologize for my intrusion. The rest of us thought that we should start heading back down to the castle."

"Ah, yes—the ball tonight. You are right," Savino said. He smiled smugly as he turned back to Marisa. "Shall we go down, my dear?"

She nodded and hastily wiped her cheeks. He took her hand and guided her across the bridge to the path and past Darian, who seemed rooted to the spot.

Finally, the gloomy-faced young man turned to follow them back down the mountain trail but didn't utter a single word until long after they reached the castle.

CHAPTER 11
PROPOSALS

"AFTER YOU'VE FINISHED BATHING and changing, you may wait in the Blue Room down the hall until you are fetched for dinner," Helinda shouted as she turned Marisa's bed down for the evening.

When the talkative woman had finally left and the quiet had returned once again, Marisa sank down into the hot water and suds of the bathtub. Enjoying its warmth after the chilly outing to the waterfall, she thought about Savino's kiss.

Although she had been falling for Darian, Savino was the one who seemed interested in her. He had only kissed her once, but it had confused her enough that she didn't know what to think anymore.

Pangs of guilt dug into her heart as she remembered the look on Darian's face when he saw them kissing. He had taken care of her when she had no one else, and it felt as if she'd betrayed him somehow. She felt ashamed of her behavior and decided that she owed him an apology. Perhaps an opportune moment to talk to him alone would arise later that evening.

Marisa climbed out of the tub and dried off. She entered the overstuffed cabinet filled with pretty clothes and sorted through the rows of dresses, considering each of them carefully. She tried on several but ended up tossing each one on the bed when it didn't fit.

Realizing that time was getting short, she started to panic. She finally settled on an olive velvet dress with long sleeves and stiff underskirts. The gown complemented her reddish-brown hair, hazel eyes, and peachy complexion.

After searching the closet for a decent pair of shoes, she finally found some that didn't match the dress perfectly but seemed to fit. She hoped that they wouldn't squeeze her toes tight all night.

Peering into the jewelry box on the table, her eyes were drawn to a garnet-and-gold necklace with matching pear-drop earrings. They were the perfect icing on the cake.

She ran her fingers through her damp hair and swept both sides up with combs. Her half-up-half-down hairdo fell in soft ringlets over her shoulders, and the pear-drop earrings sparkled in the candlelight. She found some lip gloss and mascara in her satchel and applied just a dab of both.

Who am I trying to impress, anyway?

Moving in front of the full-length mirror, Marisa was stunned by her own reflection. She appeared much older than her eighteen years and she almost didn't even recognize herself. She smiled as she imagined her father standing next to her, looking at her with pride and calling her his "beautiful Scottish lassie."

Her smile slowly faded. At a time when she should have been hanging out with roommates in the dorm, cramming all night for a test and meeting guys on dates, she found herself engaged in shooting parties, dining at banquets, and dancing at balls. In this strange world where she mingled with future kings and rulers, nothing bore any semblance to the simple life she had always known back home, and all at once she felt horribly alone.

Marisa peered out through the windows facing the courtyard and saw that it had been magically transformed into a beautiful dance floor. Decorated with candles, flame torches, colorful flags, and draping banners, the castle looked beautiful, and it seemed to radiate a warm glow. Thankfully the weather continued to cooperate on into the evening, and guests began to arrive at the main gate.

As she watched the men and women enter the courtyard dressed in their finest clothes, she sighed, knowing that she couldn't put it off any longer. She shut her chamber door and walked down the hall in the only direction she could go.

Marisa saw an open door and peeked in. It was a sitting room filled exclusively with blue furnishings and she knew it had to be the one where Helinda had told her to wait. She sank down into a blue velvet chair and fidgeted nervously.

Her eyes roamed the room in awe as they admired the sumptuous furnishings and rich oil paintings. She had always imagined castles to be old and spooky places. But with all its paintings, clocks, sculptures, and other decorative objects, this castle seemed more like a beautiful museum.

There was a knock on the door frame. She looked up and saw Darian slowly appraising her from head to toe.

"Magnificent," he whispered.

She stood. "Thank you, Your Highness. So are you."

He was wearing an elegant, black-armored suit and his face was cleanly shaven. His dark hair was combed back in soft waves, which made him appear both ruggedly handsome and elegantly sophisticated at the same time. The hilt of his sword flashed as he bowed solemnly to her.

"Shall we go down, milady?" he asked, offering her his arm.

Marisa slipped her arm nervously through his as they walked down the hall. Stunned by his handsome appearance, she knew that getting through the evening with Prince Darian would be incredibly difficult.

She heard soft music drifting up from one floor below and realized it might be her only opportunity to speak privately with him for the rest of the evening.

"Your Royal Highness, I wanted to apologize for my—um, strange behavior. I can't really explain it except to say that I tend to freak out whenever I feel like I don't have control over my own life."

"But you don't."

"Don't what?"

"Have any control over your life," he said, laughing softly. He guided her down the long staircase. "Apology accepted," he added with a smirk.

Now it was her turn to giggle.

When they reached the bottom of the steps, Marisa's smile quickly faded. The chattering ceased and all eyes in the room focused on her. As she searched for any familiar face in the crowd, her eyes finally rested on Savino's. The handsome blonde man whispered something to the small group of noblemen surrounding him and strode over to meet her.

"My darling, you look absolutely exquisite this evening." He took her hand and kissed it before twirling her around in order to see her from every angle.

She smiled shyly at him and noticed Darian watching them.

"I am of the sound opinion that you are the most beautiful woman in the land this evening," Savino said. "Tell me, Darian, how is it that you always manage to find me the prettiest ones?" He chuckled at his cousin's icy stare.

"Of course, unlike me, Lady Marisa, Prince Darian is not free to court you," he said. "Did you know that many people consider me to be the most eligible bachelor in the land?"

Marisa smiled politely and shook her head as Savino took her arm and escorted her into the dining hall. She glanced over her shoulder and saw the look of defeat on Darian's face. He was being forced to play by Savino's rules as long as he was on his cousin's turf.

The guests strolled into the dining room and assembled around a massive table. Marisa quickly counted fifty place settings as Savino took the head position at the table. He directed his cousin to sit to his right and Marisa on his left. Looking stunning in her pale pink evening gown, Lady Matilda had been strategically placed next to Darian.

"Please be seated," said Savino in a loud voice. Everyone sat in unison while the multitude of waiters assisted in pushing the chairs up to the table.

Once she was comfortably settled, Marisa scanned the faces down the length of the table. Although Darian and Matilda were sitting just across the table from her, she still couldn't hear what was being said. An elderly gentleman sat to her left, but he seemed to be off somewhere in his own little world as he blankly stared into space.

The only person for her to communicate with was Savino. After all, she was only a dumb mute and totally unable to keep up her end of the conversation anyway.

She glanced down the table and saw Arrie sitting on the opposite side, sandwiched between two elderly female courtiers who were already thick as thieves, mindlessly chattering away. By the look on his face, he didn't seem thrilled at the prospect of being trapped between them for the entire length of the meal and Marisa couldn't help but giggle. When he noticed her amusement at his ridiculous predicament, he just rolled his eyes and gave her a silly smile.

Savino proposed a toast in Darian's honor, and Marisa lifted her glass along with the other guests. Soon the grand hall began to resonate with soft chatter as the guests engaged one another in polite dinner conversations.

The waiters descended on the table with hot bowls of soup. After Marisa had finished her soup course, a waiter appeared to whisk her empty bowl away. She knew her only responsibility for the evening was to sit there, be quiet, and look pretty. She didn't mind, as long as she made it through the night in one piece.

She gazed around the room and admired the magnificent oil paintings that adorned the castle's walls. Most of them depicted battles and warriors with a few nude women. She remembered from her European history class that centuries ago it was common for members of the noble class to exhibit their wealth and power by displaying the family tapestries, candlesticks, furniture, and chandeliers for the entire world to see. From what she had seen of him so far, Marisa decided that Savino was definitely the peacock type of guy.

She studied the beamed ceiling in awe and noticed the gold leaf details around the wooden window frames. Obviously, the opulent dining room was the largest room in the castle, and Marisa had overheard guests referring to it as the Knights' Hall. She wondered what it would be like to live in such a castle and to be constantly surrounded by servants, cooks, and butlers.

The servers carried out the main course, which tasted like some kind of bland poultry. She ate it hungrily; glad she didn't have the distraction of having to talk to anyone. A little while later, another plate was set in front of her, and Marisa decided that it tasted like her uncle's favorite dessert of crème bruleé. She had already licked the sticky syrup off her fingers before deciding that it wasn't very ladylike.

When the plates had been cleared away, Savino dotted his mouth with his napkin and slowly leaned back, eyeing Darian carefully.

"Ambassador Fiore, let us conclude the business for which you have come so that we may move on and enjoy the rest of the evening," he said in a loud voice. The loud chatter in the hall came to a halt as Darian stopped eating his dessert and turned to his cousin. Marisa stared at Savino, surprised by his sudden, businesslike manner.

"As you already know, my father's health is in decline, and he is not expected to last until the end of the month," Savino began.

Darian crossed his arms impatiently.

"Our lands are teetering on the brink of war, and we both know I am the man most suited to lead the country. Practically speaking, I am also the only one capable of producing a legitimate heir in order to ensure the succession of power."

Savino took a sip of wine, pausing for effect.

"The question is, Your Excellency—what are you prepared to offer me if I agree to establish an accord and sign your peace treaty?"

Darian cleared his throat. "Your Grace, by authorization of the Crimson Court and as patriarch of the Fiore family, I am prepared to offer you in marriage the hand of my sister, Her Royal Highness, the Princess Adalina Fiore. Revered for her matchless beauty and virtue, I'm certain you shall appreciate the fact that any man in the country, whether noble or common, would give his right hand to marry her."

Marisa's jaw dropped as her fork clattered to the floor. The other guests turned to stare at her as she bent down to pick it up. She hoped that no one had seen the look of horror on her face.

"It certainly is a noteworthy offer," Savino said. "However, I am not entirely certain that your proposal is enticing enough to make me want to sign your treaty."

A flurry of whispers broke out around the table as Savino casually spread some butter on his bread and took a bite. He clearly enjoyed being the center of attention.

Savino held up his hand to silence the commotion. He eyed Marisa slowly before he continued. "If you were somehow able to sweeten the deal, perhaps then I might be persuaded."

Darian blinked. "What do you mean, sir, by *sweetening* the deal?" he asked.

"You offer me the hand of your sister, Princess Adalina, but I am of the opinion that Lady Marisa would be a much more agreeable alternative. If you were to offer me *her* hand, well, then I would have no choice but to accept and sign your treaty."

The room exploded with chatter.

Marisa gasped. She couldn't possibly have heard that right. She tapped on the earpiece and assumed that there must have been an error in the translation.

Darian stared defiantly at him. "Lady Marisa is not a part of this bargain, Savino, and she never will be. Kindly dismiss the idea from your head."

"Why don't you let her answer for herself?" Savino asked calmly. "She seems like a young woman who is perfectly capable of making her own decisions. Give *her* the opportunity to decide if she is willing to sacrifice herself for your peace deal."

Marisa shifted uncomfortably in her seat. She glanced down the table at Arrie. He appeared worried as he watched the negotiations with growing concern. She looked at Matilda. The young woman's eyes glared at Marisa's with contempt.

"You have explained how important this peace treaty is to you," Savino offered. "I am simply telling you that I am prepared to accept your proposal, or at least a *modified* version of it."

Darian shook his head with disgust as if he couldn't believe his ears.

"This girl is a nobody," Savino said, dismissing it with a wave. "She is the distant cousin of a man of next to no importance. Why should you care whom she marries?"

Marisa frowned. She didn't like where this was going.

Savino's eyes locked on Darian's. "Tell me, Your Excellency, are you prepared to throw away all you've been striving for just for the sake of a maiden of no consequence?"

Darian clenched his jaw but didn't answer.

"Unless perhaps, you want her for yourself," Savino added smugly as whispers echoed around the hall.

Slamming his napkin down hard on the table, Darian stood abruptly and headed for the door. Suddenly he stopped in his tracks. Struggling to control his anger, he slowly turned and walked back to the table.

As Darian sat back down, Savino smiled in obvious enjoyment of his cousin's discomfort. The hall became silent and Marisa imagined hearing a pin drop.

"I am not in the position to speak for the Lady Marisa," Darian said. "I am neither her father nor her brother nor her lover. She shall not be included as a factor in any agreement between you and me."

Savino sighed heavily. "So am I to assume that you are refusing my proposal?"

"No. I am simply stating that I cannot force her to marry you. Neither can I force her *not* to marry you."

"Well this is simply extraordinary—"

"The choice must be hers, wholly and completely," Darian interrupted. "I am not at liberty to offer you the hand of Lady Marisa within the framework of this peace treaty because I do not wield that power of authority over her." More whispers flew back and forth through the room.

Savino stared at his cousin in absolute astonishment.

"This is just utterly ridiculous! You are the mighty Prince Darian Fiore, are you not?" he asked loudly. "Am I to believe that the man who would reign as Supreme Ruler over all Carnelia is incapable of persuading even a common maid to accept a most advantageous marriage?"

The room erupted into peals of laughter. Marisa gazed sympathetically at Darian and her heart went out to him. He didn't deserve to be publicly humiliated in such a cruel way.

"As I said before, I do not exercise a rule of authority over Lady Marisa," Darian repeated calmly. "The decision is hers."

Savino shook his head and turned to Marisa. "Well, there you are, my dear. It appears that the choice is yours. You do not have to give me an answer right away, but I will be expecting it soon. I am a patient man, but I do have my limits."

She looked across the table at Darian, but he was clearly avoiding her stare.

Savino stood and offered Marisa his hand. "Would you care to dance, my darling?"

She exhaled a breath of air and took his hand. She had no choice but to follow him out to the courtyard. The other guests rose from the table and followed behind them. The hall was suddenly empty.

Darian remained in his seat, staring down at his half-eaten dessert. Arrie got up quickly and hurried over. "Are you just going to sit here and let this happen?"

"Just give me a moment, will you please?" Darian snapped.

"But this has already gone too far."

"I know that, Arrie! Don't you think I already know that?"

"You cannot in good conscience allow her to marry him. We have introduced her into this mess and we must get her out!"

"Just let me handle this!" Darian shouted. Arrie paused for a moment to calm the situation down. He took a deep breath as he searched for the right words.

"Your Highness, you know that I would never contradict you in the presence of others, but I must speak my peace. Dear cousin, if you do not take steps to rectify this situation immediately, you shall regret it for the rest of your life. As will I."

"Lord Macario, you are *dismissed!*"

Arrie nodded his head curtly and stormed outside to join the others in the courtyard. Darian sulked at the empty table, burying his face in his hands.

"Oh, what have I done?" he whispered to himself.

Up on the rampart, Savino pulled Marisa close in a dance under the starry skies. The guests stood around the edges, admiring the beautiful couple as whispers of an upcoming royal wedding spread like wildfire among the servants.

She glanced up into Savino's ice-blue eyes and wondered what it would be like to be his wife. It was crazy for her to be considering marriage at her age, but everything in Carnelia seemed to operate on a totally different time frame.

Did he love her? How could a person possibly love someone in such a short time? Some people married a person they'd never even met until their wedding day. There was a mutual attraction between the two of them, but Marisa knew there wasn't love yet. Perhaps it could be some day.

Although she'd managed to capture the heart of a handsome nobleman, she couldn't get her mind off Darian. Her gaze shifted toward the doors of the Knights' Hall where he stood alone in the shadows.

As his lonesome frame leaned against a pillar, Marisa was loaded down with guilt. He had done everything in his power to make the mission a success, but she'd blown it just by her being there. Although he had insisted that she stay back in Andresis, she had practically forced him into letting her come with them to Abbadon. If she had never come, his beloved peace treaty would have been a done deal by now.

She saw the smug smile on Savino's lips and it occurred to her that he was the one with the power to change the law. Darian was right. Savino had no intention of making any concessions to his cousin. For now, at least, the handsome young viscount seemed to be holding all the cards.

When the dance ended, Savino escorted her to the refreshments table and handed her a goblet of what looked like sparkling champagne. She took the chalice but then hesitated, unsure if she could stand the taste. On the other hand, she didn't want to offend her host by refusing it.

As she lifted the cup to her lips, Marisa felt a strong, warm hand on her back and she turned.

It was Darian. "Lady Marisa, would you honor me with a dance?"

She quickly scanned the room and spotted Savino over by the far wall, engaged in a private discussion. He probably wouldn't mind if she danced with other men at the ball, but with Darian he might have a problem. Marisa hesitated for a moment, but finally nodded and took his hand.

They walked out onto the dance floor where he slipped an arm around her and gently drew her close. She felt like Cinderella, but it was confusing as to which of the two men was the handsome prince.

"Please, don't say anything, but just listen to what I have to say," Darian began. She drew a breath, held it, and then gave a long sigh.

"I truly regret that you have become involved in our complicated affairs, but I'm afraid what's done is done. Savino has made you an offer of marriage, and it's an honorable one at that. If you were to marry him, you would have every luxury you ever wanted for the rest of your life."

She looked up at him but said nothing. He touched a soft ringlet of her hair as he carefully pieced his words together.

"The decision whether or not to marry Savino is yours. I shall not interfere, nor shall I influence your decision. I cannot deny that I have developed certain feelings for you, but I deeply regret that I am not at liberty to either declare or pursue them. With your sudden appearance into my life, I find myself in a most complicated and perplexing situation."

Darian's speech was methodical, clinical, detached. His eyes nervously roamed the room before finally settling back on hers.

"You are the most beautiful woman I've ever laid eyes on, and yet somehow I sense you have not even reached your full potential yet. Any man in his right mind would be a fool not to offer you the world. However, as you are already well aware, my position is extremely complicated. Had the circumstances been different—"

"Stop," she whispered, putting a finger to his lips.

Tears flooded Marisa's eyes and she took a step backward. Unable to hide the pain of her disappointment, she quickly gathered her skirts and hurried off the floor. She ran off into the shadows toward the northern rampart, and as she collapsed against the cold stone wall, her heart shattered into a million pieces.

Darian quickly followed after Marisa and then gently moved up behind her. He circled his arms around her waist and pulled her back against him. She gazed out over the mountains towering in the distance as tears streamed down both cheeks.

"You didn't let me finish," Darian whispered. Slowly he turned her around and pulled her close against him. He took her face in his hands and kissed her, softly and gently.

It was a pure kiss, utterly selfless and giving, not expecting anything in return. His lips were warm and tender against hers, and Marisa had never desired anything more in her entire life. Her hands trembled and her heart raced as she felt the blood pulsing through her entire body. She opened her eyes slowly.

Stunned to see a single tear rolling down his cheek, Marisa remembered reading somewhere that the eyes are the doorway to the soul. In that particular moment, she was staring straight into his soul. She gazed past him for a moment and saw the stars twinkling like diamonds in the night sky.

All of a sudden, the gravity of the situation hit her. "Please—let me go! I can't do this…" she said, pleading through tears.

Darian's eyes searched hers questioningly as she struggled to wrestle free from his grasp. Finally, he let her go and she raced down the stone steps and through the empty corridors. She ran up the two flights of steps to her chamber where she collapsed on her bed, gasping and sobbing.

Savino glanced into the faces of the guests congregated around the refreshments table. "Has anyone seen my bride-to-be?" he asked.

Several people shook their heads.

"Brother, I cannot seem to find my escort for this evening. Have you seen Prince Darian?" Matilda asked.

The host's eyes narrowed at his sister as a rather disagreeable realization came over him.

CHAPTER 12
DEPARTURE

THE SUN ROSE THE next morning and shone through the stained glass windows, casting a kaleidoscope of colors across the wall. Marisa rolled over and pulled the covers up to her neck. No matter how beautiful the morning may have been, she was too afraid to face the day.

She felt an awful pounding in her head. Still confused by what had transpired the night before, she sat up and realized that a full night of sleep had not provided a single ounce of perspective to her puzzling predicament. As she remembered Darian's kiss the night before, tears formed in Marisa's eyes. She had no desire to see anyone at all.

As Helinda hastily barged into the room, Marisa wiped her face and lunged for the earpiece on the nightstand. The chatty woman began to tidy up the room, starting with the olive dress that Marisa had carelessly thrown onto the floor the night before.

"Well, my dear, apparently you were the belle of the ball last night," Helinda clucked as she tossed fresh logs into the fireplace.

"The servants were all gossiping this morning, and everyone was highly complimentary of you, my dear. In fact, rumor has it that you are to be congratulated with your engagement to the Viscount da Rocha. I declare, if you were able to secure such a match, you would be an exceptionally lucky girl indeed."

Marisa smiled faintly and pulled on a heavy dress, thankful that she wasn't expected to respond. Helinda continued to blabber on as she swept the floor and poked the fire one more time.

"Imagine that, one day you shall become a countess!"

Marisa rolled her eyes as she pulled a brush through her hair.

"According to the cook's assistant, Lady Matilda is soon to be engaged to Prince Darian. Now that's a *true* match made in heaven."

Ouch.

Just when she was beginning to wonder if the woman ever stopped talking, there was a knock at the door. As Helinda opened it, Arrie stuck his head into the room. From the knowing look on his face, he'd already heard everything from Darian.

"And how are we this morning, dear cousin?" Arrie asked.

"I beg your pardon, sir, but I was just finishing up in here," Helinda said with a nod. She hastily grabbed a load of laundry on her way out and left the room, shutting the door firmly behind her.

He smiled. "So, I understand that the situation has become somewhat complicated since the last time we spoke?"

"Ha! That's an understatement. Did you hear Savino asking me to marry him? Well, actually, Savino asked *Darian* if he could marry me. Technically, he didn't pose the question to me."

"Of course I heard it. In fact, everyone in Abbadon has heard it by now," he said, chuckling.

He walked over to the dressing table and picked up a small mirror. Gazing at his reflection, Arrie smoothed his mustache. "You've been in the country for what—less than a week now? And already you have not one but two suitors chasing after you. That *must* be some kind of record," he teased.

"One suitor. The other doesn't count."

"Oh, you know what I mean," he joked. He set the mirror back on the table and sat down next to her.

"Well I'm glad someone can laugh about it."

As he studied her face, his smile faded. "What's wrong? Have you been crying?"

She avoided his eyes.

"Marisa, please talk to me."

She couldn't hold the tears back a second longer. Her hands flew to her face as hot tears stung her eyes.

Arrie gathered her into his arms. "Poor girl, you sure haven't had an easy week, have you?"

"I'm so sorry," she wailed. "But it seems like my life has totally spiraled out of control these past few weeks."

He stroked her hair. "Shhh, I know."

She gently pulled away. "No, you don't. You don't know me, Arrie. This is not me. I don't even know who *this* is any more. Right up until Dad died, I had everything under control. I got decent grades and was captain of our dance squad. I was vice president of the student body council.

"But ever since I came here, I've turned into some totally different person that I don't even recognize. I've become some weepy, wimpy girl who can't get her freakin' act together. Worse than that, I'm a dumb mute who can't even talk!"

"Don't be so hard on yourself. You've had a lot to process over the past few weeks. Your father died. You leapt into a different universe. You fell in love with a prince who is going to be king someday. All of those things are quite significant in and among themselves and don't usually happen all at once."

She smiled through her tears. "When you put it like that, it sounds pretty crazy, doesn't it?"

"All joking aside, you do have the right to question things and vent when you don't understand what is happening around you. Believe me, I know. I've been there."

She smiled gratefully at him. "Arrie, I think that you're a gift from heaven. No matter what happens, I'll always be glad that I met you."

"And I am very happy that you dropped into our lives from out of nowhere," he joked.

"Arrie?"

"Yes?"

"I know it's a stupid question, but do you think Darian would ever give up the throne for a commoner? I mean, I'm not presuming that he might do that for me, but just hypothetically speaking?"

He digested that for a moment. "I don't know. That is quite a lot to ask of a man, don't you think? It's a substantial decision with massive ramifications. Hypothetically speaking, that is."

"Yeah, I guess you're right," she said sadly.

"I've known Darian all my life, and the only time that he ever made a hasty, irrational decision, he ended up paying for it dearly. Since then, he's always followed his head and never his heart."

"What was the rash decision?"

"He more or less blames himself for the death of his father."

"*What!*"

"Oh, it wasn't his fault, of course, but he believes that it was a direct result of his actions. But I shall let him tell you about that when he's ready. He doesn't like to talk about it with anyone."

"Gosh, that's horrible," she murmured.

"As I told you a few days ago, he is an extremely complicated man. He's already had more than his fair share of heartbreak."

"Sometimes I wonder if my life will ever become less complicated," she said wistfully.

"Marisa, you must believe that if Darian could do anything about the situation, he would."

"Would he? Somehow I'm not so sure."

"Darian is an exceptionally tough nut to crack, but you might just be the young woman who could tempt him into choosing his heart over his head. But it would take a lot to get him that far. His devotion to duty runs deeply in his veins."

"I'd like to think that I'm worth giving up the throne for, and yet, at the same time, I don't think I could ever let him to do that for one reason."

"And just what is that?"

Marisa stepped over to the window and stared out at the majestic mountains in the distance. Her heart sank as she thought about how exciting her life might be if she could spend it with Darian.

"Someday he might actually come to regret his decision. He might say to himself, 'I gave up my entire kingdom for this woman, and it wasn't even worth it.' I just couldn't live with myself knowing that I had forced the man I love to make a decision that he would later regret."

"Ah, so now you *do* admit that you love Darian?" He teased.

"Naw, I don't think it's really love if you know it's not gonna happen."

"Love is love no matter what—even if you try to bind it, chain it, or hold it back. There is no choice in the matter. It is either there or it isn't. It's just so unfortunate you're not a Fiore princess."

"Helinda told me that Darian is going to marry Lady Matilda. Is that true?"

He shrugged. "Perhaps. Like most rumors flying around, usually there's some small seed of truth in there somewhere. Darian has had several opportunities in the past to pop the question to Matilda, but he's never done it yet. I don't know why things should be different now."

"Maybe he has no other choice now because the throne is at stake. I've seen how he pays special attention to Matilda during the meals, the hunting party, and the hike to the waterfall. You've got to admit Arrie, any guy would be crazy not to go for her. She'd make the perfect princess."

"Perfect maybe, but she's not you," Arrie said, smiling and poking her gently.

"Is your backhanded compliment supposed to make me feel better?" she asked, laughing.

"You are so fun to tease," he said playfully. "It's nice to see you laughing again."

"Well, all I know is that once we get back to this Crocetta, you're going to help me set up my new life. I'm starting to think that you might actually be stuck with me after all. And vice versa," she added.

"There's nobody I'd rather be stuck with more," Arrie said softly. "Now come—go wash your face off and I'll escort you to breakfast before Savino's household staff starts some wild rumor that I've run away with my cousin!"

She smiled at him. "I wish you really were my cousin."

"Yes, dearest, that's what they all say."

As Marisa and Arrie entered the dining room, everyone was already seated at the table, but Darian's seat was empty. Arrie pushed in her chair for her as Savino eyed her suspiciously.

"Well, Lady Marisa! I'm so glad to see you are up and about this morning. You ran off so quickly last night that I didn't even get the chance to bid you goodnight. Are you feeling all right?"

"Lady Marisa is not fully recovered from the tedious journey and her harrowing ordeal the other day," Arrie interjected. "Given the fact that she has not yet developed a stomach for alcohol, I'm afraid the champagne made her quite sick last night."

She put her hand on her stomach and pantomimed a sick face.

Arrie noticed the empty chair. "Where is Prince Darian this morning?"

"Hah! I can better ask you that very same question," Savino spewed, peeling an egg over his plate. "Apparently nobody has seen him since last night. Halfway through the ball he just ran off, leaving my poor sister alone without as much as a word." He took a sip of tea from a dainty porcelain teacup.

"Don't you think it's strange that Darian would leave a ball where he is the guest of honor? Very, very strange indeed."

"Perhaps he wasn't feeling well, either," Arrie offered. Lady Matilda said nothing but just stared at them coolly.

Marisa couldn't down her breakfast fast enough. As soon as she was finished, she jumped up and hurried away from the table. Arrie followed close behind and guided her over to a secluded corner of the courtyard.

"I'm afraid that things aren't going according to plan," Arrie said. "Darian must be terribly upset by all of this. Obviously, it's the reason why he didn't come down to breakfast this morning."

"Actually, I think I'm the reason he didn't come to breakfast this morning. He tried to pour his heart out to me last night, but I wouldn't let him," she said sadly.

Marisa spotted Darian standing above them on the opposite side of the rampart and their eyes locked. As he descended the steps and approached them, her heartbeat quickened.

"Good morning," Darian said without emotion.

"Morning, Your Highness."

"Good morning, friend," Arrie said. "We missed you at breakfast this morning."

"Yes, well, I seem to have lost my appetite."

There was a moment of awkward silence.

Arrie nodded. "Right, I'm off to change my clothes for whatever exciting activities Savino has planned for us today."

Darian stopped him. "No. Go pack your things. We're leaving here at once." Arrie nodded and hurried off to the castle. "Will you please walk with me?" he asked her softly.

Marisa nodded anxiously and followed him over to the northern castle wall. She watched him lean against the wall and stare out at the spectacular view of the waterfall. He seemed worried about something.

"So what happens now?"

"What do you mean?"

"I mean as far as your peace treaty is concerned."

He shrugged. "It never had much of a chance anyway. Savino isn't interested in securing peace. His only goal is to capture the throne."

"So why doesn't he just step in and take it?"

"Because he can't!" Darian snapped.

Startled, she took a step backward. He shook his head and then lowered his voice.

"Like me, he must marry a Fiore princess to ascend the throne, which is why I thought that if I offered him my sister, he might reconsider."

"And now he wants to marry me instead? But how does he expect to ascend the throne if he doesn't marry a Fiore princess?"

"Don't you understand? Savino will seize the throne any way can. I thought that by offering him the legitimate option of marrying my sister, he would accept my terms of peace."

"But wouldn't that defeat the entire purpose? I thought you didn't want him on the throne at all."

He shook his head. "As the possessor of the Fiore surname, Adalina would become queen and the Sovereign Ruler. Savino would become a token king and would have no real power."

"Oh."

"My cousin would rather wage war and sacrifice thousands of innocent lives to obtain absolute power than ascend the throne in a partnership through peaceful means."

"Does Adalina know she's been offered to Savino?"

Darian's eyes were distant. "We all must make certain sacrifices in our lives to preserve the peace. Some of us more than others."

She shook her head. "None of this makes much sense to me."

"Marisa, I'm truly sorry. Please forgive me."

"Sorry! What are *you* sorry about? This is all *my* fault. I was the one who insisted on coming along when you wanted to leave me back in Andresis."

"You are mistaken. This whole predicament is my fault."

"Whatever." She didn't feel like having an argument with him, so she quickly changed the subject. "How did the line of succession get so far off course anyway? Why are you not on the throne if you are a Fiore and he is not?"

"When Queen Elyse perished in the shipwreck, her sister Sophie was crowned immediately. Unfortunately, she didn't rule for very long because she developed a serious illness and died just seven years after ascending the throne.

"I was next in line to the throne, but because I hadn't yet reached the minimum ruling age of eighteen, Queen Sophie's widower husband Gregario assumed the throne as dowager king temporarily. Gregario is, of course, Savino's father."

Marisa shivered and pulled her cloak tight around her. She was trying to concentrate on his story but kept getting distracted by his seductive, strong accent.

"Unfortunately, Gregario has not ruled our country well because it has essentially been in a state of anarchy ever since his reign began. Ever since his health deteriorated a few years ago, Savino has been salivating at the opportunity to step in and take over the throne."

"But how can Savino take the throne if you are next in line?"

"He claims that because his mother was queen and his father also served as king, now the order of succession has shifted from the Fiore line to the da Roca line. As the firstborn da Roca, he thinks he should inherit the throne."

"But aren't he and Matilda twins?"

"They are, but technically, he's the eldest by only a few minutes. And although I am the only remaining Fiore prince, according to Carnelian Law, I must marry a Fiore princess in order to ascend the throne."

"I know this is probably a stupid question, but why did someone ever write a silly law like that in the first place? It doesn't give the heir to the throne a whole lot of options."

He smiled sadly at her. "To someone outside of the royal family, it is a valid question. But to those of us within the Fiore bloodline, we know that the law exists to protect the integrity of the family.

"You see, although I might not like the limited options the law allows for me, I can still understand and respect it.

"But why?" she asked.

"Without the law in place, it would be extremely easy for an outsider to steal the crown. Being royal is not something that can be counterfeited. You must be born with it."

"Hmm, that sounds a bit snobby to me. On Earth, all of that is changing now. Members of royal families are allowed to marry commoners, and most of them don't even marry other royals," she said.

He nodded. "It may change here as well, but it will take some time. Erasing an ancient law is not an easy task in Carnelia. It was written a long time ago when there was an abundance of Fiore princes and princesses."

"So what happened to them all?"

"Most have been killed, executed, or just died off over the years. No one could have known that the Fiore line would have withered so far down to what it is now. Savino will exploit this fact to his full advantage."

"Oh."

"As a matter of fact, the only person I can legally marry and ascend the throne now is his sister, Lady Matilda."

Her heart pounded wildly. *Here it comes.*

"Savino knows as well as I that if I were to marry his sister, I would be declared the rightful heir once and for all after Gregario passes. Nothing would stand in the way. That is precisely why he will not give his patriarchal consent for her to marry."

"So that's your only option? To marry Lady Matilda?"

"It appears to be the only option at this point." He shifted uncomfortably.

"But if Gregario is still alive, can't he give you his patriarchal consent for her to marry you?"

"That question is still being considered. It is a viable option."

So Darian would marry Matilda after all and Marisa would get on with her life. She was really starting to wish she had never come to this place at all and even regretted ever having met any of these people.

"Marisa, look at me."

Reluctantly, she raised her eyes.

"For some reason, our paths have crossed. Although you and I have both arrived at this same place at the same time, we both have different paths to follow. You must discover your own."

"But what if I have no idea where I'm going?" she asked softly.

"Savino has asked you to marry him, and he shall be expecting a reply very soon. Remember that whatever choice you make, it must be yours and yours alone. It must be a decision that you can live with for the rest of your life."

He made sure that they could not be seen from the castle windows as he drew her close in a warm embrace.

"I wish things could be different for us, Marisa. You and I both have difficult decisions to make in the coming weeks. Let us pray we make the right ones." He stroked her long, chestnut hair and then kissed her softly.

As their lips parted, his eyes searched hers. "Tell me, who do you resemble more, your father or your mother?"

"My uncle says I have the same color of hair as my father and the rest is the spitting image of my mother."

"Your mother must have been very beautiful."

"That's what my father always said." She clung to him in silence and listened to the waterfall crashing somewhere in the distance. It was almost as if they were the only two on the planet.

He took her hand. "A beautiful ring for a beautiful woman." As he softly caressed her cheek, a chill ran down her spine. They lingered for a moment before he finally broke the spell.

"Come, we must leave this place soon."

He escorted her back up to her room, and then left her alone to prepare for the journey home. "I'll meet you down in the courtyard in ten minutes," he said.

Marisa nodded to him and slowly gathered her things together. She packed an extra set of clothes in a cloth sack and ten minutes later, she was gazing around the beautiful chamber one last time. She spotted the olive dress hanging on the wall and was reminded of Darian's kiss at the ball. It was a memory she would treasure always, but one that was not bound to be repeated. She sighed in exasperation as she realized that the situation was totally hopeless.

After checking to make sure everything was in her satchel, she took one last look out the window. She saw Savino, Darian, and Arrie waiting with a group of men down in the courtyard. She closed the door of her chambers and descended the stone steps to meet the two young men waiting to return home.

Darian grabbed the reins and turned to his cousin. "Savino, we are not finished yet," he said in an icy tone. "I shall do everything in my power to stop you from hurting her. She doesn't know what you truly are."

"And just what is that, Darian?" Savino asked, challenging him with his eyes. "You are in no position to make any demands of me, my dear cousin. No one shall prevent me from getting what I want. Not even you." The haughty look on Savino's face transformed instantly to a pleasant demeanor as Marisa emerged from the heavy wooden door.

"Ah, there you are my dear. My heart is heavy because you are leaving us again so soon. The next time we see each other, I know that we shall never be apart."

Marisa forced a small smile as he stroked her cheek.

"Now, now, my dear, do not be so sad to leave me. We shall see each other again very shortly." He took her in his arms and kissed her passionately.

Darian clenched his jaw and tightened his grasp on the hilt of his sword. "Time to go," he said, stepping between them.

"Remember, my love, you still owe me an answer," Savino said, wagging a finger at her. "I shall give you a bit more time to consider my offer before I send an envoy to Crocetta."

Darian gently lifted her up onto Siena's back while Arrie quickly mounted his own horse. Talvan took the lead and rode down ahead of them toward the gate. Marisa turned to see Savino lift a hand in farewell, and she waved to him one last time. The four of them passed under the raised castle gate and made their way down through the city.

"Come, gentlemen," Savino ordered. His eyes flashed and his voice dropped an octave as soon as Darian and his friends were out of sight. "We've got work to do."

CHAPTER 13

RIPPLES

THE FOUR RIDERS EXITED through the northwest edge of the city. Marisa noticed that they were headed in a different direction from where they had originally come. The mountain road was muddy from the recent rain as the horses trudged down it until they reached a crossroads.

Talvan bid them farewell and turned around to go back up toward the castle. Once the warrior was out of sight, Darian glanced at Marisa and noticed her worried expression.

"Don't worry, we won't be traveling through any rijgen-infested forests," he said.

"How long will it take us to get there?"

"If all goes well, we should reach Crocetta within three, perhaps four days," Arrie interjected.

As the mountain slope gradually ascended, the road became so narrow that it forced them to travel single file and not much was said over the next couple of hours. Marisa was in awe of the vast mountain range surrounding them, and it reminded her of photos of the Rocky Mountains. Abbadon was situated at a high elevation, but now they were ascending even higher.

She wrapped her cape tightly around her body and pulled the hood over her head. They had been traveling just below the timberline for most of the morning, but toward the early afternoon, they began to descend from the high mountains down toward a beautiful valley.

As they approached an alpine lake, Darian announced that they would be stopping to eat along the southwest shore. He helped Marisa down off her horse and removed a blanket from his saddle. Arrie tossed him a leather pouch as he led the horses down to the water's edge for a drink. Darian spread the blanket out on the grass just a few hundred feet up from the shore.

Marisa jogged down to where Arrie stood with the horses at the edge of the lake. Rolling her head around slowly, she stretched her neck, back, and shoulder muscles that had become stiff after sitting so long in one position.

She noticed that the beach wasn't made of sand, but instead consisted of millions of tiny black pebbles. She took off her shoes and stockings and slowly dipped her feet one at a time into the cold lake.

The water was so clear that she could see the pebbly bottom and lots of tiny fish swimming just a few feet away. It reminded her of a fishing trip with her father up to Mt. Hood one summer. He had rented a small cabin for the long weekend where they had spent hours on the beautiful banks of the Upper Sandy River fishing for rainbow trout. Marisa's always seemed to jump off the hook just as she was about to reel them in.

It made her wonder what her brother and Uncle Al were doing. Were they sleeping or eating? Maybe Mark was at school. Uncle Al might be on one of his Harley road trips up to the Gold Ray Dam. She wished she could call them just to hear their voices. At this point, she'd even settle for a text message.

Marveling at the wide expanse of the large lake, she studied the mountains' inverted reflections on the still water. Her thoughts wandered to what life would be like once they reached Crocetta. She wondered if it would include Darian. With each day that passed, she was finding it even more difficult to be around him.

Knowing that she couldn't avoid him forever, Marisa returned to the grassy area where he and Arrie sat, enjoying their meal in the fresh mountain air.

"Marisa, would you like to try some wine? It comes from the Fiore family vineyard," Darian asked.

She hesitated at first but then nodded. He poured the sparkling wine into her cup as Arrie handed her a plate of food loaded with bread, cheese, and some fruit. They ate quietly, in awe of the breathtaking mountain scenery. They were all avoiding an awkward discussion of what had transpired the night before.

"You know, Marisa, before we return to Crocetta, we must figure out what we shall tell people about you," Arrie said finally.

"I'm a mute. I can't talk. End of story."

He smiled. "No, I don't think that will be required. What are your thoughts, Darian?"

"She can't continue to be a mute. It would be too complicated, and it wouldn't be fair to her," he replied. Darian took a bite of apple and chewed it slowly.

"We could find her a nice position at the palace, don't you think?" Arrie suggested. "That way, we could also keep her under our protection, eh, Darian?"

"Do I have any say in this, or are you two just gonna plan out my entire life for me?"

"Marisa, we told Savino that you are mute. He thinks that you cannot speak," Darian said, his face turning serious. "Under this pretense, he has made you an offer of marriage and will not be amused when he discovers that all three of us have deceived him. Word travels quickly here and sooner or later, the truth shall get back to him."

"To hear both of you talk, it sounds like you don't think I'm ever going home. I thought we were gonna find that Celino guy who can help me get back to Jacksonville."

Arrie and Darian exchanged uncomfortable glances.

"Marisa, we told you that to keep you from panicking," Darian said. "It would be best if you accepted this world as your new home now. As Arrie explained before, the chances of a person returning through a vortex are—"

"So you lied to me? Are you saying that there's no chance that I'll be able to return? Ever? Do you even know someone from Earth named Celino? What else aren't you telling me?" she demanded.

Both of them looked at her sheepishly. She jumped up and stormed off toward the edge of the lake. She loosened her braid and shook it out as tears pooled in her eyes and her cheeks flushed with anger.

Knowing that she should accept and embrace this new world as her home, she fought the tears that refused to stop. Not wanting them to see her crying and feel sorry for her, she kept her face toward the water.

Darian stood up and watched her as she strolled along the edge of the water and decided to give her a few minutes alone. Finally, he walked down to where she was dipping her toes into the lake.

"It's amazing, don't you think?" he asked softly.

"What is?"

He pointed at the water. "Look at the size of this lake. It's so big, and the water is so still, like a perfect pane of glass with nothing to disturb it. But all of a sudden, you appear out of nowhere and start dipping your toes in it. With that one small action, you create ripples that are felt throughout this enormous lake."

Marisa said nothing as she gazed across the lake. She was not in the mood to be polite to him.

"Please tell me what is wrong. I would like to help you if I can," he said softly.

Her face sank. "You won't understand."

"Perhaps I already do."

She sighed. "I'm only eighteen and I haven't lived my life yet. I should be in college now, learning things and having fun. But the only option I have is to marry some man I don't even know. I'm not ready to be saddled down with a husband and twelve kids yet."

"You don't have to marry him. You do realize you have the option to say no, don't you?"

"What about your peace treaty?"

"Just you let me worry about that."

"But if I don't marry him, what will happen then? If I'm the one person who could prevent war from happening, then what kind of woman would I be if I didn't try to stop it?"

"Marisa, you're assuming far too much responsibility," he said. "Savino is itching to go to war and probably will, regardless of your decision. You just make sure that you do the right thing for you and let me worry about the rest. I'll make sure you are safe."

"You can't keep taking care of me, Darian! This has got to end somewhere." She crossed her arms over her chest. She didn't want to hurt him, but it was time to cut bait.

"You are, without a doubt, the most fascinating guy I've ever known. I can't even begin to explain how exciting it is just to be around you—it's like watching some action hero out of a movie or something."

He shook his head. "Marisa—"

"Darian, look—we both know that this is going nowhere. You're a prince, for crying out loud. With a little bit of luck, hopefully someday you'll be king. And I'm just a lost girl trying to find my way home. We are literally from two different worlds. We can't change who we are."

"You're right," he said sadly as he stared out over the water.

"The sooner we each can accept that fact and go our separate ways, the better it will be."

"Marisa, in just two days, we shall reach Crocetta. Many things will change after we arrive, but one thing shall never change—how I feel about you." He moved up close and put his arms around her. As he gazed tenderly into her eyes, he removed the earpiece from her ear and spoke to her softly in English.

"I love you, Marisa."

He pressed his lips against hers and goose bumps tingled down her arms. Her heart beat so hard that it felt as if it would escape from her chest. In the safety of his strong arms, she could feel the warmth emanating from him. Her heart couldn't take any more, and if she had to live in Carnelia without him, she would rather be dead. A life without his love was no life at all.

"I know it was unfair of me to confess that right now in light of our circumstances, but I just couldn't help myself," he said. "I may not ever get the chance again." He held her tightly as his eyes wandered out over the hills.

Suddenly Darian's face lit up. "Marisa—look!"

She turned to see where he was pointing. "What? What are you looking at?"

"Come, quickly!" Darian said excitedly.

Marisa followed him as he hurried over toward the meadow. He kneeled down on the grass next to two small flowers with petals just barely sticking out above the grass. Tenderly touching one, he looked up at her and smiled.

"What is it?" Marisa asked. She bent down to look at it closer and wondered what all the fuss was about. The flower had several beautiful white petals radiating from an ugly, dark brown clump in the center.

"It's a wounded heart!" Darian exclaimed. "I can't believe it. These flowers are extremely rare, but there are two of them here."

"What's so special about it?"

His eyes sparkled. "For most of its life, the flower's center appears as it is now; brown and hard, shaped like a human heart. Do you see it?" He pointed to its center.

"Yeah? So?"

"Right now, it's just a little white flower and nothing extraordinary. But one day, the pod will open and reveal a color so spectacular you must see it to believe it."

"When will it open?"

"That's just it—for each flower the timing is different. According to the legend, on the day that one sees a wounded heart bloom, they shall find their heart's destiny at last."

"But why is it called it a *wounded* heart?"

"This flower is a symbol of hope—of second chances. You see, now it's just a small white flower with an ugly, hard center. It looks like a heart that has been wounded or broken. But one day, someday totally unexpected, the flower will have its chance to blossom into something so incredible and so beautiful that will make it stand out among all the other flowers."

"Have you ever seen one open?"

"Yes, but it belonged to another," he said. "Wait here." He ran over to remove something from his saddle and quickly returned with two metal cups.

Carefully digging the flowers out with his dagger, he placed each of them into the cups and took them down to the lake to saturate the soil with water.

"You aren't actually taking those things back with you, are you?" she asked, laughing.

"Of course I am! Wounded hearts are rarely ever found near Crocetta. They only grow at higher elevations. That should be just enough water."

He wrapped the flowers in a piece of cloth and guided her back toward Arrie and the waiting horses. "I shall never forget the things we have shared on this journey, Marisa," he said softly.

She smiled gently at him but felt pangs of sadness in her heart once again. How could she possibly find another man to fill the gap he had already created?

Impossible!

Marisa knew that she had to start pulling away from him for her own sanity. She needed to begin the painful process of tearing herself away from him before it was too late.

He helped her up onto Siena's back before mounting his own horse. She avoided eye contact with them for most of the way and spoke only when necessary. After a while, she grabbed the iPhone out of her satchel and stuck the buds in her ears, unable to hear the sound of his voice anymore.

After several more hours on the road, they stopped at sunset in a small outpost called Snowton where they spent the night at the Sleepy Eye tavern.

CHAPTER 14

FROZEN

"MARISA, ARE YOU AWAKE?" Arrie's soft voice called to her from the other side of the door. Still half-asleep, she stumbled out of bed and opened it for him.

"I am now," she answered, still groggy.

"Good morning, cousin," Arrie said. "You're molting." He smiled in amusement and pulled a feather from her hair.

"Am I going to keep being your cousin forever?"

"Would you like to be?" He grinned at her. "Come, we need to hurry and get some breakfast and get back on the road. We have a lot of ground to cover today."

Marisa groaned, falling back onto the bed. "Just give me five minutes and I'll be down," she said. "Is Darian awake yet?" She stretched her long frame and brushed her hair.

"He was up and dressed a while ago to go out on his usual morning walk, but he should have returned by now. He is probably downstairs having breakfast right now."

As Arrie closed the door and left her alone to get ready, Marisa thought about Darian. She kept learning surprising things about him all the time but then quickly remembered that she was supposed to be forgetting about him.

Marisa entered the cheery dining hall downstairs to find Darian and Arrie both engaged in a deep conversation. They stopped as soon as she sat down, and both seemed a bit unsettled. She knew that they were probably nervous about returning home after their failed mission. She adjusted her earpiece to follow the conversation.

"I trust you slept well, milady?" Darian asked.

"As well as can be expected, Your Highness."

Touché.

He wiped his mouth with his napkin and sipped the last of his tea. "We will be riding all day today, so please make sure you get enough to eat this morning."

After breakfast, Marisa stepped out into the crisp fall air and threw her cape over her shoulders. She was glad that she had decided to wear it out riding that afternoon and couldn't have imagined being in Carnelia now without it.

The autumn morning was tinged with the smoky smell of dry leaves, and she counted just six more days until her birthday. She wondered if she'd even celebrate it. There wasn't much point since none of her family would be there.

Slinging her satchel across her body, Marisa hoisted herself up onto Siena and stroked her silky mane. With everything else that was so strange and new, she was grateful to have Siena as a familiar constant in a sometimes chaotic world.

As they began the second half of their journey home, little was said. Darian seemed subdued and barely spoke at all. Arrie tried to lighten the mood by telling some of his jokes, most of which Marisa didn't understand.

As they entered a small forest, Darian assured her there would be no rijgen in the woods. He explained that they were taking a whole extra day to travel to Crocetta using a different route in the hopes of avoiding the same dangerous situations they'd experienced on their way to Abbadon.

In the late afternoon, the road wound and twisted its way around some high cliffs. Although Marisa considered herself an experienced rider, she was wary of traveling on treacherous roads with an edge that dropped off down a steep cliff.

Although she didn't like to admit it, she was afraid of heights. Whenever Siena rode close to the edge, her heart began to race, and she had to look away.

"We'll soon pass through the Styrian Ice Caves in order to get to the other side of the mountain," Darian said.

"Ice caves?"

"Yes. They're a remarkable phenomenon and quite beautiful to behold. Of course, you must be familiar with the trail in order to navigate safely through them, or you might not make it out alive," he said smugly.

She looked at Arrie. "What's he talking about?"

He smiled. "The ice caves are areas deep in the rock where ice crystals have formed and grown over the limestone over the course of several centuries. They remain at a constant freezing temperature all year round."

Marisa stared at him blankly.

"Have you ever been in a cave?"

"Yeah?"

"Do you know how stalagmites and stalactites are formed?"

"I think so, but remind me again."

"Stalactites are formed when calcium carbonate flows through the rock and starts to drip. It hardens into a ring from the top down, growing downward. The liquid that drips to the ground and builds upward hardens to form a stalagmite. When the two of them join, it forms what is known as a column."

"So why are these caves so dangerous?"

"They are covered in a thick layer of ice, making them extremely slippery. In the caverns, it is extremely dark and exceptionally cold. Unless one knows how to navigate through it, a person can get lost in there and even freeze to death within minutes."

"Sorry I asked," she muttered.

Several hundred feet up ahead, they spotted the opening of the cave where hundreds of milky-white icicles hung down. It looked like a dragon's mouth with its jaws wide open and the icicles appeared as long, sharp daggers. Marisa imagined that they were probably just as dangerous.

As they neared the cave's entrance, Darian dismounted and unsheathed his sword. In one swift motion, he knocked down the icicles to clear the way. Then he took a rod and cloth from his saddle and used them to make a torch.

After watching Arrie dismount, Marisa followed his lead and climbed down from Siena. "Aren't we going to ride through the caves?" she asked.

"Too dangerous," Darian replied. "The ceiling of the cave isn't high enough. Trust me—you wouldn't want to brush your head against one of those low-hanging blades of ice."

Darian entered the cave and the others followed behind. He held the fluttering torch as high as possible to light their way as he led Obsidian with the reins.

An icy gust of wind rushed past Marisa, and she shivered. Squinting as they entered the blackness of the cave, she strained to see anything in the dark. Once her eyes had adjusted, she gasped at the wondrous sight.

The cave was just as Arrie had described, with hundreds of stalactites and stalagmites staggered everywhere throughout the massive cavern. It reminded her of a field trip years ago with her fifth-grade class to the Oregon Caves National Monument. Everything inside these caves, however, was covered entirely with a thick layer of ice.

As the yellow limestone shone through the ice, the entire cave glittered and glowed as if it were made of pure gold. Carefully shuffling and sliding across a hardened sea of yellow crystal, Marisa was in awe of the translucent beauty of this natural phenomenon.

"Don't touch the columns, and be very careful where you step," Darian warned. "We're moving along a high ledge in the cave wall, and you wouldn't want to fall into that."

He motioned below, pointing the torch downward. She saw that there was only about eight feet of the ledge, and after that, it dropped off into a large cavern and what looked like a deep, dark abyss.

Marisa glanced up at the ceiling of the cave. Thousands upon thousands of dagger-like icicles hung down only a few feet above her head and if just one fell on her, she'd be dead. She was amazed that such a place of beauty could also be just as dangerous.

All of a sudden, her foot slipped and she started to slide away from Siena. With lightning-fast reflexes, Arrie grabbed her arm just before she slid off down into the deep cavern below.

"Marisa, are you all right?" he asked.

She nodded. Her heart was pounding wildly.

"Do be careful, Marisa," Darian said.

Stupid, stupid! Embarrassed, she scolded herself to pay better attention. For the next several minutes, she followed behind Darian as they advanced slowly but surely through the length of the cave.

She couldn't resist the temptation to take a photo of the cave's interior. She rummaged around in her satchel for her phone. She pulled it out and swiped the menu items until she came to the camera function. Holding it out to the side and angling it toward the ceiling of the cave, she pressed the camera icon.

The flash from the phone bounced around the cave and spooked all three horses. Concrete reared up and backed into her, pushing Marisa off the slippery path.

With no traction on the glassy surface, she struggled for balance. But the momentum was strong enough to send her plummeting over the edge. In a single instant, she dropped out of sight and slid down into the main cavern below.

"Marisa!" Darian and Arrie screamed in unison.

That's it—I'm dead.

As she raced down the steep wall of ice like a runaway bobsled out of control, she flailed in the darkness, trying to grab hold of anything that could break her fall. But the ice-covered stalagmites and columns were too slippery to clutch. Sharp pieces of ice sliced into her hands and arms and the cold quickly seeped through her clothing all the way to her skin.

Her body slammed into something. She was immediately jolted to a stop, caught by what felt like a large tree trunk between her legs. As she groped in the darkness, her hands encircled the cold pillar and Marisa realized that only a single column of ice was keeping her from plunging into the bottomless pit below. Her arms and legs were shaking as she strained to see anything in the dark cavern. Her body was quickly losing its warmth in what felt like a subzero meat locker.

Arrie and Darian's voices shouted down to her from somewhere far above. "Marisa! Where are you! Are you still there?"

"Help," she cried weakly.

Can they even hear me?

As she glanced high above her, she saw a small source of light dancing to and fro and realized that it was Darian's torch as he paced back and forth across the ledge.

"Marisa, you've got to show us where you are! Say something!" Darian shouted.

"I'm here," she cried softly, terrified of falling at any moment.

With no rope or climbing equipment to speak of, she knew that it would be almost impossible for them to reach her down so deep and her hopes began to fade.

The minutes ticked by, but they seemed like hours, and her thoughts started to drift. She could still hear Darian and Arrie calling to her, but she didn't have the strength anymore to answer. Her whole body shook from the cold penetrating into her skin. Arrie had said that the temperature in the cavern was low enough to freeze a person within minutes.

Without warning, a monstrous roar followed by a shrill whistle erupted from somewhere deep in the cave. Marisa's eyes flew open. She peered around in the darkness to detect any sort of movement, but it was no use. Zero visibility.

Danger! Something screamed inside her.

The roar and whistle came again, but this time they seemed much closer. The sound reminded her of the roar of the rijgen. Knowing they'd probably disturbed some monstrous beast sleeping in the cave, a fresh wave of terror rippled through her.

Garon, give me wisdom, she prayed. *Think—think!*

By some miracle, she had managed to hold onto her phone, which she still clutched in her hand. It was almost frozen between her fingers that had rapidly grown numb from the cold, but it might be her only chance. Shivering, she felt for the power button and turned it back on. Another howl and whistle.

It was definitely moving closer.

Arrie shouted something, but she couldn't understand what he was saying as the terrifying roar reverberated through the cavern.

The screen illuminated, and she waited impatiently for it to load before swiping her finger across it in search of the flashlight function. She pressed it a few times before it eventually turned on.

Once the light glowed, she raised the phone above her head and waved it back and forth as high as possible.

Another roar and shrill whistle.

Get out of there now!

Suddenly Marisa heard something large crawling down the wall of ice several feet above her. Should she switch off her phone? Was its light leading some horrible beast right to her?

Let your light shine, said a voice in Marisa's head.

Her mind was numb with fear as she heard sharp claws digging and scratching into the ice right above her, moving dangerously close.

"Marisa, I see you!" It was Darian. "Stay where you are and don't move!" he shouted, his voice resonating through the cavern.

"Please, hurry," she mouthed, her teeth chattering.

"Hold your light higher so I can see where you are! We've got to get out of here!"

Struggling to hold the phone above her head, Marisa waved it back and forth as a beacon in the darkness. A moment later, she could hear Darian digging into the ice on a shelf just a few feet above her.

There was a deafening roar from the creature that sent tremors across the cavern floor. The unmistakable sound of Darian's sword being unsheathed echoed in Marisa's ears. His blade clanged as it smashed into the walls of ice when it missed. The piercing shrieks of the beast reverberated throughout the cave.

Small chunks of ice pelted her, and she quickly covered her head with her cape. Sounds of scuffling could be heard as the beast whistled and roared in anger.

Hugging the wall of ice, she breathed on her hands, trying to warm them as her teeth chattered violently.

Darian grunted somewhere in the darkness, and the beast howled in pain. Again the sword clanged as it missed the animal and slammed into the walls of the cave. She winced as a thousand tiny splinters of ice rained down around her.

She listened to the terrifying struggle going on just above her as the creature's howls and snorts mixed with Darian's grunts and shouts. She had no idea what he was up against but could only pray he would be able to defeat whatever it was.

Suddenly, the monster screamed in agony.

Marisa jumped as the lifeless creature tumbled down past her, only visible for a second or two as the dim light from her cell phone reflected in the creature's pupils.

After an extended pause, there was a loud, echoing thud that resonated upward from the cavern floor deep below.

"Marisa! Where are you?" Darian called to her.

Unable to think or speak, Marisa couldn't muster the strength to respond. Her eyelids were drooping, and her teeth chattered. She continued to shake her cell phone light above her head.

Darian scurried down the icy slope just as fast as he could go without losing his footing. Within seconds, his head popped over the edge just above her.

"Oh, thank Garon!" He exhaled with relief as he quickly climbed down to her. "Marisa, we thought we'd lost you. We must get you out of here right away. Are you hurt?"

He looked her up and down, trying to see if she had been wounded. Her clothes were soaked and freezing, but she didn't appear to have any broken bones. In the low light of the cell phone, Darian saw that her face and hands had already started to turn a deathly bluish-white.

"Marisa? Marisa—look at me!"

Darian sounded as if he was far away, and his face was only a blur. If she fell asleep now, she'd never wake up, but Marisa no longer seemed to care.

"Put your arms around my neck. I'm going to carry you up on my back, but you've got to hold on. Do you think you can do that?"

She nodded, barely able to make out his blurry shape in the flashlight of her phone. He took it from her and slipped it under his belt to light their way.

"Now I want you to put your arms around my neck, grasp your wrist with your hand, and hold on as tight as you can. Wrap your legs around my waist, and whatever you do, don't let go. Are you ready? Let's go."

Marisa couldn't feel her feet or thighs anymore, and there was barely a hint of feeling in both hands. She locked her arms around Darian's neck and struggled to hang on. It felt as if she hadn't slept in days.

He slowly began to scale the wall using a small dagger to delve into the ice. Using his other arm to hoist them both up, he sought solid footing, bracing his boots against the stalagmites and columns. Slowly, they ascended higher above the cavern floor.

As Marisa fought to stay awake, she could feel the power of his back muscles flexing underneath her. Her body grew steadily weaker as her consciousness finally started to slip away. At last she shut her eyes.

All she wanted to do was sleep.

Darian reached the ledge where Arrie waited with an outstretched arm. He pulled her up over the slippery edge, and was startled by the bluish-white color of her skin as he peered down into her unseeing, glassy eyes.

CHAPTER 15
CONVERSATIONS

As Marisa finally regained consciousness, she awoke with a strange jostling sensation. She opened her eyes slowly to find herself sitting on Obsidian just in front of and facing Darian. Startled by their proximity to each other, she sat up quickly and glanced around.

Her legs were extended over his, and her arms encircled his waist under a white linen shirt. He had removed his armored breastplate, and his arms were stretched out around her to grasp the reins and to keep her from slipping off.

As Marisa felt his oblique muscles flexing under her fingers, she sat up straight and stared directly into his amused eyes.

"Good afternoon," he said softly.

Without breaking his horse's stride, he gazed down at her, and his eyes seemed to sparkle from within. Her face was close enough to his that they almost touched, and she had the overwhelming urge to kiss him. She decided that it probably wasn't a good idea at this point.

She squinted in the brightness of the afternoon sun and leaned out to see Arrie leading Siena at the rear. "What happened?" she asked, rubbing her forehead.

"You fell."

"Yeah, that part I remember. What happened after that?"

"You slipped and slid off down the wall of the cave. If that column of ice hadn't broken your fall, you would have tumbled over the edge into the abyss just like that *yarmout* did."

"Yarmout? Was that the hairy, freaky monster you killed?"

He nodded. "Your body temperature dropped so far that you blacked out. We got you out of the cave as quickly as possible."

"So why do I have my hands inside your shirt?"

"You became under cooled. We had to warm you up as fast as possible. Are you able to feel your hands again?"

"Yes." She blushed. "How long have I been out?"

"About an hour, I think," he said softly.

Sinking her head back into his chest, Marisa relished in his warmth. Her muscles felt weak, and she knew they'd probably be sore by morning. Sobered by the fact she had narrowly escaped death that day, she sought comfort in his firm body. As she looked down, a startling realization came over her.

"Uh, Darian—Your Highness?"

He glanced down at her from where he'd been concentrating on the road.

"I'm not wearing the same clothes that I put on this morning. These are the extra clothes I put in the sack."

He nodded. "Your garments were wet from where the ice had melted through the cloth. The only way we could warm you up was to remove them."

Marisa's eyes widened.

"We had to get you into dry clothes immediately, or we might have lost you forever. You have nothing to be ashamed of." He looked down at her with a smirk.

Her face flushed, and she quickly looked away.

In the late afternoon, they crossed a shallow river and stopped there to allow the horses to drink. Darian dismounted and then lifted her off his horse, setting her down on the ground.

"We'll set up camp back in those woods," he said to Arrie. "I'm going further upstream to find some firewood." He raced off into the woods.

Arrie unrolled the small tent he'd been carrying on his horse and cleared a small patch of ground about a hundred yards from the river. He quickly pitched the tent and built a fire pit.

Darian soon returned with an armful of wood and a giant hare he had killed. "I found us some dinner," he announced proudly.

Marisa's jaw dropped in amazement. She watched as he removed a small dagger from his belt and skinned the hare within just a few minutes. She shook her head. This guy was more like Tarzan than a prince.

Once the wood was burning, Arrie whittled some sticks to build a makeshift spit and placed the skinned rabbit on it to cook. The flames licked the flesh, gently roasting their dinner.

Marisa noticed the sun was beginning to set on the horizon, so she stood up to go wash off in the river before it got dark. As she walked through the forest toward the water, she rolled up her sleeves to examine her arms. Sharp edges on the ice had scraped her arms in a couple of places, but by some miracle, she hadn't gotten frostbitten. Although she had been bruised badly on her hip and back, Marisa was relieved nothing had been broken.

She reached the rocky stream and kneeled down next to a large boulder, gazing at her surroundings. She admired the tall trees that towered along the banks of the river and Marisa inhaled the fresh scent of pine and cedar. The tranquility of the woods back in Oregon had always provided peace for her soul and the place where they were camped out now reminded her so much of home.

She closed her eyes, and for a few brief moments, her troubles and worries seemed to melt away. The sound of the water rushing by was soothing, and Marisa realized that she was quickly falling in love with the breathtaking wilderness of Carnelia.

As she stared down at her rippling reflection and splashed water on her arms, her mind wandered back to Darian. She thought about his confession of love by the lake and was sobered by the fact that it would never happen again. She pulled her hair into a ponytail and stood up to go.

She bumped into Darian who was standing right behind her. Startled, she lost her balance. In a lightning-fast reaction, he reached out and caught her just before she fell in. She steadied herself and glared at him.

"Sorry, I didn't mean to frighten you," he said.

"Well—you did," she said angrily.

"I didn't think you should be down here alone. This area is a favorite watering hole of many large animals."

"Oh. I didn't know that."

"It's getting dark fast now. Let's return to camp."

As they walked back toward camp, she noticed that Darian seemed to be keeping his distance. Ever since they had met, he'd been something of an enigma to Marisa. Although he had opened up while they were at Abbadon, now that their mission was over, he seemed to be retreating into his shell once again.

When they reached the camp, Arrie handed Marisa a small metal plate with some food. She sat down across from him on a log. As they ate their dinner in silence around the campfire, she noticed Darian watching her thoughtfully. Arrie was not in his usual cheerful mood, and she wondered if the consequences of their failed mission would be even more serious than she had imagined. She tried to lighten things up by starting a conversation with Arrie.

"What exactly is a yarmout? I didn't get a real close look at it in the dark as it tumbled down past me, but what a horrible roar!"

"Well, a yarmout is actually quite similar to the rijgen, except that they only dwell in cold-weather places such as the ice caves," he said with a sheepish grin.

"What? Why are you looking at me like that?" she asked.

"You're not going to believe me."

"Try me."

"Have you ever heard of a yeti?" he asked.

"A what?"

"A yeti."

She blinked. "That's a car model, right?"

He shook his head. "Otherwise known as the Abominable Snowman?"

"Seriously?" Marisa laughed. "What mythical creature are we going to come across next? The Loch Ness Monster? Unicorns? Wait, I know, vampires!"

"That *mythical* creature we encountered in the caves could have easily killed you," Darian said softly in the darkness. "Lucky for you, I got to him first." His remark rubbed Marisa the wrong way.

"Well, Darian, it appears that you've saved my life yet again. By the time we reach Crocetta, I'll probably owe you my firstborn child."

When Marisa saw his crestfallen expression, she instantly regretted her words. He'd risked his own life to save her when he could have left her down there to freeze.

"I'm sorry, Darian. I just don't know what's gotten into me lately. I am grateful to you for saving me."

He gave her a curt nod and stared back into the fire. As Darian retreated back into his shell, Marisa sulked. She knew that he was probably just trying to protect himself. After all, she was doing the same thing and couldn't honestly blame him.

Arrie rolled out their mats and pointed her toward the tent.

"Marisa, your tent is ready anytime you wish to retire. You've had a pretty rough day and should probably get some sleep."

"I'm so exhausted that I could fall asleep right now."

"Don't worry about a thing—we'll be right over there," he said, gesturing toward the fire just a few feet away. "Now go try to get some sleep."

"Sleep well, milady," Darian added softly.

Marisa crawled inside her tent and lay down on the mat. The temperature had cooled off considerably in the past hour. She shivered as she thought of Darian and Arrie out in the cold and wondered if they would be warm enough. She covered herself with her cloak and finally decided they'd be okay under their cloaks and wool blankets next to the fire.

As she lay on her mat, her mind raced. She tossed and turned for nearly half an hour but still couldn't get comfortable. Realizing that the earpiece was still in place, she reached up to remove it.

Something caught her attention as she heard Darian and Arrie whispering. She adjusted the translator and strained to listen.

"Are you absolutely certain about this?" Arrie whispered.

"Quite certain," Darian replied softly.

"Have you told anyone else?"

"No, and I shall not inform the Crimson Court until after I've had the opportunity to tell my mother and Adalina first."

"I don't think I need to remind you that Savino will use all means possible to defeat you. When he finds out, he—"

"Savino isn't going to find out," Darian interrupted. "I am certain that he must be planning something, and I must act before he does. I believe he would hurt her if he ever found out. But by the time he learns of our betrothal, it will be too late."

"You're not planning to elope, are you?" Arrie whispered.

Marisa gasped.

"Of course not. I don't want that, and neither does she."

"Then I offer you my warmest congratulations, Darian. I hope that you will be supremely happy together. If anyone deserves it, it's you. When will you be making the announcement?"

"Soon—when the timing is right. I plan to invite Mattie and Savino to Crocetta as guests of honor at a ball. With all the members of the Crimson Court present, there will be plenty of witnesses should Savino try anything."

There was a long pause as Marisa held her breath. The two men said nothing for a moment, and she heard only the popping and cracking of the fire.

"What about Marisa?" Arrie whispered finally. "When are you planning to tell her about the engagement?" Marisa leaned against the tent and strained to hear Darian's reply.

"I—I don't know how to tell her."

"*What!*" Arrie said out loud.

"Shhh, you'll wake her!"

"No more games, Darian. She cares about you and has a right to know. You may be my cousin, but if you don't tell her, I will."

Darian let out a long, heavy sigh. "Just let me handle it. I will need some time to break it to her gently."

"Not too much time. You need to tell her soon."

"The poor girl has had so much to endure in recent weeks, and the last thing I want is for her to hear about it from someone else. Promise me that you won't say anything to her?" Darian asked.

Another silence.

"But when are you planning to tell her?"

"Arrie, please—just promise me."

"All right. I promise."

Marisa fell down on her mat and rolled over on her side, tears flooding her eyes. Ripping the translator from her ear, she threw it against the side of the tent, unable to hear anymore. She recalled what Darian had said just a few short hours ago:

In just two days, we will reach Crocetta. Many things will change when we get there, but one thing that will never change is how much I care about you.

Darian had never made a secret of the fact that he'd probably end up marrying Matilda. He'd told her straight out that he wasn't in a position to offer Marisa anything. Arrie said he always put duty before his heart. Why should she be so surprised?

Her father had always said that life wasn't fair. Well, there's no way she'd stick around and watch those two get married among a host of well-wishers.

Pulling the hood of her cape over her face, Marisa tried to muffle her gut-wrenching sobs and started to wish she was dead.

CHAPTER 16
APPREHENSIONS

MARISA AWOKE THE NEXT morning with a terrible headache and muscle pains that stretched through her whole body. She'd never cried herself to sleep back home, but since she'd come to this strange new world, it had become a frequent evening ritual.

Great, now I'm turning into a basket case.

She quickly dressed and twisted her hair up in a knot. She looked terrible from all the crying and the poor night's sleep, but she just didn't care anymore. She emerged from the tent to find Arrie and Darian sitting around an early-morning fire.

"Good morning, sleepyhead," joked Arrie.

"Very funny," she muttered under her breath, in no mood for jokes. "How much longer before we get to this Crocetta, anyway?"

"About eight hours," Darian answered.

"Another day of sore muscles—that's just great!" The two men exchanged puzzled glances.

She looked down at the smoky fire, avoiding eye contact with either of them. She swiped the last piece of bread and fruit, turned away from them, and gobbled it down in just a couple of minutes. After washing her meager breakfast down with a cup of water, she stood up and stomped down to the river.

As she splashed the icy water on her face and arms, Marisa shivered. She was looking forward to taking a warm bath once they got home. *Wherever home is these days,* she thought.

Once Arrie had taken down her tent, they saddled up and moved out on their final stretch of the journey toward Crocetta. They had been gone for more than a week, and tonight they would finally reach the city.

Marisa had hoped that her life would return to some sort of normalcy, but she doubted it was even still possible at this point. Although she would never admit it to anyone else, she'd be a bit sad when their journey was over. It had been a frightening yet wondrous adventure, and she owed Darian and Arrie for saving her life more than once. The three of them had been through a lot together.

No matter what happened, she'd never forget either of them, and it would be strange not having them around for moral support. They had gotten her through a rough first week after her father's funeral and even helped ease her into life in this strange new world.

She would stay friends with Arrie, but there was no way she could continue to associate with Darian once he married Lady Matilda. Not only would they move in totally different social orbits, but the pain caused by seeing him married to another woman would be too much for her to bear. For her own sake, she had to make a clean break.

Out in the open wilderness, Marisa had time to ponder many things for several hours, and she shifted her focus to planning her new life. She wondered what she could do to earn a living for herself in Carnelia. Most women seemed to marry and let the man take care of them for the rest of their lives. She wasn't so sure that was what she wanted.

The option of starting a new life as Savino's wife was still on the table, but she wasn't sure yet if she could go through with it. Helinda had said she would be lucky to have such a powerful man, but it wasn't passion and fireworks with him as it was with Darian. Although she felt tremendous pressure to marry Savino and save the country from war, Marisa needed more time before she could make her final decision on whether to marry him.

She wondered what would happen to the country if she turned Savino down. Darian had said that Savino would declare war and many people would die. Would she be hated by all as the woman who could have prevented war but didn't? She couldn't bear to think of that scenario playing out in her future.

On a more personal level, Marisa wondered if she'd ever meet another man that she could love again. She doubted it, but maybe somewhere in her future she might meet someone she could respect. Darian might be willing to find her a suitor, but that was the last thing she wanted from him. Arrie was right; she was still young, and time was on her side.

But she didn't want to find someone else, and she didn't want to settle for second-best in her life, either. What was it her father had written in his letter? *Never settle for less than that which is worthy and worthwhile.* Would her father have considered Savino as being either? She wondered.

Marisa came to the sad conclusion that she had few options in this world. She had met the man of her dreams in Carnelia but now wished she'd never even come here. The illusion of the fairytale happy ending had disappeared forever. It was probably just a gimmick used to sell books and movies anyway.

"You're much too quiet over there, cousin," Arrie said. "What's going on in that pretty little head of yours?"

"Everything," she said quietly.

"Could you be a little more specific, please?"

Marisa shrugged. "I've just been wondering what is going to happen to me. There don't seem to be many options available for a girl like me. It's not like I'm fresh out of college and can go interview for a job somewhere."

"Your prospects are not as dismal as you think, dear cousin."

"Ha! That's easy for you to say. You're a guy."

"Nonsense! You're a beautiful woman that many men would be willing to fight for," Arrie said.

He glanced over at Darian and chuckled. "Or even die for."

She made a face. "I seriously hope it doesn't come to that. I don't need any extra drama in my life right now."

"Nevertheless, I think you give yourself and, I might add, Carnelia far too little credit."

"What do you mean?"

"You don't yet know much about our world, Marisa, and you've still got a lot to learn. There are many opportunities for women in our world, believe it or not, and they *don't* all end in matrimony."

She looked at him skeptically. "Do tell."

"Women are employed here just like they are on Earth. Maybe not in the same ways, but it is possible for a woman to make her own living here. We just have a different philosophy when it comes to women."

"I'm all ears," she said dryly.

"Women are equal in importance to men, but they have different roles to play. While your world has been fighting for women's rights, emancipation, and equality for more than a century now, our world came to the conclusion long ago that men and women, though created differently and sometimes behave differently, are in fact equal."

"Somehow Savino and his warriors didn't leave me with that impression. They all treat women like they're trophies or something."

"You are most perceptive, milady. But that is a rather poor example. Savino is not your average Carnelian male."

"*That* I can believe."

Darian interrupted. "Time to stop and rest the horses."

Marisa dismounted and grabbed her satchel. She headed toward a large grove of trees and turned her back toward them, hoping that they would take the hint and leave her alone. She removed the purple diary from her satchel and felt the soft fabric on its cover.

"What is that book anyway?" Darian asked over her shoulder.

"Do you always have to sneak up on people like that? It's so annoying!"

"Sorry."

She softened. "It's some kind of diary my father gave to me. The only problem is—I can't read it."

"Why not?"

"Because it's written in Scottish Gaelic."

"Scottish Gae-lic?"

"Yeah, the language my parents spoke back in Scotland."

"Ah. May I see it?"

"Sure, I guess—why not?" She handed him the book.

He sat down next to her and began to thumb through it, stopping every now and then to look at a picture or drawing.

"Who wrote it?"

"I dunno. I was gonna ask my uncle about it but I didn't get the chance. And now I might never find out," she said wistfully.

"Well, it certainly is a beautiful book," he said as he handed it back to her. "Someone obviously spent a lot of time writing it. Such an heirloom should be treasured indeed."

"Yes, well, I've managed to hang on to it so far. And even if I'm never able to get it translated, at least I still have something that belonged to my father."

"Yes, but what a pity you can't read it," he said thoughtfully.

Feelings of loss and regret washed over Marisa as she thought about all the influential people she'd lost in her life. She glanced down at the ring and tried to remember the mother she had barely known.

"I would be extremely careful with that ring if I were you," he said. "It must be of great value and there are many who would try to steal it."

"I'm real careful with it. I don't ever want to sell it, no matter how much it might be worth."

He nodded. "Some things are too valuable to put a price on."

Somehow, she didn't think he was talking about the ring. She quickly turned away. She was still upset by what she'd overheard the night before. It had been dishonest of him to play with her affections when all along he'd been engaged to Lady Matilda. If she just kept that thought in front of her at all times, it would remind her never to get too close to him again.

But deep down, she knew she only had herself to blame. Darian had never lied to her. He had told her straight out that he could never have any kind of deep connection with her, but she hadn't taken it seriously. Neither of them had planned on any of this happening. They had just gotten in each other's way.

"What were you thinking about just now?" he asked softly. "You seemed somewhere very far away."

"Oh, nothing important. I'm just anxious to get to Crocetta and start a new chapter in my life. Who knows, I might even decide to move on once I get the lay of the land."

Darian studied her thoughtfully. "You shouldn't decide that now. Wait until you've gotten to know Crocetta a little better. Arrie and I would like to help you get settled and introduce you to all the right people. I hope that you'll allow us to do that for you."

She glanced at him. Maybe he was starting to feel guilty after all. Maybe he thought that if he helped her get established in Crocetta, he would have done his duty and could go off and marry Lady Matilda. But after the way he had hurt Marisa, she didn't think she should let him off the hook so easily.

"Unless, of course, you're planning to marry Savino. Then none of that would even be necessary..." he trailed off.

"Look, Darian, I appreciate all you've done for me, but I just want to make it on my own. You don't owe me a thing, and I don't expect anything from you. Honest I don't."

"I'm just trying to help, Marisa."

She sighed. "I know you are, but my father always said that one of the things he admired most about me was my sense of independence. I just want to make him proud of me."

"Marisa, your father is already proud of you. In fact, I hope to have a daughter someday with half the spirit and independence as you," he said, twirling a long blade of grass between his fingers. As she looked at him, Darian blushed, and he quickly changed the subject. "We should be leaving soon if we want to make it home by sundown."

Arrie was already mounted on his horse as Darian and Marisa approached him. They saddled up and quickly got moving on the hilly road once again.

As the hours passed, Marisa realized that each step toward Crocetta was one step closer to a new life without Prince Darian. The first chapter in her life was coming to a close. She hoped that the next would be a significant improvement.

No matter what the future held in store, she was resigned to accept one point as fact—there could never be a happy ending with Darian.

CHAPTER 17

CROCETTA

As they rounded the bend of a large hill, a great, walled city loomed in the distance. Strategically situated on top of a mountain, the citadel resembled Abbadon, but even from a distance, it was obvious that Crocetta Castle was much larger in scale than Savino's fortress.

When she smelled the saltwater air, she looked and saw that the hillside sloped down to meet a bustling harbor far below them. The masts of at least a dozen ships moored at the docks jutted up from the water as wagons transported people and goods from the port up to the city. The cries of seabirds pierced the skies as she glanced up to see them circling in search of food.

Waiting for them on the road was a large company of more than fifty soldiers dressed in dark, elegant uniforms with shields, swords and helmets. As they sat patiently on their horses, Marisa wondered how the men knew that they were coming and how long they'd been waiting for them. Arrie must have read her thoughts.

"These men are guardsmen of the Order of the Crimson Paladin Knights," he whispered. "They have probably been awaiting our arrival since early this morning."

A dark-haired, handsome man in the lead moved toward them.

"Your Highness, Lord Arrigo, the kingdom is pleased to welcome you both back safe and sound," he said.

"Lord Domenico," Darian said with a smile. "It's good to see you, my friend." He gave him a friendly slap on the shoulder.

Marisa's jaw dropped. If she had been standing further away, she would have thought he was Darian or at least his brother. With roughly the same build as Darian, Lord Domenico had the same dark hair and square jaw. She guessed they were about the same age and noticed he wore the same military uniform.

"So, Darian, aren't you going to introduce me to this beautiful young maiden whose heart you've obviously already captured?" he asked, eyeing Marisa mischievously. "How do you ever expect the rest of us to keep up with all of your conquests?"

She turned to Darian with a puzzled expression.

"Ah—right. Lord Domenico, it is my honor and privilege to introduce to you the Lady Marisa," Darian said. The man who could easily have been his clone maneuvered his horse alongside Siena and took Marisa's hand.

"I am most enchanted to make your acquaintance, milady," Domenico said. He kissed her hand gently as his eyes flirted with her.

"Pleased to meet you, sire," she answered in English.

Domenico raised an eyebrow. "And just how did you manage to stumble across such an exotic gem, Your Highness?"

"Lady Marisa was—we found her stranded near Andresis. She comes to us from a land far away."

"Are you two somehow related?" she asked, pointing at them.

Darian and Domenico exchanged amused glances. "No, Lord Domenico is no relation to me whatsoever," Darian said. "However, we are often asked that same question."

"The likeness is uncanny!"

"Yes, well, some have said that Lord Domenico is my alter-ego," Darian joked.

"What Prince Darian means to say is that I'm his better half," Domenico said with a chuckle.

"Lady Marisa, I would beg you not to believe a word this man says," Darian said. "For he loves to mix truth with falsehoods in such a way that one never knows when he is joking and when he is serious. But enough with the introductions—I am eager to return to my home."

As the company turned to escort them into the city, Marisa studied the faces of the young soldiers. The men were roughly the same age as she and they were all unusually tall and broad. She wondered if there were certain height and weight requirements to serve as a Crimson Paladin guardsman.

It was already late afternoon as they entered the outer edge of the city. The houses, shops, and halls surrounded the massive citadel on three sides in the shape of a crescent moon. The fortress sat on the highest point of the mountain and towered above all the other buildings.

Crocetta was teeming with people that mingled in groups at the side of the road and individuals that hurried down the street on their way to somewhere important. The men, women, and children were all dressed in beautiful garments, and just like the soldiers, they also seemed sturdy and tall. Deciding that they must be some kind of super race of people, Marisa was stunned to note that most of the women were at least six feet tall or more.

People stopped their daily business to bow and courtesy to Darian, clapping and cheering as he passed. Most people just stared at Marisa—not in a rude way but more out of curiosity.

Once they reached the citadel, she stared in awe up at the fortification walls towering high above them. Unlike the gate at Abbadon, the iron portcullis of the citadel at Crocetta was raised, allowing people to move in and out of the castle freely. Here, the guards didn't seem to stop anyone from entering.

They passed under an impressive stone archway and through a long tunnel under the rampart wall that ended in a large stone courtyard. The massive ramparts were at least sixty feet wide. Inside the walls at the highest point of the hill was a large fortress with seven round turrets and four larger turrets in the middle around a central tower.

In the main courtyard, several rows of colorful banners containing various coats-of-arms were draped along its walls. Arrie whispered to her that each of the banners represented a nobleman's family crest from different provinces all across the land. She couldn't identify some of the strange beasts on the crests.

Since the time she'd visited Disneyland at the age of five, Marisa had imagined castles to be pretty buildings with quaint pink-and-blue turrets. But now as she stood in the main courtyard of Crocetta Castle, she felt an invisible force surrounding the mighty stone citadel and the stereotype was instantly shattered.

Massive in size and constructed from the hardest rock, it was an absolute fortress and the most imposing structure she'd ever seen. The castle walls dwarfed them all in size, and all of a sudden she felt small and insignificant.

"So, what do you think of your new home?" Darian asked.

"Very impressive," she said. "But I'll only be staying for a few days until I can get a place of my own. Any longer than that and I might get spoiled."

Arrie laughed. "Maybe that's the whole idea."

Darian escorted Marisa up a long purple carpet leading toward the main door of the castle. She started to giggle.

"Just what is so amusing, milady?" he asked with a smile.

"Oh, I'm just in another one of my surreal moments. I'm being escorted down a red carpet—uh, purple carpet by a handsome prince into his fantabulous castle. Yep, this kind of thing happens to me all the time."

Darian chuckled as he gestured them all to go inside. As soon as they entered the Great Hall, Marisa's jaw dropped.

The dark brown beams supporting the wooden roof were enormous and ran the entire breadth of the hall. The ceiling itself was a dark shade of indigo with intricate curls of gold trim around the edges. Beautiful stained glass windows near the vaulted ceiling cast vivid colors with the last rays of sunshine.

The hall was graced by eight golden chandeliers fitted with thousands of crystals, giving the room a particularly grand feel. The walls inside were a pale, polished stone, and the bricks themselves were several feet wide each. As Marisa was admiring the castle's interior, three men and a woman approached and nodded to Darian.

"Lady Marisa, I would like to introduce you to the members of my household," Darian said. "This is my head political advisor, Faustino, but we all call him Tino."

A tall man in his early fifties with a mustache, graying sideburns, and a beard stepped forward. He smiled warmly at her and he exuded confidence as if he knew everything and everyone in Crocetta like the back of his hand.

"I am very pleased to meet you, Lady Marisa," the man said with a bow.

"Nice to meet you, sir," Marisa answered in English.

Everyone looked at her with surprise and Darian raised a hand to reassure them.

"Please do not be alarmed. Lady Marisa comes to us from a land far away, and she is our honored guest here in Crocetta. I would appreciate it if you all made her feel welcome."

Tino nodded to her. "Milady, you are most welcome here in Crocetta, and I pray that you will afford me the honor of assisting you in whatever way I can."

"It is an honor to meet you, milady," said a fair salt-and-pepper-haired woman in her early fifties. She stepped forward to curtsey.

"This is Cinzia, the Baroness Macario, and member of the royal household," Darian said, smiling at the woman. "She is the mother of Lord Arrigo, and I call her aunt, even though she is of no blood relation to me,"

Marisa smiled at Arrie's mother. The woman was so beautiful for her age, and she admired her grace and elegance. She remembered to curtsey and made a mental note that she needed to practice that evening.

"The baroness lost her husband years ago in the shipwreck that took most of the royal family—the one I told you about," Darian explained. "And please meet Bruno, my Paladin military advisor."

A handsome young man with sandy blond hair and brown eyes bounced forward. He bowed to Marisa and took her hand to kiss it. She noticed he was wearing a military uniform and breastplate that was similar to Darian's.

"This is indeed a great pleasure, milady," Bruno said with a lopsided grin. Somewhere in his late twenties, the young man's expression was friendly and flirtatious. He took a step backward but didn't take his eyes off her.

"And finally, this is Cozimo, my historical advisor, head of the royal household and my personal mentor," Darian said. "He's been at the castle for nearly sixty years now, assisting other royals before me."

An old man in his early eighties wobbled toward them and slowly bowed. Trying to keep his balance, Cozimo took Marisa's hand and kissed it before raising his wrinkled face to study her.

"Eyes so beautiful—I remember eyes such as these when I first came to the palace..." Cozimo gazed intently at her and blinked several times before his eyes glazed over.

Marisa curtseyed and tried to suppress a giggle. Arrie motioned silently that the old man was a bit eccentric.

Darian said, "You will meet my mother, sister, and the rest of my staff later, but for now, you may go and rest before dinner. Baroness Cinzia will show the way to your chambers."

As the baroness smiled gracefully and took her arm, Marisa felt clumsy. The woman led her down a vaulted corridor that emptied into a magnificent lobby. A grand staircase split in the middle and curved gracefully up on both sides to the second floor. The marble floor contained intricate mosaics of battle scenes and there were several life-sized portraits hanging on the walls.

As they ascended the stairs, she studied the paintings' subjects and noticed that they all seemed to possess similar traits. It was downright eerie the way the faces in the portraits seemed to be staring right at her.

After they had reached the second-story landing, the baroness led Marisa down a plush, carpeted corridor. From the ornate details on the ceiling and walls, it was obvious to Marisa that these were the rooms where important guests stayed. The doors were hand-carved with nature scenes of trees, rivers, and flowers. Every bit of available space along the wall was covered with a royal portrait. Her eye caught on a particular painting when she suddenly recognized a face.

In the portrait, there was a much-younger version of the baroness standing next to a strangely familiar young man. Marisa studied the painting. He looked a lot like Arrie.

"Is that..."

Somehow Cinzia understood what she was asking.

"Yes. That was my husband and I just after we were married. He was Arrigo's father," she said sadly.

As Marisa listened to the translation, she felt sorry for this woman who had lost her husband so young. She suspected there was more to the story but since she was unable to speak Crocine, Marisa could only nod to Arrie's mother.

The baroness walked to a door half way down the hall with an intricate flower carved into the wood. When Cinzia opened it, Marisa was astonished by what she saw.

The chamber was a bedroom and living room suite all together with a fireplace, a separate bathroom, and a dressing room. Although it was slightly smaller than her room at Abbadon, it was much more exquisite. There was a wooden four-poster bed large enough for two people but not nearly as large as the ridiculously oversized one she'd slept in at Savino's castle.

After the coolness of the corridor, the room felt like an oven. Marisa struggled to unhook the clasp of her cape but impatiently pulled the whole thing over her head. Realizing the clasp had gotten caught in her hair, she groaned and tried to work it loose. Finally free of the cape, Marisa threw it over the back of a chair and explored the magnificent room.

"Beautiful," she said, admiring the comfortable sitting area. There was a couch and bookcase filled with all kinds of books written in what Marisa guessed must be Crocine.

Cinzia opened a side door and showed her a smaller bedroom where a young woman sat. "This is Anna. She will help you during your stay at the palace," she said.

The young girl with long dark hair jumped to her feet and curtseyed to them. Marisa nodded warmly. Cinzia moved to a large set of floor-to-ceiling windows that opened out onto a large stone terrace. She opened them and the two women stepped outside. Noticing that her room shared a balcony with rooms on either side, Marisa wondered who the occupants were.

The sweeping vista beyond the citadel walls was spectacular. Because her room faced west, Marisa had a magnificent view of the setting sun as it slowly dipped behind the distant mountains. She spotted the nearly-full moon rising on its path across the sky. The heavens were turning pink and purple with slight tinges of orange.

Still in awe of the amazing view, Marisa walked over to the railing and leaned over. Everything below her began to spin and she hastily drew back from the edge. She closed her eyes and willed the dizziness in her head to stop.

"Lady Marisa, you must prepare for dinner now," Cinzia called to her.

Marisa walked to the cabinet to find something to wear for the evening and began ruffling through the dresses. Her hand flew to her ear when she realized the earpiece was missing. Guessing that it must have fallen out when she was messing with the cape, she dropped to the ground and began searching the floor. When she finally found it under the nightstand, she put it back into her ear and froze.

Marisa glanced at Cinzia. "Were you just speaking English a minute ago?" she asked.

Cinzia just looked at her, smiling and shrugging her shoulders, clearly not understanding what she was saying.

"Okay, that was weird," Marisa muttered.

"Dinner will be served shortly, milady. We will fetch you once you've had the opportunity to freshen up."

Cinzia had been speaking Crocine all along, so how could she understand her? Marisa listened to the English translation in her right ear as she smiled and curtseyed to Cinzia.

As soon as Cinzia left her room, Marisa peeked into Anna's room and motioned she wanted to take a bath. Anna scurried around to fill the tub.

Strolling out onto the balcony, Marisa watched as the sun disappeared behind the mountains and the stars began to twinkle. Below her window, the night watchmen were lighting torches along the walls of the citadel, creating a soft glow across the courtyard.

A door shut loudly behind her. As she saw a candle being lit in the room next to hers, Marisa drew back quickly into the shadows. She slowly leaned over and peered through the window.

Sitting on the bed at the far side of the room was a beautiful young woman slightly younger than Marisa. She had dark eyes and an olive complexion, and her long, black hair was twisted into an elaborate braid down the entire length of her back. She wore a dark blue dress and a single strand of sapphires around her neck. From the elegant way she was dressed, Marisa guessed she must be a member of the royal family.

The young woman was engrossed in reading a letter. Marisa leaned over to get a better look. Her earpiece dropped from her ear and bounced across the stone floor of the balcony. The young woman glanced up at the windows and Marisa quickly pulled back. She waited a couple minutes before she stepped over to retrieve the translator. When she peered into the room again, the letter lay crumpled up on the floor next to the bed. The woman was sobbing pitifully into her pillow. Marisa knew those tears could only have been caused by a man.

Nobody is immune to shattered dreams, she thought.

CHAPTER 18
ENCOUNTERS

ANNA HAD CHOSEN AN elegant evening gown for Marisa. Although she thought it looked too formal, she didn't feel like second-guessing the young woman who seemed to know her way around a closet.

Marisa had slipped into the gown and was quickly running a brush through her hair when she heard a soft rap at the door. She opened it to find Arrie washed, dressed, and looking dapper.

"So what do you think of your room, milady?" he asked.

"It's amazing."

"Perhaps we can persuade you to stay for a while?"

She shook her head. "Only until I can get a place of my own."

"Darian and I have been discussing that, and we have a few ideas. We'll talk about it after you've had the opportunity to settle in."

Marisa looked at him but said nothing. She knew Arrie had been charged with keeping Darian's engagement a secret. The idea of him marrying Matilda was so depressing that she immediately pushed it from her mind.

"I shall not be joining you all for dinner this evening," he said.

She frowned. "Why not?"

"I shall be dining with my mother. We shall see you all later this evening."

"Wait a minute. Who am I eating with?"

"Darian, his mother, and his sister," Arrie replied.

"He's introducing me to his *family?* Great!"

"Now, Marisa, don't work yourself into a frenzy. Everything will be fine. Just remember to duck when you face the firing squad."

"Very funny," she said, rolling her eyes.

As Marisa entered the dining hall on Arrie's arm, she was sweating from nervousness. They strolled over to the gigantic fireplace where Darian was chatting with two women. Marisa saw the formal dinner gowns the other ladies were wearing and was immediately grateful to Anna.

"I shall see you later," Arrie said, excusing himself with a bow.

The women turned toward Marisa and she sucked in her breath. One of them was the unhappy young woman who'd been crying an hour before in the room next to hers.

"Lady Marisa, please grant me the pleasure of introducing you to my mother, Her Royal Highness Princess Helena Arras of Ottaviano," Darian said.

Princess Helena had dark eyes and hair, with clear skin and few wrinkles. She had the unmistakable air of entitlement and privilege about her, and Marisa guessed she was probably in her early fifties.

Marisa curtseyed as deep as she possibly could as Darian's mother observed her carefully.

"And this is my sister, Her Royal Highness Princess Adalina Fiore," Darian said.

The young princess smiled warmly at Marisa as both women curtseyed. Marisa wondered if Princess Adalina even knew that she'd been offered to Savino as his bride but had been rejected. Maybe it was the reason she'd been crying. If that was the case, making it through dinner might be difficult.

"Lady Marisa, my brother has told me all about you and I am so glad to meet you," Adalina said, smiling.

Marisa heard an echo in her earpiece, and she did a double-take.

She tapped her right ear and glanced at Darian, who nodded, already knowing what she was thinking.

"But how...?" Marisa asked.

"My mother felt it was just as important for my sister to learn English as it was for me," Darian said. "She may not speak it as well as me, but then again, I've had more opportunities to practice this past week." He winked at her.

"But how do you know about me?" Marisa asked Adalina. "We just got here a couple hours ago."

"Yes, well, my brother was so excited when he arrived home that he came right away to speak with us. Apparently much has happened since he met with Savino and Mattie at Abbadon—"

"Yes—thank you, Adalina," Darian interrupted. "Shall we go to dinner now?"

Darian offered his mother an arm as Marisa and Adalina followed them down into the Knight's Hall. As they all sat down for dinner, he helped each of the ladies into their chairs.

Marisa admired the pewter plates and crushed glass goblets sparkling in the lights of the candelabras. She felt intimidated by all the formal dinners and liked the fact it was just the four of them now.

"Marisa, we don't usually take our meals in the Knight's Hall. But for tonight, I wanted you to have the special experience of eating in the most historic room in the castle. We've moved in here from our usual dining chamber."

"It's beautiful," Marisa said. "And so *big*. I think you could easily squeeze the entire gym from South Medford High in here." Her eyes roamed the interior of the great hall.

There were several banners and royal crests hanging high in rows along the walls. A large, blazing fireplace gave the hall a cozy feel and there were beautiful paintings of coronations and battles decorating the room. The table was piled so high with food that Marisa felt as if she could have been dining with King Henry VIII.

On the far wall, there were several groups of swords arranged in geometric, circular patterns. The handles were on the outside with their blades pointing inwards toward a coat-of-arms in the center. Some of the pie-shaped circles had more swords than others.

Darian saw Marisa's puzzled face. "You are probably wondering about the swords." he said.

"Yeah. Why are they like that?"

"It reminds us of our history," Adalina explained. "Each of those circles of swords represents a different family that has ruled the land of Crocetta."

"Some of them have only a few." Marisa commented.

"Yes," Darian said, "each sword represents one ruler or a generation of one particular dynasty. Some lasted longer than others."

"And the row of swords along the bottom?"

"Those are the rulers whose dynasty didn't last beyond themselves. They had no children, or their heirs all died."

"So it's considered a shame to be on the bottom?"

"Yes," Darian said. "The sovereigns represented by the swords in the single row are not looked upon with the same favor as those placed in a circle."

"Oh," she said. "Which one is the Fiore circle?"

"That one, over there on the left."

"You mean the one with the red coat-of-arms?"

"No, the one just above it. The blue one." He pointed.

Marisa counted them. "There are only five swords."

"That's how many Fiores have ruled in our dynasty so far."

She quickly did the math. "But from what you've told me, there should only be four up there, right?"

Darian and Adalina exchanged glances. "That is correct. One of them does not belong." He stared up at the circles of swords and Marisa silently wondered if Darian's sword would ever be up on the wall too. She knew it would depend on how things ended with Savino.

The dinner was served and the subject seemed to have been

dropped. There was no mention of Darian's failed mission and most of the dinner conversation consisted of small talk. Marisa wondered if Darian's mother and sister even knew about the outcome of the trip. Maybe he'd told them the whole story, and they were just being friendly because Marisa might someday be Savino's wife.

Helena and Adalina filled Darian in with all the latest gossip since he'd left Crocetta. Marisa didn't care that she didn't know who they were talking about—she was just enjoying being around other women again.

After dinner, the four of them retreated into the library for drinks and a game of cards. The cards were octagonal shaped with four different numbers on every other side. Marisa couldn't follow the rules on how to play, so Helena and Adalina played while Darian sat with Marisa.

When Marisa saw his sister and mother stealing glances at her, she wondered if they thought he might be forming an inappropriate attachment with Marisa. She wished she could set their minds at ease. If they didn't know already, they'd be hearing soon about his engagement to Lady Matilda.

Darian poured a glass of red wine for Marisa and suggested they enjoy their drinks outside. He unlocked a set of French doors and the two of them stepped outside into the crisp night air.

Marisa already had felt completely out of place in the palace, but it was only getting worse. She had to remain emotionally detached from them until the opportune moment arrived for her to make her escape. Maybe the others already knew about Darian's engagement and they saw her as some kind of threat. Perhaps they resented Marisa for even being there. If they did, at least they were doing a marvelous job of keeping it concealed.

"You are unusually quiet this evening, Marisa," Darian said.

She shrugged. "There's been an awful lot to absorb over the past few days. I think I may be suffering from sensory overload. It's not every day that I meet royalty, you know."

He smiled. "I'm sorry if this seems overwhelming to you. I easily forget that I've grown up in the palace all my life but you have not."

Yeah, go ahead and keep the gulf between us right out there in front as a constant reminder. "You seem pretty chipper tonight," she said. "Have you heard some bit of good news since you've been back?"

"Chipper? What does this mean?"

"It means happy, in a good mood."

He smiled. "Ah, no, it's nothing like that. I suppose that I'm just happy when I'm at home surrounded by the people that I love."

She shifted uncomfortably. "Yeah, I know what you mean. I really miss my family. I wish they could be here to see all this," she said, pointing to the walls. "Uncle Al would just die if he saw this castle. He's always been crazy about knights, castles, and damsels in distress. Not that you would have any idea of what I'm talking about..." she trailed off.

"Uncle Al?" Darian said, puzzled. "What an unusual name. Is it short for something?"

"Yeah—well, actually, his name is Alistair, but he's always been Uncle Al to us. My father's name was Alan. Did I tell you that they were twins?"

"Yes, I believe you did," he said, sipping his wine. "Do they have any other siblings?"

"Nope, our family is pretty small. I never even knew my grandparents. They died long before we were even born. I do have relatives from our clan back in Scotland that I've never met, though."

"Did your father or uncle ever return to this Scotland since they moved to America?"

"No. But my uncle has promised to take us back someday. I've heard it's absolutely beautiful."

Darian gazed into the dark courtyard below. "How do you like your room? Did you know my sister's room is next to yours?"

"Yeah, I like it, it's comfortable. And Adalina seems like a sweet girl. You're lucky. I always wanted a sister."

She gazed up into the mountains and tried to think of something else to say. It was becoming increasingly difficult for her to be with him and she couldn't seem to concentrate on anything else when he was around.

"What you are thinking about?" he asked.

"I, uh—I was thinking about Savino," she said finally.

As the smile disappeared from Darian's face, she immediately regretted her words. She hadn't even thought about Savino much lately and she wondered what had compelled her to suddenly blurt out his name.

"Is it safe to assume then that you wish to accept his offer?" he asked in a flat voice.

Marisa tried to think up a noncommittal response, but her mind kept coming up blank. She knew her silence would only confirm Darian's suspicions.

Silence.

"I see—"

As he gulped down the last bit of his wine, his face transformed into the cold, stony Darian she'd met on the way to Abbadon. She could feel a palpable tension but decided she shouldn't fight it as long as it helped keep the distance between them. If he wasn't going to be honest with her about Matilda, then she wasn't about to discuss Savino with him.

He leaned back against the stone wall and stared out into the darkness. When he turned to her a moment later, his face had suddenly softened.

"Marisa, would you please allow me to take you to a quite remarkable place tomorrow morning?"

She sighed. "I guess. What time do you wanna leave?"

He brightened. "Please be ready to go after breakfast. We'll meet in the library at eleven."

"Eleven it is."

"Cheer up, you might even enjoy it," Darian added smugly. He led her back inside to his mother and sister, who were still playing cards. After kissing them both on the cheek, Darian offered Marisa an arm.

As they walked up the stairs and down the corridor leading to her room, neither said a word. Marisa felt guilty for brushing him off, but she knew it was the only way to keep from getting too close.

"I'll see you in the morning, sire," she said finally.

"Milady," Darian answered with a nod. He walked down the corridor and disappeared into a side hallway.

As soon as Marisa was inside her chambers, she kicked off her shoes and collapsed on the bed.

She was dreading tomorrow.

CHAPTER 19

BEAURIÉL

MARISA WAS JOLTED OUT of her sleep. The room was pitch-black and she tried to remember where she was. Her heart was racing from her very real dream about Mark and her uncle. They had been out searching in the woods and calling her name. But every time she tried to answer them, she would open her mouth and no sound would come out.

She stumbled across the room, groping for the entrance to the water closet. Her hands found the sink and she pumped out a glass of fresh water. On the way back to bed, she noticed how brightly the moon shone through the windows and something caught her eye.

The display of her phone was lit, and Marisa saw that the date read September 27, 4:38 a.m. In just three days, it would be her birthday. No cake, no gifts, and no family.

She climbed back into bed and sighed. Her finger felt dry and itchy where she had been wearing her mother's ring, so she slipped it off and carefully placed it on the nightstand. Distracted by the pulsating light on her phone, Marisa stuck in her ear buds and swept through her playlists. She listened to music for a few hours before finally drifting off to sleep.

When she awoke, Marisa glanced at her phone and saw that it was already 10:38 a.m. She suddenly remembered that Darian was expecting her at eleven and quickly jumped out of bed.

He had asked Marisa to dress comfortably and warmly, so she chose a complete riding habit with a full skirt, blouse, boots, hat, and riding jacket. Although she knew spending more time alone with Darian would only complicate matters further, her interest had definitely been piqued by whatever it was he wanted to show her.

At exactly eleven o'clock, Marisa entered the library and found Darian already there waiting for her. Out of his usual armored suit, he was wearing a dark green tunic, beige pants, and brown riding boots.

Why did he have to be so handsome, she thought.

"Ready to go?" He offered her an arm.

"Lead on, Your Highness."

They started down the corridor, but Marisa stopped abruptly when they reached the main staircase. "Hold on a minute, something looks different here," she said, glancing around.

"What do you mean?" he asked.

"I don't know—it just looks different for some reason."

"You sure notice details, don't you?" Darian chuckled. "As a matter of fact, they took down a couple of the paintings here that are due for restoration."

"Hmm, that must be it. I knew there was something different."

Darian just smiled and shook his head as they reached the ground floor. He guided her through a large doorway that led to the main courtyard.

"Where are we going anyway?"

"Patience, please, milady. You shall see."

They went outside and Darian pointed across the central courtyard to another set of stone steps leading down. She glanced up and saw dark storm clouds covering the sky.

As they entered the lowest level of the citadel, Marisa recognized the pungent odor of wet straw and manure. When she saw Siena, she hurried over to her stall and stroked the animal's chestnut-colored mane.

"Hey, Siena, do you want to go out for a ride, girl?"

"We're not going on horseback, Marisa."

She looked at him in surprise. "Well, why did you bring me down here, then?"

"A carriage awaits us, milady." He extended his hand toward the other side of the stable where two horses, a large covered carriage, a driver and a footman all waited for them.

"Oh, wow," she exclaimed.

The exterior of the carriage was black with gold trim and the door was embellished with the Fiore royal crest. The large spokes of the wheels were tipped with gold accents and two glass lanterns decorated each side.

"Today it's quite cloudy, and I didn't want to get soaked in the rain. I'd much rather be warm and dry, wouldn't you?" Darian asked.

She nodded to him and skipped over as Darian chuckled. The footman helped her up into the carriage and she sat down on the seat that faced forward. Darian climbed in and took the seat opposite her that faced the rear.

The interior walls were upholstered in dark blue velvet. Marisa ran her hand across the softness of the seat and noticed it was covered with the same fabric but then in black. The footman closed the door with a solid thud, sealing them off in their own private world.

"There is a blanket under your seat in case you get cold," Darian said. He lifted a small hatch underneath and showed her a storage compartment filled with blankets. Smiling mischievously at her, he pulled down a lever to ring a little bell, and soon they began to move forward.

As the carriage made its way down the courtyard and through the tunnel under the ramparts, Darian studied her with an amused smile.

"Have you ever ridden in a carriage, Marisa?"

"Nope. First time."

The carriage passed under the portcullis of the citadel wall. Marisa stared at all the shops and watched the people milling about in the street. The city was bustling as its citizens went about their daily business. There was a high wall surrounding the outer gates of the city and once the carriage passed through it, they entered the open countryside with rolling hills and small forests.

Marisa heard a clopping noise behind them. She looked out the rear window of the carriage and spotted four soldiers following them on horseback.

"Those are the royal bodyguards," Darian said. "I'm afraid we can't be totally alone today." He winked at her playfully.

"So why didn't you have bodyguards on your trip to Abbadon?" she asked.

"I had no need of them."

"Why not?"

"I was on a diplomatic mission as His Excellency Darian Fiore, Ambassador and Plenipotentiary to Abbadon," he said, rolling his eyes.

"I don't get it. Are you a prince or an ambassador?

"Both, actually. In my capacity of ambassador on a diplomatic mission to Abbadon, I carried with me official papers of protection. If anyone dared threaten or harm me while I was on my journey, they could be executed."

"Executed?"

"Yes. But now that I'm back to being His Royal Highness, I am required to have bodyguards with me even if I venture outside the citadel."

"Why? Is it that unsafe?"

He shrugged. "Members of the royal family are always facing some threat or another. But just between you and me, I would sooner choose my sword over a small piece of paper." He chuckled, peered out the window.

It felt like an awkward first date, although Marisa knew it wasn't. Her hands fidgeted nervously as the carriage bumped along the unpaved road. The country scenery was breathtaking, but as if from the force of a magnet, her eyes were constantly being pulled back to Darian.

When the front wheel suddenly sank into a deep pothole, she lurched forward into his lap. His arms moved quickly to catch her, and shyly she moved back onto her seat.

"I'm so glad you came with me today, Marisa," Darian said softly, his crystal eyes beaming at hers. "I hope you like where we are going."

Ancient trees covered the road to form a tunnel of green as the road entered a dense, forested area. The carriage stopped in front of a rusting, wrought-iron gate that guarded the entrance of a gravel driveway. From the way the road had been completely overrun with weeds, Marisa could tell that it probably hadn't been used in years.

"Remain here, please," Darian said. He stepped out of the carriage and opened the gate with a small key. When the carriage had passed through, he closed it again and they continued up the long, tree-lined road.

The driveway came to an end as the carriage veered off to the right and made a broad arc around a circular driveway. The footman jumped down and opened the door for Marisa, lifting his hand to assist her. Her boots touched the grind driveway and she stared up in amazement.

The small castle reminded her of a photo she'd seen somewhere of a very old French chateau. It was built of alternating gray and red-colored stone, with several windows of stained glass. It had thirteen chimneys and there was a large fountain in the circle of the driveway that had been dry for some time. It was surrounded on three sides by towering trees that reminded her of the California sequoias in her backyard at home.

"Shall we?" Darian asked. They ascended the front steps to a heavy oaken door where he took out a set of keys and unlocked it. He slid the metal bolt aside and turned the heavy iron ring. It made a loud creaking noise as if the door hadn't been opened in years.

"After you, milady," he said, bowing.

They stepped into an octagonal-shaped hall with a sweeping staircase and hand-carved banisters winding gracefully up to the second floor. The floors were made of marble and a large crystal chandelier hung down from the lofty ceiling.

Marisa was speechless.

Silently he took her hand and led her through a door toward a sitting room with large windows facing the front of the house. Although the room was quite spacious, the furnishings had been arranged in such a way as to create a warm, cozy atmosphere.

"Shall we take a tour?"

Marisa nodded, still in awe. They toured all the rooms on the ground floor, and in each one she saw that all the furnishings had been covered with cloths. She gently lifted a sheet up off a couch and spied its beautiful golden upholstery underneath. There were various works of art adorning the walls as well as handcrafted clocks, books, crystal and porcelain dishes, and other decorative, eye-catching pieces.

As they entered the large formal dining room just off the living area, she gasped as she saw two crystal chandeliers hanging from the ceiling. There were several beveled glass doors opening out onto a large stone terrace, with extensive gardens beyond. When Darian saw her peeking outside, he unlocked a large set of doors and opened them.

She walked across the stone terrace and admired the beautifully landscaped gardens. There was a reflection pond with a large grassy area just beyond it and a rose garden on the left side with paths to admire the blooming flowers.

"This reminds me of a hotel where I stayed with my family in California," she said. "It's so beautiful!"

The footman approached them carrying a large wooden box.

"What's that?" she asked.

"Keep watching," Darian said. He spread a blanket across the stone table and began to remove from the box small bundles of food wrapped in cloth. As he whisked out a bottle of wine and two crystal glasses, it reminded Marisa of a magician pulling objects from his hat.

"Here you are, milady. I hope you're hungry."

"*Very* hungry. I skipped breakfast."

He raised his glass in the air. "*Ap eirie!*" he said.

"Cheers."

"So, what do you think of the house?"

She took a bite of bread. "It's incredible. Whose is it?"

Darian grinned. "Yours."

Chapter 20
Dowry

Marisa coughed, nearly choked on her bread. She struggled to clear her throat and searched his face. "What did you say?" she demanded.

"You heard me. You can move in whenever you wish."

She took a sip of wine. "You're *giving* it to me?"

Darian nodded.

She shook her head in disbelief. "But I can't accept this! It's a *castle* for cryin' out loud!"

"Did you happen to notice the coat of arms above the front door? This house is one of several belonging to the Fiore family. As such, it is my property, and I can give it to whomever I please."

"Yeah, but no—Darian, I can't accept this!"

"Why not?"

She made a face. "C'mon, get real. It's just too much. You want to give me a book, okay, fine—that I can accept. But this..." She pointed to the mansion, exasperated.

"The house is empty. There's no one living in it, and there hasn't been for several years. To have someone managing and maintaining it would be extremely beneficial. In fact, we should pay you to stay here."

"Uh, Your Royal Highness, I can't just take a house belonging to the royal family."

Darian stared at her. "Marisa, Castle Beauriél is a gift from me to you, from one friend to another. How do you say it in English? No strings attached. I beg you—please do not insult me by refusing my gift."

Her eyes roamed the expansive gardens. It would be difficult to pass up such an incredible offer. The house was gorgeous and she could certainly imagine living there. But she wasn't comfortable accepting a house from him. The whole thing was, as her father used to say, just not kosher.

"I don't need such a humongous place," she whined. "What am I supposed to do with twelve bedrooms? I'm gonna end up like Cinderella, having to clean the place twenty-four/seven—"

"How did you know that?" Darian asked.

"Know what?"

"That there are exactly twelve bedrooms."

"I don't know, lucky guess, I suppose," she sighed. "Your Highness, I don't think I can accept this gift."

He turned to her as if he wanted to say something, but when he saw her determined face, he said nothing and quickly looked away.

Without a word, he lifted his glass off the table and walked down to the edge of the terrace. His back was turned to her as he stared into the garden in quiet contemplation.

Just then, it occurred to her that the house was meant as a peace offering. Located far enough outside the city, Beauriél would conveniently keep her out in the country and a considerable distance from the palace after Darian and Matilda were married. Obviously, it was what he wanted, and it would be best for everyone if she just accepted the house.

Marisa crossed the terrace to where he stood. "I can see that this is one battle I'm never gonna win, Your Highness. I am grateful to accept your extremely generous gift."

Darian turned cautiously. "Really?"

"Really."

"Wonderful! We'll make sure you have enough servants, butlers, cooks, and maids to manage the estate. Please don't worry about a thing."

"Whoa, hold on there. I didn't agree to an army of people living out here with me."

"You didn't think you could live here on your own, did you?"

"Well I haven't had much time to think about it now, have I?"

He chuckled. "Consider it an early birthday present."

"I sure as heck won't be getting a car this year. I'll just have to settle for a house then," she said dryly.

Darian smiled and took a sip of wine. "Marisa, my family would like to hold a ball."

"Sounds nice."

"On your birthday."

"*My* birthday?"

"Yes. People from all over the country will be there. Lady Matilda and Savino would be the guests of honor. If that's acceptable to you, of course," he added.

Her heart sank. He was looking for an opportunity to announce his engagement to Lady Matilda. After all he'd done for her, she couldn't refuse him now. "Sure, I guess."

"Great! I'll have my staff start the planning right away."

She quietly sipped her wine. She'd probably agree to almost anything Darian put in front of her right now just to keep him happy.

"You know, Marisa," he began, "Savino will be expecting a response from you soon. Have you made your decision yet?"

She shrugged noncommittally. "If Savino is coming to the ball, I'll talk to him then."

"He doesn't know you can actually speak."

"True. But if I don't marry him, he'll never know."

He gazed at her thoughtfully. "Marisa—I, uh..."

"What?"

"I know I told you back in Abbadon that this marriage proposal is your own choice to make, and it is..."

"But?"

He avoided her eyes. "As your friend, I feel I must warn you that you should be extremely careful with Savino. He does not accept things interfering with his plans, and he is quite notorious for his tempers. Promise me that you'll warn me before you give him your answer?"

"Why? Are you assuming I'm gonna refuse him and then he'll beat me up? I appreciate your concern, Your Highness, but I can take care of myself. You've got enough problems of your own."

"Savino *is* my problem!"

Marisa frowned. She probably deserved that.

Darian clenched his jaw and dusted the crumbs off his hands. "Would you like to see the rest of the house?" he asked.

"Yes," she said softly.

As he led her upstairs, Marisa felt as if a wedge had just been driven between them. Clearly, he was distancing himself from her. If the tables had been turned and she had been engaged to Savino, she would have been doing the same thing. They went from room to room as he pointed out the features in each of the various bedrooms.

Half an hour later, they came back down the large staircase, and he locked the wooden door behind them. Marisa hurried across the driveway and stepped into the carriage just as fat drops of water started to pelt the carriage windows.

She glanced over her shoulder at the house one last time. It was the perfect place for her to begin a new life out from under the royal shadow of the palace. She would push Darian to let her move out of the castle as soon as possible.

As they traveled through the open spaces of the colorful countryside, neither one spoke as both were each lost in their own thoughts. Observing the houses, farms, windmills and trees on their way back toward the city, she pondered his comment about being just friends. She hoped that they could still part that way.

Although Marisa knew she wouldn't see Darian after he married Matilda, she was determined to stay civil to him until her birthday. Right then, she promised herself she would attend the ball for his sake. It was the least she could do for him after saving her life. The ball would be the perfect opportunity to announce the engagement and allow Marisa to bow out gracefully. Then, she could release him forever.

Marisa had been resting quietly in her room but was jolted by a brisk knock at the door. She opened it to find Cinzia and two other women.

"We are here to take the measurements for your ball gown, Lady Marisa," the baroness explained. "By royal decree, it shall be a masquerade ball."

Marisa motioned the ladies to enter and they began to strip all of her clothing right down to her underwear. An elegant woman in her mid-sixties stepped forward.

"Marisa, this is Leonora, and she is here to create the perfect gown for you to wear," Cinzia said. Leonora simply nodded to her and got right down to business by taking her measurements.

Marisa fought to stifle her giggles as the woman measured every conceivable inch of her body. By the time the ladies were finished, it was already three o'clock.

Cinzia dismissed the other woman before beckoning Marisa to sit down between she and Leonora on the couch. She opened a large book filled with hundreds of colorful drawings of various dresses of all sizes and colors. Leonora opened the other book filled with numerous swatches of different fabrics.

"Choose one, my dear," Cinzia said. "Leonora is the best dressmaker in all of Crocetta, and she can make you anything you wish."

Marisa took the book in her lap and carefully flipped the pages. Never in her life had she seen so many beautiful dresses. After narrowing her choice down to three gowns, she tried to guess which dress her father would have liked.

In the end, she decided on a floor-length, dark purple dress with ivory and gold panels on the bodice and front of the skirt. It had a square neckline that flattered the shoulders, trimmed with pearls and sparkling gold embroidery.

Cinzia smiled. "Perfect."

After Cinzia and Leonora had finally left, Marisa wondered which jewelry she should wear with the dress and she froze. She glanced down at her finger and remembered she'd taken her mother's ring off in the night. She hurried over to the night stand.

Gone.

"*Noooo!*" she shrieked.

She searched frantically under the bed and all over the floor, but there was no sign of it anywhere. After combing the entire room for more than a half hour, she fell onto the bed, sobbing in despair. Both her father and Darian had warned her about losing it, and she knew she'd been careless.

Hearing Marisa's sobs, Anna came rushing into the room, clutching the book she'd been reading. Through tears, Marisa pointed to her ring finger as if to ask if Anna had seen the ring, but she shrugged her shoulders and shook her head. Anna honestly didn't seem to know where it was.

There were at least three other women who'd been in her room that afternoon. It was possible that one of them had taken it when she wasn't looking. But who?

Cinzia didn't seem the type who would steal another woman's ring, and clearly Leonora was wealthy enough to buy everything she wanted. Perhaps Leonora's helper, the other woman had taken it. No matter what, her chances of finding the ring again were probably slim to none.

Frantically she hurried down the stairs and asked everyone in sight if they knew where Arrie was. When nobody was able to understand what she was asking, she became frustrated and ran outside into the courtyard. She climbed the rampart steps and collapsed against the stone wall as she sobbed in utter despair.

"Marisa, what are you doing out here?" Darian asked as he saw her tear-stained face. "The servants came to find me after you ran away upset."

"My mom's ring is gone," she bawled. "Somebody stole it from my room. I took it off last night and laid it on my nightstand, but when I came back today, it wasn't there."

"Don't worry, we shall find it. I will investigate this and post a reward. We'll make sure your mother's ring is returned to you. Please try to calm down."

Arrie hurried over. "What's wrong, Marisa? I heard a commotion among the staff, and they told me that you were out here." He looked at Darian for an explanation.

"She cannot find her ring—it appears to be missing. I was in a meeting of the Crimson Court when they called me out, but I must go back in. Arrie—will you stay with her for a while?"

"Yes, of course."

"I shall check on you later," Darian said to her.

She didn't respond.

"Marisa, look at me!"

She looked at him slowly, and his eyes locked on hers. "I promise you, we shall find your ring. Do you hear me? I promise."

She nodded sadly and Darian hurried back into the castle.

"Come on, let's go have a warm cup of tea," Arrie said. "That will cheer you up."

He gently steered her across the courtyard and back inside where they found a cozy sitting room. He offered Marisa a handkerchief and asked the maid to bring them a pot of tea.

"I heard you went out to Castle Beauriél this afternoon. What did you think of it?" he asked.

"It was amazing," she said. "But I can't believe he just gave it to me. There's got to be a catch somewhere." She wiped her eyes, blew her nose, and sighed.

He shook his head. "Darian is an exceptionally generous man where his friends are concerned. He doesn't hold back."

"Arrie, just cut to the chase and tell me what's going on."

"What do you mean?"

He stared at her uncomfortably as the maid returned with a tray. As he poured the tea, the porcelain cup shook on its saucer.

"I mean the way Darian has been acting. The first thing he tells me—emphasizes to me—is how unavailable he is. The next thing I know he's kissing me, acting like a jealous lover toward Savino, and then today he gives me a house. An entire house! All the while he's keeping me at arm's length." She took a sip of the hot spiced tea. "Please tell me I'm not going crazy."

"Marisa, there is much to ruling a country and Darian is under tremendous pressure at the moment. While I do not claim to understand all of the methodology behind his actions, I do know that he is struggling to walk the line between doing his duty and doing what is right for him."

"What does that even mean, Arrie?"

"As I told you when we first met, Darian almost always sacrifices his own desires for the sake of the kingdom."

"Yeah, so?"

"Where you are concerned, he just wants to make sure that you are taken care of. In giving you Castle Beauriél, Darian means to make life in Carnelia a bit easier for you."

Marisa eyed him accusingly. "That's not considered normal where I'm from. A guy doesn't just give a house to some girl he barely knows—unless he's maybe some rock star from Beverly Hills."

Arrie chuckled.

"Look, Arrie—I can't help but think he's expecting something from me in return. It feels as if he's tryin' to bribe me or something."

He shook his head. "Things are not always as they appear."

"Meaning?"

"I understand the situation may seem a bit—strange to you at the moment, but there's more at work here than either you or I see. You've managed to burst into our lives during probably the most critical time in the history of Carnelia."

"What do you mean?"

"Simply that Darian's future could rise or fall over the next several weeks. If he manages to ascend the throne, the situation may just turn around for the good of the country. But if Savino were to end up on the throne—well, things may not turn out so well, I'm afraid."

"But Darian told me that the only way he could ascend the throne would be to marry a Fiore princess. We all know that there's only one woman right now who fits the bill…"

She cornered him with her eyes. All at once he was quiet and she knew he couldn't reveal anything about the engagement even if he wanted to.

Wondering if she could squeeze the truth out of him somehow, something suddenly occurred to her.

"Darian *wants* me to marry Savino, doesn't he?" she asked.

Arrie shifted uncomfortably.

The wheels were already spinning. "Those two have already worked out a deal," she said, thinking out loud. "If Darian can broker a marriage between us, then Savino would agree to sign the treaty. Darian would marry Matilda, and they ascend the throne together. End of story."

"Marisa—"

"That's it, isn't it?"

"Ah, I—"

"Savino expects Darian to deliver me as his bride," she said.

"I'm truly sorry, Marisa—but I'm not at liberty to discuss any of this with you."

"I can't believe this."

"Sometimes we must just accept that some things are out of our hands. After all, it is impossible to outrun our destiny."

She held up a hand to silence him.

"Don't talk to me about destiny. I've just about had it up to here with all of that." She walked over to the window, barely able to contain the anger bubbling to the surface. She crossed her arms and stared out at the bustling port below. Darian's fate had already been sealed a long time ago, but she never dreamed hers was as well.

Marisa spun around angrily. "Castle Beauriél isn't a gift meant for just me, is it? It's my dowry to marry Savino. And when Darian marries Matilda, it will make him my brother-in-law." She shivered.

Arrie stared at the floor in silence.

"I'm sorry, Arrie, but I'm not feeling well. I'm going up to my room for a while."

"Milady." He nodded soberly.

CHAPTER 21

INTRIGUES

WHEN MARISA REACHED THE sanctuary of her room, she broke down in tears. She plunked down at the dressing table and saw her almost unrecognizable reflection in the mirror. This was no longer the same girl who could take any challenge and use her smarts to find a way through it. She couldn't make it all better by studying harder or practicing on the field a little longer. This wasn't high school anymore.

This was life.

The longer she lived in this strange and bewildering world, the less sure of herself she became. Carnelia had shown her a new reality in just a matter of days, but already she was worn down by the tears, sick of the pain, and desperately wanting to wipe it all away. After all that had happened in her life, she had finally been stretched to her breaking point.

"Why am I!" she shouted at the mirror. She dropped down on her knees next to the bed and sobbed into the blankets. Her father was gone. Her uncle and brother were gone. Her best friend Danielle was gone. There was no one she could talk to.

Her mind wandered back to the first day she had landed in Carnelia. She thought about what Darian and Arrie had told her about Garon, and in her desperation, she began to pray through tears:

Garon, if you're really out there like Darian and Arrie say you are, please tell me what to do. Because I just don't know anymore. My life is being planned out by people I don't even know, and I have no control over anything. I feel so alone. I need help. I don't know what I'm supposed to do. If you care about me even in the slightest way, please give me a sign that you are there. Amen.

Marisa opened her eyes.

Silence.

Nothing.

She waited several minutes in the quietness of her chambers for something to happen, but everything remained just as it was. No bolt of lightning. No booming voice in the sky. No bright light that blinded her.

Her eyes roamed the peaceful stillness of her chambers.

Nothing.

"Well that just figures!"

The tears streamed from her eyes as she jumped up and threw open the balcony doors. Shivering as a blast of cold air hit her face, she took a step outside and inched slowly across the balcony.

The closer she got to the edge, the more her hands trembled from anxiety. She was going to overcome her fear of heights if it was the last thing she ever did.

The last thing she ever did.

Her hand wiped away the tears. She leaned out slowly and peered over the edge. It was a long way down to the courtyard below. Maybe ten or twelve stories. Nobody could survive a fall that far.

Marisa bit her lip.

She glanced over her shoulder and spotted a wooden chair. It looked sturdy enough. She walked back into the room and tried to lift it. Too heavy. The legs of the chair scraped across the stone floor as she threw her weight against it and pushed it out onto the balcony. Someone must have heard that, she thought.

She stepped up onto the chair and looked straight down.

Her eyes traced the length of the citadel walls. The courtyard appeared deserted and there was no one in sight except for two watchmen on the northwest and southwest corners of the ramparts. They were too far away to notice her. If she did it quickly, nobody would even see it happen.

As the tears streamed down her cheeks, her will to live was fading fast. She stared out across the Crocine mountains and saw a thin layer of snow lightly dusting the highest peaks. When she realized she wouldn't be around to see the Carnelian springtime flowers Arrie said were so spectacular, she began to think about all the things she'd never experience. No more falling in love, no children of her own, and none of the life her parents had experienced with each other. Nothing but a dark, endless void of nothingness after she was gone.

Or was it?

Darian was going to marry another woman. There was no future for her in Carnelia. Her past on Earth had ended in pain and disaster. She had nothing left to make life worthwhile. Nothing good could ever come from her miserable existence. Savino was right—she was a big nobody. After she was gone, she wouldn't even be missed. They probably wouldn't start to look for her until someone happened to notice the splattered mess on the courtyard.

Her heart wrenched in pain, but her head was filled with a strange numbness. She glanced down and knew it would be over in seconds. She probably wouldn't even feel it. Quick and painless.

It will all be over soon.

She moved closer to the edge and lifted her foot up onto the wall. Tears dripped from her eyes and splashed onto the chair.

Do it. Do it now before you lose the nerve.

Suddenly, a strong breeze whipped up around Marisa and she felt a large, invisible hand pushing her back from the edge. A strange, comforting presence enveloped her as a deep inner voice impressed words upon her heart:

My child, I care very much, and I am with you forever. Trust in me always with hope, and do not be afraid.

An urgent pounding at the door interrupted her thoughts.

"Lady Marisa, are you there?" asked Princess Adalina from the corridor. "Please open the door! Lady Marisa?"

Marisa gasped. She jumped down from the chair and quickly pushed it back inside. She hastily wiped her tears with the skirt of her dress and took a deep breath. The door swung open to reveal the worried look on Adalina's face.

"Oh, thank Garon," said Adalina, relieved. "I was just resting before supper when, all of a sudden, I had the most horrible dream about you. It seemed so real that I just had to come and make sure you were all right."

Marisa appeared calm on the surface, but inside her emotions were raging. "Well, Your Highness, I'm safe and perfectly sound, just as you can see," she said. "But I appreciate you coming to check on me."

"Are you indeed?" Adalina asked. "Milady, have you been weeping?"

"I'm fine. I have a small headache, but I should be okay once I've had something to eat."

"Would you like to accompany me to dinner?" asked the young brunette in near-perfect English.

Marisa hesitated. "Can you give me a minute?"

"Certainly. Shall I meet you at the staircase in five?"

"Fine. I'll meet you there."

She shut the door and leaned against it. As a wave of peace washed over Marisa and reached down into her soul, she knew it couldn't have been a coincidence. For the first time in her life, she was sure things would turn out all right, no matter what her future held in store.

Her father had told her once that all experiences in life, whether good or lousy, somehow built a person up from the inside out. That one small pearl of wisdom struck home with her and suddenly she knew she had a choice. She could choose to just give up and fade away or she could allow the pain, loss, and suffering to propel her through a spiritual growth spurt.

She had the power of choice.

The fear and anxiety began to drift away. Deep down in her heart, she knew Garon was real and not just some fanciful idea people used to make them feel better. Her parents had trusted in Garon all their lives. He had always been real to them.

They walked down to the dining room together and joined the others already sitting at the table. Helena, Cinzia, Arrie, Adalina, and Marisa enjoyed the delicious meal that had been prepared. But so far, there was no sign of Darian.

Arrie and Adalina spoke English to accommodate Marisa during dinner, translating for Helena and Cinzia whenever necessary. They recounted their adventures on the way to Abbadon, and the women were captivated by the story as Arrie described the escape through the woods from the rijgen. He told them about Marisa's fall in the ice caves and Darian's heroic rescue of her from the yarmout.

Marisa noticed Darian's seat remained empty through the main course and even into the dessert. She wondered what could be so urgent as to keep him away from a meal with his family.

"Where is Prince Darian? Is he not eating?" she asked finally.

"The Crimson Court convened early this morning," Arrie replied soberly. "He has been leading the members in discussing urgent matters all day. Unfortunately, he will not be joining us this evening,"

"Oh," Marisa said, trying not to sound disappointed.

The others exchanged knowing glances around the table. She blushed, embarrassed, and quickly changed the subject. "What exactly is the Crimson Court?"

"The Court is the absolute authority and power of Carnelia," Arrie said. "It's comprised of twenty-four Paladin knights—noblemen of distinction knowledgeable in the history of Carnelian law."

"Paladin knights?"

He nodded. "They typically deal with specific issues, such as the laws of succession, declaring war, and other difficult situations that arise. The governing ruler is the twenty-fifth member of the court."

"So the king doesn't have absolute authority?"

"Yes and no. The king, or queen—whatever the case may be—has the power to veto any resolution or amendment set forth by the Court as long as he or she can prove it is in direct violation of Carnelian law. The Supreme ruler remains the governing body and makes most of the day-to-day decisions except when it pertains to the ruling party itself."

"So why is Prince Darian leading it if he is not the king—uh, Supreme ruler?"

"The court voted almost unanimously to appoint Darian as the acting ruler on behalf of Gregario who is too ill to preside. Savino is the only other person who may serve as acting ruler."

"Why isn't he here?"

"He has been summoned, but the court couldn't wait any longer in light of Gregario's worsening condition."

"What are they deciding now?" Marisa asked.

The others exchanged uneasy glances.

"They are discussing the question of the succession of the throne once Gregario passes," Adalina said finally.

"Oh."

Silence.

Arrie brightened. "Shall we adjourn to the Green Room for refreshments?" The small group rose from the table and walked the long corridor.

As they entered the opulent room, it was immediately apparent to Marisa why it was called the Green Room. The panels were made of a carved, dark wood, and the walls above them were painted dark green. The emerald-upholstered furniture was pleasantly arranged in front of a large fireplace.

There was a strange, squarish-shaped object in the front corner of the room, and Marisa realized it was a sort of piano. She hurried over to Princess Helena and curtseyed as the others settled down with a glass of wine. "Your Highness, may I play that instrument?"

Adalina translated as her mother smiled and nodded to Marisa.

She sat down at the piano, and her fingers gently pressed the keys as she established its scales. It was more or less the same as the piano back home in their parlor, except that all the keys on this piano were made of smooth, dark wood.

When Marisa finally had a good feel for the notes of the keys, she concentrated on hitting the right notes and began to play a lively, upbeat tune her dance team had performed to during the halftime basketball game at school.

She made mistakes as she translated some of the notes incorrectly, but her captive audience didn't even seem to notice. Adalina encouraged her to play another song as Arrie set a glass of wine down next to her. When Marisa finished, she rested for a few minutes.

For her final song, she chose a classical piece that had been one of her father's favorites. In the final weeks of his life when he was too weak to retire to his bedroom, her dad had looked forward to the evenings when Marisa would sit down to play for him in the parlor. He would lie on the couch and huddle under an afghan while she played all his favorite songs.

It wasn't her intention to dredge up the sad memories of her father's last days, but as her fingers floated over the keys, strong emotions erupted to the surface. She fought to keep the tears at bay as she focused on hitting the correct notes.

After the song had ended, the final note resonated throughout the room and she rested her hands in her lap. Everyone was frozen in their chairs, mesmerized by the somber, haunting melody.

Marisa looked up with tearful eyes and saw Darian standing near the back. His applause broke the spell, and a single tear rolled down her cheek. She wiped it off with her hand.

Sensing it was a private moment, Helena and Adalina both stood to leave. "My mother and I are retiring to bed now. Thank you, Marisa, for your beautiful music and delightful company at dinner," Adalina said. Helena simply smiled and nodded to Marisa.

Arrie stood up and offered Cinzia an arm. "Good night," he said as he escorted his mother out of the room.

All of a sudden, Darian and Marisa were alone in the room.

"Marisa, that was extraordinary," Darian whispered. He noticed the sadness in her face. "Are you all right?"

"I'm fine, Your Highness."

He sighed. "I wish you would not call me Your Highness. Please do me the honor of addressing me as Darian."

"I'm sorry, sire—I can't."

Awkward silence.

Warmth from the fireplace radiated to fill the chamber as the soft orange glow bounced around, throwing shadows across the walls. The room was still except for the popping and hissing of the freshly-cut firewood.

"Are you angry with me? Have I offended you in some way?"

"No," she said softly.

"Arrie is under the impression that you are angry with me. He says that you think I've been deceiving you. Is that true, Marisa?"

Unable to meet his eyes, she stared down at the keyboard. Deciding it would be best to say as little as possible, she shook her head.

"You know I would never lie to you," he said. "As a friend, I have never been anything but honest with you."

"Oh really?" she asked, raising her voice. "Completely honest? Isn't there something you're not telling me?" She wondered when he was planning to tell her the truth about Matilda.

"What do you mean by that?"

Long pause.

"Oh, never mind," she said, exasperated. "I'm tired and I've had a really rough day. I'm going to bed." She turned to leave, but he grabbed her arm.

"What do you mean?" he demanded.

"Nothing! Let me go!"

She wrestled her arm loose and ran into the empty corridor, but he hurried after her. "May I please walk you back to your chambers?"

"Fine, whatever," she said in a huff, practically running.

He followed her as she moved quickly down the long corridor and hurried up the staircase toward the guest chambers.

Halfway down the hall, Darian stopped and took her hand before she could slip away. He raised her hand to his lips as he searched her eyes. "Are you angry with me, Marisa?"

"No," she lied.

"I shall not be able to sleep tonight if I know you're angry."

"I'm not angry. Just a little frustrated maybe."

"Sleep well, milady."

"Night."

So close, and yet so far.

CHAPTER 22

CELINO

ARRIE HAD PROMISED TO take Marisa to see Celino the sorcerer after breakfast, and she was surprised to find she was actually looking forward to it. When Arrie came to get her, she grabbed her cape and draped it over her dress. The weather was getting chillier with each passing day.

Since Celino's house was only a few hundred yards from the palace gates, they set out on foot, passing the heavily-armored guards at the citadel's main entrance. Once they were outside the castle walls and had entered the narrow, cobblestone streets, she breathed a sigh of relief.

Marisa was amazed by all the fascinating paradoxes she saw in Carnelia. As they walked through the streets and observed various aspects of the city, it struck her that things were not crude and unsophisticated but functional, well thought out, and elegant. The clothing styles, the hair styles, and the tools and wares being sold were familiar and yet so different too. Carnelia was a fascinating world, and Crocetta was a beautiful sort of retro-futuristic city.

They moved at a snail's pace as she stopped to examine each interesting object that caught her eye. She laughed at the row of strange hats in a shop window and admired the women's beaded slippers on display. Arrie just chuckled and patiently stopped to wait each time she wanted to take a closer look at something.

"Marisa, wait—you've got to try something here," he said as they passed a small shop.

"What is it?"

Arrie grinned. "Come inside," he said.

They entered the store and her eyes widened as she spied a variety of candy and delectable treats in a rainbow of colors. There was a shopkeeper behind the bar helping a woman with two young boys who were fighting over the biggest lollipop. The little old man behind the bar raised a hand in greeting and flashed Arrie a kind smile. The young boys were still arguing about something as their mother herded them out of the shop. The shopkeeper just rolled his eyes and chuckled.

Arrie whispered something to the white-haired man who wore an apron and a funny-looking hat. The man disappeared into the back and quickly reappeared with two round, brown balls on sticks. He handed one to Arrie and then gave one to Marisa. Arrie took a bite and urged her to do the same.

She smiled and took a bite. As the familiar taste spread through her mouth, she exclaimed with delight, "It's a caramel apple!"

"My favorite!"

"How did you know I love caramel apples?"

"Doesn't everybody? I discovered caramel apples in a candy store in Paris. I had never tasted anything like them, and when I came back to Carnelia, I showed him how to make them. They've been a hit ever since," he said, taking another bite.

"Oh, this tastes so good," she moaned with delight.

"He can't even keep them on the shelves, but I have a special deal with him. If he's sold all the ones in the shop, he always keeps a couple in the back should I happen to stop by." Arrie laughed and winked at the shopkeeper.

"How wonderful!"

"Come, let's go. Celino is expecting us."

They left the shop and strode through an open-air market where vendors sold fruit, vegetables, fabrics, jewelry, hats, and other items. She hurried to follow Arrie but stopped abruptly when she saw a necklace in a shop window.

"Oh, Arrie, look at that. Isn't it beautiful?"

The necklace was made of rose gold and it showcased several teardrop-shaped amethysts. The larger, central stone was darker than the others and its facets sparkled in the morning sunlight.

"Why don't you try it on?" Arrie asked.

"Really?"

"Well, go on!"

They stepped inside the shop and Marisa's eyes popped. There were so many unusual but beautiful pieces of jewelry out on display. Most of the pieces looked antique, but a few of them almost seemed to have a distinctly modern flair.

Arrie pointed to the rose gold set in the window, and the jeweler unclasped the necklace for her. She carefully draped it around her neck as the shopkeeper offered her a mirror. She inserted the earrings and gazed at her reflection.

"It's so beautiful! It must cost a fortune, though."

Arrie looked at the price tag. "Too much for either you or me to afford," he said, chuckling.

She frowned. "Oh—Arrie, my ring. We've just got to find it. It's the only piece of jewelry I have that belonged to my mother."

"Don't worry—Darian is doing all he can to find it. Come, we really must be going now," he urged.

"Oh, yeah, I'm sorry, Arrie. It's just that it's been a long time since I've been shopping."

"We'll come back another time."

Marisa removed the necklace and earrings and handed them back to the shopkeeper. They stepped outside, and Arrie led her down the main street. He stopped when they came to a modest stone house with a blue front door and rang the bell.

The door opened only a few inches as the face of an old, unsmiling woman with wild eyes and frizzy hair peered out at them. She eyed Marisa with intense suspicion.

"Good morning, we're here to see Celino," Arrie said.

The woman muttered something under her breath as she motioned them inside and down a dark, cramped hallway. Marisa stared in wonder at the hundreds of diagrams, models, and intriguing objects covering the tables, walls and corners.

In every room, there were plans, drawings, schematics, and prototypes of all manners of contraptions and curious inventions. They reminded Marisa of the Leonardo da Vinci drawings she'd seen in her European history textbook.

At the end of the hallway, there was a door leading outside to a postage-stamp courtyard. The woman pointed to two wooden chairs and disappeared inside. Arrie dusted off one of the chairs with his cloak and offered it to Marisa.

A few minutes later, the woman returned with a pot of tea and poured them each a cup. She mumbled something unintelligible and sauntered back into the house.

"What did she say?" Marisa asked. "I didn't quite catch that."

"She said Celino would return in a few minutes," he said. "He went out to get something, but she expects him at any moment."

She took a sip of tea and winced, nearly burning her lips.

Arrie set his teacup on the table. "Be careful, it's hot."

"Yeah, I already found that out."

A graying, fifty-something man stepped into the garden and stuck his hand out to Arrie. "Lord Arrigo! It's good to see you again!"

"Celino! How have you been?" Arrie said, smiling.

"When Prince Darian came by yesterday, he mentioned that you'd found quite a gem on the way to Abbadon, but he neglected to describe how incredibly beautiful she was," Celino said playfully, winking and grinning at Marisa.

She stared at him in surprise. Darian had visited him? She thought he had been sequestered in the Crimson Court all day. Why hadn't Darian mentioned his visit to Celino?

"Celino, please allow me to introduce Marisa MacCallum. She is a citizen of your native country and is particularly keen to meet you."

"Well, my, my. If I'd met a girl as charming as you in America, I never would have left home." He grinned at her.

"It's nice to meet you, Mr. Celino sir."

"Oh, please, just call me Celino. My name is actually Cecil Weingarten, but I changed it to fit in around here. The locals have given me the rather dubious distinction of being some sort of sorcerer," he said, chuckling.

"A *sorcerer?*"

"I'm not really, you know. Actually, I'm a physicist, a PhD from Caltech in physics and astronomy, but everyone around here seems to think I'm some sort of magician." He poured a cup of tea. "Everyone except Arrie here, of course."

"Yes, I've promised Celino not to ruin his reputation around here," Arrie said, grinning. "Might spoil his livelihood."

"What Arrie means is that I've been able to make a decent living by developing all kinds of devices and contraptions and selling them. Every now and then someone asks me to develop a specific, complex mechanism for them."

"What kinds of mechanisms?" she asked.

"Mostly just practical, basic things you and I take for granted. Last week I helped a farmer complete a waterwheel that pumps water to his crops," Celino said proudly. "And the palace pays me a monthly stipend to keep me on retainer," he said, winking at Arrie as he took a sip of tea.

Marisa leaned forward. "Celino, I think I understand the concept of a parallel dimension, but one thing I don't get is why this civilization is so far behind ours."

Celino cocked his head at her. "Say again?"

"Well, I guess people have probably roamed Carnelia just as long as people have been on Earth, so why are we so much further advanced in science and other stuff?"

"Don't let them fool you, Marisa. Although this world may seem as if it's a couple of centuries behind ours, it doesn't mean they aren't an advanced society."

"Advanced society?"

"Yes. This isn't the Dark Ages. In fact, our world could learn a lot from them, especially when it comes to infrastructure and society. Women became fully emancipated far earlier here than they did on Earth."

"Yeah, that's what I've been told." Marisa looked at Arrie.

"It's true that the civilizations in Carnelia have been slow in making technological advances. Gunpowder has not yet been invented, and this has halted the so-called 'march of armaments.' Battles are still fought hand-to-hand with swords, longbow and arrows, and other crude weaponry," Celino said.

"But how does that affect technology?" she asked.

"More than you can imagine. The arms race has always fueled the technology race. If somebody from Crocetta were to discover gun powder, this kingdom would become a fearsome force to be reckoned with. Another rival kingdom would rush to discover the secret of gunpowder as well as create a better gun with which to retaliate.

"In the process, mechanical processes are discovered which can be used for peaceful purposes. Before you know it, someone invents the steam engine and Carnelia has an industrial revolution on its hands."

"Oh."

"More of that another time. Now, let's get down to brass tacks," Celino said, gulping down the last of his tea. "Since you're sitting here with us, you've obviously made a leap through a vortex." He looked at her expectantly.

"I guess so."

"You probably witnessed the whole deal—three bright flashes of light, a tornado-like force sucking you in, etcetera?"

"Yeah, it was pretty scary."

"First tell me a little bit about yourself and how you got here. I don't know anyone else in Crocetta who's been to earth, except Arrie here. You and I'll have loads to talk about."

"Well, I'm from Jacksonville, Oregon. I graduated from South Medford High last June." Marisa paused. "My dad died almost two weeks ago—"

"Aw, I'm so sorry to hear that," he said, interrupting.

Her eyes were moist. "Thanks," she said.

"How did he die?"

"Prostate cancer."

Celino shook his head soberly. "Somebody's just got to discover the cure for cancer. That would be the most important scientific discovery of our generation."

She nodded.

"But you were telling me how you got here..."

"Anyhow," she began, "after the funeral, I went out riding in the woods. There were all these weird lightning strikes and a freaky tornado came down on top of us. I blacked out after that and Arrie and Darian found me along the side of the road, so I tagged along and came back here with them."

"That's the short version, I assume. Tell me, were you by any chance up in the woods north of Gold Hill when you encountered the vortex?"

Marisa's eyes widened. "How did you know that?"

"That area is known for its vortex activity," Celino said. "In fact, members of the Latgawa tribe have refused to enter the area for years now."

"Yeah, my dad always warned us not to go up there. I've always heard those woods were cursed, but I just thought it was superstitious nonsense."

"You're not the only skeptic. For the longest time, I've been trying to prove my theory that there is a higher frequency of vortices occurring between the fortieth and forty-fifth parallel."

"Why is that?" asked Arrie.

"It all has to do with the gravitational pull of the earth and the fact that it is halfway between the equator and the North Pole. Of course, altitude must always be taken into account as well."

"Oh."

"I've had a hunch, though, that the largest concentration of vortices in the world is located inside the Bermuda triangle. It would explain why most of the boats, planes, and people that have gotten sucked in over the years have never been found."

"Celino, Marisa is curious to know if there's any chance of her returning to Earth," Arrie said.

"Hmm. That's a difficult question." he answered. "And you're not the first one to ask it."

"How did you travel through a vortex, sir?" Marisa asked.

"First of all, none of that *sir* stuff. Call me Cecil or Celino, but no sir. I'm no knight. Second, in answer to your question, I arrived here through a vortex that I predicted myself," he said proudly.

Arrie's jaw dropped.

"But how?" she asked. "I thought you just said it was a difficult question?"

"I said it was a difficult question—but with an easy answer. And the answer is, yes, it can be done because I have done it."

"But how can you predict a vortex?" Arrie asked. "It's my understanding that there is no way of knowing when and where one will open."

"Without giving away too many trade secrets, I can tell you with reasonable certainty that it is possible to predict when and where a vortex will occur using my own algorithmic method of statistics and probability. Of course, it only has a 96.7 percent standard of accuracy, but in my book, I'd call that pretty accurate."

"So you *can* predict when another vortex will open," she said.

"Oh, most definitely. However, the tricky part is predicting when the right vortex you need will open."

"What do you mean?"

"Well, I'm sure Arrie has already explained to you that there are at least four other existing worlds. And those are just the ones we know of. When a vortex opens, you only have a one-in-four chance that it will lead toward Earth and not one of the other three worlds."

"So, how are you supposed to know which is which?"

"Yes, that's the difficult question, now, isn't it?" Celino smiled.

She threw up her hands. "So basically we're back to square one, aren't we?"

"Not necessarily. After years of studying the paths and predictability of vortices, I just recently made a significant breakthrough. I need to test my theory just one more time, and if it works, I can officially label myself a genius."

"So there's still hope for me yet?" she asked.

"Oh, I think you could safely say that, yes," Celino answered smugly.

Marisa suddenly brightened.

"However," he warned, "you must never share this information with anybody in Carnelia. The power to predict a vortex would be a tremendous leap, scientifically speaking. But it could negatively impact Carnelia and alter its course forever."

"In what way?"

He shrugged. "Someone could introduce a Howitzer. Or they might bring across some dangerous biological agent such as smallpox that could wipe out the entire population."

"I never thought of that," she said.

"There are countless ways in which one civilization can negatively impact the other. We're just fortunate that nobody from our world has yet been able to tap into this incredible power source. Can you imagine what would happen if they did?"

Marisa shook her head.

"Well, I wouldn't worry about it. Back on Earth, the vortex wormhole theory is still in its infancy. Scientists are still trying to prove that there's more than one universe out there and yet, here we are, sitting in Carnelia and proving that theory as fact."

Celino paused for a moment as he scratched his head and reached for his reading glasses on the table.

"Scientists cannot completely disprove the possibility of time travel through the wormhole. But most of them scoff whenever anyone suggests utilizing a vortex as the quantum event to transport a person or object to another universe."

"Hasn't anyone ever tried to prove it?" she asked.

"Some have tried. I've devoted a substantial part of my life to researching and understanding this virtually unknown phenomenon. In fact, my thesis at Cal Tech was on something I call the vortex leap theory. It is real, my friends, as you both discovered for yourselves."

"How long will it take to finish the testing phase?" she asked.

Celino smiled at her. "In other words, you want to know how much longer you're stuck here."

Marisa nodded sheepishly.

"Well, I can't say for certain, but I should know pretty quickly here once I'm able to test it." Celino slapped his hands on his thighs, signaling the discussion was over. "End of the science lesson for today. Who wants more tea?"

"No thanks, I've had enough," she said.

"I think we should probably be getting back now," Arrie replied.

"Well then, I guess I'll be seeing you two at the masquerade ball in a couple of days?" Celino asked.

"Oh," said Marisa, "I didn't realize the invitations had already gone out. So you're coming, right?"

"I sure hope so, if my research doesn't interfere. I'll look forward to having a dance with you, my dear," Celino said, kissing her hand.

"Thanks again, Celino. We'll be back again soon," Arrie said.

CHAPTER 23
RESIGNATION

ARRIE AND MARISA HURRIED up toward the castle just as it was beginning to pour. The heavy rain soaked through their clothes within a couple of minutes. Laughing, they ran into the Green Room and stood with their backs to the fire.

"That was an interesting morning," Marisa said. She removed her cape, hung it over a chair next to the fire. "Thanks for taking me."

"You're welcome. Celino is quite an intriguing man. One of these days, we'll go back for another visit and he can tell you one of his crazy adventures."

"Arrie, can you please find out if anyone has found my ring?" she asked. "Every time I think about it, I get sick to my stomach."

"Yes, I will," Arrie promised. He removed his cloak and shook his wet hair like a dog. Marisa laughed at him as she wrung her hair out on the marble floor.

All of a sudden, Tino burst into the room.

"Ah, Lord Arrigo, there you are. I've been searching all over the palace for you for the past hour. Please forgive my intrusion, milady, but I must speak with Lord Arrigo immediately."

"Of course," she said with a nod. Marisa watched curiously as they whispered in the corner. Tino said something she couldn't hear and Arrie nodded with a grim look on his face. Tino left the room and hurried down the corridor.

"What's going on?"

"Bad news, I'm afraid. Tino has just informed me that Gregario passed on this morning."

"Savino's father?"

Arrie nodded. "This is the news we've been dreading, though none of us expected it to happen so soon. I must go to Darian right away. Will you please forgive me?"

"Yes of course—go, go."

Arrie rushed out of the room.

Marisa went upstairs to change her clothes. She opened the door and was surprised to see her nearly finished ball gown hanging from a wooden peg.

Anna curtseyed. "There you are, milady. Your dress is almost completed, but we need a final fitting. I will go fetch Leonora. Would you please be so kind as to put it on?" she asked.

As the young woman ran off, Marisa moved closer to examine the dress. The fabric had an almost reflective sheen on its surface and the intricate beadwork curled and twisted across the bodice. She ran her fingers ran along the small, ivory pearls sewn onto the edges of the neck, shoulders and sleeves. The gown was a work of art.

She slipped off her clothes and lifted the purple, ivory, and lavender gown over her head just as Anna returned with Leonora. After Anna had fastened the dress in back, Leonora carefully took in small folds of fabric, sticking pins around the waist and bust area.

The gown was hemmed to the perfect length, and Leonora made sure the sleeves flared out from the elbow at exactly the right length. Finally Leonora nodded in approval, apparently satisfied that everything was correct. Marisa removed the dress and handed it to Leonora who scurried off to complete her work.

Marisa's thoughts turned to Savino. Wondering if he even knew that his father was dead, she quickly did the math in her head. It had taken them three days to travel back to Crocetta from Abbadon. If Savino had left for Crocetta two days ago, there was no way he could know about Gregario's death yet.

Both Arrie and Darian had said it would be disastrous if Savino became king. She thought about her own unique position in the country's politics. The fact that Savino's father was now dead had undoubtedly kicked things up a notch or two. It was highly likely that she would be forced to decide much sooner on whether to marry him.

Marriage?

How could she even consider it? She was only eighteen and not ready for that kind of commitment. She hadn't even dated that much, but in this strange world, people were engaged from birth.

Could she marry Savino to save the land from war? And how was it possible that the fate of an entire country could rest on whether an eighteen-year-old girl would accept an ordinary marriage proposal?

It blew her mind.

Savino, Lady Matilda, Talvan, and his entourage of thirty-something warriors were less than a day from Crocetta when they were met by a royal courier sent to convey the sad news of Count Gregario's death.

Raising his sword victoriously, Savino shouted, "Hail the new king of Crocetta! You shall be witnesses at my coronation in less than a fortnight! The king is dead! Hail to your king!"

"Hail, King Savino! The king is dead! Long live the king," the men shouted in unison.

"Show you no remorse for our father's death, Savino?" Matilda asked, tears in her bright blue eyes. "Have you forgotten about Prince Darian? It's still possible that he shall ascend the throne instead of you."

"The only way for that coward to ascend the throne, dear sister, would be if, by some miracle, you should agree to marry him," Savino replied with a wicked smile.

He turned to the royal courier and motioned to dismiss him.

"Go back and report to Prince Darian. He is commanded to prepare for the king's arrival in Crocetta tomorrow. Tell him that I am coming to claim my throne."

"Will Prince Darian be joining us for dinner?" Marisa asked as Adalina sat down at the table. The rest of the royal family had not yet arrived.

"I'm afraid not, Lady Marisa. The Crimson Court called another emergency meeting this morning, and they've been in session all day. There are many preparations for the funeral tomorrow. I have not seen my brother all day."

"So it's true then? The funeral will be tomorrow?"

"Yes, but don't worry," Adalina said. "It shall not affect your birthday ball. We're all looking forward to the masquerade the day after tomorrow."

Marisa looked at her sheepishly. "I actually wouldn't mind if the ball were cancelled altogether. You all seem to have a lot more important stuff going on at the moment anyway."

Adalina looked horrified. "Nonsense, Lady Marisa! Everyone has been looking forward to the ball, especially Darian. I happen to know that he plans to make an announcement."

"What sort of announcement?" Marisa asked casually.

"He hasn't said exactly," Adalina said, her voice chiming like a bell, "but he is insisting that Matilda and Savino both be present." She leaned in close. "Just between you and me, I think my brother is secretly engaged, and he's going to announce it."

Marisa coughed. "What? Engaged to whom?"

"Who do you think?"

Marisa nodded but said nothing. Darian's family must have been thrilled with the news of his engagement. Arrie, Helena, and Cinzia all sat down at the table and began to chat politely over dinner.

She stared blankly at her plate and thought about her promise to attend the ball as a last favor. It would be a relief to finally escape the drama and go live at Castle Beauriél.

Marisa placed her napkin on the table and stood up. "I'm going to take a walk around the palace," she said.

Arrie cocked his head at her. "Are you all right, Marisa?"

"I'm okay. Meet you down in the Green Room in a little while?"

"Certainly," he said. "Don't get lost."

She smiled faintly. "I'll try not to."

As she wandered the empty corridors of the palace, it seemed to be deserted. The only sound was the hollow click-clack of her shoes as she walked across the marble floors. Gazing up at the high, vaulted ceilings, she shook her head, unable to fathom how people could live in such an enormous place.

She studied the paintings along the walls and marveled at the painstaking details worked into each one. The time and attention the artists had spent creating just the right amount of light bouncing off the objects was incredible. The royal portraits appeared especially lifelike.

As the stoic figures of the royals gazed down at Marisa in their full regalia from their lofty realm upon the wall, they seemed to wonder what she was doing there among the country's elite.

"I'm just a common girl from a faraway place, with no idea what I'm doing here," she said out loud.

She entered a cozy room with a fire burning in the fireplace and immediately noticed a small piano in the corner. She sat down on the bench and began to play a song she hadn't sung in years.

As the notes flowed through her fingertips to the keys, she sang in the most beautiful voice she had, her heart exploding with both joy and sorrow at the same time.

Startled by a large silhouette in the doorway, she stopped. When she realized it was Darian, her heart beat quickened. She dotted her eyes with a handkerchief.

"Good evening, milady" he said softly, easing his muscular frame into a chair. "You are very talented, you know."

"You startled me. I thought I was alone."

"I apologize if I frightened you. I found the others in the Green Room, and they said you were out somewhere roaming the castle. Then I heard the music, and thought I'd come down to listen."

"Oh."

Awkward silence.

"I guess you've been pretty busy with important stuff lately, huh?" she asked.

"Yes, there's much to be done with both a funeral and a ball taking place within twenty-four hours of each other," he said, rubbing his temple. His face was pale from exhaustion, and he looked as if he hadn't slept in days.

"Are you feeling okay?" she asked.

"I'm just a bit tired." He looked up at her. "Arrie said he took you to the city to visit Celino today. What did you think of that?"

"I had fun. I enjoyed looking in the beautiful shops, having a caramel apple, and sipping tea with Celino."

Darian smiled faintly. "I wish I could have been there. I would have enjoyed watching you discover our city."

"Does Savino know his father is dead?"

He sighed. "After Gregario had passed, we dispatched a messenger to intercept Savino's company on its way here for the ball. We're assuming the courier has reached them by now and are expecting Savino's attendance at the funeral tomorrow."

"And Lady Matilda?"

He avoided her eyes. "She is traveling with Savino as we speak."

"Your Highness," she began, "I would understand completely if you decided to cancel the ball."

He cocked his head at her. "Why would I do that, Marisa?"

"Well, I'm no expert when it comes to royal etiquette, but doesn't it seem sorta out of place?"

Darian looked at her questioningly.

"I mean, since Gregario is being buried tomorrow and all? Shouldn't there be a period of mourning or something?"

"If there is anything this country desperately needs right now, it's a reason to celebrate," he said. "There will be plenty of time for mourning tomorrow. And unless I am completely mistaken, the man closest to Gregario will not shed even a single tear for his own father. No, we are *not* cancelling the ball."

Marisa said nothing as she stood and moved toward the fireplace.

Darian let out a deep sigh as he rose from his chair. "I'm sorry. That was perhaps unfair of me."

"No, he's your cousin. You know him better than me."

He brightened. "You do know that your birthday ball is being billed as *the* social event of the year, don't you?"

"Actually, I didn't." She smiled faintly. "I guess life in Crocetta must be pretty dull if the most thrilling thing around here is to come and meet someone like me."

"Your reputation has already surpassed you, milady. Every nobleman from here to Terracina is eager to cast his eye on the mysterious young woman the royal family has taken under its wing."

"How does everyone know me already?" she asked. "I've only been here a few days."

"Well, apparently you made quite an impression on Lord Domenico..." he teased.

"Ah, Lord Domenico."

"Yes. He is a man of refined tastes and is not easily impressed. Any time a woman earns his favor enough to be mentioned, it's usually enough to arouse the interest of half the kingdom. The male half." He chuckled.

Marisa smiled. "Listen, Darian," she began. "I know I owe both you and Arrie a lot for all you've done for me, but I also realize you've got a full plate right now. You need to be concentrating on running the country, not entertaining me like I'm here on some kind of vacation or something. I don't want you to worry about me anymore."

"What are you saying?"

"Only that I think your time is better spent elsewhere."

Silence.

"*Elsewhere?* Marisa, I don't understand what you mean."

She swallowed hard. "On the night we first met, Arrie told me that I was a 'distraction' you couldn't afford to have. Although I was a bit offended when he said it, now I'm beginning to realize just how right he was."

He stared at her in disbelief. "You make it sound like I'm all work and no play. Marisa, whatever you think of me, please remember that underneath all the fancy titles, I'm just a man. I have my own dreams and desires like everyone else."

So he only considers me a bit of play before settling down with Matilda? Suddenly, Marisa's mind was made up.

"Your Highness, I need to tell you something."

"What is it?"

"I have decided to accept Savino's marriage proposal."

Darian blinked. "Are you absolutely certain?"

"Yes. I've been thinking about it a lot over the past few days, and it's my final decision. I just thought you should know."

"I see. When are you planning to tell him?"

She shrugged her shoulders.

"Are you in love with him?"

Marisa stared at him in shock. She had no answer.

Darian's face was flushed. "I—I," he stammered, "That's none of my business."

She shrugged and looked away.

"Milady, I am truly sorry for all you've endured in recent days. None of us planned things this way, least of all me. I wish the circumstances had been different for all of us."

A tear rolled down her cheek. "You don't have to apologize for anything—I'm the party crasher here. But don't worry, after the ball you won't be seeing me again."

He grabbed her by the shoulders, forced her to look him in the eye. "You are *not* a party crasher, whatever that means. Don't you understand that you've managed to turn everything upside-down just by coming here?"

She looked at him sadly. "I didn't mean to."

"I know you didn't. But make sure you are making the right decision for *you.*"

"Marrying Savino is my decision," she said firmly.

Darian said nothing for a moment as he studied her face. He moved in close to her but when she realized he was going to kiss her, she pulled back suddenly.

"Your Highness, would you please tell the others that I'm not feeling well? I just want to go back and go to bed."

He nodded and turned to escort her to her room.

"I'll say goodnight here," she said quickly. "I'd rather walk alone if you don't mind."

"As you wish," he whispered.

As Marisa hurried away through the deserted palace corridors in the direction of the main staircase, the only sound she heard was that of her heels clacking across the marble floor. And in her haste to get away, she never even noticed the tears in Darian's eyes as he watched her go.

CHAPTER 24

GLIMPSES

MARISA LIFTED HER SKIRTS and descended the stairs for breakfast in her all-black mourning gown. An army of palace servants rushed up and down the corridors in the middle of their various tasks, all of them making sure the funeral preparations were completed by two o'clock that afternoon.

She sat at the nearly-empty table in the dining hall and smiled at Adalina, who was quietly eating her breakfast. Darian's sister looked beautiful in black as it complemented her dark hair and fair skin.

"Did you sleep well, Lady Marisa?"

"Yeah, thanks."

"We grew concerned last night when you didn't join us. Later my brother told us that you weren't feeling well. Are you feeling a little better this morning?"

"I'm fine, Your Highness, thanks. Where is everyone anyway?"

"Preparing for the funeral. My brother slept only a few hours last night. The Crimson Court convened until four o'clock this morning."

Marisa eyed her curiously. "Adalina, how old are you?"

"I turn sixteen in a few months, milady."

"You're almost the same age as my brother Mark."

"I wish I could meet your brother," Adalina said. "What a shame he won't be at the ball."

"Yeah, I'll miss him. He's always the life of the party."

"Darian says he's planning to throw a ball for my sixteenth birthday and invite all the eligible men in the land."

"Your brother's a generous man."

"I'm so lucky to have him. Since our father died six years ago, he has sacrificed a lot for my mother and me. He even postponed marriage for our sakes."

Marisa look at her, stunned. "He postponed *marriage?*"

"Yes. He didn't feel right about getting married and ascending the throne. He thought he wouldn't be able to take care of us and he refused the throne when Queen Sophie died. He could have married Lady Matilda then and been ruling as king today."

"Prince Darian refused the throne?" she echoed. "But he told me he wasn't old enough to become king. That's the whole reason why Count Gregario had to step in."

Adalina shook her head. "No, he only told you part of the story. Darian was seventeen when Queen Sophie died. The Crimson Court voted to confirm him as prince regent until he could assume the throne on his eighteenth birthday.

"Our father had just passed on and he felt responsible for our mother and me, so he exercised his right to veto. The court was left with no choice but to appoint Count Gregario as temporary ruler."

"And the only way he can regain the throne is to marry Matilda?"

Adalina shrugged. "A few months ago, my mother told him not to delay marriage any longer for our sakes. She even made him promise he'd be married by his twenty-third birthday. Just between you and me, I think she's eager to become a grandmother," she whispered.

Marisa's shoulders sank. "He deserves to be happy."

"He just turned twenty-two, so it doesn't give him much time. It's been a running joke in our family who will be married first—him or me," Adalina said, giggling.

"I don't understand. Is Prince Darian required to find you a suitable husband, or are you allowed to choose for yourself?"

"Are you asking if I must marry a Fiore prince? Well, the answer is no, but he must be of noble blood," Adalina said, setting her teacup down gently on the saucer.

"So, basically, your options are pretty limited, then."

Adalina nodded. "Darian has been combing the entire kingdom for an acceptable suitor. But in the end, he always says that no man is ever good enough for me. Personally, I think that's *his* excuse for never marrying. No woman is ever good enough for Darian Fiore."

Marisa stared at her plate. She wasn't hungry anymore.

"Can you keep a secret?" Adalina whispered.

Marisa nodded slowly.

"I've had a secret love for several months—Gervasio. I can't marry him, though. He's a common man. I was ready to run away with him even though it would have hurt Darian and my mother."

"What happened to him?"

"He left on a ship bound for Terracina. I received a letter from him a few days ago. He refused to see me ever again—not because he doesn't love me but because he doesn't want to stand in my way of finding happiness with someone worthy of me."

"Oh, Adalina, I'm so sorry."

"When I received his letter, it nearly broke my heart."

"I know," Marisa said sympathetically.

"*What?*"

"I mean, I know how you feel. Falling in love with a person you know you can never be with is pretty devastating."

"Neither my mother nor my brother know, Lady Marisa."

"I won't say a word to anyone, I promise."

"Thank you, Lady Marisa."

"Please—just call me Marisa."

"All right, Marisa."

"Oh, uh, Princess Adalina? About the funeral—I don't know what I'm supposed to do or where to sit or anything."

"Don't worry, I'll make sure Cozimo comes to brief you before the ceremony starts," she said, getting up to leave.

"Thank you, Adalina."

"You're welcome, Marisa."

Marisa just had to get out of the palace for a little while.

She decided to go out riding on Sienna before the pomp and ceremony later that afternoon. As she hurried back to her room to change into her riding clothes, she peeked outside at the storm clouds brewing and hoped she wouldn't get drenched.

A few minutes later, she lifted her skirts and dashed through the main corridor as quickly as possible. It wasn't very ladylike, but Savino was expected to reach the castle at any moment and she wasn't ready to face him yet.

Everyone in the palace seemed to be adhering strictly to the rule of wearing black out of respect for the monarch's death, so she hoped she wouldn't cause a stir by wearing her brown riding outfit. The palace servants all seemed too busy to notice her as she slipped down to the lowest level of the citadel.

She entered the stables and maneuvered carefully around a pile of manure toward Siena's stall. Her feed trough was empty. Spotting a storeroom filled with burlap sacks, she slipped in to find some oats. One of the sacks was open and as she reached down to get a handful, the door of the storeroom fell shut.

Suddenly she froze.

The sounds of men's voices and horses' hooves on the cobblestones grew louder as she heard them entering the stables. She stepped up closer to peek through a slit in the door and saw a man removing his saddle. It was Savino plus another man she couldn't see. She moved to the rear of the storeroom and hid behind some sacks of oats.

The other man led the horses into their stalls and secured the iron locks. He was saying something to Savino, but all she could hear was static. The earpiece was unable to translate above the clanging noise.

"Are you're sure that no one suspects anything?" Savino asked.

"Yes, Your Grace," the man said. "Rest assured that everything shall go according to plan." She recognized his voice. It was Gaspar.

"Well, you must make sure that the poison does not find its way into the wrong goblet. We cannot afford any mistakes at this point. One slip-up and the entire plan falls. This is war."

"I understand, sire."

"When I am at last seated on the throne, you shall be elevated to knighthood, Gaspar."

"Thank you, Your Grace."

She tapped on her earpiece as the men left the stables, but there was no further translation. They must have been out of range. She waited a few minutes before she cautiously peered outside. There didn't seem to be anyone around except the guards posted down at the main gate. Darian had to be told about Savino's plan before it was too late.

She glanced up toward the citadel and spotted Bruno crossing the courtyard toward the Knights' Hall. She dashed up toward him and grabbed his arm, pulling him behind a low wall. After checking to make sure they could not be seen from the castle windows, Marisa turned to him, still struggling to catch her breath.

"Milady, what is this? How may I be of service?" Bruno smiled suggestively at her.

"Go get Arrie," she managed, heaving. He looked at her with a puzzled face but didn't move. She rolled her eyes. "Arrigo," she said simply and motioned toward the citadel. All at once he understood her and bowed briefly before dashing off.

She waited impatiently until Bruno returned with Arrie.

"What is this, Marisa?" Arrie asked, panting. She looked at Bruno to excuse him so they could talk in private. But like a bellhop waiting for a tip, he just stood there and stared at her, waiting patiently for some sort of thank you.

Knowing he wouldn't leave any other way, Marisa finally gave Bruno a quick peck on the cheek and shooed him off. He laughed as he left and she smiled in spite of herself.

"Now what's this all about?" Arrie asked.

"Come! Follow me down to the stables first," she said.

Marisa hurried down to the stables as Arrie followed her with a puzzled face. She checked all the stalls and storeroom to make sure they were alone and then grabbed her tack.

"Savino and Gaspar arrived here just a few minutes ago. I was spying on them in the stables and overheard them discussing a plan to poison someone." She unlatched Siena's stall. "I think they were talking about Darian."

"*Poison?*" Arrie asked. "Are you sure you heard them correctly?"

"Oh, yeah. Savino told Gaspar to make sure the poison didn't 'get into the wrong goblet' or something to that effect." She fitted the bridle around the horse's muzzle and looked at Arrie. "Savino also mentioned something about being at war. What are we going to do?" she asked.

"*We* are going to do nothing. I will go and alert Darian of Savino's plan. I'm not yet certain what he's up to, but if he's discussing poisoning someone, that's not good."

Arrie stopped. "Wait—where are you going?"

"I was gonna go out for a ride, but now I'm starting to have second thoughts. Maybe I shouldn't leave the castle."

"Don't worry about anything," he said. "Go and take your ride, but be back by twelve-thirty. Cozimo will come to your chambers at one o'clock to run through the protocol before the ceremony starts. I shall go find Darian and inform him right away."

"Okay, I'll be back in a little while."

"Do you know where you're going?"

"I thought I'd ride out to Castle Beauriél," she said, mounting Siena. "I wanted to take another look before I move in."

"Well, please be careful. Do you remember how to get there?"

"Yeah, I think so."

He pointed toward the edge of town. "You just keep to the main road out of the city for about three miles, and at a certain point, you'll see the gates on the right side. Wait just a minute."

Arrie felt around in his pockets and then finally pulled out a small brass key. Smiling, he handed it to her. "Here you go."

"What? You just happen to have a key to Castle Beauriél in your pocket?" Marisa asked, laughing.

"It's a skeleton key. It will open nearly all of the doors at the castle and some of the royal residences. Nobody's supposed to know I have it, though, so whatever you do, don't lose it!"

"I know, I know," she said.

"Now, get going. I'm off to tell Darian."

Marisa pulled the hood of her cape over her head and dug her heels gently into Siena's belly. She rode through the rampart tunnel and passed under the portcullis into the main street.

After a few hundred yards, she recognized the house with a blue door and realized it was Celino's. She quickly tied Siena's reins off at the gate and knocked on the door. The old woman opened it and stared at her blankly.

"Master Celino is not at home. He's gone away for a few days, and I can't tell you when he'll be back." The woman shut the door.

Puzzled, Marisa walked back up the short path and loosened Siena's reins. Celino had promised to come to the ball the next day. Why would he suddenly decide last minute to go on a trip?

She climbed back up on Siena and rode down to the outer walls of the city. After they had passed through the gates into the countryside, she was stunned by the emerald hues of the rolling hills. She thought about her trip out to Castle Beauriél with Darian just a couple of days before and it hit her how much she enjoyed his company.

Now that she had decided to marry Savino, Marisa resigned herself not to dwell on Darian any longer. But the memories of their journey together kept creeping back into her mind. She didn't want to shut them off.

At last she reached the iron gates of Beauriél and climbed down off Siena. As she continued on foot, the wide lane flanked with mature trees seemed longer than she'd remembered. The branches above swayed in the breeze and the only sound she could hear was the wind blowing through the trees. It was peaceful stillness that refreshed her soul after the frantic, busy days of the palace.

As the façade of the castle slowly came into view, she gasped at the sheer beauty of it. The autumn leaves were piling up all around the house and they would need a gardener to trim back the trees and shrubs that had gotten too big, but basically the house was ready to move in.

She secured Siena's reins around a large tree and ascended the steps to the front door. Thanks to the small skeleton key from Arrie, she entered the grand foyer effortlessly and admired its decorative details for the second time.

Marisa had only been inside for less than a minute when she felt a sick feeling in the pit of her stomach. The wave of nausea spread out through her entire body until she had the sensation of being squeezed by a boa constrictor. Her breathing became labored as she collapsed at the bottom of the stairs. She fought for air and a wave of panic gripped her.

What is happening to me?

She rested her chin between her knees and tried to take long, deep breaths. She concentrated on slowing her breathing down as the words from her father's letter suddenly popped into her head:

You will be confronted with many choices in your life, but always strive for what is good and right, and never settle for less than that which is worthy and worthwhile.

Marisa began to wonder if she'd made the right decision about marrying Savino. She didn't know him very well and she wasn't sure she could spend the rest of her life with him. Her thoughts turned to Darian and Arrie. Being around them seemed so natural that she couldn't imagine not having them in her life anymore.

She quietly began to pray.

Garon, I don't know which path to choose. Show me which way to go. Both ways seem like a dead end. If it isn't possible to share a future with the man I love, should I go with the other? I don't want to make the wrong decision, and I need help. I will try to trust you to help me find my way. Amen.

Still trying to keep her breathing under control, she grabbed the railing and slowly pulled herself up. She walked into the adjacent room, but the deathly stillness made her jittery. Somehow, being at Castle Beauriél without Darian felt eerie and the stillness of the house seemed unnatural. And all of a sudden, Marisa couldn't imagine living in the castle alone.

Her eyes roamed the room. It was a large living area that connected to a dining hall. She peeked in and saw the long table that would seat at least sixteen people. Her fingers felt the smoothness of the table as she admired its hand-carved legs and matching chairs.

She pulled out a chair to feel its velvety cushion and suddenly the entire room sprung to life. The table was instantly filled with all kinds of foods and decorated in a festive manner for the holiday season. Each chair was occupied by a different family member as they all sat down to enjoy Christmas dinner.

The room was filled with laughter, smiles, and the mixed fragrance of delicious food and warm company. A young mother sat at the table facing her, and Marisa was stunned to see it was an older version of herself. Several children, aunts, and uncles were talking and laughing, enjoying the holiday feast together.

The vision of the family faded away, and in the place of the young mother, Marisa saw herself as an old woman sitting alone at the long table on Christmas Eve. She moved closer to observe her old self, but the wrinkle-faced woman was oblivious to her.

A servant brought her food on a silver tray, but the old woman didn't even seem to notice as she sipped her wine in lonely silence. Marisa could smell the stench of regret hanging in the air as she reached out to touch the old woman's face. Her hand went right through her as if she was a ghost and she quickly pulled it back again. The old woman could not see or hear Marisa as she dined alone in her solitude.

All of a sudden it occurred to her that she was seeing a glimpse of two distinct pathways for her life. One of them was just a possibility, and the other was destined to be.

But which was which?

The vision of the old woman faded away, and she moved to the glass doors to view the expansive gardens. Another vision materialized as she gazed outside and saw herself tossing a ball to her young son on a bright spring day. The boy was laughing, and she smiled to him while a little girl ran to grab her around the legs.

The three on the lawn slowly faded away, and instantly she saw the old woman version of herself resting in a chair on the terrace. She was bundled up in a blanket as she stared blankly into the forest. Dried leaves blew across the grass as the woman sipped her tea. Her face was worn with grief and loneliness. A tear rolled down Marisa's cheek and she quickly looked away. When she looked again, the old woman was gone.

Marisa climbed the steps to take a look upstairs. The antique boards creaked under her weight as she walked down the long hallway and peeked into each of the bedrooms. When she came to the large chamber at the end of the hall, she stopped. The room was filled with luxurious furnishings and there was a large bed against the far wall. There were four large windows that looked out over the front of the house onto the driveway.

As she looked at the bed, Marisa saw herself once again as a mother reading a story to four small children all squashed under the covers on either side of her. When the story was over, the mother chased them all down the hall into their own bedrooms. Marisa watched with a smile as she kissed and tucked each one in.

Turning back toward the master bedroom, she saw herself as an old woman again, lying alone in the big bed. The woman had been reading, but she stopped to stare out the window just as the rain began to hit the window panes. She crept out of bed and sauntered down the hall, peering into each of the empty rooms. The woman's lip quivered in melancholy and sadness as Marisa followed her down the hallway.

Unable to take anymore, Marisa flew down the stairs and out the front door. Slamming it shut, she quickly locked it with the key and ran over to her horse, desperate to get away as quickly as possible.

As Siena galloped up the gravel road as fast as she could, Marisa glanced over her shoulder and saw the old woman staring at her from the upper bedroom window and she shuddered. She dug her heels into Siena's belly, pushing her as hard as she could go.

Once they were back on the main road toward town, she slowed Siena to a normal walk, still unable to shake the haunting visions. In her head, she was debating herself on whether she should still marry Savino. Certainly marrying him would be better than being alone for the rest of her life.

What am I thinking?

Savino was plotting to kill someone with poison. How could she marry a man like that? She sighed, completely confused about everything. Carnelia certainly was a strange place, and nothing was as it seemed.

Up ahead, a man was herding some sheep across the road but most of them had stopped right in the middle and were blocking it. The animals didn't appear as if they were planning to move anytime soon.

The man turned his attention from his sheep and smiled gently at her. In his early thirties, the young man was dressed in old farming clothes, with a dark beard and large hat. He was tanned as if he had spent most of the day outdoors. Although his face was rather plain-looking, there was something pleasant and familiar in his expression. He smiled warmly at her.

"Good morning, milady. What are you doing out here on this chilly afternoon?" he asked.

Marisa dismounted and approached him cautiously. She shaded her eyes with her hand. "I came out to take look at my house," she said. "It's the big one over there with all the chimneys and the really long driveway," she said, pointing to the forested area behind them.

"Ah, yes," he said.

She stopped. "Sir, can you understand what I am saying?"

He nodded at her and smiled.

"Have we met?" she asked. "I have the strangest feeling that I know you from somewhere."

"My name is Eman, milady. I'm exceedingly pleased to meet you," he said with a low bow.

"I'm Marisa. Do you live nearby?"

"I reside over there, just beyond those trees—up on that hill."

"Excuse me, sir, but how do you know English? Have you ever been to Earth? Maybe you know my friend Celino?"

Eman stared out into the hills, ignoring her questions. "What were you running away from just now?" he asked.

"Oh, I—uh, I was afraid."

"Afraid of what?" His sparkling brown eyes seemed to dance.

"I don't know—it's kind of complicated. I guess I was worried about my future," she said finally.

"Today has enough problems of its own. Do not worry about tomorrow, for it will take care of itself," he said.

Marisa just nodded.

"The next time you are out here from the city, milady, I would be most honored if you would come visit me for tea," he said softly.

"I'd like that. I'll be living out here permanently starting the day after tomorrow, so I guess we'll be neighbors. I can come once and borrow a cup of sugar," she said dryly.

Eman smiled. "You had better be getting back now, milady. It is going to rain soon." He herded his sheep off the road.

"Thank you, sir. I'll come visit you the next time I come back."

"Milady, the pleasure was all mine," he said, tipping his hat.

CHAPTER 25
BURIALS

ON THE WAY BACK to Crocetta, Marisa thought about Eman. She knew she'd seen him before, but she couldn't remember where and it was driving her crazy. The shops were all closed in respect to the king's funeral, and there were only a few people still milling about on the city streets. Most were making their way back home.

She entered through the main gate and headed straight toward the stables, on her guard in case she should bump into Savino. Once Siena had been secured in her stall, Marisa snuck up to her room through the servants' corridors which passed along the wine cellars.

Once she was back in her chambers, Marisa noticed that Anna had laid out a different gown for her to wear to the funeral. It was all black and made of a stiff material that reminded her of taffeta and it was much more formal than the dress she'd worn that morning.

The time on her phone read 12:43 p.m. She only had a few minutes before Cozimo would come to give her instructions. The water was cold as she quickly gave herself a sponge bath, but she didn't have time to wait for hot water from the kitchen. She scrubbed her face and dried it before asking Anna to help her fasten the stiff corset. With the young woman's assistance, she slipped into the black dress and Anna quickly braided her hair.

Marisa frowned when she looked in the mirror and saw the deathly pallor in her face. Still in shock from what she'd seen at Beauriél, she pinched her cheeks for a bit of color. There was a soft knock at the door.

Anna opened the door and Cozimo entered with the help of a walking stick. He bowed slowly, and Marisa remembered to curtsey.

"Milady, this shall be brief as the funeral is set to begin shortly," he began slowly. "You shall assemble down at the main staircase thirty minutes from now. There shall be a short procession consisting of two rows that shall lead the funeral guests down toward the Knights' Hall."

He blinked absently as if he'd forgotten what to say.

"Leading the two lines will be His Royal Highness Prince Darian and the Viscount Savino da Rocha, followed respectively by Her Royal Highness Princess Adalina and Lady Matilda. The rest of the royal family and advisors shall follow in rank order. You shall walk with Lord Arrigo Macario, so if you have any questions, he shall be there, ready to assist you."

The old man coughed several times and seemed to be having trouble breathing. Marisa was just about to call Anna to get him a glass of water when he cleared his throat loudly and continued with his instructions.

"Once the procession has reached the interior of the Knights' Hall, everyone shall sit in the royal pews in the exact order they entered. At the conclusion of the service, the procession shall depart from the Knights' Hall and cross the main courtyard.

"There, the casket shall be placed on a royal carriage and the procession shall make its way down through the city. This will allow the citizens of Crocetta ample time to offer their final farewell to His Royal Highness. Then it shall wind its way back up to the royal Crimson sepulcher, where the coffin shall be laid to rest."

The old man stared at her. "Do you have any questions?"

She ran over the order of the events in her mind. It all seemed straightforward enough. "*Nyoit*," Marisa said. She had managed to pick up a few basic words in Crocine.

"At the conclusion of the funeral service, which is expected to close at approximately four-thirty, a funeral banquet will be held. Again, you shall sit next to Lord Arrigo Macario at the place marked especially for you. When the feast has reached its conclusion, you shall be free to leave. Questions?"

The old man seemed to be out of breath as she shook her head.

"No?" Cozimo asked, giving her a curt nod. "Then that will be all. Milady, I shall see you at the banquet."

He wobbled over to the door and bowed his head. She curtseyed to him and gently closed the door.

With still a few minutes before she had to report downstairs, her thoughts drifted back to Darian. He was probably used to briefings every day that mapped out his entire schedule minute-to-minute. It would be enough to drive a sane person to total madness. She was starting to understand what Darian had meant when he said he had no control over his own life.

Her father had always taught her never to judge a person until she had walked a mile in their shoes. But after just a few days at the castle, she was already starting to get calluses on her feet. Next to the importance of Darian's life, her own insignificance became painfully clear.

In that moment, she suddenly wanted more. She wanted to be important—not for her own sake, but to make a difference. What good was a person's life if they didn't make some sort of positive impact for the better? Even the favorite toast of Carnelia had to do with a person fulfilling his destiny. But what was her destiny? And what role did she have to play in all this?

Marisa jumped as she noticed the time on her phone. She closed the door behind her and jogged down the hall as fast as she could move in the bulky dress. As she descended the grand staircase, sounds of loud chatter echoed up the vestibule. She was startled to discover a dense crowd of people waiting below to start the procession. As soon as she appeared, everyone stopped to stare.

Both Savino and Darian watched her from their spot at the front of the procession. The two men seemed to juxtapose each other perfectly, one with hair as dark as night and the other as bright as the sun. Marisa quickly found Arrie and he offered her an arm.

"Are you ready to endure another funeral so soon?" he asked.

"I guess. I didn't know Gregario, so it shouldn't be too difficult."

"He was a lot like Savino," Arrie whispered. "In so many ways."

She strained to see Savino's face through the crowd but was only able to catch a glimpse of the back of his head.

Without warning, the bells in the citadel tower began to crash loudly, startling everyone. Pealing long and steady and slow, they clanged in a funerary melody as the procession started to inch forward.

Arrie gave her a quick squeeze. "Here we go," he said.

As Marisa followed the young woman ahead of her, she concentrated on not stepping on her dress. When they crossed the courtyard outside, she could see Darian and Savino at the front leading the line of noblemen and women.

The procession entered the Knights' Hall where the pews had been set up in rows of four, each one facing the center of the hall. The casket in had been placed in the very center. Marisa and Arrie quickly found their assigned places as the bells continued to peal.

Once the service began, Marisa found it difficult to concentrate. Recent memories of her father's burial at the Jacksonville cemetery rose to the surface, and a wave of grief came rushing back. After just a few minutes, she had to remove the translator from her ear, unable to listen to any more tributes or eulogies. A few of the people around her sniffled, further intensifying the somber mood.

They stood and sat down several times, and when the ceremony had finally ended, the bells in the citadel tower began to peal once more. Everyone in the hall stood around chatting until it was time for them all to file out.

She scanned the crowd for Savino but instead saw Lady Matilda's grief-stricken face. Knowing exactly how she was feeling, Marisa's heart went out to Matilda. She felt the need to comfort her with a hug, but with the dense crowds of people packed into the hall, it would be almost impossible to reach her at that point. She decided to find her after the ceremonies and offer her condolences.

Darian's broad figure caught Marisa's eye as he strode across the hall and she watched as he pulled Matilda into a firm embrace. As the beautiful young woman sobbed into his chest, Marisa flashed back to the road near Abbadon where Darian had comforted her in that same manner just a few days before.

Although she had always known deep down that she could never be with Darian, it had never stopped her from hoping.

But now as he held Matilda in a private, tender moment, Marisa released the last sliver of hope still clinging to her soul. There could be no denying the mutual love and respect that existed between them, and she felt as if she was intruding on their intimate moment.

A tear slid down Marisa's cheek. Matilda would be the woman he needed to face his prominent role in history. For the first time since she'd come to Carnelia, she was finally sensing closure on a turbulent time with Darian. Once a tentative question mark she had hoped might end as an exclamation point, Darian would simply become the period at the end of the chapter. Prince Darian Fiore would wind up as nothing more than a small footnote in the story of her life—

"Marisa, are you okay?" Arrie eyed her with concern.

She shook her head sadly.

As a tear rolled down her face, he brushed it away and gathered her in a warm hug. Arrie knew the real reason for her tears. From coping with her father's death to falling hopelessly in love with Darian, he had remained her one true friend through it all, and she trusted him entirely.

"Here, take this," he said, handing her a handkerchief.

As the trumpets sounded, Marisa wiped her damp face and turned to see Darian watching them questioningly. She quickly looked away and pretended not to notice him.

The mourners jostled back into their places as the procession began to crawl forward. The Crimson knights were dressed in suits of armor and stood at attention in two rows facing each other with their swords drawn. Gregario's casket passed under them as it left the Knights' Hall for the last time. Behind it, the long procession of royals and noblemen filed out of the hall in a somber fashion.

Once they were outside, the carriage crossed the central courtyard and rolled down toward the main castle entrance. It passed under the rampart walls and down into the city streets. Marisa glanced up and saw the black storm clouds rolling in from over the ocean to cover the skies. Gray and somber, just like the mood.

The people of Crocetta bowed in silence as the casket passed them by and they paid their last respects. Her eyes scanned the worn, weary faces of the people and she wondered what would become of the city. There was still a chance to save them, but it would mean marrying Savino. When she saw the face of a tired mother trying to comfort her crying baby, her heart broke.

The funerary procession wound its way down through the streets of the city and meandered back up again until it found its way back to the castle gate. As the coffin reached the royal Crimson sepulcher, the procession stopped, and it was ceremoniously removed from the carriage by six members of the Crimson court.

After the casket had been solemnly laid to rest inside the sepulcher, there was silence in the kingdom for two full minutes. The only sounds that broke the stillness were the flags whipping in the wind and the distant peals of thunder rumbling across the skies. Soon the bells in the tower rang out, marking the end of the entombment ceremony.

"Come, Marisa, it's time to go to the banquet," Arrie said.

The Knights' Hall had been transformed into a splendid banquet room with tables full of food. After several minutes of searching among the commotion, Marisa and Arrie found their places and sat down. Scanning the crowds to find the others, Marisa noticed a beautifully carved chair between Darian and Savino.

"Who sits between Darian and Savino?" Marisa whispered.

"No one, it remains empty," Arrie answered somberly. "It's left that way in honor of the deceased. It's a reminder to all that he no longer walks among us."

As the bountiful feast was served, Marisa picked at her plate, but she wasn't hungry. She leaned forward in her chair to see Savino flirting shamelessly with a young woman at the next table and her face twisted with disgust.

She looked at Darian as he passed a plate of food to Matilda and sighed. He was so handsome in his black armor. No matter how hard she tried, she would probably never be able to erase him completely from her heart.

He looked at Marisa and their eyes locked for a brief moment. He smiled thoughtfully and cocked his head as if to ask what she was thinking. In the midst of the noisy conversations going on all around her, she just smiled faintly and then quickly looked away.

She knew she would never fit into the rich lifestyle of titled people of privilege and nobility. It was a completely different world and one in which she did not belong.

Later when a maid approached Savino to pour more wine into his glass, she saw him give the young woman a naughty smile as he patted her on her backside. She had seen enough.

"Is it okay for me to leave now?" Marisa whispered.

"Yes, our duty here is done," said Arrie. "Would you like me to walk you back to your chambers?"

She nodded sadly. Arrie pulled her chair back for her, and as they made their way through the noisy hall, Darian and Savino turned to watch them leave. She avoided their stares as she mentally closed the book on a most difficult chapter of her life. One of the two men sitting at the head table Marisa could never freely love and the other one could never freely love her.

They entered the empty palace corridors and suddenly she felt exhausted. She stopped to remove her shoes and slowly leaned back against the wall. Her feet hurt from all the unexpected walking that afternoon.

"Arrie, you know that I'll miss seeing you every day, but I sure won't miss any of this," she said, pointing toward the Knights' Hall.

"I will be very sad to see you go, cousin," he said softly. "Are you certain there isn't a way to talk you out of it?"

"No, there isn't."

The marble floor was cold under her bare feet, but Marisa didn't care—at least she felt free. As they climbed the grand staircase, she studied the faces of the royal ancestors. It struck her how old, haggard, and worn out they all appeared. She decided that being a royal probably took years off a person's life.

Once they reached her chambers, Arrie turned to leave.

"Would you mind staying for a few minutes?" Marisa asked, grabbing his arm. "I could really use some company."

"Of course. How about a nice glass of wine?"

"Hmm, okay, maybe half a glass." They entered her suite just as Anna was laying out a clean nightgown.

"Would you please bring us some wine?" Arrie asked.

"Yes, sir." Anna curtseyed and hurried off.

Arrie dragged a couple of chairs out onto the balcony as Marisa slipped her cape around her shoulders. The sun was already starting to dip underneath the storm clouds on the horizon. A few minutes later, Anna reappeared with some white wine and two glasses.

"So, are you ready for your big birthday ball bash tomorrow?" Arrie asked, carefully uncorking the bottle.

"Honestly, I'm not even looking forward to it. I might not go. I'm just trying to get through the next thirty hours or so until I can get out of this castle for good."

He stopped pouring the wine. "What do you mean? The party is going to be fantastic! Why won't you come to your own party?" he asked, handing her a glass.

"Arrie, you already know why."

"Remind me."

She rolled her eyes. "I can't be around *him* anymore. I just want to start all over and put the last two weeks behind me."

"You'll never be able to do that, you know."

"What? Put the past behind me? I'm sure gonna try. The memories are just too painful."

"Marisa, this whole thing we call life is just a series of painful, not so painful, happy, and joyful memories. Everything we experience, for better or for worse, shapes us into who we are."

"Believe me—I have tried to stay positive about everything. But at this point, the last thing I need is another bad memory."

"I heard a marvelous saying back on Earth once—something about making lemonade?"

"When life hands you lemons, you make lemonade?"

"That's it!"

"Yeah, well, I'm all out of sugar. Losing my mom's ring was the last drop in the bucket." She turned to him. "I don't suppose you've found it yet?"

"No, but we're not giving up just yet. Marisa, many people have gone to a lot of trouble to honor you on your birthday."

"I never asked for a party."

"Promise me that you'll come? Just for my sake?" He looked at her with his saddest puppy-dog eyes.

Marisa laughed. "Well, when you put it that way, I'd be pretty heartless to say no."

"I thought I heard voices out here," said Adalina.

"Would you care for some wine, Your Royal Highness?"

"I know you're teasing me when you say it like that, Arrie. And no, I don't care for any wine, but thank you for asking. What were you just saying about someone being heartless?"

"Marisa's not coming to the ball," he said.

"Arrie!" Marisa groaned. She shot him a dirty look.

"What?" Adalina said, horrified. "But it's going to be the ball of the season! Don't you know everyone is dying to meet you? Why won't you come?"

Marisa scrambled for an answer. "Uh, I don't know. I guess I've never been comfortable with being the center of attention."

"Speaking of uncomfortable, these shoes are really killing my feet," Adalina said, distracted. "What I was thinking wearing these shoes on cobblestone streets?"

"Yeah, mine are hurting too," Marisa said.

Adalina removed her slippers and rubbed her feet gently. She tucked them under a blanket and turned to Marisa. "I suppose you aren't accustomed to always being the center of attention. But once you get used to it, it's not so bad."

"What's not so bad?"

Marisa froze as she heard Darian's voice behind them.

"We were just discussing royal life," Adalina explained. "This has been a very full day for you, hasn't it, brother?"

"Indeed it has," Darian said with a sigh. He picked up Arrie's empty glass from the table and poured some wine.

"Marisa doesn't want to come to her own party tomorrow," Adalina pouted. "Won't you help us persuade her to come?"

"What's this?" Darian asked.

Marisa sighed heavily. "Look, you guys, I don't want to seem ungrateful, because I'm really not, but it just feels like it's not my party anymore."

"What do you mean?" asked Arrie.

"I know Lady Matilda and Savino and tons of other people will be there, but my dad, Mark, and Uncle Al won't. It just isn't the same."

She looked at their sullen faces and pangs of guilt began to eat at her. It would be best to sever all ties with the Fiore family while she still could. Marisa didn't really want to, but she was in survival mode now.

"I deeply regret the fact you don't feel at home here with us," Darian said, swirling the wine in his glass. "I had looked forward to dancing with you tomorrow night."

"Been there, done that," Marisa muttered under her breath.

Awkward silence.

Arrie motioned to Adalina, and without a word, the two of them stood up and went inside. Marisa pulled the cape around her and lifted the hood over her head as tears stung her eyes.

"I thought you were fitting in quite well, all things considered," Darian said as he stared out over the horizon. "I'm sorry to hear you don't feel welcome."

"I never said I didn't feel welcome."

He finished the last of his wine and set the glass down on the table, sighing heavily. "Now that we're alone, what is the real reason you don't want to go to the ball?"

Marisa swallowed hard. He was calling her bluff. "I already told you.

Since none of my family will be there, I just want to move on and start a new life on my own."

"But why *before* the ball? It's only one more day."

"Your Highness, you've done a lot for me, and I appreciate it, honestly I do. But you're royalty and I'm not. I'm not a member of your family, and I never will be."

Unless I marry Savino.

Darian pulled his chair closer. "I hope you'll reconsider and come tomorrow night."

"I can't make any promises," she said softly.

"If you do not wish to stay in the castle beyond tomorrow, we can arrange for your arrival at Castle Beauriél the day after tomorrow. But at least allow us to celebrate your birthday with you. Won't you please do that for me?"

Marisa remembered her promise. She owed it to him.

"I promise," she said quietly.

"Good, I'm glad to hear it," Darian replied.

"But after that, I'm gone."

He shifted uncomfortably. "I should probably tell you that Savino was inquiring after you this afternoon. He seems rather anxious to see you."

"Oh."

"That reminds me—I believe I owe you a word of thanks for informing us about the poison. In fact, I may just owe you my life."

"Now we're even," she said, remembering their encounters with the rijgen and the yarmout. "Did you find out what Savino is planning?"

"Yes. He's trying to kill me." He stood abruptly. "Good night."

"Darian, wait—"

He stopped in his tracks. "Yes?"

"I, uh, mean Your Highness," she stammered. "Are you okay with me marrying Savino?"

Darian paused. "Why should it matter what I think?"

"Because we're friends. I care what you think." *Give me a reason—give me a reason not to marry Savino.*

Long pause.

"Marisa, I told you that I cannot influence your decision one way or another. You need to do what is right for you."

Silence.

"I bid you goodnight, milady. You have a big day tomorrow, so make sure you get some rest."

"Goodnight, Sire," she said flatly. Darian turned to go back inside. Marisa stared up at the full moon and it seemed to almost tease her. She went into her chambers and took off the black dress. Slipping the nightgown over her head, she blew out the candles around the room and climbed into bed.

As she lay waiting for sleep to come, she could still see the bright light of the moon shining through her window. Savoring the fact that she would be eighteen when she woke up the next morning, her mind wandered for a while before at last she drifted off.

At last, she would be calling the shots.

CHAPTER 26
SURROGATES

THERE WAS A LOUD, impatient knock at the door. Still half-asleep, Marisa squinted at her phone and groaned. It read 6:23 a.m. She stumbled across the room and opened the door. It was Arrie, shifting uncomfortably with a look of worry on his face.

"Marisa, I am terribly sorry to wake you so early, but something rather serious has happened during the night. Would you please get dressed as quickly as possible and come downstairs?"

"Can't it wait?" she asked, irritated.

"No, I'm afraid it's extremely urgent. Shall I wait for you down in the Blue Room while you dress?"

"Yeah, okay, hang on." Marisa sighed. "I'll be down there in a few minutes." She wondered what sort of crisis would make him drag her out of bed so early.

She pulled on the first dress she could find and hastily braided her hair. Reaching for one of the slippers she'd worn the day before, she flung it across the floor in frustration when she couldn't find its mate. She grabbed a different pair of shoes and hurried down to the Blue Room in her bare feet. Marisa opened the door.

"Surprise!" People shouted from around the room.

"Oh, wow!" Her hands flew to her flushed face.

"Well, I guess you weren't expecting that, were you?" Arrie said, laughing. Adalina, Darian, Helena, and Cinzia all smiled in amusement at the bewildered look on her face.

"What is all this?" she asked, punching Arrie playfully in the arm. She saw the pile of wrapped presents. The table was dressed with a white linen tablecloth and a perfect, two-tiered birthday cake with pale yellow icing stood in the middle as its centerpiece.

"I became familiar with the surprise party tradition during my time on Earth, and we all decided it would be fun to throw you one," Arrie explained.

"But we're already having the ball. Why do I need a party too?"

Darian stepped forward. "You said it wouldn't be the same without your family here to celebrate," he said, smiling at her. "So for today, we want you to consider us your family."

Marisa stared at him, stunned. "I don't know what to say. This is one of the nicest things anyone has ever done for me."

"Happy birthday, sister," Adalina said, laughing. "Now come open your presents. Here, the first one is from my mother and me."

Cinzia beckoned to Marisa to sit next to her on the sofa.

Marisa removed the pretty purple fabric to discover a hand-carved music box. She opened the lid and listened as it played a beautiful melody.

"It's so beautiful! Thank you so much," she said to Adalina and Helena. Next, Cinzia handed her a present wrapped in silver and blue fabric. Marisa peeled off the beautiful covering to find a lovely purple mask covered in sparkling beads and feathers with a long satin handle.

"It matches your ball gown, my dear," said Cinzia.

"Thank you, Baroness! I can't wait to wear it tonight!"

"Time to open my gift, Marisa," Arrie said, handing her something heavy wrapped in brown parchment.

"Hmm, feels like a book."

"Hey, how did you guess?" Arrie asked, disappointed.

She smiled and tore the paper off. "It's *The Jane Austen Treasury.* Oh, Arrie! How did you know that I love Jane Austen?"

He smiled proudly. "It was just a wild guess. I know how popular Ms. Austen's writings are back on Earth, so I figured you probably liked her as well."

"But where in the world did you ever find this?"

"Celino had a copy for me."

"Thank you—I love it!" Marisa said, kissing him on the cheek.

"Marisa, there's one more gift on the table," said Adalina. "I think you can probably guess who it's from." She nudged Darian. He picked up the gift and shyly handed it to Marisa.

"You already gave me a castle. I don't think there's any way to top that," Marisa said. She briefly ran her fingers along the canary-and-white striped fabric before she removed it. Inside was a hand-carved, square wooden box.

Lifting the velvet-lined lid, Marisa gasped when she saw the same amethyst necklace and earrings set that she had tried on in the jewelry store. The purple stones glittered and sparkled as they caught the rays of morning sunshine.

"I don't know what to say, Your Highness. It's so beautiful."

"I am told they match your gown perfectly," Darian said, beaming at her.

"Thank you, sire." Impulsively, she kissed him on the cheek.

"Happy birthday," he whispered softly in her ear.

The hairs on Marisa's neck stood on end. Not wanting to give his family the wrong impression, she quickly stepped back. "Thank you, everyone," she said, her voice cracking with emotion. "I'm so honored to have you as my surrogate family today."

"Now let's eat a piece of that cake before we go down to breakfast," Adalina said, laughing.

After everyone had eaten a slice of the delicious cake, they all headed down to the dining room. Darian escorted Marisa down the corridor and helped her with her chair at the table. There was no sign of Savino and Matilda, so they started without the da Rocas. A half hour later, Savino and Lady Matilda appeared in the doorway.

"Ah, there is my darling," Savino said. He strode over to Marisa and kissed her sensuously on the mouth.

Adalina and Helena's jaws dropped in shock. Darian grabbed Savino's arm tightly. "Milady was just leaving the table, Savino. Today is her big day, and she has much to prepare for," he said, scowling.

"Now what kind of welcome is that for your cousin, Darian? Am I not even allowed to kiss my own fiancée?"

"You assume too much, Savino," Darian shot back angrily. "Come, Lady Marisa. I will show you back to your chambers."

Savino watched them leave with a stunned expression.

Once they reached her door, Darian turned to leave. "Milady, I shall see you later."

"Do you want to come in for a few minutes?" Marisa asked.

Darian hesitated. "Perhaps just for a few minutes." He sat down on the couch and spied her ball gown hanging in the corner. "You are going to look very beautiful in that dress this evening."

She smiled. "Leonora did an amazing job."

"Anna, may we have some tea?" Darian asked.

"Right away, Your Highness," Anna said. The young woman curtseyed and soon they were alone.

He looked at her with a serious expression. "Marisa, I really want to apologize for my neglect of you over the past few days."

"Neglect?"

"Well, I haven't been a very good host since we came back to Crocetta. Unfortunately, I've been occupied with extremely urgent matters."

"I understand, sire."

"Are you becoming acquainted with our way of life?" he asked.

Marisa studied him thoughtfully. His guard had been raised once again and now he was just making small talk. All of a sudden, she felt foolish.

"I guess. But I think it's gonna take me awhile to get used to things. I like Castle Beauriél and am planning to move in tomorrow morning if that's still possible."

"Tomorrow?" he asked, surprised. "Still you are so anxious to leave us? Marisa, are all the members of my household staff treating you well?"

"Yes, no—that's not it. Everyone's been just great."

"I deeply regret the fact that we got off to a rough start a few weeks ago. I've been trying extremely hard to make it up to you."

"I know you have," she answered.

Anna returned with a tray of tea and gently set it on the table. Darian quickly dismissed her. He poured a cup and handed it to Marisa.

"We've been through quite a lot together, and it feels almost as if you've become a member of our family." He stirred his tea and paused, searching for the right words. "Marisa, I would like to say just one more thing. No matter what happens this evening, I want you to know that I shall never forget these weeks we've spent together. And I shall always treasure your friendship."

She nodded and took a sip of tea. The regret in his eyes was clear. This was his way of saying good-bye. She'd once heard that if you love something, you should set it free. It was time to set him free. *But I love you, Darian, and I don't want to let go.* She choked down her tears.

"Why are you crying?" he said. "You cannot cry today—it's your birthday."

"I always cry on my birthday. Why break tradition?"

"Oh, that reminds me—before I go, I have something for you."

"I don't want anything else," she said.

"Just wait until you see what it is." He hurried out the door but returned a few moments later holding a terracotta pot with a small white flower. "Marisa, please take this to remember our time together. It is my sincere hope that it blooms for you soon."

"It's the wounded heart," she said, laughing through her tears.

She set the pot down and embraced him tightly knowing she would never find another man to equal him.

"I really must go back down now. I promised to take Lady Matilda for a walk after breakfast. Don't forget that we're all meeting later today for a trip out on the lake. Arrie shall fetch you."

Marisa nodded and shut the door. She gazed down at the wounded heart. The flower was still shut tight with its ugly brown center. The irony of the plant's name didn't escape her. Her own heart had been mortally wounded.

As Marisa sank down into the soft mattress, she thought about her birthday the year before, and how her father, brother, and uncle had all surprised her with a birthday party. She missed them all so much. The thought that she might never see them for the rest of her life filled her with an overwhelming sadness.

Marisa stood all alone in the garden at Beauriél, soaking in the peace of the country air and admiring the lushness of the trees. The spring flowers were already starting to bloom once again as she quietly sipped a cup of tea.

Without warning, a rijgen rushed out of the forest and bared its teeth as it charged straight toward her. Her porcelain teacup fell onto the stone terrace and shattered into a thousand pieces as her screamed pierced the peaceful stillness.

Just as the beast was about to pounce on top of her, Darian leapt between her and the beast and swept his sword in a broad arc through the creature's midsection. The animal's body fell forward on the terrace.

Frozen in fear, she watched as it slumped to the ground, its blood quickly spreading across the stones. She turned to thank Darian for saving her but his stony eyes glared at her with a cold stare.

Suddenly a man shouted her name, and Marisa turned to see Savino coming out of the castle, striding toward her with orange flames shooting out from his eyes and mouth.

Terrified, she turned back to Darian, but both he and the slain beast were gone. There was no sign of the creature's body or the blood. Savino continued to advance toward her menacingly as he shouted her name.

Marisa awoke with a start. Her palms were sweaty and shaking. The nightmares had been occurring more frequently. She took a sip of water from the cup on her nightstand and tried to slow her breathing. The image of Savino breathing fire had been burned on her retina and was not one she could easily forget.

As the mid-afternoon sun streamed through the windows of her room, she lunged for her phone and saw that it read 2:38 p.m. The afternoon outing would be getting underway in twenty minutes, so she didn't have much time to get ready.

Rushing to her closet to find something warm to wear, she scolded herself that she'd slept so long. She slipped into a pumpkin-and-brown dress with a camel riding jacket and hat. She splashed water on her face and loosened her hair from the braid, hastily brushing it out. Deciding it would be windy on the lake, she braided it back up again.

Marisa tapped on the earpiece twice to make sure it was working. She was thankful for the small device. As she finished getting ready, there was a hasty knock at the door.

"Is the birthday girl ready to go?" Arrie asked, smiling cheerfully and offering her his arm.

"As ready as I'll ever be," she said with a sigh.

CHAPTER 27
EXCURSION

THE CASTLE WAS BUSTLING with activity as Marisa followed Arrie across the ancient courtyard. She was amazed at how the citadel had been totally transformed from the somber, dreary house of mourning the day before into a festive, party-like atmosphere for her birthday ball.

Colorful, velvet banners hung on poles all the way from the castle gate up to the entrance of the Knights' Hall. The purple carpet had been rolled out, and in just a few short hours, guests would be lining up for their chance to walk down it to attend the masked ball. Anybody who was anybody would be arriving soon in their fancy costume, ready to mingle with royalty and the country's elite.

"I gotta say, I'm pretty intimidated," Marisa said.

"Nonsense!" Arrie replied. "You're the most exotic creature these people have ever seen."

"They must not get out much."

"Now, remember—we must keep up the pretense that you are a mute around Savino, his minions, and Lady Matilda, at least until this evening," he cautioned her.

"What happens this evening?" she asked curiously.

He held his finger to his lips as they approached and entered the stables. Inside, there was a small circle of guests waiting to go on their outing. Savino saw her approach and rushed over with a sly smile.

"Marisa, come—you must ride with me in my carriage."

He took her hand and led her over to a white carriage. She noticed Darian was engaged in a private conversation with Lady Matilda and she quickly looked away.

On the surface, Marisa was calm and smiling, but deep down she was trembling with fear. The nightmarish images of Savino were still fresh in her mind. Perhaps she had only imagined it, but when he took her hand, it felt like a chunk of ice. She glanced over her shoulder at Arrie and relayed a silent SOS message to him.

He saw her plight and strolled over. "I will be acting as my cousin's chaperone this afternoon," Arrie said sternly.

Savino's jaw dropped as Arrie hopped in and plunked down across from them. When Gaspar climbed in and sat down next to Arrie, Savino was unable to hide his disappointment and he turned to stare out the window. Marisa breathed a sigh of relief as she realized she wouldn't be forced to ride alone with him.

The carriage lurched forward and Marisa peered through the rear window. Darian's attention was focused on Lady Matilda. He helped her into the carriage and sat down next to her. Helena, Adalina, and Cinzia stepped into the last carriage at the rear.

As they rode in a convoy down through the streets toward the edge of the city, the people stopped to look, bow, and wave. Savino ignored the crowds, calling them "peasants," but Marisa and Arrie waved politely to the people as they passed.

Savino held Marisa's hand in the carriage, but for the most part, he remained formal toward her. Arrie stared at him during the journey, almost daring him to make a move. Marisa tried not to giggle at the frown of disapproval on Arrie's face. His antics in playing the role of the austere chaperone were highly entertaining.

She glanced out the window as they passed the gated entrance to Castle Beauriél. She exchanged knowing glances with Arrie.

"Is there something interesting to see here?" Savino asked suspiciously.

"Only if you're a Fiore," Arrie said.

Savino exhaled a puff of air and stared out the window. She smiled at Arrie when she saw his triumphant smirk. Clearly he didn't like Savino any more than Darian did.

Thirty minutes later, the three carriages arrived at a boat landing on the edge of a large lake. The water was surrounded on three sides by mountains, and it reminded Marisa a little of Crater Lake. She stepped out of the carriage and gasped as Arrie pointed to the royal ship moored to the dock.

The beak of the galleon rose and fell slightly as the waves lapped softly against the hull. Three tall masts were connected by a tangled mass of ropes and ladders. A royal standard whipped in the wind at the peak of the tallest mast. Crew members scurried all around the ship, preparing to set sail.

Darian led the guests down to the dock and invited everyone to board. Savino had not let go of Marisa's hand since the moment they'd first stepped into the carriage. As each guest crossed the narrow gangplank to board the vessel one by one, she finally had the excuse to wrestle free of his grasp. She noticed that Darian and Savino seemed to be avoiding each other like the plague.

Once everyone was aboard, Darian gave orders to set sail, and the captain signaled the men to unfurl the sails. The burgundy-colored canvas unrolled to catch the wind and a cold wind hit Marisa's face.

The oak timbers creaked and groaned with every rise and fall of the ship. She gripped the railing firmly as she admired the view of the high, snow-capped mountains on the other side. The weather was cloudy but dry, and her cape flapped in the breeze as the wind whipped across her face and hair.

On the opposite side of the ship, Darian and Matilda were engaged in deep conversation. Unable to watch them together, Marisa turned to stare out across the cold waves. Hopefully, she wouldn't be expected to attend the royal wedding. The worst thing she could imagine would be to stand by and watch the man she loved marry someone else. She needed time and space away from Darian to allow her heart to heal. Although she was happy for him and wished him well, she could not bear to stick around to watch him pledge his life to someone else. *Just a few more hours and you won't have to see the two lovebirds anymore.*

Cinzia noticed Marisa standing at the railing alone and she approached her cautiously. "Why is there such gloom on this beautiful young face?" she asked so the others couldn't hear.

Marisa hesitated, not sure if she could share her secret. Finally, she glanced over her shoulder at Darian and laid her hand over her heart, motioning the thumping rhythm of a human heartbeat. A single tear slipped down her cheek.

Without a word, Cinzia followed Marisa's gaze to Darian and Matilda. The intimate manner in which the two of them conducted themselves could not have been mistaken for anything else except mutual love and respect and the source of Marisa's pain was all too apparent. The middle-aged woman who had lost her husband years ago was sympathetic to all forms of unrequited love.

Although the two women's circumstances were different, they were bound together though their own versions of heartbreak and disappointment. Marisa knew in that instant that even after she left the palace, she would still have true friends in Carnelia. It energized her with fresh hope.

Arrie found Marisa and Cinzia and offered to escort them below for afternoon tea. They descended the steps into the spacious captain's quarters at the rear of the ship, where a large table had been set with an assortment of exotic food and drinks.

Savino coaxed Marisa to sit next to him at the end of the table. Darian, Matilda, and Darian's mother sat and the opposite end. Unable to hear the conversation on the opposite side, Marisa decided that it was probably for the best. Darian stood and raised his glass to make a toast.

"First of all, I would like to welcome you all for joining us today. We've all withstood some very difficult times, but tonight we will be celebrating a new start for our country. This afternoon is simply a taste of things yet to come."

Savino coughed loudly.

Darian ignored his cousin's thinly-veiled distraction. "Second of all, I hope that you will all join me in wishing a supremely happy birthday to our lovely guest, Lady Marisa. *Ap eirie!*"

"*Ap eirie*," everyone shouted in unison as they all stood to toast.

Marisa stood and raised her glass as she dipped a small curtsey. Everyone around the table raised their glasses and took a sip of wine. As he sat back down, Arrie missed his chair. His hand flew out to catch himself, but instead he accidentally knocked over Matilda's wine and water goblets. The wine quickly bled into the linen tablecloth, and a servant appeared to clean up the mess.

"Oh, do forgive me, Lady Matilda," Arrie said as he scrambled to sop up the dampened tablecloth with his napkin.

"No harm done, Lord Arrigo," Matilda said sweetly. The steward quickly replaced her empty glass with a full one as Marisa looked at Arrie and giggled.

When the meal had concluded, Darian suggested they all try their hand at fishing before returning to the dock. Everyone jumped up from the table and hurried outside on the deck.

"Marisa, you are going to love this!" Arrie said excitedly as he shoved a fishing rod in her hand. "Have you ever caught a fish with *wings?*"

Her eyes widened. "*Wings?*"

"We call it *flegan* fishing. Flegan means flying in Crocine. The fish are quite large, sometimes as large as a man, and they have enormous wings they use when trying to get away. If you aren't careful, they can pull you right up out of the boat!"

Arrie laughed at her stunned expression and stuck a chunk of bait on the hook. "Now, let's see if you can fish," he said, squinting into the sun as he tossed the line into the water.

Marisa's eyes scanned the deck. Savino had gone below and everyone else was on the other side of the ship. "Arrie," she whispered, "have Darian and Matilda set a wedding date yet?"

"What are you talking about? What gave you the idea those two are to be married?" He glanced over his shoulder and watched as Darian helped Matilda slip the bait on her hook.

She lowered her voice. "C'mon, Arrie, I'm not stupid. I can see what's going on here."

"What are you talking about?"

"If you don't tell me right now what's going on, I'm gonna go to Darian and ask him."

He glanced around nervously. "Please, Marisa—I'm not supposed to talk about this. You don't understand what's at stake."

"You're right, I don't, but I'd sure like to."

"I can't explain it right now. Trust me—I want to, but I can't."

Her shoulders sank. "All right, I won't make you break your promise. You've been such a good friend to me."

He stopped. "Wait a minute. What promise?"

"Arrie, I know everything. I heard you and Darian discussing the engagement that night after I fell in the ice caves. I was in my tent, and you were lying next to the fire. He made you promise not to say anything."

A look of realization came over him. "Oh, that. Wait a minute—you heard *that*?"

She nodded at him knowingly.

He sighed. "How much did you hear?"

"Enough to know that Darian is secretly engaged to Matilda."

Arrie rubbed his beard, eyeing her thoughtfully. His expression turned serious. "Marisa, you must promise to keep silent about all of this. Savino must not discover this or there will be extremely serious consequences for Darian."

Just then, Savino ascended the steps and approached them. Right before he came within earshot, she whispered, "I promise."

"Well, it appears that I've interrupted something here," Savino said suspiciously as his gaze shifted between their faces.

She gasped at the sharp tug on her fishing pole. If she hadn't been holding it so tightly in her hands, it would have been ripped right out of them.

"Marisa, you've got something on your hook!" Arrie cried.

He grabbed the pole to help her steady it. Her rod bent over into a C as the fishing line disappeared down deep under the boat. They struggled to hold on as the others ran over to their side of the boat.

"Let go of the pole!" Arrie yelled.

Marisa let it go. Arrie was yanked up and over the side of the ship just as an enormous fish with webbed wings burst out of the water and took flight. The gigantic, blue-green sparkling fish whipped its wings furiously as it tried to escape its captor. Arrie laughed and whooped as he was pulled through the air behind the monstrous fish. He screamed at the horrified spectators below.

"Look at me! *I'm flying!*"

All of a sudden, the fish dove down into the water, pulling Arrie along with it. For a moment, there was no sign of either fish or man. The people on the boat scanned the water's surface for any sign of Arrie, but it was calm.

Without warning, the fish burst up out of the water. Marisa was relieved to see Arrie still clutching the pole as he gasped for air. He coughed and sputtered, shaking the water from his head. The fish shot upwards and Arrie was dragged once more up into the sky.

Darian spun around and ran down into the ship. He reappeared seconds later with a long bow in one hand and six arrows in the other. He drew the bow and aimed it carefully, letting the first arrow fly. It missed the fish, shooting past it, and Darian quickly reloaded.

Shooting once again, the second arrow pierced the fish near the tail, but it didn't wound it enough to bring it down. The third arrow struck the fish just under the wing, and the mighty creature fell down to the water.

Both the fish and Arrie hit the surface with a gigantic splash. The large beast began to sink beneath the waves, but Arrie was nowhere in sight. Cinzia and Marisa stood helplessly at the ship's railing as they leaned over and scanned the water in search of the redheaded young man.

Finally, Arrie broke the surface and inhaled a gulp of air. Darian tossed him a rope which he quickly tied around his waist. Several members of the crew pulled him back onboard. He collapsed onto the deck, drenched and exhausted.

Taking deep breaths, Arrie slowly rose to his feet and strutted across the deck toward Marisa. He grinned triumphantly at her and handed Darian the fishing rod, which was still intact.

"Milady, I have risked life and limb to catch for you a choice delicacy to be served to your birthday guests this evening. Are you not pleased with my efforts?" He bowed proudly to Marisa, grinning at her and dripping wet.

She laughed and hugged him, shaking her head.

Arrie saluted Darian and dismissed himself to go change his clothes below decks. The captain collected everyone's fishing gear in preparation to return to the docks. Everyone watched as the crew drug the giant dead fish out of the water and heaved it into the boat.

Gazing out over the water, Marisa hated to admit it, but she was going to miss the outings, carriage rides, beautiful dresses, lavish dinners, enchanting balls, plus all the other amazing perks that came with royal life. It certainly had its charms.

Without warning, the sounds of someone retching filled the air and everyone turned to look. Matilda was buckled over the railing and vomiting heavily over the side. Darian hurried to her side and offered her his handkerchief. "Mattie, are you all right? Are you seasick?"

When she turned to him, her face was as white as a sheet. "Why yes, I am a little queasy, I must be—" Unable to finish her sentence, she threw up over the side again and again. All of a sudden, she sank to the deck.

Darian moved to catch her and he carried her down into the captain's stateroom. The guests huddled together as they exchanged concerned glances. A few minutes later, Darian emerged.

"Matilda is seriously ill and in need of a physician's attention. I'm afraid we must cut our trip short and return immediately."

A somber mood fell over the ship as they moved full speed ahead back toward the dock. Within minutes, the ship had returned to their starting point. As soon as the ship had berthed and the lines had been secured to the dock, Darian quickly carried Matilda ashore. The waiting carriage sped off the moment the door closed behind them.

While everyone quietly and calmly disembarked the ship to return to their carriages, Marisa was troubled by Matilda's sudden illness. Not a word was spoken as the carriage sped back to Crocetta.

When it came to a stop inside the stables, Savino hopped out and extended his hand to Marisa. "I shall see you again this evening, but for now I must go tend to my sister," he said, hastily kissing her hand.

She nodded at him. Savino and Gaspar hurried out of the stables and up toward the citadel. Marisa just stood there quietly, still trying to decide what to make of it all.

Arrie's face was puzzled. "What was all that about?" he asked.

"I don't know—but he was sure acting strange."

"You mean more than usual?"

She stopped, bothered. "You don't think he would poison Matilda intentionally, do you?"

"What? Poison his sister? Don't be ridiculous."

"I'm just sayin…"

"To be certain, the man cannot be trusted, but I do not believe he would try to kill his own flesh and blood."

She shook her head. "I've been deep-sea fishing enough to know that she wasn't seasick."

"Why do you say that?"

"Seasickness comes on more gradual than that. Matilda was chatting and laughing one minute, and then, bam! The next minute she's losing her lunch over the side."

"Hmm, perhaps…"

"Did you see that pastiness in her face? When someone is seasick, they have that nasty yellow or green tinge, but never that pale color."

"But what could his motivation possibly be?" Arrie asked.

"Maybe he'd rather see Matilda dead than married to Darian."

"Savino cares too much about his sister to kill her."

Marisa shook her head. "In any case, we've got to let Darian know. He could still be in danger. I just hope it's not too late for Matilda."

"She'll recover. If he had actually intended to poison her, she would have been dead on the boat."

"Not necessarily…"

"I still think it was seasickness."

"Not me. I'm not convinced."

"Marisa, it's getting late now. I think you should go get ready for the ball while I find out what's going on."

"Okay. Wait—do you think the ball is even still happening with her being sick and all?"

"I'm certain it would not be cancelled on such short notice."

"Why not?"

"There are far too many people who have traveled from considerable distances. Now please don't worry about a thing. I shall meet you at the main staircase at half past six."

CHAPTER 28
MASQUERADE

WHEN SHE RETURNED TO her chambers, Marisa saw that Anna had cleaned the room and there was a pleasant smell. She was feeling sleepy and the fresh linens on the bed were beckoning to her, but there was no way she could get out of going to the ball.

She collapsed on the bed and stared up at the ceiling. The lavishly furnished suite was decidedly different from her room back home. Thoughts of Jacksonville drifted into her mind as pangs of homesickness hit her once again. She wondered what her best friend Danielle would say if she knew she was the guest of honor at a masquerade ball thrown by a rich prince. Marisa smiled to herself. No one back home would ever believe her in a million years.

Motioning to Anna to draw her bathwater, she stepped out onto the balcony for some fresh air. She wasn't thinking about Darian or Savino or about Matilda getting sick but about what her life would be like the next day.

As she spotted a full moon on the rise, somehow she knew she'd always look back on this birthday as being the key turning point in her life. Although there were hundreds of question marks still hanging in the air all around her, only one seemed important at the moment.

She took a deep breath and bowed her head in prayer.

Garon, I don't know where my life is going, but one thing I do know is that I need purpose. I want my life to matter. I'm afraid of what will happen tomorrow. I'm afraid of being on my own. Please give me courage to stop doubting myself and give me wisdom to recognize the truth. Point me in the way I need to go. Amen.

Marisa exhaled deeply and opened her eyes. She heard a commotion down in the courtyard and leaned over to take a look. Far below her, Darian was stepping into a carriage. Even from where she stood high above him, she could still recognize his tall frame as he ducked his head. The carriage rolled down toward the gate. A wooden wagon followed it across the courtyard.

When the carriage and wagon had disappeared under the ramparts, she went inside to take her bath, wondering where Darian could be going so late in the day. Hopefully he wouldn't arrive too late at the ball he was hosting.

As she sat in the tub and reflected on all that had happened since she'd landed in Carnelia, time seemed to stand still. She thought about meeting Darian and Arrie on the path, their night in Andresis and when they were chased through the forest by the rijgen. She remembered how shocked she was by the size of the warriors and how the incredible landscape of the country had stunned her. There was the hike to the waterfall, the bizarre negotiations at the dinner table, and the ball at Abbadon where Darian kissed her. And then on the trip back to Crocetta, who could forget their stop by the lake and her brush with death in the ice caves?

After she had retraced their entire journey from start to finish, she was feeling nostalgic but her bathwater was cold. She washed and rinsed her hair until it shone. It was important she look special on the night she would say farewell to them all. She stepped out and dried off.

Anna fastened her into the corset and pulled the strings so tightly that she almost couldn't breathe.

"It must be tight for the gown to fit correctly," Anna said.

Marisa wondered how she was supposed to eat, drink, and breathe wearing such a constrictive undergarment. Anna gently lowered the ball gown over her head and Marisa marveled at the most exquisite dress she'd ever worn. Tailored to fit the slender curves of her body perfectly, the purple, lavender, and ivory colors complemented her reddish-brown hair, hazel eyes, and fair skin. She slipped into a pair of matching shoes encrusted with purple beads and she was relieved to discover that they fit her size-ten feet perfectly.

On the dressing table lay the wooden box from Darian containing the beautiful necklace, earrings, and bracelet set. She fastened the solid gold choker at the nape of her neck and gasped at its beauty. Anna worked on her hair, twisting several pieces into a flowing style and fastening them on the top of her head. Marisa struggled to fasten the bracelet using just one hand and inserted the dangling earrings.

Anna eyed her from top to bottom. "Now remember, don't put on your gloves until right before you go down," she said. "You look so pretty in that dress, milady. Enjoy yourself this evening."

"Thank you, Anna." The young woman smiled at her before leaving the room with a small curtsey.

Marisa inhaled deeply and strode over to the full-length mirror. She was a tight bundle of nerves and her palms were sweating again. Unsure of whether she could make it through the entire evening, Marisa secretly hoped it would pass quickly. Then she remembered Savino.

He would be expecting her to dance with him for most of the ball. He would also be expecting an answer to his proposal. She already knew how she felt about him in her heart, but she was still trying to frame an answer in her head.

She gazed into the mirror and gasped as she saw her mother's reflection staring back at her. In that moment, it felt as if Marisa was peering directly into her past. She covered her face with the feathered mask. It was suddenly a painful fact to Marisa that neither her father nor her mother was alive to see her.

She jumped as she read her phone's display of 6:27 p.m. She grabbed her gloves and gathered up her skirts before hurrying down the corridor toward the main staircase. As she heard Arrie and Darian's hushed voices at the bottom of the vestibule, she stopped abruptly.

"…can't believe Savino is capable of something like that. Why would he kill his own sister?" Arrie whispered.

"He would prefer her dead than married to me. That should tell you just how determined he is to take the crown," Darian said softly.

Marisa's heart sank when Darian mentioned Matilda, but she quickly reminded herself that she only had one more night to get through.

"Are you still planning to make the announcement? Even though Matilda won't be present?" Arrie whispered.

Darian hesitated. "I believe I have no choice. Her life is in even greater danger now than it was just a few days ago. We must make sure we can protect her."

"Have you taken the necessary precautions?"

"I've already arranged for double guards posted throughout the citadel tonight," Darian whispered. "Some are disguised as guests standing by just in case."

"Who knows how he'll react to your announcement."

"I've learned not to underestimate my cousin."

Marisa wiped her sweaty palms on the skirt of her dress and exhaled. The tightness of the corset prevented her from breathing normally and she was already starting to feel lightheaded.

"You did ask Marisa to be here at 6:30, correct?" asked Darian.

"Yes, she should be here any minute now."

She didn't want them to know she'd been eavesdropping, so she waited for another minute or two. Unable to put it off any longer, she slipped on her gloves and lifted the mask to her face. She inhaled as deeply as the corset would allow and descended the grand staircase. Her dainty-gloved hand slid down the polished wooden railing as she fought to keep her shaky knees from buckling under her. The last thing she needed was to take a nasty tumble down those stairs.

When they heard the rustle of her skirts and the clicking of her heels on the marble steps, Darian and Arrie both turned. The two young men who had discovered a lost and frightened girl just a few weeks ago were now spellbound by the same beautiful woman floating down to them with grace and poise.

Darian's face was half-covered by an elaborate mask, but Marisa's heart skipped a beat as soon as she saw him. The most handsome man she had ever known waited at the bottom of those stairs, but when the night was through, she would never see him again.

Darian stretched out his hand to her. "You are the most beautiful woman in the world tonight," he said, drinking her in from top to bottom. Blushing at his words, she smiled shyly as he escorted her down the long corridor toward the Knights' Hall.

Arrie smiled. "Smashing, cousin. Simply smashing."

"You're just saying that because you're my cousin." She giggled nervously. They reached the door to the hall and she looked at Darian. "By the way, how is Lady Matilda?"

He lifted his mask. "Mattie is expected to recover but is still terribly sick. She will not be joining us this evening."

"I'm so sorry, sire."

"Please, Marisa, do not call me that."

"Ugh! I'm sorry—I meant Your Royal Highness." She shook her head, embarrassed. "Don't worry—you'll only have to put up with me for one more night."

"That's not what I meant," Darian said with a sigh. He placed his hand on the enormous door handle. "Ready?"

She nodded nervously like a debutante at her coming-out ball. As he guided her into the noisy hall, large crowds of people all turned to stare and a hush fell over the room. The eyes of the Carnelian nobility were all fixed on Miss Marisa MacCallum from Jacksonville, Oregon.

Spotting Adalina and Helena, she began to move toward them but Darian stopped her as a uniformed man with gray hair marched forward. He carried a long stick made of bronze and wood and slammed it to the ground three times, commanding the attention of the entire room.

"Ladies, gentlemen, knights, and lords! Announcing His Royal Highness Prince Darian Fiore and the Lady Marisa MacCallum!"

271

She fought to suppress a giggle. The man was shouting so loud that everyone inside the hall and probably outside the hall could hear him. All the guests bowed and curtseyed to Darian and Marisa as they moved to the front of the hall.

"Now that the first part is over, shall we have something to drink before we meet the guests in the reception line?" Darian whispered.

"Reception line?"

"Of course," he answered with a smile. "You didn't think you were off the hook yet, did you?"

"I was kinda hoping..."

He smiled at her. "Many powerful people from all parts of the country have come here tonight to meet you. And they won't leave until they do."

He handed her a crystal goblet filled with sparkling fruit juice. She chugged it down nervously as he stared at her in shock and amusement.

"You didn't finish that already, did you? No, Marisa—you must sip it slowly. It's wine from my family's vineyard. Very sweet, but you have to be careful," he said, chuckling. "Come, let's welcome our guests."

She felt giddy as she followed him toward the throne platform where the guests had already lined up to meet them. She watched as the gray-haired man approached them again.

"He will announce each of the guests by their name and title," Darian whispered. "When they bow and curtsey, you only need to smile and nod your head in acknowledgment."

"I don't curtsey?"

"No—you would grow tired very quickly with several hundred guests. Unless you want to try," he joked.

Marisa's head was swimming as the man announced each of the guests one by one. Sometimes he would introduce a couple together. There seemed to be far more men at the assembly than women.

Each man stepped up to kiss her hand as they were introduced as dukes, earls, barons, counts, marquises, and lords. Marisa would never be able to remember all their names and titles, but that didn't stop her from trying. The line moved along slowly and she nodded to each of the noblemen and women as they filed on past. Her corset was starting to seriously hamper her movement and it became increasingly difficult for her to breathe.

After greeting the last guest in the line, she was extremely grateful for her beautiful yet sensible shoes. Her back was stiff, and she wanted desperately to sit down.

It dawned on her that if Matilda had not gotten sick, she would have been standing alongside Darian as hostess now instead of Marisa. She was beginning to wonder if Matilda's brother still planned to come to the ball.

"No sign yet of Savino?" she asked.

Darian's smile faded. "Not yet. He usually likes to make an entrance." He led her to the center of the floor and took her hand in his.

"This is the part where we kick off the evening with a dance."

"Thanks for the advance warning," Marisa muttered. Her eyes roamed the crowds of people craning to get a better look. They were all wearing masks so it was difficult to see their expressions.

As he led her effortlessly across the floor, she recognized it was the dance that Arrie had taught her at Abbadon. She was trying to concentrate on her steps, but the corset was becoming increasingly uncomfortable underneath her dress. Darian seemed to notice her anxiety.

"Just imagine they're all stone statues and we're the only two real people here," he whispered. "It's what I always do when I get nervous about speaking in public."

"You nervous? Somehow I find that hard to believe. Especially after watching how shy you are about mowing down the rijgen and the yarmout," she giggled.

He chuckled. "That's a little different."

As they danced close together, Marisa's heartbeat quickened. She reminded herself that he was engaged to another woman but his irresistible charm and charisma held her attention like a powerful magnet. The mask hid the upper half of his face, but she could still see a smirk playing around his lips.

"And just *what* is so amusing, sire?"

He grinned, displayed his perfect, white teeth. "Oh, I was just remembering the first time I saw you with that lost, scared look on your face. I knew I could not remain suspicious of you for very long."

"It was all just an elaborate act, you know," she teased. "How do you know I'm not spying for Savino after all?"

He lifted his mask. "Call it royal intuition."

"Royal intuition?"

"Yes, it's a kind of sixth sense—you just know that you know something. You don't know how you know, but you just know that you know."

"Yes, I can see the logic in that."

He spun her around and she saw the crystal chandeliers sparkling above her like a thousand tiny diamonds. It was a night she would never forget. She didn't want to think about starting her life over without him so she pushed it from her mind. For one more night, she wanted to be Cinderella before making her escape at midnight.

The song ended but Darian didn't let go. When the spell finally broke, they looked around and noticed they were the only two still out on the floor. He offered her an arm and they walked to the refreshments table.

"Are you hungry, milady?"

"Yeah, starving actually."

"What would you like to eat?" He pointed to the buffet table filled with food. "How about some of Arrie's flegan fish caught with much effort in your honor?"

Marisa laughed as she pictured Arrie flying through the air, only to be dragged back down under the waves by the giant fish. She followed Darian's lead and loaded her plate with food. Some of the other hungry guests noticed them and began to help themselves.

"Would you like to go outside?" Darian asked. He was balancing two goblets of wine in one hand and his full plate in the other.

"I'd like that," she said softly.

He led her under the stone archway, across the courtyard, and up the rampart steps. The sounds of the music and ball drifted further into the background until she felt as if they were the only ones there.

Marisa set her plate down and began to eat. She was hungry, and the food tasted good on her empty stomach.

"I haven't seen Celino yet. I thought that he'd been invited."

Darian pulled off his mask. "He was invited. I was expecting him to arrive very soon, in fact. I hope nothing is keeping him."

"Well, it's a shame if he doesn't show. He's one of the few people I can actually have a conversation with," she said, frowning.

She gazed up into the night sky. She couldn't see the stars behind the dark rain clouds and hoped the impending rain showers wouldn't make it too difficult for the guests to get home later.

"So, have you given Savino an answer yet?" he asked.

"I, uh—no, not yet," she said. "I've actually been having second thoughts about accepting his offer."

Darian clenched his jaw. "Second thoughts?"

"Yeah, I just don't think I can go through with it," she said, stroking the feathers on her mask. "I'm not ready to get married, and besides, I don't love him."

He took a sip of wine. "Someday the right man will come along and you'll be glad you waited."

"Yeah, well, I'm not holding my breath."

You are the right man for me, Darian. If only that stupid law didn't exist. If only you weren't a prince.

"Your Highness," she began, "I just wanted to say I'm glad we bumped into each other. I wouldn't have gotten through these past few weeks without yours and Arrie's help. Thank you."

"You are very welcome, milady."

Awkward silence.

He pulled the mask back over his face. "I think we'd better get back in to the guests now."

She nodded and finished her goblet of wine a little too quickly. As they returned to the ball, all eyes followed Marisa as she floated over to Adalina and Helena.

"Are you enjoying the ball, Marisa?" Adalina asked. She was

breathtaking in a scarlet gown and matching jeweled mask. Her raven-black hair was swept up onto her head, and her ruby necklace and earrings sparkled in the candlelight.

"It's amazing, Your Highness."

Out of the corner of her eye, Marisa suddenly saw him. Dressed from top to bottom in an ornate silver and white outfit, Savino stood head and shoulders above the other guests. His eyes roamed the crowd and stopped when he saw Marisa. She quickly turned her back and ducked down behind some guests as she scanned the room for Darian. When she spotted him in the far corner chatting with some men, she groaned. He was too far away to see her plight—

"Lady Marisa—may I please have the honor of this dance?"

Slowly, she turned to see Lord Domenico grinning and bowing to her just as Savino was approaching. Savino quickly took a step back, but there was a flash of jealous fury in his eyes.

Marisa smiled and curtseyed to Domenico. As they strolled out onto the dance floor, she deliberately avoided Savino's stare.

"Although I cannot speak your language, milady, I was delighted to hear from Prince Darian that you are learning ours," Domenico commented softly.

She smiled and nodded. Her eyes darted around the room, searching for Savino. There he was—over by the refreshments and still watching them closely. No matter what happened, she could not let Savino see her lips moving.

"It has been many months since I danced with such a beautiful woman," he continued. "I'm afraid I might be a little out of practice."

Something in Domenico's voice made her forget about Savino for the moment. She looked in his eyes and saw hope. This was a man with his own story. He wasn't Darian's clone—he was distinctly his own person. He had endearing features such as the dimple on his chin and the crinkles in the corner of his dark brown eyes.

"What is your first name, Lord Domenico?" she asked.

He stared at her, puzzled.

She pointed to herself, *"Marisa MacCallum."* Then she pointed to him. *"Domenico—"*

"Ah, yes. My name is Luca. Luca Domenico."

"Luca." She smiled. "Luca Domenico. What a nice name."

He grinned. "Although I do not understand half of what you are saying, milady, when you speak my name, it sounds so intriguing."

Marisa smiled at him and realized there might just be life post-Darian after all. She had to admit she was attracted to Domenico and wanted to know him better. Perhaps she would get the opportunity once she left the castle. But she was getting way too ahead of herself.

"I hope you shall afford me this pleasure again in the future," Domenico said with a broad smile. After the dance had ended, he kissed her hand and Marisa was amused. He certainly was charming.

A cold hand touched her shoulder.

"Lady Marisa—may I have the honor of this next dance?"

Marisa turned and sucked in her breath. Even with a mask almost covering them, Savino's ice-blue eyes were hypnotizing. She curtseyed and he led her to out to the dance floor. Her hands were trembling.

"Alone at last," Savino joked as he saw the crowds of people watching them. "You are absolutely stunning this evening, Lady Marisa. Was this dress of your own design, or did my cousin pick it out for you?"

Marisa motioned that she had chosen the dress.

"It appears that everyone in the kingdom has come to your birthday party," he said. "People are exceedingly curious to know who you truly are."

She raised the mask to her face and avoided his gaze. Unable to see his expression, she was glad he couldn't see hers.

"I'm so looking forward to getting to know you better once we're married. And I'm especially looking forward to the *wedding night*," he whispered.

At his words, she cringed. The wine had gone right to her head and she was starting to feel groggy. She searched the sea of faces but couldn't find Darian anywhere. A wave of nausea filled her head. She had to get out of there and find someplace to sit down.

Savino stopped as a look of recognition registered in his eyes.

"Do you know, I have the strange feeling that we've met somewhere before," he said suspiciously. He stared into her face as he tried to remember where he'd seen her before.

Marisa shrugged nervously, tried to act casual. She scanned the room frantically but still there was no sign of Darian in the packed hall.

He was here just a minute ago—where did he go?

Savino shook his head. "No, I must be mistaken. I'm quite certain we've never met before you came to Abbadon, so I must be thinking of someone else."

A sense of panic began to rise up inside her as she thought about her dream earlier that afternoon. She knew what Savino was thinking, and what he was about to ask, and what she was going to say, and how he'd react—

"So, I believe it's time for you to give me an answer to my proposal, Lady Marisa," he said. "Will you be my bride and share the throne with me as my queen?" He bowed deeply before her as several people ceased their conversations and turned to watch. The hall suddenly grew silent.

Marisa gulped. *Garon give me strength. Don't leave me now.*

She stopped dancing and took a step back. All sets of eyes in the room were fixed on her. Her hand shook as she slowly lowered her mask to gaze into Savino's crystal blue eyes—beautiful eyes that she knew were connected to a cold heart. Dipping into a deep curtsey of respect, she shook her head and stared at the floor, too terrified to see his reaction.

Savino stopped and his body stiffened. He said nothing for a moment but then raised himself up to his full height and glared at her like a stone statue.

Marisa slowly lifted her gaze. The expression on his face was the same one she'd seen in her nightmare that afternoon.

And now it was coming true.

CHAPTER 29

DISCLOSURE

"*WHAT!*" Savino shouted at her in anger. She took a step backward as a flurry of whispers shot back and forth across the room. A wave of nausea, which had begun in her stomach, was now slowly rising toward her head.

"How *dare* you reject me, you ungrateful wench!"

"Savino—stop this at once!" Darian said loudly, rushing to Marisa's side. "She has a right to answer you any way she so desires."

"This is your fault, Darian," Savino screamed. "You have made her refuse me!"

"I've done nothing of the sort," Darian said, removing his mask. "The decision is her own."

"There shall be no peace treaty, and neither shall you ascend the throne. This is an act of war, and I hold you both responsible!"

"Cousin, lower your voice. Let us discuss this in private."

Savino ignored Darian and approached Marisa, stabbing angrily at her with his finger. "You have humiliated your future king. I shall *never* forget this," he hissed.

Darian motioned to the guards. "Arrest this man, but do not remove him until he has heard what I have to say."

The guards moved to shackle Savino's hands together. As he struggled to resist, he was still spewing venom at Darian.

"Cousin, you too shall regret what you did here today!"

Darian ignored him.

"Lords, knights, ladies, and gentlemen—may I have your attention, please?" he announced in a loud voice.

The storm of chatter and whispers quickly died down.

"As you all are already aware, tonight you have been invited here to celebrate the eighteenth birthday of a remarkable woman, the Lady Marisa MacCallum. I would like to thank you all for coming to meet her and to help us celebrate on this joyous occasion.

"What you aren't yet aware of is that we are also gathered here to celebrate a new beginning and a new chapter in the history of our country."

Marisa's legs wobbled underneath her as she fought to remain standing. The queasy feeling in the pit of her stomach had already risen to her head, and everything was starting to swirl around her. Her eyes searched the room for an empty chair as Darian continued.

"For too many years, our lands have suffered in a state of turmoil. For too long, our nation has suffered from a lack of leadership and under the banner of oppression." The guests were becoming restless as noisy whispers resonated through the large hall.

Darian held up his hands to silence the crowds.

"Tonight everything is about to change. This evening we shall begin uniting the country once again and picking up the pieces."

As the crowds broke out into spontaneous cheering and clapping, Marisa wanted to fade into the woodwork.

I'm gonna hurl right here in front of all these important people.

"It is especially fitting that we are celebrating tonight with a masked ball, for this evening represents the literal unmasking of the future of our country. It is my highest honor and privilege to present to you our true sovereign ruler who, by the mercy and might of Garon, has been returned safely to us—"

The bile rose in her throat as she scanned for the nearest exit.

"—Her Royal Highness Princess Maraya Fiore; daughter of Queen Elyse Fiore and King Alano Macario; future queen and Supreme Ruler of all the lands of Crocetta and Abbadon."

Darian moved in front of Marisa and solemnly sunk down on one knee. Gasps erupted from every corner of the great hall as the guests watched Adalina and Helena follow his lead. Mother and daughter lowered themselves into a deep curtsey in front of Marisa.

Marisa was speechless as a wave of sound and motion rippled through the Knights' Hall. Every person was either bowing or curtseying to the simple girl from Oregon.

Except one.

In a stance of defiance, Savino eyed her coldly.

"Impossible!" he hissed. "This is all madness and lies! Princess Maraya drowned years ago when the *Carnelian* capsized. There is no possible way you can prove this ordinary girl is Maraya come back from the dead!"

Marisa felt detached, almost as if she were watching some scene unravel in front of her like a movie on TV. Her mind simply refused to accept what was happening. Both her mind and body became paralyzed with shock.

Darian rose to his feet and lifted a velvet pouch in the air.

"Princess Maraya has returned, and with her, she has brought back the lost Fiore Veritas ring, which will show you all the truth."

He emptied the contents of the pouch into the palm of his hand and held it out for Marisa to see.

"My mother's ring! You found it!" she cried.

Savino stared at her in horror. "You can speak? What is that strange language? What is this chicanery?" he shrieked.

The guests chattered loudly as they all tried to catch a glimpse of the ring. Darian held the sparkling diamond up for everyone to see. Taking Marisa's hand, he slipped it on her finger, and immediately the stone transformed from clear diamond to a deep purple. A wave of commotion exploded through the hall as people in the crowds began to shout. "It's true! She is the rightful heir!"

Marisa stared down at the ring, mesmerized by the pulsating violet-colored gem on her finger. She looked up at Darian and shook her head in disbelief.

He nodded to her softly. "Marisa, it's true. You are the Princess Maraya Fiore, rightful heir to the throne of Crocetta and the young lady to whom I was betrothed when we were just children."

"This is trickery! Prince Darian is using witchcraft to fool us all!" Savino cried.

"*Savino—hold thy tongue!*" a man's booming voice shouted from the entrance of the Knights' Hall.

Marisa froze. Her eyes widened as she turned to see the face belonging to the voice she already recognized.

"Uncle Al?" she asked weakly. "What are you doing here?"

Cinzia was weeping. "Alessio? Is that really you?" she cried.

Her uncle's eyes locked on Cinzia and a broad smile spread across his face. The crowd parted as the man that Marisa knew as Uncle Al strode across the room toward Cinzia. She flung herself into his arms and everyone smiled as they locked in a tight embrace.

Marisa watched dumbly as Arrie ran over to hug Uncle Al. Then she noticed another familiar figure casually sauntering over to them.

"Mark! How did you get here!" she squeaked.

Suddenly she couldn't breathe. It could have been from the tightness of the corset, the wine, or from just complete shock. But whatever it was, the last thing she saw was the glittering chandeliers above them. A curtain of blackness fell in front of her eyes and all the sounds going on around her faded away into silence.

Darian lunged to catch her as she slumped to the ground.

Marisa's head was swimming. She opened her eyes to find she was lying in a large antechamber with Princess Adalina next to her, holding her hand. She heard the muffled sounds of music, people and laughter in the adjacent room.

"Oh, Marisa, I am so glad you're all right. Please don't move while I go fetch my brother."

Adalina ran from the room, returning a couple moments later with Darian, her uncle, Cinzia, Arrie, and Mark. Uncle Al was the first to reach her.

"There you are, my darlin' Risa. Are you feeling a little bit better now?" he asked, stroking her hair. "This must all be pretty overwhelming for you."

"Uncle Al, how did you get here?" she whimpered.

"Shhh—just be quiet now. You need to relax so you can go back to the party."

"Hey, sis! Just what have you managed to get yourself into here?" Mark asked, grinning at her.

"But *how* did you two get here?"

"Celino came and got us," Mark said. "I was freakin' the day you disappeared, but Uncle Al kept sayin' things would be okay and that we would find you."

"I'm so glad to see you," Marisa said. "You have no idea."

She leaned around Mark and saw Darian standing at the back of the room, quietly listening to the conversation. She looked at him knowingly. "How did you do it?"

Sensing it was a private moment, the others quietly slipped out.

Darian shrugged. "It wasn't me—Celino brought them here. He deserves all the credit. But Marisa, are you ready to return to the ball? There are many people out there who have come a long way to meet you," he said.

"Darian, is this really true?"

He leaned in close to her. "Everything I said out there is the truth. You are the Princess Maraya Fiore."

"Why can't I remember any of it?"

He shook his head. "I honestly don't know. But you were very young when it happened. Perhaps you simply purged it from your memory."

"But why didn't you tell me sooner?" Marisa demanded. "All this time we've been together, and you never said a word. Why?"

Darian softly caressed her hand. "The timing wasn't right, and you weren't ready to hear the truth. You wouldn't have believed me if I'd told you."

"How long have you known?"

"Mmm, probably since the day we met. I thought I recognized you that first day on the road—you looked so much like your mother. And that same evening at the inn when I saw the ring, I figured it couldn't be a coincidence. There were so many added clues along the way—your father, Uncle Al, Mark, and of course, your mother's royal diary."

"The book was my mother's?"

His eyes sparkled. "Do you remember the morning we broke camp with the warriors? I was in your tent and found your mother's diary. When I saw your Crocine record of royal birth stuck between the pages, it confirmed what I already knew to be true—that you were indeed Maraya."

"But why would you—"

"Marisa, although I would love to keep you all to myself right now, I'm afraid we must rejoin our guests at *your* birthday party."

"Yeah, you're probably right."

She got up and moved toward the door but he pulled her back into his arms. He tilted her chin to face him and his eyes were serious.

"Maraya, you were born a princess and shall one day become queen. But just so there is never any doubt, I would love you forever if you simply remained Marisa MacCallum for the rest of your life."

He pulled her to him and pressed his lips firmly against hers with such depth and passion until she was finally convinced it wasn't a dream. As they slowly parted, she noticed tears in his eyes.

"I've wanted to tell you for so long now," he said softly.

"I just can't believe this is happening."

"Yes, I know—another surreal moment." He grinned. "I don't know what I've ever done to deserve getting you back again."

"Darian, what happens now?"

"Well, after the proper training, you become queen."

"No, no—I mean—are we still engaged?"

His face was serious. "Only if you want to be. There is no law against you ruling as queen without a husband."

"There isn't?"

A mischievous grin spread across his face. "You could banish me from your sight if you wanted to. But you would break my heart forever if you chose that option."

She punched his arm playfully. "Do you have any idea how often I've beat myself up over you? You knew I loved you and yet you never said a word."

"You are mistaken, my dear. Although I confessed my love for you not only in words but in actions, you did not do the same for me. In fact, your words and actions seemed to confirm the opposite. I had no way of knowing what was going on in that pretty little head of yours."

"I still don't get it—why didn't you just tell me about our engagement?"

"Two words: free will. You expressed to me almost as soon as we met that you could never marry someone out of an arranged marriage. It was then I knew I would have to fight to win you.

"Patiently, agonizingly, I waited for you to discover if you could ever feel anything for me. The last thing I ever wanted was to force you into marrying me out of some sense of duty or obligation."

"So I guess I can eat my own words now."

He chuckled. "Are you ready to go back in?"

"Do I even have a choice?" They laughed as he hoisted her to her feet. He put his arm around her and steered her through the door leading to the Knights' Hall.

As the subjects bowed and curtseyed to their new princess, she mumbled softly so that only Darian could hear.

"I don't think I will ever get used to this."

"Yes, you will," he whispered. "I will help you. And now, Your Supreme Highness, may I have the honor and extreme pleasure of the next dance?"

"Only if you promise not to call me that again tonight."

As they clung to each other in a romantic, slow dance, the guests gathered around to catch a glimpse of their soon-to-be king and queen. Marisa savored the night as one she'd never forget for the rest of her life.

As she pressed her cheek against Darian's chest, Marisa noticed that Uncle Al, Mark, Cinzia, Arrie, Helena, Tino and Adalina were all chatting and watching the two of them together. Uncle Al had one arm around Cinzia and her head was resting on his shoulder.

"So how do my uncle and Cinzia know each other?"

Darian burst into laughter. "Do you mean Baron Alessio? Why, they're married, of course!"

"*Married!*"

"Yes! Years ago, the baroness was too ill to travel with your family on the voyage aboard the *Carnelian*. Since Alessio disappeared along with the rest of the ship, those two have been separated until today."

"It's so strange to hear you call him that."

"You'll be hearing a lot of strange things from now on."

Her eyes widened. "The painting!"

"The painting?"

She nodded. "When Cinzia took me upstairs to the guest chambers for the first time, I saw the portrait of she and her husband and I knew I recognized his face. But I just assumed it was because he looked like Arrie. But the young man in the painting is Uncle Al!"

He laughed. "Indeed."

"I don't know why I didn't see it sooner," she muttered, shaking her head. "But how did all of us get from here to Earth?"

"I shall allow your uncle the privilege of telling you *that* one."

"How do you know so much?"

"Patience, my darling. You don't need to know everything all at once. In fact, it would be much better if you received the news in little bits," he said.

"Little bits?"

"You've already had so much to process in recent days, and there will be plenty more in the days to come. We wouldn't wish you to suffer from—what do you call it again? Ah, yes—sensory overload."

"Too late for that!"

When the dance ended, Darian and Marisa rejoined their families. She was surprised to hear her uncle speaking fluent Crocine.

"Uncle Al, why didn't you tell us sooner?" she chided him.

His eyes glistened with tears. "Oh, Marisa, believe me, I wanted to so badly. But your father made us all promise never to reveal anything about Carnelia to either you or Mark."

"But why?"

Uncle Al sighed. "I don't exactly know. Perhaps he didn't want you to go through life always feeling as if you didn't fit in."

"But I've always felt different."

"You were different. *Are* different."

"And now you've broken your promise?"

Uncle Al sighed. "Your father felt it was best if you never found out about this past since you would never get to see it anyway. Or at least, that's what he thought. In light of what's happened, I feel duty-bound to tell you anything you want to know. It's what he would have wanted."

She turned to her brother. "And why aren't you freaking out like I did when I first got here?"

Mark shrugged. "Uncle Al told me what had happened to you the very first night."

"You already knew where I was?" she asked her uncle.

"When Mike Stevens called to tell me that your Mustang was parked up at the stables but there was no sign of you or Siena, I knew something was up," said Uncle Al. He nudged her gently. "Why do you think we always warned you to stay out of those woods?"

"Anyhow," Mark continued, "I kept asking questions—like why weren't we calling the police. Finally, he spilled the whole story. At first I didn't buy it. And I still didn't believe it right up until the time that Celino brought us back—"

She interrupted. "He told me he was working on something in the testing phase. Where is Celino, anyway?"

"He was so excited about it all that he wanted to go home to write up his notes while they were still fresh in his mind," said Uncle Al.

She turned to Darian. "So you probably paid Celino a king's ransom to go back and pick up Uncle Al and Mark and bring them here. Why would you do that?"

"The reason should be obvious, Marisa. You are the rightful heir to the throne. I could not in clear conscience keep this knowledge to myself. That plus the fact that I might have an extremely difficult time proving your identity without your uncle's help," he chuckled.

Marisa decided to drop all the questions and just enjoy the rest of the evening. There was still plenty of time to ask questions and Darian was right about taking the time to absorb the information.

Everyone danced late into the night, and when the last guests had finally left, Darian escorted Marisa back to her room. He hadn't let go of her since making the big announcement.

They climbed the grand staircase and Marisa noticed the missing portraits had been hung back up on the walls. In a prominent spot, there was a magnificent, life-sized portrait of a young woman. She gasped when she recognized the face.

"That's me!" she exclaimed, pointing at the painting.

"It's your mother," he said softly.

The beautiful young monarch was dressed in a luxurious cream satin dress. Except for her hair which was nearly black, the woman bore an uncanny resemblance to Marisa.

She studied the painting in awe, noticing the subtle details such as the glints of light sparkling in her diamond tiara and the graceful curve of her hand as it rested on a marble stand. Tears formed in her eyes as she stood face-to-face with the mother she had lost so long ago.

"This portrait was commissioned for your mother's eighteenth birthday, just before she ascended the throne," Darian said. "She was about the same age as you are now when it was completed. Of course, I had to order the staff to remove it when we arrived so you wouldn't see it."

"I don't think I can take anymore," she said weakly.

He put an arm around her. "Come, let's go have a cup of tea and calm you down so you can sleep tonight."

Once they entered her room, Darian asked Anna to bring them some tea. He grabbed her cloak, slipped it around her shoulders, and led her outside onto the balcony. Gently he pulled her towards him and rested her head against his chest.

"Darian?"

"Yes?"

"There's something I still don't understand. Why did you tell Arrie that you were engaged to Lady Matilda? I overheard you talking that night after I fell in the cave."

"Did you hear me state plainly that I was engaged to Matilda?"

She looked him in the eye. "Well, no—but it was implied..."

A smile spread across his face. "Yes, you see, the inherent danger in eavesdropping is that you can almost always be certain you will misinterpret the true meaning of the words spoken."

"Say what?"

"Indeed I *was* speaking to Arrie about being engaged to a young woman, but that woman wasn't Lady Matilda."

"Oh."

"I told you that afternoon by the lake that I loved you and I knew no other woman would do."

He took her face in his hands and covered her soft lips with his firm ones. It was a kiss so tender that it made her want never to be apart from him. *This is not a dream—this is actually happening.*

"Just tell me one thing," she said. "That first day we met—why did you seem so disgusted with me?" She searched his face. "You seemed to hate me with everything you had. I couldn't understand what in the world I'd done to deserve it."

He smiled, shrugged. "I don't know, I was in shock, I suppose. When I saw you there, lying on the road unconscious, I honestly believed my eyes were playing tricks on me."

"But how did you even recognize me after so long?"

"You looked exactly how I remembered your mother, Queen Elyse. In my heart, I wanted to believe it was you, but the reason in my head told me it couldn't possibly be you.

"Those first few days, I hated you for owning the face I'd lost so long ago. But by the time I knew with absolute certainty it really was you, it was too late. I had already fallen deeply in love."

She smiled softly.

"Then Savino appeared in your life. When I saw him kissing you near the waterfall, I was sure I'd lost you forever. And when he proposed marrying you instead of Adalina, my torment was complete. And I had no one else to blame but myself.

"From the very beginning, I had made myself utterly unavailable to you. I'd convinced myself that I had to shut you out for my own protection. Because I could not yet reveal your true identity, I also could not make any promises. I tried to conceal my feelings, but I failed miserably.

"Knowing I'd locked myself away for far too long, you had every right to refuse me in favor of Savino. But I still prayed that even if you could not love me, you would never marry him. I had to wait for you to make your decision about Savino before I could even try to win your heart."

She shook her head. "Incredible."

"You have really tried my patience, woman."

"I think it's gonna take me a while to get over the shock of all this."

His face softened. "You have no idea of the agony I suffered that day you informed me of your plans to marry Savino. But I knew I only had myself to blame."

"I just can't believe what I'm hearing," she said, shaking her head. "I have been searching nonstop ever since I came to Carnelia for some kind of guidance—for some sort of direction in my life. But on the day I think my entire life is falling apart, the pieces are flung into the air and they all fall neatly into place. It's just too good to be true. There's gotta be a catch."

"There's no catch. With Garon, all things are possible, and everything happens for a reason. I know this."

"So you're saying there's no such thing as coincidence?"

He cocked his head at her. "Just what do you think the odds are of us ever finding each other again after all these years? And after living in separate worlds?"

"Hmm, I see your point. Probably about a million to one."

"I'd say about a billion to one," he said with a smile.

"Darian, I don't know if I can do this. I don't know how to be a queen. You've grown up in the palace, but I haven't."

"Don't worry, I will help you. We'll take it step-by-step, and you will learn everything at your own pace. Don't forget you'll have my mother, Adalina, Cinzia, Arrie, and your uncle to help you too."

"But it's such a huge responsibility. How am I supposed to rule a country I don't know anything about?"

"You won't be the first ruler to have asked those very same questions. But I do have a quick answer for you—pray for wisdom," he said.

"Why are the Knights of the Crimson Court gonna want to listen to some eighteen-year-old girl from another world?"

"Just think of it. You are part of an extraordinary legacy that has managed to transcend worlds and survive against all odds. That never could have happened without the blessings and protection of Garon. You are the rightful heir to the throne of Crocetta and *this* is your birthright. You must step up and claim it."

She just stared at him, unconvinced.

"Marisa, I love you, and you have what it takes to be queen. I've seen it. Your father saw it, too. We have our whole lives ahead of us and we shall accept this challenge together. We've got each other and we've got Garon. Both of those things can carry us through."

"I love you, Darian," she whispered. "It almost killed me when I thought we could never be together. But now that I know the truth, I can only do this if you'll be there with me."

"I'm not going anywhere. Remember, it was you who left me, after all." He chuckled, pulled her in a tight embrace. "This has been a highly emotional day for you, and now you need to rest."

"What an understatement."

"There is much to be done in the coming days, weeks, and months, but we shall take it one day at a time," he said as he led her back inside. "Your Royal Highness, I bid you good night and shall see you first thing in the morning. Sleep well, my beautiful princess."

"Good night, sweet prince." She pulled him close to kiss him one last time. Darian grinned at her as she slowly shut the door.

Marisa fell back onto the bed feeling drained and exhausted. She wriggled out of the dress, ripped off the corset, and pulled her nightgown over her head.

As she snuggled deep under the covers, her mind began to replay the most fantastic birthday she'd ever experienced. A wave of exhaustion quickly consumed her, and for the first time in weeks, she sank into a deep and restful sleep.

CHAPTER 30

MARAYA

THE NEXT MORNING, MARISA awoke to a light tapping sound in the hall. She grabbed the earpiece from the nightstand and slid out of bed. She tiptoed across the cold stone floor and peeked out in the hall. There was a young man hanging a picture on the wall and as soon as he saw her, he bowed.

"I apologize, Your Royal Highness. I hope I didn't wake you."

She shook her head and gave him a reassuring smile. As she closed the door, the events of the previous day came flooding back. The fact that she had no memory of ever being a princess totally boggled her mind.

She climbed back into bed and snuggled under the warm covers. What was it that Darian had said the night before? *Only if you want to be* was his response when she'd asked him if they were still engaged.

She gazed down at her mother's ring. It seemed to be glowing and pulsing from within. Curiously she removed it and saw it return to its clear diamond color before she slipped it back on again and watched it transform into a deep purple. So many questions swirled in her head. Now that she and everyone else knew she was a princess, it was going to be a busy day.

After she had bathed and dressed, she took one last look in the mirror before heading down the corridor toward the dining room. Once she had sat down at the table, members of the kitchen staff practically fell over one another as each one tried to please her. Obviously they had recently become aware of her position and had no intention of screwing things up for themselves.

Darian had told her from day one that he always questioned the motivations of the people surrounding him. Marisa wondered if people would be falling over themselves for her all the time now. She had only been a princess for a few hours but was already beginning to understand the complexities of Darian's life as a royal.

The door creaked open as he entered.

"Good morning, Your Supreme Highness," Darian said. His baritone voice echoed in the airy hall as he leaned down to kiss her.

"Okay, we're going to have to make some kind of deal that you don't call me that. I can deal with hearing it from just about everybody else, but not from you," she said, returning his smile.

He laid the napkin in his lap. "Yes, dearest, but actually, protocol demands that I address you as such because now you outrank me," he teased, tugging a lock of her hair.

"This is gonna take some getting used to," she said with a sigh.

"Of course you shall start right away with the language lessons. That will be a challenge in itself," he said in a mock serious tone.

"Language lessons?"

"But of course. How else are you supposed to communicate with your subjects? You shall learn Crocine as well as three other dialects," he said, spreading butter on his toast.

"Okay—stop! Too much information already," she said with a laugh, lifting her hand in protest.

"Stop what?" Uncle Al asked as he sat down at the table.

"Darian was just telling me I'm gonna have lessons in at least four different languages. I've already got English and French—don't they count for something?"

"Neither of those languages will do you much good here, darlin'," Uncle Al replied, stirring his tea.

"Where's Mark?" she asked.

"Do you mean *Prince Marcus?*" Uncle Al corrected. "He's still asleep, I think."

Okay, I need some answers," she said. "And I need them now."

The two men exchanged glances. "Fire away," said Uncle Al.

"First of all, how did our family get to Earth?"

Uncle Al stared down at his plate for a moment. He took a sip of tea and leaned back in his chair.

"You were only four and Mark almost three when your parents, Queen Elyse and King Alano, set out on a diplomatic mission to the neighboring kingdom of Terracina. Your father and I were born there, and it was the desire of many in both houses that we would foster an even tighter alliance with our uncle, the king. With our kingdoms combined, we could better defend our lands from the kings of the east, who were determined to annex and rule both our countries.

"My wife, Cinzia, and I were both asked to join the voyage while Arrie stayed behind. But knowing it would be a long trip both ways, your mother refused to leave you and your brother in Crocetta. The night before we were to set sail, Cinzia became terribly ill, and only after I insisted she wasn't in a state to travel did she decide to stay here in Crocetta."

"Cinzia is my aunt, right?" Marisa asked.

"Yes, and she's really looking forward to getting to know you."

She smiled. "I've always wanted an aunt."

"Anyway," Uncle Al continued, "the next day, the *Carnelian* set sail to cross the Sea of Pyrgos. We'd been gone for about four days when the ship hit a severe storm in the early evening. It lasted for several hours, and we were tossed and turned violently by the sea.

"I was so relieved that Cinzia had stayed behind. But your mother just sat on her bunk, hugging you and Mark, trying to calm you both down. You were so frightened. Later that night, a member of the crew spotted a maelstrom, and before we knew it, we were being sucked down. There was terrible thunder and lightning all around us. Every last man and woman on that ship began to pray to Garon for mercy."

Marisa became engrossed in the story as Uncle Al recounted the haunting images burned on his retina forever. Adalina, Arrie and Cinzia entered the room one by one and quietly and sat listening to Uncle Al's account.

"Just as the ship was being sucked down into the maelstrom, there were these strange blue-light flashes of lightning. The wind swirled all around us and the last thing I saw was a shining full moon and a high wall of black seawater coming straight for us.

"Just when I was sure it was all over, the ocean suddenly became calm—just like that."

He snapped his fingers and his eyes widened. He stared at Marisa with a look of disbelief. "Although we didn't know it at the time, the ship, passengers, and crew had all passed through a vortex."

"All of you? Everyone survived?"

He shook his head sadly. "Not everyone. A young couple and their baby were swept overboard and drowned. We weren't able to save them," he said sadly.

"So what happened then? What did you do?"

"Well, fortunately, when we came through the other side of the vortex, the ship was not far from shore. In the early hours of the morning just before dawn, someone spotted a rugged coastline only a few miles away. We had no idea where we were. At that point, it didn't matter. Everyone was just glad to put their feet on solid ground once again.

"When we got close to the shore, your father sent four men out as a landing party. They came back and reported that although it seemed to be a remote area, there was a road running parallel to the sea. The ship had landed off the coast of Oregon in a place called Cape Ferello. Although we didn't know it at the time, not only had we landed in a different country, we had wound up an entirely different world," he chortled.

"So what happened next?"

"Lucky for us, the *Carnelian* ran aground near a secluded stretch of beach, and we were able to salvage enough food and supplies from her to survive for the next few months. It was summer so we didn't have to worry about freezing at night. Thankfully, nobody spotted us down there in the cove, or they could have alerted the police.

"We made makeshift tents from the ship's sails, found fresh water, and had enough food from the ship to last us for weeks. We removed all traces of the *Carnelian*, eventually burning the last of her for firewood. After that, we began to move inland, disguising ourselves as foreign immigrants. Some of us who were gifted in languages were able to pick up just enough English to get jobs and support the rest."

Suddenly he looked at Marisa and tears filled his eyes.

"Your dad took on the weight of the world during those first few months and years. He became our community leader and held himself personally responsible to make sure each of the thirty-some Carnelians survived. Both your father and your mother had been born to a pampered life of royalty, but in that world, they were nothing more than immigrants. Working by the sweat of their brow, your mother became Alice and your father Alan."

"All those years, I had no idea." Marisa stared at him in amazement. As she listened to the story, the puzzle pieces of her life finally began to click into place. It was all coming together.

"I'll never forget the day your dad and I met a man in a small grocery store up in the mountains. He asked us if we were from Scotland and made some remark about us sounding just like his grandfather who'd emigrated several years ago. We decided then to tell all outsiders that we were Scottish immigrants. Our family changed its name from Macario to MacCallum, and anytime someone wondered why we were slightly different and talked funny, we had an excuse.

"After that, we moved to Jacksonville and made a fresh start. The adults sealed a pact never to reveal who we were and where we'd come from. Everyone changed their names to sound more American and vowed to raise the children as Americans. We tried to blend into the community as much as possible, but we still had secret meetings where we could speak Crocine and fellowship together."

Marisa just sat at the table, stunned. She started to realize why she'd always felt like an outsider in Jacksonville.

"And now you know the truth," Uncle Al said softly.

"Does Mark know?"

He nodded. "I told him the whole story the day after you disappeared. Somehow I knew what had happened to you. Of course, Mark didn't believe me at first. But then, sure enough, the day before yesterday, Celino came looking for us. He gave me twelve hours to get our affairs in order before we both followed him up into the woods.

"There were three flashes of light, a vortex of wind, and the next thing we knew, we landed somewhere down in the valley west of here. It was quite a hike up to the city, and by the time we finally made it to the citadel, your birthday party had already reached its high point, with Savino yellin' and screaming."

"That's right—I forgot all about him," Marisa said. She turned to Darian. "Where is he now?"

"He's being escorted back to Abbadon by a group of warriors," Darian said. "But don't you worry. Talvan has an eye on him in case he tries anything. We'll be forced to deal with him soon enough, though."

"Hey, what'd I miss?" Mark asked, sitting down at the table.

"Everything," Marisa said with a laugh. "So, now tell me about this ring. It actually *glows*. How does it do that?"

"Only when it touches the royal skin of the rightful heir to the throne of Crocetta does it revert to its true color and become the rarest of rare Ambrogia," Darian said. "It's extremely valuable."

"But when I first put it on several months ago, it was just a pretty diamond. And up until a few days ago it was still clear. Now the color is a deep bluish-purple. Why now? Why all of a sudden?" She slipped the ring on and off her finger, watching it change from to clear diamond to deep purple and then back again.

"Because," Darian said with a smile, taking her hand, "when you first wore the ring, you were still seventeen and you were on Earth. Once you landed in Carnelia, the closer you became to being the royal succession age of eighteen, the darker the stone became. Only, you didn't notice the color changing in recent days because I had, ah—*borrowed* it."

"So, it's only glowing purple like that in Carnelia?"

"Yes," said Uncle Al, "and it must be on the hand of the rightful heir. Your mother wore it at all times, but on Earth it became a diamond."

"How is that even possible?"

Her uncle shrugged. "No one knows. The gem is carved out of an Ambrogia stone, which doesn't even exist on Earth."

Marisa turned to Darian. "*You* took my ring!" she said accusingly. "You knew where it was the whole time and you didn't say a word!"

"I had to. You would have noticed the changing color and started to ask too many questions. I also couldn't take the chance that Savino might see the ring turning purple. If he had discovered you were the princess, he could have kidnapped or even killed you. I needed the ring to prove you are the real Princess Maraya."

"Is that what you're gonna call me from now on?"

He smiled. "That's up to you. Remember, you will be the queen soon, and you can call yourself anything you want. Maraya is your true name, given to you by your father and mother, but it's up to you to decide what people will call you."

"Queen…"

"Well, technically, you're still a princess until your official coronation. Only then we may call you queen," Darian answered.

Arrie finally spoke up. "You want to know what the best part of all this is, Your Highness?" A small smile played about his lips.

"No, but I'm sure you're gonna tell me," she said with a giggle.

"You actually *are* my cousin!"

Everyone around the table laughed, and she grabbed Arrie's hand and gave it a warm squeeze. For a week that had started on such a depressing note, her situation had improved beyond her wildest dreams.

And for the first time in her life, she had a true purpose.

"And now," Darian interrupted, "If you all would excuse us, I would like some time alone with Princess Maraya."

He stood up from his chair, bowed formally to her and offered his arm. They strolled down to the stables where the footman was waiting next to the open door of the carriage. Filled with a joyful sense of contentment, Marisa sat down on the seat. Darian settled down next to her and pulled the wool blanket over them. The carriage rolled out of the citadel and down to the dark tunnel under the rampart wall.

As Marisa rested her head on Darian's shoulder, she listened to the echoes of the horses' hooves on the cobblestones. The carriage entered the city and people stopped to bow and curtsey as it passed them by. She waved to the people lined up on the streets and suddenly realized they were bowing to her.

"What a difference a day makes, don't you think?" he asked.

"I keep pinching myself, sure that I'm going to wake up. I know this is all happening, but it's still so surreal to me," she said. She heard horses' hooves clopping behind them and turned to peek out the rear window. There were six horses with riders following behind the carriage.

"There are your bodyguards again. I guess we still can't be alone," she said, teasing.

"Wrong. Those are *your* bodyguards," he chuckled.

"Where are we going, anyway?"

"To *your* house."

She smiled at him and snuggled close under the blanket. Soon they turned off the road, and the carriage stopped at the iron gates. Darian hopped out and opened the gate for them to pass.

As the carriage rode up the long lane, Marisa leaned out to see the stately Castle Beauriél. It no longer seemed eerie to her now.

"I came here alone a couple of days ago on Siena, and it scared me to death," she confessed.

"What do you mean you came out here alone?"

She looked at him sheepishly. "I wanted to see the house again. Arrie gave me a key to get in, so I came down by myself. It was kind of creepy, though, and I thought I was seeing things."

"What kinds of things?"

"I don't know, people, visions. Glimpses of the future, I guess."

The carriage pulled up the driveway and came to a halt. She climbed out and stared up at the façade. "It's so strange, Darian, but somehow I feel as if I've been here before. I mean—before you brought me here."

"But you were here before, Marisa. When I say this is your house, it truly is. You lived here with your parents from the day you were born until you were four."

She was stunned. "This was our home?"

"Look carefully up there, just above the door. Don't you recognize that coat-of-arms? It's the same one on the clasp of your cloak. It's the Fiore family crest."

"That's where I've seen it before!" she exclaimed. "It was driving me crazy when I was here before, but I never made the connection."

"And you're the one with an eye for detail?" he teased.

"Yeah, I guess I'm slipping a bit."

They walked up the stairs to the front door. Darian pulled a key out of his pocket and led her inside. She stared at the foyer in amazement. Everything that had previously been covered up with sheets was now on prominent display.

Hand-carved pieces of furniture, paintings, sculptures, and antiques adorning every wall and corner had breathed life back into the house. It was all so striking and just as Marisa had dreamed the house should look.

"Oh, Darian—it's so beautiful! Did you do all this?"

He nodded proudly. "You told me you would be moving out of the castle today, so I had to prepare for the eventuality that you might actually leave me." She smiled and gave him a playful nudge. Her eyes roamed the room, admiring all the ornaments and details.

They entered the family living room where she had envisioned a large Christmas tree in the corner. The room was perfect for a family to sit together to read, play a game, or enjoy each other's company.

As her eyes drunk in the details of the room, she noticed a brand new piano in the corner and she shrieked with delight. She hurried over to examine it.

Darian beamed. "What do you think of it, Marisa? Will it do?"

"Will it do? This is *amazing*!"

She lifted the lid and tapped on the keys. It was a beautiful instrument and she couldn't wait to sit down and play on her own again. She lowered the lid and hurried over to the window.

"Darian, look at this! You can see the whole garden from these windows, and the trees—"

She turned to see him kneeling down in the middle of the room. His sword was unsheathed and extended out toward her.

"What are you doing?" she asked.

Without a word, he extended his sword further and motioned to it with his eyes. She just stared at him with a confused expression.

Darian rolled his eyes and grinned at her. "Marisa MacCallum, would you please do me the extreme honor of accepting my hand in marriage?"

Only then did she notice something on the tip of the blade. She looked closer and saw that it was a ring. Her eyes widened and a smile slowly spread across her face. Gingerly, she removed it from the tip of the sword. It was a golden ring with a large emerald surrounded by several smaller diamonds. Darian took it and slipped it on her finger.

"It belonged to my grandmother, Queen Aya Mondor," he said. "King Petrus Fiore gave it to her as a wedding gift."

Marisa screamed as she leapt and threw herself around him. She pulled his face down to meet hers, kissing him passionately on the lips. The love coursed through her lips to his, and she could not give enough nor get enough of his love. She held him tight, never wanting to let go.

Darian gently drew back and took her chin in his hand.

"So, does this mean yes?" he asked.

She wiped away a tear. "Yes," she said.

"I am now officially the happiest man in Carnelia," he said, beaming and kissing her again. He pulled away and looked at her mischievously. "I have one more surprise for you," he said.

She pushed him away, laughing.

"No, Darian, I don't think I can take any more surprises right now. Don't you think that I've had enough to last me for a while?"

"Ah, but this one I think you'll like," he said mysteriously. He pulled her over to a table near the window and pointed to a terracotta pot containing a small white flower. "Look, Marisa, do you recognize your flower now?"

"Oh! Is that *my* flower?" she asked through tears. He nodded solemnly and she bent down to study it closer.

The small plant had bloomed into the most beautiful flower she had ever seen. Long, glowing tendrils of red floated and extended from the stem, and pinpoints of white light shot out from its center. Although the white petals on the outside had remained unchanged, the heart of the flower was alive, rolling and undulating in slow motion like seaweed on the ocean floor. She watched in fascination as the scarlet threads pulsated with color.

"But when did it open? When you gave it to me yesterday, it was still closed."

He looked at her sheepishly. "Yesterday after I deposited Matilda in her suite, I went to your chambers to gather a few of your things for the move to Beauriél. It was then that I noticed it was already starting to bloom. The moment I saw those scarlet petals, I knew you loved me."

"It bloomed on my birthday?"

"Yes. I knew it last night at the ball. I knew I was your true love even before you did."

"Darian, I don't know what to say. This is too incredible."

"Then don't say anything. Just enjoy it." He caressed her cheek softly as he kissed her lips.

It was the only place in the world she wanted to be.

Standing in the very room where her life had begun eighteen years earlier, Marisa MacCallum wiped the tears of joy that blurred her vision and smiled at the man destined to share her life and her legacy.

EPILOGUE

DARIAN SAT WITH A puzzled expression. He was deeply engrossed in Queen Elyse's diary when a soft knock at the door interrupted his reading.

"Come in."

"Your Highness, you asked to see me?" asked Uncle Al.

"Yes, but please, dispense with the formalities whenever we're alone. Would you care for some tea?"

"No thanks. How can I be of service?"

"Well, I've been reading Queen Elise's diary, and I've stumbled across some rather disturbing passages."

Uncle Al shifted uncomfortably. "Where is Marisa now?"

"She went out riding to Beauriél."

He eased back in his chair. "Good. Which entry do you mean?"

Darian pointed. "Here, this very last entry is extremely troubling. Please read it and tell me what it means."

Uncle Al put on his glasses and began to read out loud:

Sunday, August 6, 9:34 p.m.

I have decided to end my life, so this is my final opportunity to say goodbye. My dearest Alano, I've loved you since the day we met in Terracina all those years ago and I could have spent forever with you. But my heart is heavy and I cannot go on any longer.

I have found the transition to our new life too much to bear. Please watch over little Marisa and baby Mark and give them extra love in my absence. I wish I could hold you all just one more time before I depart from this world.

Please forgive me,
Alice

Uncle Al sighed heavily as he folded his reading glasses. He closed the book and handed it back to Darian, crossing his arms in quiet thought.

Finally, he leaned forward and sighed heavily. He glanced up at the young man and his eyes wore a grim expression.

"There are some things that happened during our time in the other world that you should be aware of. But you must promise me never to reveal them to either Marisa or Mark."

ACKNOWLEDGEMENTS

There are several people to whom I owe a debt of gratitude and without them this book would never have become a reality.

First, I would like to thank my beta readers Christy, Debbie, Jennifer, Ken, Amy, Jan, Candace, Adrienne, Shirley, and Melodie for their insights in helping make a fantastic story even better. Thanks also to my good friend Janice for serving as an unstoppable source of moral support and prayer.

I would also thank my husband, Jan and our children, Amy, Vincent, Joshua and Marcus who all showed an incredible amount of patience as this book went through editing, after editing, after editing. I love each of you very much in your own special way.

I also owe a word of thanks to the staff of WestBow Press who patiently guided and encouraged a debut author all the way through the lengthy process of transforming a story from the concept stage to the physical book.

Lastly, I want to thank my two cheerleaders, Debbie and Christy for believing both in me and in this story from square one. Without their constant supply of encouragement and support, the story of Marisa and Darian would never have seen the light of day. I love you both, and remember to keep your fork—the best is yet to come!

- CLK

Coming in 2013

THE CARNELIAN TYRANNY

For news and updates, please visit
www.CherylKoevoet.com

Follow Cheryl on Facebook:
www.facebook.com/AuthorCherylKoevoet

Twitter: @CherylKoevoet

www.CarnelianLegacy.com

CPSIA information can be obtained at www.ICGtesting.com
Printed in the USA
BVOW07s0352051113

335449BV00002B/122/P